The Priest of Santa Maria

ALEXANDRA KLEANTHOUS

For my Father, the Sleeping Lion.
He was my secret fan.
May He Rest In Peace.

ACKNOWLEDGEMENTS

I would like to thank my family for all their support during the writing and publishing of this book. Also, my first mentor, Andrew Ellis, who worked with me through the first stages of the book. Yehudi Gordon for helping with Angelica's medical history. Fiorella, who was my initial adviser on all things Italian for the first few chapters of the book. Our dear family friend, Lina Anacreonte, for help with all things Italian after I had finished the book. Lawrence Bradbury, who sadly passed away in 2016, was my dearest friend and mentor. An accomplished writer and genius of a man, whenever I needed any advice, he was a Skype call away. I would have struggled without him. I am eternally grateful that we met that day at the London Book Fair. My editor, Dennis Hamley, was my rock during the final stages of editing. He taught me a great deal more than any writing course, and I am so thankful for all his encouragement and time. A big thank you to Elene Neocleous, my hero who saved me from tech hell! She is also a highly talented artist. And, I mustn't leave out my furry pal, Rosie, who sat on the windowsill every day as I wrote this book. Her companionship was her encouragement. I am eternally grateful for her unconditional friendship and love.

✦ Prologue ✦

Babylon, Circa 7 BC

A subtle breeze wafted through the open shutters, caressing the nape of Jannara's neck like the soothing whispers of a woman. It was a welcome respite from the relentless desert heat of the day. The night always brought with it a sigh of relief. The light from three Roman lamps on his workbench guided his eyes as he scribed the last of his instructions onto a piece of parchment. The open shutters behind him framed the scintillatingly starry sky, while the breath of the wind frolicked with the lambent flames and contorted his silhouette on the whitewashed walls. He completed his task and signed off with his name and seal – a star with his initials in its centre.

It had been an extraordinary few weeks, which involved many painstaking hours fashioning a block of cypress into a receptacle that was not only pleasing to the eye but also matched his technical requirements. He had exceeded his expectations on both counts. Before him was an item of sublime beauty – a rectangular trinket box consisting of a hinged lid and base, every detail handcrafted by Jannara himself with the dexterity of a master craftsman. A sliding wooden panel had been built inside the lower framework of the box, safely concealing a strip of white linen. On the underside of the lid, a cuneiform message had been etched into the wood with directions on how to unlock the secret compartment within it.

He dusted the lid and held it closer to the light, narrowing his eyes. The lid itself had an intricate design – a map – chiselled on its surface. This would play an integral role in liberating the secret compartment. The blaze highlighted a flaw that had gone unnoticed. With his carving tool in hand, he etched deeper into a section of the map, blowing the dust and brushing it away with his fingertips. He nodded contentedly, opened the box and, to ensure there were no imperfections in the lettering, ran his fingers along the inscription on the underside of the lid.

Satisfied, he slid the wooden panel open, removed the fabric, held it between praying hands, and with closed eyes muttered inaudibly. After completing his supplication, he touched the tips of his fingers to his forehead, kissed the fabric and placed it back in the box, sealing it beneath the wooden panel.

The haunting *kew-wick* of a solitary owl pierced through the window; a male hunting for rodents in the desert dusk. Jannara sat up, made circles with his head and pinched his back to relieve the aches provoked by his continuous crouching. His mouth felt like sand. He sipped water from the cup by his side before opening the secret compartment to reveal a complex geared mechanism rather like an astrolabe. A device with three principal dials stacked one upon the other.

When the parchment was dry, he folded it into a neat square, tucked it into a space within the compartment, and moved his attention to the dials. He turned the smallest one first, a hundred and eighty degrees to the right; then the middle dial ninety degrees to the left. He moved the top dial forty-five degrees to the right, pushed it down firmly, twisted it sixty degrees to the left, and pressed it down once more. Breathing deeply, he shut the lid and lowered his ear to the box to hear the clicking sound that confirmed the contents were locked and secure. He attempted to pry it open, but it remained sealed.

Jannara smiled, pleased with himself. 'And so it is done.'

Twenty-First Century, Geneva, Switzerland

'Moosh-am, are you home?' Kurush tossed his jacket on the coat stand and dropped his keys on the hallway table.

'In the kitchen, Papa.'

He continued through the hallway carrying a paper bag blotched with grease. His daughter, Frya, was sitting at the table, her laptop open. Beside it was a sandwich with mouse-like bite marks around its circumference. She looked at the paper bag and smiled. 'Let me guess – pain au chocolat.'

'You know I can't resist.' He placed the bag on the bench. 'I bought one for you too. Coffee?'

She nodded, watching him endearingly as he prepared the coffee machine. How his hair sparkled like graphite in the sunlight! His every movement seemed imbued with an intrinsic nobility as modest as a gentle breeze.

He caught her gaze from the corner of his eye. 'And what's so interesting?' he said.

'You seem different.'

'Different how?'

'Like a man on the verge of a breakthrough.'

'That's cheating. You know exactly what lies ahead of us this evening.' He put the pastries on a plate and placed them on the table. 'Now, wait for your coffee and me,' he said with mock sternness.

'I know the ritual.'

He placed the coffees on the table and sat down. 'What are you working on?'

'Just checking emails,' she replied with a mischievous grin as she lifted a wrapped package from her lap and placed it on the table. 'Happy birthday, Papa!' She stretched out her arms and hugged him, kissing his cheek.

'Moosh-am!' He took the gift, smiling and patting her arm. 'Where did you find cuneiform wrapping paper?'

'I'm a very resourceful woman.'

'That you are,' he said, with a raised brow. 'I don't want to tear it. It's a present in itself.' He took a knife from a drawer and meticulously sliced the tape.

Frya watched, noticing a nervous tremor in his hand.

The paper parted without a single tear to reveal a black gift box. He lifted the lid to find a tie with a matching tie clip and cufflinks. 'Pietro Cavallini's *Gifts of the Magi!* Another bespoke item?'

4

'And it has the mosaic effect. You can see it on the cufflinks and the clip.'

He nodded, holding the tie up to the light. 'I love it. Every item.' He kissed her cheek.

'So,' she said, dropping a lump of sugar into her coffee, 'you're keeping a calm exterior, but I can tell you're bursting inside.'

He nodded with fevered excitement as he placed the tie back in the box.

'I've never seen you like this.'

He took a sip of coffee. 'If I'm honest I have a flood of conflicting emotions coursing through my body. Fear of disappointment that it will be an anticlimax. The excitement that after two thousand years of ancestry we are the chosen ones. It has to carry some importance, surely.'

'Are you afraid you won't rise to the challenge?'

'What if there is no challenge? What if it's nothing?'

'Then the wait will be over. We will be disappointed for a while, but we'll carry on with our lives. Where's the box now?'

'In my office. Beneath the skylight. Facing the heavens.'

'You know I've waited my entire life, too.'

'I know you have. I filled your head with stories about the box from the moment you were conceived. I would lean my head to your mama's bump and recount the tales of our ancestors.'

'And you never stopped until I began finishing the stories for you.' She smiled reminiscently.

He chuckled for a moment before his smile faded and his

eyes moistened. 'I just wish your mother were here to share this moment with us.'

Frya placed her hand over his. 'She is, Papa.'

He patted her hand. 'Look, whatever happens tonight, I want you to know that you're not obliged to be involved.'

'Papa, stop. I've already taken a sabbatical from the hospital. I've let go of the flat, and I've left Zurich to come to Geneva and spend time with you. There are other doctors just as competent as I am.'

'I doubt that.'

'Oh, you're just biased… Listen, I don't want you to become too excited. You're right; it may turn out to be nothing.'

'I see the same doubting whispers have been circling your mind,' he admitted.

She rested her hand on his. 'So now we wait. What's another few hours, hey?'

He nodded; a burdened glint in his eyes.

Later that evening, Frya entered the lounge in search of Kurush who was sitting in his favourite armchair, sipping coffee, his gaze riveted on the blank television screen.

'Papa, it's time.'

He looked up at her with a glint of adoration in his eyes. She was a beauty like her mother, Nāzanin – refined in stature; eyes like the moon; skin golden silk.

'It's close to midnight,' she said.

He looked down, saying nothing.

'I've never seen you like this.' She walked over to him

and knelt by his side, placing her hands over his.

'This story has been the focal point of my life. It was my only purpose after your mother's death. I'm afraid…'

'That you'll have nothing to live for after this?'

'Yes, and that my life has been a waste of time.'

'Papa, you're a highly praised and published Professor of Babylonian Studies. You raised me after Mama died. Tell me what part of your life has been wasted?'

He nudged his forehead into hers. 'Jāné del-am, you were always wise, even as a child.'

'How about we hold hands and walk upstairs together? Whatever happens, we'll face it together.'

He took a deep breath. 'It's time.'

'It's time,' she repeated.

They reached the bottom of the stairs and stopped for a moment to gaze up the short staircase that led directly to the study.

'The journey of a thousand miles begins with one step,' said Frya.

'If it's good enough for Lao Tzu?' said Kurush.

They nodded and smiled at each other, each lifting a foot onto the first step.

As they ascended the staircase, Kurush turned to her. 'You know that an important part of Jannara's riddle is still a mystery.'

She said nothing until they reached the top and stopped outside a closed door. 'I have a feeling that's intentional… Now, after you,' she said, motioning towards the door.

He yielded with a nod and they entered a room with the ambience of an antiquated library. To their right was a desk, where Jannara's box took central position beneath the skylight. Ahead of them was a patio door with a telescope positioned skywards. Kurush pulled the door open, revealing the night sky. Then he took his place behind the telescope and peered through the eyepiece. 'How long until midnight?' he asked.

Frya looked at her watch. 'About three minutes.'

'Let's go over Jannara's inscription. What's baffling to me is this *unknown*.'

Frya opened a desk drawer and removed a notebook. 'Here we go,' she said, flicking to the first page. '*I am Jannara. On the fiftieth year of my second and final incarnation, follow the status of each Royal through the sign of stauros, to the unknown, where what I have concealed can be retrieved by my hand only, at the hour that seals the night.*'

'In the name of Zarathustra's Royals!' exclaimed Kurush, moving his eye away from the telescope.

'What is it?'

Kurush stumbled over his words; his saucer-shaped eyes wide with moisture.

'Papa?'

'I… I can't believe this.'

'Can't believe what, Papa? Talk to me.'

'It's…' He shook his head.

'Papa!'

'A star, Frya. It's a star.' The words seemed to find their own way from his lips as if he was too amazed to speak them

8

himself. He stood up and grasped hold of her shoulders. 'Whatever this is, it's huge!'

'What do you mean, *a star?*'

'The *unknown* is an uncharted star!'

'Are you sure?'

'I've watched the stars for over thirty years. I'm positive.'

'Let me see.' She bulldozed past him to take a look through the eyepiece. 'What am I looking at? Where?'

He gently prised her head away from the telescope. 'It's as unmistakable as the hand of God. Just there, beneath the Pole Star.' He pointed to its position. Frya followed his pointing finger, and there, just beneath Polaris, shone a resplendent star of huge magnitude.

Her mouth dropped open as she stared up at a gleaming crystal as large as the eye of a giant. Before she could speak another word – it blinked at them. She shot a look at her father with a half-smile that was unwilling to believe what had just happened.

Kurush rushed to his desk with unbridled excitement. He took a seat, turned on his table lamp and pulled the box towards him. 'Pass me a pin,' he said as he flexed his fingers.

Frya pulled one out of a box and handed it to him, then turned back to the star.

'Is it still there?' he asked.

'It is, but… This is unreal. It's flickering – I think. Could it be a countdown?' she said.

'As inconceivable as that sounds, you may be right.' He reached for a magnifier and held it over the box. The spiral design carved by Jannara had four stars etched into it – one each at the top, bottom, left and right sides of the spiral.

He moved the pin to the star at the crown. 'What's happening with our uncharted star?'

'It's still blinking. Astronomers across the world must be going nuts.'

'Yet it's a message intended just for us. If only they knew.'

With a look of impenetrable concentration, Kurush moved the pin to a microscopic hole at the centre of the star and left it momentarily suspended in the air. His forehead was a film of perspiration. 'Here we go,' he said through a mouth as dry as sandpaper. *'Aldebaran.'* He plunged the pin into the hole.

A clicking noise followed that sounded like the gears of a lever being released.

His head shot up – his excited eyes meeting Frya's before moving his attention back to the box. With a slight tremor in his hand, he wiped his perspiring brow, held the pin over the star at the base of the spiral and took a deep breath, pushing the pin into the tiny aperture. *'Antares,'* he announced with a firm push. Another click followed.

'I can't believe this.' He continued to the left star, plunged the pin into it without hesitation and once again named the star. *'Fomalhaut.'*

To their ears, the clicking sound was as melodious as a church choir.

'Tell me what our *unknown* is doing,' he said.

'Still signalling.'

'After this last star, the sign of *stauros* will be complete.' He planted the pin into the infinitesimal hole at the right of the spiral. *'Regulus,'* he said, stabbing it in.

The fourth click sounded. A piece of wood at the centre of the spiral collapsed, and in its place, a larger star rose from beneath it.

Their eyes met in astonishment.

'Is there another hole?'

Kurush checked through the magnifier. 'There is.' He poised his hand over the centre of the spiral and looked up at the flashing star in the sky. Its extensive size and unmatched illumination stood out like a king amongst his kingdom. Regal. Proud. Authoritative.

'It's speeding up,' said Frya.

Kurush bit his lip, his mouth parched and his hand quivering over the hole. He grabbed it with his free hand, holding it steady as he inserted the pin, returning his attention to the sky.

With a firm push, the pin penetrated the hole and the star in the heavens gave its final wink before vanishing, for good.

Three pronounced clicks followed.

Their eyes met again.

Time slowed to stillness, along with their breaths.

He gently gripped the box with both hands and tugged lightly on the lid. It opened with surprising ease.

Inside, tucked amidst the clockwork structure, was a piece of folded parchment. Kurush removed it and looked at Frya in nervous anticipation.

'We've come this far,' she said.

He nodded, carefully unfolding it with tremulous hands.

Frya stood over him, enraptured by the streams of recognisable characters. 'Ancient Greek?'

Kurush stared at the paper in his hands, chuckling and shaking his head in disbelief. 'It is.'

Four Years Later, Italy

Fortuna cautiously poked her wizened face out of the doorway, slanting her head to the right. Seeing no one, she beckoned to Angelica to follow. They tiptoed over Enzo's unconscious body, into the hallway, down the stairs and out of the building.

The streets were as black as the cosmos. It was as if the entire village was midway through a hundred-year slumber. There was not a light in sight, but for Fortuna's little torch, which shed just enough for their actions to remain covert.

They hurried through the Lilliputian streets, which wound round the hilltop village like the perfect peel of an orange – manoeuvring between the cars and mopeds which were parked with tight precision along the irregular stone pavements. They reached a cobalt Fiat 500, stationed outside a house with a matching blue door that looked too small to allow the passage of a normal-sized person.

Fortuna entered the driver's side while Angelica, wearing an exaggerated, grey hood which concealed her appearance, crouched in the back. The car eased itself away, gently, silently, down the sinuous avenue, leaving behind it the quietude of averted eyes and barricaded ears.

Hours later, Angelica stirred. Sunlight flooded through

the windows as the car pulled up to black iron gates so high and imposing that it was as if they concealed the most secret of locations. Above the gates stood an unimposing sign in black serif font that read, *Santa Maria L'adorata*. Above the sign was a metal structure, intricately constructed in the form of the Virgin Mary holding the baby Christ in her arms.

The car entered and the gates glissaded to a close.

Part One

The Convent

✦ Chapter One ✦

One Year Later, Italy

Christiano stood at the entrance to the alleyway where the taxi had left him. The blazing sun, which highlighted the lustrous blue-grey flecks of his almond-shaped eyes, dazzled his vision. He used one hand to shield the blinding rays and scratched beneath his left eye with the other – distorting the mole in the shape of a cruciform below it. A rosary of perspiration had formed on his olive-toned skin, above his collarino, and jewels of sweat glistened across his forehead.

He popped a ginger sweet into his mouth, picked up his luggage and continued to walk down the alley until he reached a small fifteenth-century townhouse with a crooked but pristinely polished white door. He knocked and waited, breathing in the remnants of fresh paint.

An old man of about sixty-five with smiling eyes greeted him at the door. His full head of hair was as alabaster white as his freshly painted door: a sharp contrast to his sun-baked skin and deeply furrowed features.

'Hello, I am Father…'

'Father Abbadelli!' he interrupted. 'Welcome! I am Marcello Franco. Please come in.'

Christiano stepped inside, extending his hand expecting it to be shaken, but instead, the old man kissed it. Christiano's face flushed.

Inside, the house offered a cooling shelter from the scorching rays. Christiano bent his head curiously, noticing that it was not just the door that was crooked; the entire interior was lopsided, the low ceiling and staircase askew.

His mouth salivated at the wondrous aroma wafting throughout the house.

'Welcome, Father!' A stout old woman wearing an apron imprinted with the Virgin Mary in prayer came out of the kitchen. A tea towel was tossed over her shoulder, and she walked with a hobble. Her grey hair was worn in a bun, accentuating her vibrant green eyes. The couple stood together, the taller of them only five feet seven inches, smiling up at Christiano, a six-footer.

'Father, this is my beautiful wife, Agostina.'

'Father.' The old woman bent forward and kissed his hand. 'Are you hungry?'

'How can I resist such a wonderful aroma? Minestrone?'

'Yes,' she replied.

'My favourite.'

'Ah, then you're in for a treat,' said Marcello. 'My wife makes the most delicious summer minestrone, with homemade pasta and a generous dollop of freshly made pesto. But first, I'll show you to your room.'

Christiano followed Marcello, looking surprised to see him open a door to the side of the staircase. He stooped to enter and followed him down a steep flight of steps to a door. Marcello opened it to reveal a deceptively large basement room shaped in a perfect square. Very little light entered the room through a row of windows running along the top of the entire side of one wall. The sun was obscured by the buildings opposite; the windows opening at pavement level. The youthful sounds of play and laughter echoed through the glass and landed with reminiscent charm on Christiano's ears.

'I will tell the children to stop playing outside your window. They are good boys; they will listen to me.'

'There's no need. It reminds me of my carefree youth.' He looked round the room as he continued to speak, 'Besides, it's unlikely I'll be here during the day.'

In one corner was a vintage wardrobe that looked like something out of the twenties, and, next to it, a half-open door. On the next wall was a double bed with working fans on both the bedside tables. A cheap, commercial painting of Christ hung on the wall above the bed. It depicted a handsome, young Jesus with a goatee beard. He wore a white tunic with a red heart imprinted in the centre. His eyes were penetrating, and a shimmering halo circled his lustrous long hair.

Opposite the bed was a desk, also with a working fan, and, on it, what appeared to be a shrine: the photo of a teenage boy surrounded by candles and a crucifix.

'I hope the room is to your satisfaction, Father. You have

your own en-suite bathroom here.' He pushed open the door next to the wardrobe.

'It's perfect. Thank you.' He smiled. 'May I ask who this is?' He pointed to the photo of the boy.

'He was our son, Nicolas. He died in a boating accident when he was fifteen. This was his room… Father, if you don't mind blessing him every now and then, we would be very grateful.'

'Of course.'

'Thank you, Father. I can tell you are a true man of God… Please, when you are ready, come and eat with us.' The old man left the room.

Christiano undressed and entered the shower cubicle. He twisted the gauge to the coldest temperature and immersed himself under the jet of skin-numbing water. He gasped beneath the icy stream.

'The Abbess told us that you are only at Santa Maria for a year, Father Abbadelli,' said Marcello.

Christiano, who had spooned a mouthful of minestrone, swallowed it quickly to reply. 'Please, call me Father Christiano… Yes, Monsignor Luka Basso requested that I give my services for twelve months.' He dabbed his lips with his serviette.

'So you are on loan?'

He smiled. 'It would seem so. The priest who was to take on the role had a car accident breaking a few ribs, both his legs and an arm.'

Marcello made the sign of the cross. 'And if you were not here, Father?'

'I was to continue my studies for a Doctorate in Theology.'

'Ah, I see,' said Marcello, looking impressed.

'What do you do, Marcello?'

'I am the janitor at Santa Maria.'

'So I shall see you every day. Do you attend mass at Santa Maria?'

'Yes, the Abbess permits me to attend with Agostina on Sundays. Father Cavallo is a wonderful minister, but he was forced to retire, due to his hip. Such a bad fall. I was right there when it happened. It was as if an invisible force pushed him down the stairs. He had just one more step to take before reaching the ground.'

'So the priest who should have taken his place had a nasty accident, and Father Cavallo fell down the stairs. What a strange chapter of accidents has brought me here!' said Christiano. 'He retires in one month, yes?'

'As far as I know, Father, he has already retired, and you are his replacement. But while his sister is preparing his room, he is staying on to help you settle into your new role. It would seem you are now officially the priest of Santa Maria.'

'More zuppa, Father?' asked Agostina.

'No thank you, that was delicious.'

'How about some homemade gelato?'

'Thank you, but I never eat dessert. After dinner, I like to go for a walk. I find that it not only helps me to digest, but I sleep better. Would you like some help in the kitchen before I go?'

'I would not hear of it, Father. Enjoy your walk.'

Christiano left the house and walked along a freshly tarred road, through a dimly lit village. The street lamps emitted a red-orange hue that drenched the surroundings in a sepia tone, like an old Victorian photograph.

He walked past a gaggle of teenagers gathered outside a cafe that was closed for the night. The boys and girls quickly stamped out their cigarettes, waving their hands in front of their faces to disperse the smoke. The young girls gazed lustfully at his athletic torso and exchanged dreamy looks.

'Hello, Father,' they said in unison; though he thought he detected a couple of provocative voices among them.

Nodding his head dutifully, he said, 'God bless you!'

He continued down a winding road. The uneven pavements became narrow dirt tracks. Soon he could hear the ripple of the ocean and smell the salty sea air. He pushed his handkerchief against his nose and popped a ginger sweet into his mouth, turned on his heel and briskly walked uphill towards the village centre. He turned right down a deserted lane, lined with clothing boutiques and shoe shops. Suddenly, he stumbled upon an old man sitting in the middle of the road holding a quarter-full bottle of whisky and muttering nonsensically.

The man looked up, saw the priest and said, 'Forgive me my sins, Father.'

Christiano helped him to his feet, walked him to the parade running the length of the shops and sat him down on the pavement. 'Seek confession, and it is done.'

'They told me you were coming.'

'Who?'

The man laughed, rising from the ground. He looked straight at Christiano. His laughter died. Then he said, in a hushed voice of wonder, 'You bear the mark.' He set off round the corner without another word.

A curious Christiano pursued the mysterious drunkard, but he had vanished. Instead, there ahead of him was a large stone wall with black iron gates in the shape of a pointed arch. As he walked closer, he could just make out the sign under the subtle street lighting: *Santa Maria L'adorata*. He reached the gates and attempted to catch a glimpse of what lay behind the dense barricades, but they were unrelenting. He finally looked away and instead fixed his gaze on the looming image of the Virgin Mary set against a purple-blue, starlit sky.

✦ Chapter Two ✦

Christiano awoke to the smell of freshly brewed coffee and a room immersed in darkness. He turned on the table lamp, yawned as he scratched his chest, and checked the time on his alarm clock. It was 5.30am. He kicked the sheets away and rose out of bed. True to his word to Marcello, he approached Nicolas's photo, where he lit a candle and muttered a prayer.

When he'd completed his blessing, he switched on all three fans, pulled a mat from his suitcase and placed it on the cemented floor. He took a seat, positioned himself into lotus pose, shut his eyes and took a few deep breaths before moving into a handstand. He then brought his legs up and over his head to finish with the soles of his feet on the crown of his head – *Taraksvasana pose.* He continued to perform various yoga poses before finishing with a cold shower and proceeding to breakfast.

Agostina greeted him with a wide smile. 'Good morning, Father.'

'Good morning. No Marcello?'

'No Father, he already left.'

The breakfast table was loaded with *cornetti*, bread rolls, jam and figs. Christiano was suddenly hungry.

'Did you have a good sleep, Father?' said Agostina as she placed a cup of espresso on the table.

'Thank you… Actually, I was a little restless. I met a drunkard in the street last night and…'

'Oh, so you saw Philippe,' she said. 'He has had a great sorrow in his life. Did Marcello tell you about Nicolas?'

'He did. I am sorry for your loss.'

'Thank you, Father. Philippe's two sons were with Nicolas, and they also drowned. He lost his wife a week later. Grief-stricken, she took her own life.'

'A tragedy.'

'Yes, Father. It was a difficult time.'

'What happened?'

'A freak storm, Father. The sea claimed our children. They would have been a little older than you now.' Agostina's eyes glistened.

'I will pray for you all.'

'We appreciate that, Father.'

Christiano strolled through the stone-brick village towards the convent, which, in daylight, he could now see towering above the rest of the suburban buildings on the crest of a hill. The bell tower sprouted defiantly above the gates as if determined to be seen. Standing at the highest point, it rang proudly, summoning all to its call.

The morning was warm and fresh with a crystal blue sky

that promised another scorching day. He walked beneath the Romanesque arches, which formed columns connecting the opposite buildings to each other. The narrow streets curved and undulated round the small suburb which was crowded with buildings constructed on an old medieval fortification.

With each turn, he chanced upon a hidden treasure of quaint village streets and alleyways, and the bustle of people starting their day. He strolled by shops selling fishing tackle, trinkets and fine embroidery. A market was just opening its doors. He chose a different route from the previous night's walk, stumbling upon Piazza di Nettuno, lined with cafes, restaurants and bakeries brimming with queuing customers. In the centre stood an impressive fountain with a hefty stone statue of Neptune sitting on a rock, his trident in hand and his hair and beard carved like the waves of the ocean.

Two children sat on a stone bench bordering the fountain, each munching on a cornetto. The chocolate filling trickled down their chins. 'Morning Father,' they said happily as he passed.

'Bless you, children.'

Others sat having breakfast at the tables around the piazza. A man in an apron swept the floor outside his restaurant, while another set the tables. Each person greeted Christiano with a polite hello and a nod.

He strolled with his head held high, his spine as straight as an arrow and his hands at his sides, responding to each greeting with a gracious smile and a nod in return, until he reached the gates of Santa Maria. He dabbed his perspiring brow with a handkerchief as he pressed the buzzer.

'Welcome to Santa Maria L'adorata. How can we be of service?' replied the polite female voice.

'Father Christiano Abbadelli to see Father Franco Cavallo.'

The gates opened and Christiano entered the courtyard. An old brick well stood in the centre of the grounds with an antiquated wooden bucket suspended above it. Ahead of him was the entrance to the abbey where double doors formed a Gothic arch doorway. To his left, fenced by an arcade, was a pathway; an entire wall of modern windows spread its length, revealing a library where a few nuns were reading. To his right stood another arcade, and through a circular window, he could see two nuns sitting at their desks. The arcades bloomed with climbing rose bushes of red, cerise, white and yellow – pruned with precision, so they only lined the stone walls. It was clear the buildings to his left and right were modern extensions while the arches were remnants of the original building.

An aged nun stood patiently at the doorway. She wore her black serge habit pinched in at her slender waist by a white rope. She gave Christiano a mild greeting smile. 'Welcome, Father Abbadelli. I'm Sister Celeste. Father Cavallo is waiting for you in the chapel. Please follow me.'

'Sister.' Christiano nodded as he stepped into the corridor. He gasped when he saw his new surroundings.

Stone bricks the colour of rust and burnt sienna – some cracked and chipped from age – formed irregular walls and gave a cold but characteristic feel to the abbey. Directly ahead of him was a water fountain that had been carved into the wall, forming part of its structure. It was overlaid by fading mosaic tiles which spread to the wall above, forming the image of a famous painting.

'Tell me sister, is this based on *The Crowning of the Virgin by the Trinity*, by Velásquez?'

'I think so.'

'A beautiful representation,' he said and paused to study it more closely before following Sister Celeste.

She turned right and opened a wooden door that led to a generously sized cloister skirted by a Romanesque arcade. A cypress tree stood erect in its centre. Two nuns sat reading on stone benches bordering the square. They did not look up. To his left was a two-storeyed building that he assumed were the nuns' dormitories.

Sister Celeste continued along a short corridor with white-washed walls and rooms hidden behind closed doors. She reached a set of arched doors and pushed them open, leading Christiano to the chapel nave.

He was at once plunged into a cool penumbra, soothing after the sun's bright glare. Stained-glass windows high in the chapel walls were the sole source of natural light. The sun streamed a potpourri of hues through the coloured glass, exposing dust that clung to the air and created a mystical atmosphere. There was a tranquil silence throughout the basilica that seemed to diffuse a feeling of peace on anyone who entered.

Sister Celeste nodded and left.

A rotund old priest holding a cane slowly hobbled towards him with a smile that did its best to disguise discomfort. 'Greetings, Father Abbadelli.' Father Cavallo extended his hand and Christiano received it with a slight smile.

'Have you settled well into your dwellings?'

'Yes, Father. Thank you. Marcello and Agostina are good, pious people.'

'Yes, they are pure of heart.'

He studied Christiano's face with a reminiscent glint in his eyes. 'You know, I remember my first day fresh out of the seminary. I was desperate to begin my work; a young whippersnapper eager to preach the word of God and change the world. Oh the years, how indiscriminately they pass and with such speed. How old are you, Father Christiano?'

'Twenty-seven.'

'And a great life ahead of you, I have no doubt… Well, this is our chapel. The convent dates from 1157, and as you can see the chapel has maintained most of its original, Romanesque features.'

'Beautiful,' said Christiano as he stared up at the patterned herringbone ceiling.

'As you can see Our Lady of the Chapel stands to prayer above us.'

A monochrome sculpture of the Virgin Mary was suspended eight feet in the air. She wore a compassionate expression as she gazed down at the congregation, her hands clasped in prayer.

He stood awestruck. 'Was she made by a famous sculptor?'

'No, back then the abbey was a dwelling for monks. They

moved to the Abbey of Fossanova to join the friars there in the sixteenth century, and the monastery became a convent. It was one of the monks, a talented Friar Rodolfo back in the twelfth century, who sculpted Our Lady from the local mountain stone... Did you have much of a chance to look around?'

'A little as I walked.'

'Well, we have a very talented group of nuns at Santa Maria. The dear sisters are successfully running an organic vegetable and herb garden, they embroider the most magnificent tablecloths and bed sheets, they make jam from our very own orchard, and they make pottery.'

'Yes, I hear.'

'The abbey shop is just opposite.' He motioned to his right. 'It runs by the side of Via Scala... Well, the Abbess is keen to meet you before lunch.'

Father Cavallo hobbled to a wheelchair parked by a pew. 'If you don't mind pushing, I will direct.'

'Of course.'

Father Cavallo led Christiano across the cloister.

'It's very quiet. I've only seen a handful of sisters,' said Christiano.

'Most are attending to duties in the convent, and some are out amongst the community. You will meet most of them at lunch.'

They reached the end of the cloister and took a sharp left. Father Franco rapped lightly on a door with his cane.

'Enter!'

They entered a rectangular office. Light flooded through

a skylight that formed the entire roof. A tall, distinguished, elderly woman walked towards them, her head held high and her hands overlapping at her navel. 'This must be Father Abbadelli. Welcome, Father. I am Abbess Francesca Rossini,' she said with a welcoming smile.

'It's an honour to be here,' he replied, shaking her hand. From the corner of his eye, he caught a glimpse of a collection of iconographic sketches pinned to a cork board on the wall. One of the drawings had an incredible likeness to the Abbess. All the drawings were in monochrome, except for one, which was a richly coloured sketch of the entrance to the abbey, with the climbing rose bushes in full bloom. Christiano was captivated by the artwork.

'Marcello tells me that you have settled in well. He likes you very much.'

'Yes, it's a peaceful home,' he said, forcing his gaze away from the sketches. 'I do so enjoy the meditative life.'

'Indeed. Here at Santa Maria many of our sisters like to practise spiritual silence. Not all of us have taken a vow of silence, but generally, words are few and only spoken with good intention.'

Christiano nodded. 'What is more important than allowing time for prayer and quiet contemplation with the Lord?'

'You most certainly seem an ideal replacement for our Father Franco, even if it is a temporary position. He will be greatly missed, though.'

'I will do my best to fill his humble shoes… I must say, the convent is quite beautiful.'

'Please, allow me to give you a tour.'

'If you don't mind, I'll be on my way,' said Father Cavallo. 'Father Christiano, it has been a pleasure. I shall see you at lunch.' He wheeled himself away leaving Christiano with the Abbess.

'Let us walk and talk,' she said.

As they stepped into the corridor, they met the nun who had greeted him at the front gate.

'You've met Sister Celeste,' said the Abbess.

'I've had the pleasure.'

Sister Celeste nodded politely and continued past them and down the corridor.

'I don't know what I would do without her. She is my right arm.'

Christiano smiled.

'As you have no doubt noticed, the architecture is an eclectic mix of periods and influences, but we think it adds character.'

The Abbess led Christiano back towards the chapel. They passed through the cloister and walked down a corridor until she opened the door to a frugally furnished recreation room. The overpowering scent of fresh thyme, rosemary, basil and lavender wafted through open patio doors and circled them like buzzing bees. In the garden, two nuns collected herbs and placed them in a woven basket, while two others did the same in the vegetable garden.

The two of them walked onwards, meandering through a fragrant grove of lemon, quince, cherry and fig trees, rampant with delectable, ripe fruit. At the end of the grove was a cemetery, which led to a pathway, after which they re-entered the corridors via a side door by the preserve kitchen. Inside, nuns prepared homemade jam. They continued through to the embroidery and pottery rooms and reached a storage area.

Shelves were lined floor to ceiling with tablecloths, dried herbs, jam, bed linen, biscuits, vases and crockery. From there, they entered a quaint shop that had the familiar characteristic stone brick walls. A large iron crucifix hung on the wall above the till, and to the left a large tapestry of the Virgin Mary.

'Ah, a representation of the *Sistine Madonna* by Raphael; commissioned by Pope Julius II in 1512,' said Christiano.

'You know your art, Father.'

'A great love of mine. The Madonna is holding the Christ Child and at her sides are Saint Sixtus and Saint Barbara. They stand on clouds, and two distinctive winged cherubs rest on their elbows beneath her. Stunning!'

The nun working in the shop shut and locked the door leading to Via Scala.

'Lunchtime already,' said the Abbess.

They retraced their steps to the preserve kitchen and from there into the corridor.

'Such a creative and productive community,' said Christiano.

'Yes, we keep busy. Personal time for prayer and contemplation is important, but we also believe that it can be accomplished through artistic pursuits.'

'Exactly my reasons for my love of art. I look upon a piece, and it's as if I'm staring into the face of God.'

'Are you an artist?'

'Alas, no. I can only admire, not create.'

'Perhaps, if you had been an artist you would never have entered the priesthood.'

'That will have to remain a mystery.'

They both chuckled as they reached the refectory where Father Cavallo and a group of nuns sat around a long wooden table. The dining room was plainly furnished but modern, with smooth white walls, one of which had large windows overlooking the cloister.

As soon as the Abbess entered, the nuns rose in venerable salutation, their hands in prayer and bowing their heads.

The Abbess introduced Christiano.

As he sat at the table, he saw out of the corner of his eye a woman, not dressed as a nun, but in a long, grey hooded cloak. She came out of the kitchen with a large pot of soup and laid it on the table. He eyed her curiously, unable to see her face; just young, smooth, olive-skinned hands, long and delicate, with a gold, heart-shaped ring on the little finger of her left hand. She disappeared as swiftly as she had appeared – without a word, her head still bowed.

'Father Christiano, we would be honoured if you would say the lunchtime prayer,' said the Abbess.

'The honour would be mine.'

They all bowed their heads.

'Bless us Oh Lord, and these thy gifts, which we are about to receive, from thy bounty, through Christ, Our Lord. Amen.'

✦ Chapter Three ✦

The next morning, Christiano entered the narthex of the chapel with a bible in his hands. As he reached the nave, he slipped, skidded on his rear a fair way across the floor and collided with a bucket. A cascade of water splashed over his face and chest. He gasped as he wiped his eyes and opened them to gaze into large, oval eyes that gleamed like black pearls, a small pert nose and full pronounced lips. The woman with the familiar grey hooded cloak peered over him with a mop in her hand. The Virgin sculpture in the background seemed almost to be standing watch over her.

He lay motionless and dazed, gazing up at a flawless face that looked down at him like a frightened deer staring into the headlights of an oncoming vehicle. She grabbed the bucket and sped out of the chapel, leaving him breathless.

The rest of the day drifted by in a haze. Christiano was unable to erase those penetrating eyes which seemed to have found their way to his soul.

That evening at dinner, he pushed some food to the side of his dinner plate.

'You don't like seafood, Father?' asked Agostina in surprise.

'To be honest, it's not my favourite. I'm that rare person, a fisherman's son who doesn't like fish. I say we should leave the poor creatures in the ocean where they belong.'

'Oh Father, you should have told me. Can I get you something else?'

'No. Thank you. To be honest, I'm not very hungry this evening.'

'And what did your father think when he discovered your aversion to his livelihood?' asked Marcello.

'He was very disappointed, but the local priest, Father Guido, a mentor of mine, spoke to him. I soon discovered he was very proud of my decision to become a priest. Besides, I have an older brother who has inherited the family business.'

'So at least one of you became a fisherman.'

He smiled… 'What brought you to Santa Maria, Marcello?'

'Oh, it's a long story. I started out as a locksmith. The abbey has always been a place of mystery and intrigue since childhood. One day, tasked with replacing the locks to the convent shop, I met Father Cavallo, and it was as if we were old friends catching up. I invited him to dinner, and we became great friends. After the death of Nicolas, I didn't have the strength to work. He helped us through it.'

He grasped hold of Agostina's hand.

'Unable to face my job I ran into debt. The position of Janitor at Santa Maria became available, and he offered me the job. I took it, hoping that a holy place would help me find solace. On my first day as I walked into the abbey, a feeling of peace washed over me. That was twenty years ago.'

'A story full of both wonder and sadness,' said Christiano.

'Father,' said Agostina, 'he went into that place a broken man who hardly spoke a word to me and returned the very first day with a bunch of flowers, showering me with kisses. Santa Maria is a very special place.'

'It's a pity Philippe did not have the same fortune,' said Christiano.

'Oh we tried to introduce him to Father Cavallo, but we had each other, he had no one. His burden was three-fold.'

They sat in quiet contemplation for a moment before Christiano broke the silence. 'Will you both be attending mass tomorrow?'

'Oh yes, we look forward to it,' said Agostina, rising from her seat and collecting the dishes. 'Will you be conducting the service?'

'No, I will leave the pleasure to Father Cavallo. Despite my new position, I feel it is still his church. Until he has left, that is.'

The next morning, Christiano helped Father Franco prepare for mass.

'How are you enjoying Santa Maria?' asked the old priest.

'An enchanting, tranquil place, but a momentary pause in my life.' He placed the chalice on the altar and the bible onto the lectern.

'Well, don't be so sure, she may grow on you yet. Our

Lady is a very persuasive woman… Ah, our sisters arrive.'

As Father Cavallo conducted mass, Christiano took a moment to survey the congregation. Marcello and Agostina were listening to the liturgy in devoted musing, but the Abbess, he noticed, had a pained and anguished expression as if her attention was on another matter. He stared at her for a while, wondering what it might be. Then, several rows behind her, as though a tinted figure in a monochrome photograph, he caught sight of the mysterious young woman. Her grey hood fell over her shoulders to reveal an angelic face and long hair the colour of onyx and as straight as a poker. Her skin was the colour of shimmering bronze highlighted by a single golden hue emanating from the stained glass directly above her. It was as if tiny particles of glitter were ingrained into her flesh.

She sat in quiet devotion at the back of the chapel, her eyes transfixed on Father Cavallo. As Christiano stared, she looked up to meet his gaze. He quickly looked away, his face turning crimson. From that moment, he kept his eyes firmly on Father Cavallo and attended to his duties until the very end, when he dared to look her way once more.

The space where she had stood was empty. Christiano felt a strange sensation of loss.

Gradually, the nuns dispersed to attend to their chores and Christiano approached Father Cavallo. 'A wonderful service, Father. One I'm certain I cannot match.'

'Oh brother, you are being humble. Monsignor Luka speaks very highly of you. He tells me that you were his best student.'

Christiano's face flushed. 'Well, I have always had an aptitude for study. I enjoy it very much.'

'So, you have delayed your doctorate for twelve months?… I do hope this diversion isn't causing anxiety.'

'A little at first, but God has chosen me for this task, and he has his reasons. I am but his humble servant, after all.'

'Indeed. As we are all… Would you like to take confession this afternoon?'

'I would like that very much.'

It was late afternoon, and Christiano was down to his last confession of the day. He heard the fumbling sounds of someone settling into the seat and slid the grille open.

'Forgive me, Father, for I have sinned. It has been one year since my last confession,' said the female voice behind the confessional blind.

'Sister, why have you abstained from confession for so long?'

'I am but an old nun, Father, and now, after all these years, I find myself stricken with grief and envy.'

'What is the cause of this anxiety, Sister?'

'The youth around me, Father. I have a burning desire to tell my young sisters to flee the convent and seek a normal life. To marry and have children.'

'Do you regret becoming a nun?'

'If I am honest, after all these years I am suddenly full of grief and longing for a child I will never have.'

'Why did you become a nun?'

'My parents insisted, and I was young and pleasing.

Now, I have the tongue to speak my mind, but it's too late.'

'Sister, while I'm sorry to hear this, I feel it's important that you make the distinction that what happened to you did not necessarily happen to your sisters. They chose this calling of their own volition.'

'Indeed, Father. My apologies. I am blinded by my own bitterness.'

'Are you from these parts?'

'No, Father. I am not. I had my eye on a young man back in my hometown, and he was keen on me. I never saw him again. I have never passed the convent gates since my arrival more than forty-five years ago. Sometimes I cry at night, feeling the emptiness in my womb... Do forgive me for speaking so bluntly, Father. I would never say such things to Father Cavallo for fear that he may recognise my voice.'

'Do not worry yourself, Sister. I feel for your loss. I too have taken a vow of celibacy and will never father a child. It is the choice we make. While I understand that it was forced upon you, do you truly feel that your years of service to God have been wasted?'

'So much so that sometimes I feel to take my own life.'

Shock coursed through his body. Suddenly, his thoughts were interrupted by a scream. He ran from the booth, out of the chapel and into the hallway where a group of nuns surrounded someone who was lying unconscious on the ground. He approached them – and saw it was the grey-hooded woman who lay on the floor. The Abbess pushed through the small crowd and knelt beside her, waving smelling salts under her nostrils. 'Angelica, can you hear me?'

she said. Angelica opened her eyes, and the Abbess tilted her head forward to receive water.

Christiano, appalled and concerned, watched as she was gently raised and helped away by the Abbess and Sister Celeste.

'That's all there is to see here!' said the Abbess. Her voice was sharp, and as she left she looked at Christiano for a second, it seemed to him almost suspiciously. He stood, staring as they disappeared down the dark corridor and then turned to see that all the nuns were gone and the hallway was empty. He walked back to the chapel and noticed that the door to the confessional booth was ajar and the chapel was empty.

A dark shadow descended upon the nave as the sun went down. An eerie silence hovered in its place. Christiano suddenly felt uneasy and narrowed his eyes, glancing from side to side as if sensing a presence.

'Sister, are you still here?' He looked in the confessional booth to find an empty chamber. A whimper sounded by way of reply.

'Sister!'

He flicked the light switch. The bulbs emitted a warming, flame-like light that lined the entire stretch of the nave. He searched around as the cry continued, looking under the pews and pausing in the transept crossing.

As he stood there, he felt droplets of water fall on his head. He looked up at the Virgin sculpture towering above him. Another drop landed beneath his left eye. He picked up a flickering candle and grabbed a nearby chair, raising himself higher, for a closer look. He held the candle as far up to her face as he could reach. It appeared the tears were flowing from the Virgin's eyes. He rubbed his own eyes in disbelief and lifted the candle towards the ceiling, searching for a leak. The wan light revealed nothing. On tiptoe, he cautiously stretched his hand up, feeling the area beneath her eyes with the tips of his fingers. The stone felt wet beneath his touch.

As suddenly as it had begun, the whimpering stopped. The chair beneath him wobbled, one of the legs snapped, and it toppled over.

Christiano crashed to the ground.

✦ Chapter Four ✦

Entering the convent infirmary was like walking through a time warp. Jagged cracks ran along the neglected whitewashed walls, and iron bedsteads looking like leftovers from the First World War lined each side of the room. The pungent odour of disinfectant took Christiano's olfactory senses hostage as he looked round the ward for the nurse, while the incessant drip… drip… drip from leaky taps shrilled in the silence.

A buxom face with rose-flushed cheeks poked out of the bleached surgical curtains that concealed a portion of the room.

'I'll be with you shortly, Father Abbadelli. Please take a seat on the bed, over there.' The nurse signalled with her head as she spoke.

Christiano reached the bed and noticed a small television set nearby – a relic from the seventies. He switched it on and twisted the volume knob all the way down, to mute the sound.

'Father Christiano!' called the Abbess from the doorway.

She walked in, arm-in-arm with Father Cavallo whose face was straining from the climb up the stairs.

'Sister Celeste informed me that you had arrived. How are you feeling after a few days' rest?'

They reached his side, and she beamed a warming smile, while Father Cavallo dabbed the sweat from his forehead and tried to catch his breath.

The Abbess inched closer to Christiano. 'May I take a look at the wound?'

'Of course,' said Christiano. 'It's just a graze. I was lucky. Sister Carmina said that my head must be made of steel... Father Franco, you should not have climbed the stairs in your condition.'

'Nonsense, I refuse to be an invalid. It is good to see you well, my friend.'

'Do you remember what happened? Why you were standing on a chair?' asked the Abbess. 'With all the fuss I didn't have a chance to ask.'

'I was just clearing cobwebs from Our Lady when the chair gave way.'

'Really Father, we have a ladder and a dusting brush for that. At least you could have waited until daylight,' said Father Cavallo.

Christiano's lips pursed in mild amusement.

'It seems that any priest who works here meets with a mysterious accident,' said Father Cavallo. 'I am glad to retire. It has become a perilous job.'

'And what will you do, Father Franco?' asked the Abbess, amused.

'Well, if I'm honest I'll be bored out of my wits. I'll need a new hobby. My preference is to lead a cloistered life among my brothers, take a vow of silence and write my memoirs – somewhere where they make fine wine. The reality, however, is a hip replacement and rehabilitation under the supervision of my sister, Fiorella – a woman of deep compassion but a teetotal, strict disciplinarian.'

The Abbess and Christiano laughed.

'Santa Maria will be a dull place without our jolly Father Franco and his shenanigans,' said the Abbess.

In mid-chuckle, Father Cavallo stopped. He leaned towards Christiano and put his spectacles on. 'How extraordinary. Your mole has a cruciform shape. Right there beneath your left eye.' He pointed. 'I've never noticed it before. Have you, Abbess?'

The Abbess cocked her head and moved in closer with a squint in her eye. 'Oh yes. How odd. Were you born with it?'

'I think so. I have had it for as long as I can remember. People are always intrigued.'

'Well, it's certainly fitting for a priest,' said Father Cavallo.

The surgical curtains parted with a jingle and Sister Carmina stepped into the ward, followed by Angelica, whose luminous presence seemed to transform the room into a starlit sky.

The Abbess shifted uneasily, and her face suddenly appeared burdened. 'Father, I must leave. Please take it easy today.' She walked towards Angelica and chatted for a moment with Sister Carmina.

'I must go, too,' said Father Cavallo. 'I wish to pop to the library. I shall see you in the chapel in due course. Be ready to take confession.'

Christiano nodded. 'Do you need help with the stairs?'

Father Cavallo shook his head and waved his hand in the air in a dismissive manner.

Christiano smiled and shook his head in astonishment as the old man, cane in hand, limped with surprising speed to the door.

He turned his attention to the women but found himself distracted by the fuzzy television screen to his side. A black limousine was passing through the gates of the Vatican. The back seat window was slightly open and a man with a full head of lustrous silver hair, on top of which sat a red skullcap, smiled and nodded at the cameras. The headlines at the bottom of the screen appeared with the words, *Cardinal Cäsar Beltz, 'Prefect of the Miracles Commission', leaving the Vatican after a meeting with His Holiness Pope Leo XIV.*

'How are you feeling, Father?'

Christiano turned to face Sister Carmina, 'Much better, Sister. Thank you. Marcello and Agostina kindly took turns and watched over me the night of the accident. I slept like a log. Unfortunately, they did not.'

'Well, you could have stayed here. I should have insisted, but you were adamant to leave. How stubborn you can be, Father Abbadelli!'

'My apologies if I appeared abrupt and rude. It was the fall, I am sure.'

'You were quite spooked as if you'd seen a ghost. It seems the psychological impact was worse than the physical damage.' She inspected the wound. 'Well, it's practically healed. As I said, head of steel.'

He smiled. 'Thank you, and I'm sorry for being so much trouble. I shall keep my feet firmly on the ground next time, unless, of course, I want another two days' rest.'

'Ah, humour! You're definitely better.'

Christiano left the infirmary and made his way to the chapel, hoping to be alone for a while. His hopes were dashed by a nun in the front pew kneeling before the Virgin sculpture. To his relief, she got up to leave. She bowed her head as she walked past him.

'Sister.' He nodded and waited until she was gone before he entered the transept crossing. His large pupils gawped in wonderment at the stone sculpture that only days ago had seemed to come to life.

As the Venerable Mary returned a loving gaze of motherly affection, the image before his eyes lost all focus. Christiano was sure he caught a fleeting flicker – a flash of Angelica's anguished face metamorphosed over Mary's.

He blinked, and it was gone, like a rogue slide in a roll of film.

'Christiano!' followed in a whisper. As unmistakable as a bolt of lightning, his name reverberated through the old bones of the timeworn basilica. The room seemed to spin.

He grasped hold of the altar table and stood aghast as his cheeks drained of life and his breath laboured in his chest.

'Father Christiano!' announced Father Cavallo as he

entered the chapel. 'Still looking for cobwebs?'

He turned to him and tried to gain his composure. 'I think I got them all,' he replied weakly.

'Are you all right? You look quite pale. Has Sister Carmina given you a clean bill of health?'

'I'm fine, Father Franco, and ready to resume my duties.'

'Well, if you're sure.' He continued to look at him; clearly concerned... 'Our sisters are due at any moment. Would you like to take the booth?'

'Yes, of course.' He entered the cubicle and collapsed on the seat, his head in a whirl. Perspiration seeped from his forehead like a running tap of water. He wiped it away with his sleeve and took deep breaths to calm himself.

As his breathing normalised, he heard the shuffle of someone enter the confessional and take a seat. The nun cleared her throat. He slid the grille open and caught the movement of black, and little else.

'Forgive me, Father, for I have sinned. It has been three days since my last confession.'

His eyes widened as he heard the familiar voice. 'What is the nature of your sin, Sister?' he asked with a steady tone.

'Father, why do you think God favours sinners over the pious?'

He rubbed his temple, nervously. 'I do not think that he does. A partial quote by Matthew 5:45 describes it best. "...He causes his sun to rise on the evil and the good, and sends rain on the righteous and the unrighteous..."'

'Do you think Jesus fornicated with a prostitute?'

'Sister, how are you feeling since the last time we spoke?'

He squinted his eyes and looked through the grille, but the image was a formless blur.

'Father, it is fruitless to try to recognise my voice as I am holding a piece of fabric over my mouth.'

'I have come to recognise your expression, Sister. That is all… Now name your sin or be gone. I know that you are not here for lessons in bible study.'

'Why would God favour a dirty whore over a nun?'

His jaw clenched. 'I ask you to moderate your tone, Sister.'

'My apologies, Father. Polite rhetoric has left me nothing but barren.'

'Sister, I'm afraid for you. There is something in your tone that is beyond reasoning.'

'Perhaps it's too late to save me, Father.'

'I will nevertheless try if you would give me the opportunity.'

'It is far too late for that. It is through idle hands that Satan does his bidding, and I kept mine busy with prayer for over forty years. I prayed devoutly, and it has left me nothing but bitterness and anger. God never spoke to me. He never answered my prayers or saved me from the demons that tormented me every day of my life. I wanted to feel a man's touch; a man's love. I wanted to experience a child growing inside me, to give birth and to see my child grow into an adult, but instead, he cursed me and forced me to watch his predilection for whores.'

'Sister, I ask you again to watch your tone.'

'All men prefer whores, and you are no exception.'

Christiano punched his fist against his thigh. 'Enough! Instead of coming to me full of penitence and begging for God's forgiveness, you continue to sin. I have tried to help you, to give you hope, to listen to your dilemma, but you continue to dishonour our Lord and me. It is time to see the error of your ways. You must seek help! You must repent!'

There was silence.

Christiano pounced up from his seat and burst out of the booth to find the door open and the chamber once again empty.

Mystified, he looked quickly round the chapel.

Father Cavallo, who was speaking with a group of nuns, looked at him with a worried expression. 'Father Christiano, are you okay?'

Christiano hastened to the entrance, into the corridor and then ran along the hallway to the cloister.

The sun filtered through the antiquated, stone arches, highlighting Angelica's presence in the corridor. The cook, Sister Immaculata, pointed a finger in Angelica's face, as if in rebuke.

When he saw them, he stopped, quickly hid behind one of the pillars and glanced furtively round the stone column.

Angelica was motionless, clutching something to her chest. Finally, the cook withdrew her finger and walked away.

With slow, hesitant steps, Christiano moved away from his hiding place.

Angelica whipped her head round.

'Don't be afraid... Is everything okay?'

From the narrowing distance between them, he noticed, clutched to her chest, sheets of paper, and on the back of one of them was a sketch. 'You're an artist?'

Angelica gave a slight, irresolute nod.

He continued to move towards her, delicately. 'Your style resembles some sketches in the Abbess's office. Are they yours, too?'

Once again, she nodded, saying nothing.

'You are very talented… May I look?' He gently reached his hand towards her, but Angelica took a giant leap backwards and ran down the corridor. She paused just once to look back before she disappeared into her dormitory.

Christiano lifted his hand to his cheek as if in reaction to a bitter sting from a slap. He stared down the empty corridor, his heart beating like a racehorse's and his mind befuddled with intrigue and curiosity.

Later that evening, Marcello sat at the kitchen table, which had been attractively set for dinner. He read a newspaper while Agostina prepared dinner. Freshly made spaghetti lay on a towel in wait for the pot of water on the stove to reach boiling point. A flaming red sauce bubbled, filling the kitchen with a sweet, peppery aroma. She waved away the steam and placed a lid on the pot.

'Do you think he'll have dinner this evening?' asked Agostina.

'I don't know. He's not been himself since the fall.'

The clomping of steps silenced them as they looked eagerly at the kitchen entrance.

Christiano appeared. 'I am off for a little walk.'

'No dinner, Father?'

'Maybe later, if it's not an imposition?'

'Not at all, Father. I'll put some aside for you.'

He nodded politely and left. Agostina and Marcello turned to each other. Marcello shrugged.

Outside, the intense heat of the day had surrendered to the subtle evening breeze, and the most dominant sound was the incessant buzz of mosquitoes overpowered by the odd car or scooter speeding by. The air was filled with the smells of home cooking. Garlic, basil and tomato wafted through the air as people dined alfresco on the front porches of their homes.

He walked in deep contemplation. Every now and then he took a glimpse at the happy families gathered round their dinner tables. 'Join us, Father,' called out one man.

'Thank you, another time. God bless you,' he replied, as he continued his journey.

He entered Piazza di Nettuno, which was bustling with punters enjoying their wine and feasting on a smorgasbord of food, and sat with eyes closed on a bench by the fountain.

'Father!' announced a deep, croaky voice.

He opened his eyes to see Philippe staggering towards him.

'Philippe, how are you?'

'You know me, Father?'

'Any friend of Marcello and Agostina is a friend of mine.'

'We lost our children, Father.' He slumped down on the

seat next to him and wiped the silent tears from his eyes.

Christiano nodded sympathetically. 'I am aware of your tragedy, and I am deeply sorry for your loss.'

Philippe continued in a low murmuring sob. He drowned it in a swig from his bottle of whisky. 'I sometimes think God punished me by taking my sons and my wife. I never appreciated what I had until they were gone.'

'The acknowledgement of your sins is the first step to forgiveness.'

He took another gulp of his drink. 'Yes Father, I confess, I was a bastard to them. I used to stay out late. I sinned against my wife. I was a bad role model to my sons. I showed no love, nor care.'

'Philippe, while confession is what you need, it must not be made in your current state of inebriation. Perhaps if you would take steps to sobriety, I could take your confession and…'

'I'm a lost cause, Father. If only there was a way to redeem myself.' He stood up and turned to face him. 'You know, Father, shortly before your arrival I began to have visions.'

'What kind of visions?'

'They told me you were coming – the man with the mark of Christ. They are calling on you soon. Be ready!'

'Philippe, what are you talking about?'

Philippe staggered away without another word, leaving Christiano dumbfounded by the day's events.

A heavy sigh left his lips.

+ Chapter Five +

The next day as he passed through the abbey forecourt, he saw the Abbess, Sister Celeste, and Father Cavallo chatting outside the admin office.

'Hello, Father,' called out the Abbess. 'Are you well today?'

'Fully recovered, thank you!'

'I shall see you in the chapel shortly,' said Father Cavallo.

He nodded and walked on. A few moments later, he paced the aisle towards the Virgin sculpture. With yesterday's events still weighing on his mind, he dropped limply onto the front pew and heard a faint rustle. He turned to his side to find that he had sat on a piece of paper.

He picked it up and blinked as if his eyes deceived him. He was looking at himself. Each boldly drawn line flowed masterfully into the next, flawlessly incorporating light and shade in a complexity of strokes that formed a sketch that was as lifelike as staring into a mirror.

With the drawing in his hand, he left the chapel and walked hurriedly into the cloister, where he looked round in all directions. Two nuns sitting in meditation were the only people to be seen.

He continued towards the kitchen, carefully opened the door and peered inside. Sister Immaculata and the other nuns, who were preparing lunch, looked at him questioningly. He shut the door in disappointment, looked again at the portrait and marvelled at its brilliance.

The door to the recreation room swung open and three nuns entered the hallway. They each greeted him with a nod. He smiled and nodded in return as he took hold of the door and entered the room. The scent of fresh herbs wafted through the open patio doors, mingling with the mouth-watering vestiges of syrupy coffee.

Across the way, in the orchard, Angelica sat on the grass, sketching.

He made his way towards her, stopped unnoticed behind her, and continued to watch fascinated as she added the finishing touches to her drawing of a golden, fuzzy bumblebee in rhythmic union with a flaming poppy.

'Bees…' he said.

Startled, she turned her head and raised herself from the ground.

'I didn't mean to alarm you.'

He pointed to her drawing which now lay discarded on the ground. 'The providers of God's sweet nectar. Such intelligent creatures. Did you know that they have super-vision? Take a television screen, for example. To us the images are fluid, but a bee can differentiate each individual frame.'

Angelica smiled.

'Also, so much of the foods and beverages we enjoy would not be possible without them. Take coffee, for example, and watermelon…

Her smile turned into a soundless giggle. He stopped and looked a little embarrassed. *Was she gently mocking him?* He quickly changed the subject.

'You drew this, didn't you?' He held the sketch up.

She nodded.

'It's a masterpiece. Where did you learn to draw like this?'

There was no reply, just a stare with eyes now soft and welcoming. After a short silence, she pointed to her mouth and waved her finger as she shook her head.

'You have taken a vow of silence?'

She removed a whiteboard from beneath her sketchpad and with a black marker began to write on the board.

Christiano's eyes widened in wonderment.

When she had finished her scribble, she held it up before him.

He mouthed the words on the board. *I lost my voice in childhood.*

'Oh, I'm sorry,' he replied. 'What happened?'

She took a step back, crossed her arms over her body and averted her gaze to anywhere but Christiano.

'Angelica!' sang a voice that interrupted their exchange.

They turned to see Sister Immaculata in the herb garden. 'Hello, Father, did you find what you were looking for?'

His face flushed.

'Angelica I'm in need of your help.' She walked towards

them, looking suspiciously at Christiano. 'Sorry to interrupt, Father Abbadelli. I have been searching for this girl everywhere. Angelica, you were supposed to be helping in the kitchen. We spoke of this yesterday. Whatever is the matter with you, lately? Bring yourself over here and collect some vegetables and herbs for lunch and dinner.'

She shook her head. 'Excuse us, Father.'

The nun continued to berate Angelica as they walked away, wagging her finger at her. 'You know, Angelica, it is with idle hands that Satan does his bidding…'

Her voice trailed away, but the familiar words spoken only yesterday in confession rose to his throat like vomit.

✦ Chapter Six ✦

The portrait, which now took pride of place above Christiano's bed, seemed to take on its own persona, like his trapped shadow with its own secrets and longings. He found himself mesmerised by these new eyes; ones that seemed to be telling him a different story from those he saw in the mirror every day.

He turned away from them, walked to his yoga mat and took a seat. The unflinching eyes watched as he manoeuvred with deft agility into *firefly pose* – balancing on his hands and stretching out his legs in front of his body.

With resolute strength and an indomitable stare, he held the position as sweat dripped from his rigid frame to form a small pool on the mat. After a few minutes, he dropped his feet and used them to propel upwards, into a standing position.

He wiped his face with a towel as he entered the bathroom, where he bathed beneath a shower of arctic cold water.

As he dressed in the morning stillness, the wan light

projected through the ceiling windows of his basement room, where it seemed to remain, floating above him like a cloud obscuring the sun.

As he left the room, he picked up a book that lay in wait on his bedside table, bounded up the stairs, and peered round the door to find Agostina at the kitchen table, sipping espresso.

'Can I get you some breakfast, Father Abbadelli?'

'No thank you, Agostina. I shall get something at Santa Maria.' He nodded in appreciation and left the house.

Fifteen minutes later, he strolled into the convent and then quickened his steps to the chapel. As he reached the cloister, he found himself immersed in the sonorous, flute-like chirping of songbirds perched on the cypress tree at the heart of the grounds. Their melodic sounds seemed to transport the listener magically to a tropical paradise.

As he walked, he could see Angelica between the gaps of each archway. She sat on a bench, immersed in the sweet melodies – her head positioned reverently to the heavens, her eyes closed, and her face wearing a deeply contented expression.

He stopped at the entrance to observe her for a moment before he approached her. His lofty stature cast a shadow over her face. She opened her eyes and her lips spread into a delighted smile.

'I have a gift for you,' he said.

Remaining as ever silent, she gestured with her hands and a pleasantly surprised expression, as if to ask, *what is it?*

'It's a book that has everything about the history of art.

It belongs to me, but I want you to have it. It's a little worn, but only from years of study.'

She accepted the gift with a look of fascination. As she examined the front cover, she ran her hands along its surface and flicked through the pages. She scribbled a message on her board and held it up to him. *A meaningful gift that I will treasure. Thank you!*

He nodded and motioned to leave, but instead, turned back to face her. 'I'm going to cut some fruit from the orchard. Would you like to join me?'

With an enthusiastic nod, she rose from the bench.

As they walked together, their steps clumsy and uncertain, they glanced coyly at each other every now and then before coming to a stop at a fig tree.

Christiano pulled a penknife from his pocket, grasped the antique brass handle and pulled on the blade.

Angelica scribbled on her board. *An unusual item for a priest to possess.*

He smiled as he peeled a fig. 'A gift from my grandfather, whom I loved dearly. I am never without it.'

He split the fig open and offered it to her.

She took it, scraped the insides and licked her lips, her eyes beaming with satiety. He peeled one for himself and consumed it in one mouthful. They watched each other, their eyes communicating the messages they wanted to convey.

He cautiously reached his hand to her cheek, and seeing the permission in her eyes, he wiped a tiny remnant of fig from her skin.

'Father Abbadelli!'

They turned to see the Abbess, her brows contracted to form a scowl.

She marched towards them. 'Angelica, we have an appointment, remember? Go and wait in my office.'

Angelica did as instructed and Christiano was left with the glowering Abbess.

He wiped the blade of his penknife with a handkerchief, folded it back to its closed position, and placed it in his pocket.

'Father Abbadelli, I do not have the time to discuss this with you now, but I wish to see you in my office later. This is a serious matter, but for now I am the only one privy to what is transpiring. Find the time to see me when I return.'

Without waiting for a reply, she stormed off, leaving him with a feeling of dread coiling its way round his guts as an unexpected realisation snaked its way to his consciousness.

Back at the chapel, Father Cavallo prepared for morning mass. As he opened the Bible, ready to place it onto the lectern, an envelope fell out, landing on the altar table.

He picked it up and examined the writing on the front. *To Father Abbadelli.*

As he inspected the handwriting, a drop of water landed on the letter *A*, causing the ink to disperse and the trickle of a little blue tear to his thumb.

Instinctively, he looked up at the ceiling and felt a drop on his hand. Readjusting his focus, he moved directly beneath the Virgin Mary's face.

To his astonishment, her eyes blinked, her mouth moved, and a sound like the cry of a gentle bird, as rapturous as a children's choir, emanated from her lips.

There he remained, rooted to the spot as the teardrops rained from her benevolent eyes onto his face.

Clutching at his heart, he took short sharp breaths and collapsed to the ground.

✦ Chapter Seven ✦

A dejected Christiano dragged his feet through the chapel narthex. Suddenly, he experienced a change in him which seemed physical in its strength. An inexplicable feeling as warm as a loving caress consumed his senses. He looked up, and his moistened eyes panned round the room for the source.

A delayed image flashed through his mind. He retraced his gaze to the Virgin sculpture where he caught sight of what appeared to be a hand sprawled across the irregular, stone floor in the transept crossing.

'Father Franco?' He sprinted towards the unconscious priest who lay on the ground, knelt by his side and vigorously shook his body.

He called into his ear. 'Father Franco!' There was no response. 'Help in here!' he shouted as he placed his index and middle fingers on the Father's carotid artery in search of a pulse.

There appeared to be no life in the old priest.

He turned him on his back and made a compression to

his chest, followed by a succession of fast and hard pushes, counting each one until he reached thirty.

He stopped, put his palm on Father Cavallo's forehead, gently tilted his head back and lifted his chin forward to open his airways. He put his ear close to the priest's mouth and checked for a waft of warm breath.

To his dismay, nothing greeted his skin.

He made another pleading whisper, 'Come on. Please.' His wide eyes were suffused with panic. He pinched the old man's nostrils and puffed a second long breath into his mouth and watched his chest for movement.

There was none.

'Help in here,' he shouted before blowing a second breath into his mouth. He watched in nervous anticipation, and muttered, 'Come on. Come on', anxious for the influx of his breath to kick-start the old man's vital organs.

He hollered for help again. His screeching echo reached all the way to the bell tower where his voice seemed to ricochet off the bell, causing a deep, solemn gong that sounded like a mourning toll.

'Don't you give up,' he said, performing thirty more compressions. Another puff... 'Come on! Come on!' He followed with another breath and looked eagerly at the Father's rib cage... 'Wake up! Wake up!' he screamed as he banged his fist on Father Cavallo's heart with almighty fury.

Suddenly, a spasm which seemed almost exaggerated lifted Father Cavallo's upper torso inches off the ground. He drew his breath in sharply.

Relief made Christiano's heart heave in his chest, and he

felt tears starting in his eyes. 'I thought I'd lost you, my friend.' He affectionately cupped his cheeks.

The Father's face glowed crimson. 'I... It... Our Lady. She spoke to me,' he said with surprising vigour.

Christiano's face remained blank.

The old man jerked up into a sitting position and yelled, 'Did you hear what I said?... Our Lady spoke to me. It was like a choir of angels, their soothing voices vanquishing the crude foibles of human nature... Then she cried – a cascade of warm, gentle tears that were like an angel's touch relieving me of all pain... The last thing I remember is my heart exploding with joy.'

'Let me help you to your wheelchair,' said Christiano.

'I can walk!' he said, pushing Christiano's hands away.

'Now is not the time for independence, Father Franco, please allow me to help you to your seat.'

'No... I mean I can really walk. All the pain has vanished. I can move. Look.' He shot to his feet and tap danced out of the transept crossing and into the chapel nave.

Christiano's mouth dropped open.

'It's a miracle!' shouted Father Cavallo. 'She told me that I had performed my duty and thanked me. Then she told me that I must return to the earthly realm as I am needed at Santa Maria.'

The doors to the chapel swung open, and a concerned Sister Celeste and Sister Carmina entered, followed by a swarm of inquisitive nuns.

Father Cavallo ran towards them, his arms outstretched ready to embrace his sisters with exuberant jubilation.

The nuns looked stunned, two of them fainted, and the rest made the sign of the cross while muttering prayers.

He rushed out of the chapel like a galloping horse. 'I must tell the Abbess.'

It was late afternoon when Christiano found himself, unwillingly, at the Abbess's door. He knocked, meekly.

'Enter!'

He opened the door and entered the office.

'Please sit down, Father Abbadelli.'

He took the seat opposite her and rubbed his tense brow. 'Abbess Rossini, it is not…'

'Firstly,' she interrupted, 'I want to thank you for saving our dear Father Franco. If you had not been there…' She shook her head. 'I dread to think.'

Christiano nodded, modestly.

'Since knowing you I have thought of you as an honourable man, but my recent observations have forced me to see you in a different light.'

'Abbess Rossini, please…'

She shut her eyes as if to hush him. He stopped mid-sentence.

'I know what I saw, Father, whether you realise it or not… Need I remind you of your priestly vows?'

He lowered his gaze in shame.

'I have decided not to report your conduct to Father Franco or Monsignor Basso. Instead, you will make a request to leave Santa Maria by the end of this week, so as not to arouse suspicion. You will simply tell everyone that since

Father Franco's miraculous recovery, you have decided to pursue your studies. Is that clear?'

He nodded. 'As you wish.'

'And you are to say nothing of this to Angelica. In fact, do not so much as look her way between now and the moment you leave the gates of Santa Maria, for good.'

A hard knock sounded at the door.

'Enter!'

A buoyant Father Cavallo entered.

'Father Franco!' said the Abbess delighted. 'Back from the hospital full of mirth, I see.'

'Indeed, the doctor said it was a miracle. If only he knew!' He chuckled. 'I told him that some treatment with a chiropractor had worked well for me. He was miffed, but what could he say when the very truth was standing before him.'

'I had a call from Monsignor Basso; he heard of your recovery and is coming for a visit tomorrow. Apparently, he is bringing a prestigious guest, and we are to prepare for an arrival fit for royalty.'

'Fit for royalty, hey.' His eyes brightened. 'Perhaps the Pope has heard of my miraculous recovery and is coming to see the miracle for himself,' said Father Cavallo excitedly.

'I have no idea, but I have instructed Sister Immaculata to make her exquisite *crostata di frutta*.'

'In that case, I must go and prepare, also. It has been a day of hospital visits, has it not?'

The Abbess's eyes widened.

'Ah… Father Christiano,' said Father Cavallo, his cheeks

glowing, 'I'm sure the Monsignor will be happy to see how well you have settled in at Santa Maria.'

Christiano feigned a smile and rose from his seat. 'Will that be all, Abbess Rossini?'

'Yes, thank you, Father Abbadelli.'

He nodded politely and left, reaching as far as the refectory when Father Cavallo caught up with him in the corridor. 'With all the fuss, I forgot to give you this.' He handed him the envelope. 'While I was preparing for Mass this morning, I opened the Bible, and it fell out.'

Christiano examined the envelope.

'It seems someone had the gall to place it between the pages of the Holy Bible. I am most disturbed. Do you know who it's from?'

'I have to admit, Father Franco, I do not.'

He tore the envelope open.

Darkness engulfed his face as he read the note. '*Father Abbadelli, You will not hear from me again. I have set in motion the wheels that will expose Santa Maria as the unsavoury, unholy place it has become. The Abbess, like you, favours the sinful above the pious. She will pay for her clandestine actions and so will you. His Holiness should laicise you both. It appears that it is up to me to right the wrong. Sister Anonymous.*'

'Is everything okay?' asked Father Cavallo.

Christiano's face contorted. Without uttering a word, he marched past him, towards the kitchen. As he reached the door, it opened. Sister Immaculata just managed to stop before a collision occurred.

'Father Abbadelli, what can I do for you?'

He waved the letter in her face. 'You tell me, Sister!' His hostility was met with bewilderment.

'If you are looking for Angelica, she isn't here.'

'Know this, Sister. I am aware of who you are. If anything happens, it is you who will find herself exposed.' He stormed off.

Sister Immaculata's face turned a violent shade of red.

That evening, Christiano finished typing his letter and saved it to a memory stick before turning the light off and fidgeting for a comfortable position in his bed.

Finally, he settled on top of the sheets. The fans offered a refreshing alternative to the ambient humidity. The streetlights outside his windows threw a haunting array of sinister shapes on the ceiling above his bed, creating shadow creatures that looked poised to devour him. He stared at them half-hypnotised, as he drifted to sleep.

✦ Chapter Eight ✦

The next morning, when Christiano arrived at Santa Maria, his first stop was the admin office, where he asked Sister Celeste if he could use the office computer and printer.

After printing out three letters, he made his way to the Abbess's office, knocked on the door and waited for approval before entering. 'I brought you a copy of my resignation letter.' He placed it on her desk. 'I have a copy for Father Franco, and I will be giving the Monsignor his letter when he arrives today.'

He turned to leave.

'Father Abbadelli, please understand, this is for the...' As she spoke, her voice trailed away, her eyes fixed down on her desk.

He followed her gaze to a pile of letters by a newspaper called, *Il Cospiratore.*

She picked up the paper and scrutinised the front cover before pressing the intercom button at her desk. 'Sister Celeste, did you drop the mail in my office this morning?'

'Yes, Abbess Rossini.' The reply echoed through the loudspeaker. 'Is anything wrong?'

'Come to my office, please.'

With a mortified expression, she looked at Christiano. 'I'm sorry, this matter will have to wait.'

'Is everything okay?' he asked.

The door opened, and Sister Celeste entered.

'Please Father Abbadelli if you will…' The Abbess motioned to the door.

He nodded politely and left for the chapel.

The oratory was as busy as a train station. A group of sisters knelt in prayer at the gate of the transept crossing while others sat in the pews behind. Father Cavallo was at the altar table preparing for mass. Christiano felt relieved that Angelica was nowhere to be seen. He walked to the altar table to offer his assistance.

'Ah, there you are. The Monsignor and his prestigious guest arrive at any moment and—'

'Fathers,' interrupted Sister Celeste, 'the Monsignor has arrived.'

'And we are so very unprepared!' said Father Cavallo as he made his way out of the chapel. An unenthused Christiano followed behind him.

The Abbess was already at the door watching the Monsignor pull in and park his little blue Fiat close to her own car. A gleaming black limousine entered behind him and parked confidently in front of the entrance.

The Monsignor, a man of small, slender stature with a

wide grin, left his vehicle and stood at the door of the limousine. He wore a black cassock with red trim cord and matching buttons, and a magenta fascia tied at his waist.

A fair-haired chauffeur, whose athletic torso complemented his black suit, stepped out of the limousine and proceeded to open the back passenger door.

A lofty, rotund man emerged, dressed in a black simar with a scarlet sash. His hair was a lustrous silver-grey; springing wildly from beneath his skullcap like an unkempt bush. Three others, dressed in civilian clothing, followed behind him: two men and a woman. They each carried two large black cases.

'A Cardinal!' said Father Cavallo.

'With an entourage,' said the Abbess.

Christiano narrowed his eyes, wondering where he had seen the Cardinal before.

The two men greeted each other, the Cardinal like a giant towering over an ant. The Monsignor gestured for him to proceed ahead, while his entourage followed behind them.

When they reached the arched entrance, the Monsignor was the first to greet them. 'It is good to see you all. This is His Eminence, Cäsar Beltz: Prefect of the Miracles Commission. As you can see, he has brought with him a team of scientists who will be running various tests on the sculpture of our Venerable Mary.'

'Your Eminence,' said Father Cavallo. He genuflected and kissed the large oval ruby at the centre of the Cardinal's gold ring. 'This is rather unexpected.' He raised himself to standing.

'Yes, please forgive us,' continued the Monsignor.

'Please do not be alarmed,' interjected a voice with a heavy German accent, 'Father Cavallo, is it?'

'Yes, Your Eminence.'

The Cardinal proceeded to speak while Christiano and the Abbess genuflected and kissed his ring. 'It is the job of the Miracles Commission to investigate all claims of miracles through healing. Believe me, if it was the case of a weeping Madonna, for example, we would not be here; we leave that sort of thing to the locals. However, I am told that you were about to have a hip replacement. Am I correct?'

'Indeed you are, Your Eminence.'

'Then it seems that I am witness to a miracle!' He smiled a twisted grin that made Father Cavallo uncomfortable.

Christiano noticed. 'Your Eminence,' he said, 'I believe I saw you on television. You were leaving the Vatican.'

'Ah, yes. Unfortunately, there is no escaping publicity. Nowadays, even the Church needs PR.' He turned to Father Cavallo. 'Tell me, Father. Is the Monsignor's report absolutely accurate?'

'Yes Your Eminence, you have my most trusted word. Father Christiano is my witness.'

Christiano nodded. 'It is true, Your Eminence.'

'Then I believe you.'

'Your Eminence, Monsignor, please, follow us to the chapel,' said Father Cavallo.

'Do you reside at the Holy See, Your Eminence?' asked the Abbess as they walked.

'Not exactly. However, I do reside in Rome, in a humble

home generously provided by the Vatican.'

The Monsignor watched Father Cavallo fast and steady on his feet; not a limp in sight. 'Father Franco,' he said, 'you speak the truth. The last time I saw you, you were in a hospital bed, and the doctor's prognosis was anything but promising. It is a miracle.'

'I knew it would be a sight you would need to see with your own eyes,' replied Father Cavallo with a broad grin.

'And you, Father Christiano, how are you settling in at Santa Maria? I have heard only good things.'

'I could not have imagined a more fitting assignment. Unfortunately, I must request leave to continue my studies. Now that Father Cavallo is no longer retiring there is no need for my presence.' He handed his resignation letter to the Monsignor.

'I am sorry to hear that, Father,' replied the Monsignor as he accepted the letter.

'And so am I,' said Father Cavallo. 'I had hoped you would finish the year.'

They reached the chapel, and Father Cavallo pushed the doors open.

A drift of peace as fluid as water washed over them.

The guests sighed simultaneously, marvelling at the sight of the Virgin sculpture. 'She is indeed, quite magnificent,' announced the Cardinal.

'Sisters,' the Abbess called out.

The nuns stood in response and turned to face them, each one of them kneeling on one knee – their heads bowed.

'Thank you all for your continued devotion, but we ask

that you leave the chapel,' announced the Abbess.

The nuns stood and walked in pairs down the nave, turning their eyes to the ground as they passed the Cardinal, until the chapel was empty.

Without wasting a moment, the three scientists laid their cases down on the front pews and proceeded to put on white coats and surgeon face masks. The woman unravelled a tool belt filled with instruments of various kinds, which made her look more like she was on an archaeological dig. She removed a sharp palette knife and a vial from one of the cases and proceeded to enter the transept crossing.

Father Cavallo gasped.

The Cardinal turned towards him. 'She has permission.'

Father Cavallo nodded, 'Of course, Your Eminence.'

He watched as she began scraping a small area of the sculpture and placing the peelings in the vial. One of the men had charge of a small handheld device that he was passing along the body of the sculpture.

'It's probably best to let them get on with their work. Meanwhile, I would love a tour of your wonderful convent,' announced the Cardinal.

'Of course, Your Eminence,' said the Abbess. 'Please.' She gestured with her hand and genuflected as he left the chapel.

Father Cavallo took one last look at the scientists and shook his head as he left.

'A very tranquil place,' said the Cardinal as he closed his eyes and immersed himself in the sonorous sounds of the birds in the cloister. He opened them. 'I hear the sisters make the best preserves for miles around. Is that so?'

'Why yes, Your Eminence,' said the Monsignor. 'Perhaps the Abbess would be so kind as to give you a tour of the kitchens.'

'I'll even manage a gift of any preserves of your liking, Your Eminence,' she said.

'Most kind of you. Do you have quince?'

'We do, Your Eminence,' replied the Abbess. 'Perhaps a tour of the orchard, as well.'

As they walked towards the preserve kitchen, the door to the recreation room opened, and Angelica entered the corridor holding a basket filled with fresh herbs and vegetables. She stopped, surprised by the group before her.

Christiano immediately averted his eyes. The Cardinal, however, seemed to falter. The blood seemed to drain from his face, and his eyes grew rigid with terror. He raised his hand to shield his vision as if a blinding light bore through him.

'Your Eminence?' said the Monsignor.

He stumbled, turned and ran back towards the cloister where he collapsed to his knees by the cypress tree.

Christiano was the first to reach him. He helped him to the bench. 'Are you okay, Your Eminence?'

Straining to catch a breath, and tears trickling from the corners of his eyes, he managed to nod between ponderous breaths. The others reached them, each wearing the semblance of concern.

'Whatever happened?' asked the Monsignor.

The Cardinal caught his breath, his plump face

resembling an aubergine. 'My apologies to you all, but I must leave. I'm afraid that my health is not its best at present.'

'I am sorry to hear that, Your Eminence,' said the Monsignor. 'I will instruct your chauffeur to take you to the nearest hospital. I insist on a check-up before you make the journey back to Rome. I will go with you, and your chauffeur can return for your team later.'

'That won't be necessary,' replied the Cardinal.

'Please, Your Eminence. I insist. What would His Holiness think of me if I neglected to see you well before your journey home?'

'Of course. You are correct,' he replied. 'To the hospital it is.'

'Come, Your Eminence, I will assist you to your car,' said Christiano. He helped him up from the bench and supported the old man's weight as they made their way to his limousine, where he instructed the chauffeur to wait for the Monsignor.

Inside the limousine, the Cardinal opened his briefcase and stared briefly at the front cover of *Il Cospiratore* – a copy of the same newspaper that had arrived on the Abbess's desk that morning. He shut the lid just as the Monsignor entered the car.

✦ Chapter Nine ✦

Asmoky haze coiled its way towards the ceiling of the fourteenth-century cellar where an opulent fresco, spanning its entire length, featured Aquilon, god of the north wind. A ferocious gale blasted from his bearded mouth, which, with the aid of the drifting smog resembled a billowing wind bearing down on the restaurant beneath it.

A waiter delivering a plate of steaming linguini made his way beneath archways and beams, each step intensifying the trepidation he felt. It was a hazardous job: one wrong move; a spillage of wine; a hot beverage in a lap; or simply catching a word or phrase that could end his life. He kept the secrets contained, like the old Tuscan building in which he worked – secrets that he left behind each day when his shift was over, safely enclosed within the solid stone walls.

He reached a table surrounded by men. Ricardo made no acknowledgement as the waiter placed the plate carefully, silently, on the table beneath the newspaper he was studying intently. 'You need to look at this,' said Ricardo, addressing Don Primo, a man with steely blue eyes, to his left, clearly the head of the family.

Enzo, a man in his fifties with a deep scar running from the bottom of his right eye to mid-cheek, was sitting to Don Primo's left. He stopped mid-munch and looked at Ricardo in amusement.

Don Primo raised his head, that formidable glint escaping his eyes, that characteristic smirk on his lips. 'You're mistaken, I think. I need nothing. If, however, you think there is something I might like to see, *you* need to address me with some respect!'

Enzo smirked and started munching again, while the men around the table sniggered.

'My sincere apologies, Don Primo, it's just that there's something here I think you should, err, might, like to see.'

Don Primo accepted the newspaper, grinning to his cronies. Then his face changed.

'What is it Boss?' asked Enzo.

Don Primo remained silent as he read. When he finished, he put the paper down on the table, and with his index finger on the article of interest, he slid it over to him.

Enzo gawped, his gaze transfixed as he read.

The rest of the table was silent – each man's attention on Enzo.

When he finished reading, he raised his head and visibly gulped. Then turned to his Boss.

'You two,' said Don Primo, pointing first to Ricardo, then to Enzo, 'go to this convent and let me know what you find. If it's her, I want her back, unharmed. Is that clear?'

'Yes, Boss,' said Enzo standing up.

'Yes, Boss,' repeated Ricardo rising from his seat.

'And Enzo…' Don Primo fixed him with a malign stare. 'Don't fuck this up!'

'No way Boss,' said Enzo, making sincere eye contact.

Don Primo's steely gaze remained steady on Enzo, who was growing more uncomfortable with each ticking moment. With a brusque tone, he snapped, 'Go!'

The two men flinched, turned and quickly headed for the door. Enzo shot a scathing look at the back of Ricardo's head.

A loaded silence stifled the air as the car gunned its way along the motorway at the dead of night. Enzo scrutinised the newspaper article while Ricardo drove the car, puffing on his cigarette. His eyes sharply focused on the road ahead.

Enzo removed his mobile phone from his pocket and ran an internet search for Santa Maria L'adorata. His rough, oversized finger hit the relevant find. His search was interrupted by the ringing phone. He looked at the screen and hit the answer button. 'Yes, Boss… No problem Boss… I've got this.'

He hit the end button and went back to his research.

'What did the Boss want?'

Enzo maintained a steady gaze on his phone. 'None of your business, that's what.'

Ricardo's face contorted with scorn. 'It's because I'm an outsider, isn't it?'

Enzo turned to Ricardo with a peevish look on his face. 'What is?'

'The reason you don't like me.'

Enzo returned to his phone. 'That's about right.'

'Why?'

'I don't trust you!' he snapped.

'I've given you no reason to doubt my loyalty to Don Primo.'

'I've seen what happens to your friends.'

'The Baldi family?'

Enzo ignored him and continued to read the information on his phone.

'They were no friends of mine. They killed my parents. I was just a kid. I got in with them to get even. Don Primo gave me respect for what I did. I wiped out his competition.'

'I don't care about your shit. We're not friends here. We have a job to do. That's it.'

'Okay, I understand.'

'No you don't! You don't get it at all. You've filled Don Primo with hope. If it's not her, what do you think he'll do to us?'

Ricardo remained silent, anxiously staring at the road ahead.

'He'll have our guts removed and fed to the pigs, that's what. And I'm his brother-in-law.'

'Well, maybe it's her. Don't you want to redeem yourself? She escaped on your watch.'

'You think I don't know that? That bitch made me look like a fool, and she's gonna pay... And, what is that shit it said in the article? You believe that?'

Ricardo shook his head. 'No. When I saw it, I don't

know. It just sounded like it could be her.'

'Well, you should have kept your mouth shut and come to me first. I would have checked it out, and if it was her I would have told him.'

'I didn't think of that. He was there. I told him.'

'And you've opened up a big can of worms. Now, if it's her, we have to find a way to get her out of a fucking convent, without shooting a load of nuns in the process.'

'We'll work it out, Enzo. We'll work together, and we'll work it out.'

'I'm warning you to watch that rash temper of yours and that trigger-happy finger. Do I make myself clear?'

'You got it, Enzo. You're calling the shots.'

Enzo went back to his phone and maintained his brawny, seasoned veneer, despite his guts twisting like a tornado.

A few hours later, Ricardo pulled up to the hefty gates of Santa Maria where the innocence of the morning shone its gentle warmth on the slumbering streets surrounding the convent.

They peered out of the front windscreen, awestruck by the sight of the Virgin Mary poised over the impenetrable gates that lay ahead of them.

'How the hell we gonna get in there?' said Ricardo.

'There's a shop on a road called Via Scala, we'll find a way through there,' said Enzo. He pointed to the steep, sloping road. 'There it is.'

Ricardo continued forward on to Via Scala and parked opposite the shop.

Without a word, Enzo got out of the car and made his way to the door.

The opening times were on the inside window, on a typed laminated board that was worn and slightly faded by the relentless daily assault of the sun's rays. He squinted his eyes, ran his index finger down to the correct day of the week, and returned to the car.

'It opens in about an hour.' He looked at his watch. 'They're probably finishing morning mass as we speak.'

✦ Chapter Ten ✦

Daylight streamed through the stained-glass windows, highlighting motes of dust that descended upon the congregation like bounty from heaven. Christiano faced his parishioners with open arms. 'May almighty God bless you.' He made the sign of the cross and continued, *'in nomine Patris et Filii et Spiritus Sancti.'*

An almighty 'Amen' intoned through the chapel, creating a weightless serenity.

He joined his hands together. 'The Mass is ended, go now in peace to love and serve the Lord.'

'Thanks be to God!' responded the nuns in melodic harmony.

Many remained genuflected in prayer, while others sat in quiet contemplation. Their movement was slow, as if reluctant to leave and attend to their daily chores, choosing instead to bask in the trail of sacrosanct bliss invoked by the ceremonial prayers.

Father Cavallo had insisted that Christiano should

conduct morning mass, as he was leaving and it was to be a quiet withdrawal.

Throughout the service, a disconcerted Christiano found his gaze bound to Angelica as if his eyes were drawn to a magnificent painting. The Abbess noticed, boring a hole through his skull the size of the moon.

Angelica rose from her seat and made her way to a pew close by the confessional booth, where she lingered, waiting for Christiano.

He noticed her intention. But he was also aware of the Abbess's surveillance all the way from the narthex. He avoided her expectant stare. Instead, he entered the sacristy to remove his liturgical vestments.

Back at the car, Ricardo vigilantly eyed the shop door while Enzo skilfully puffed out smoke rings that drifted to the end of their lifespan and dispersed into a grey cloud.

A nun appeared at the shop window, flipped the closed sign and pulled the door open.

'That's our cue,' said Enzo. He stamped his cigarette into the ashtray. 'You distract her while I find a way in.'

They entered the shop to find the nun brushing the top shelves with a long duster, displacing flecks of dust that now avidly circled the air in search of a new home.

She paused and turned to them with a bright, welcoming smile.

Ricardo approached her with a forced grin and a glint of uncertainty in his eyes as he scanned the shop for a topic of distraction. He spotted the jars of preserves that lined the shelves.

'Tell me, sister, ah…' He looked at her name badge. 'Sister Clara! What a beautiful name…'

Enzo noticed a gap behind the till and managed to slip through unseen, into what looked like the shop's storeroom. He searched for a way out and soon spotted a little light filtering through the windowless room from a door slightly ajar. He poked his head through the gap to look upon a deserted kitchen. His mouth involuntarily salivated from the sweet medley of fruit preserves lingering in the air. He walked through wearing a humorous expression that suggested this was all too easy.

By the time Christiano emerged from the vestry, Angelica's seat was empty. He took a lingering blink and made a heavy sigh.

'Is everything all right?' asked Father Cavallo.

'Yes, I am just a little tired today.'

'A sleepless night? Or are you eager to resume your studies?'

'Probably a bit of both.'

'Would you like to join me in the refectory, where we can talk? We have so little time left.'

'I would like that very much.'

They reached the corridor the same moment Enzo was leaving the preserve kitchen.

'Can I help you?' asked a bemused Father Cavallo, unable to avoid a fixed gaze on the man's scar.

'Ah yes, where's the latrine?'

'I beg your pardon? Are you aware that this is a cloistered community of nuns?'

The Abbess was walking towards them. 'What's going on here?' she demanded.

'Nothing,' said Enzo. He gestured with his hands to calm the situation. 'I made a wrong turn, that's all.' He spun himself round and re-entered the kitchen.

'I'll make sure he leaves,' said Christiano, following behind him.

The Abbess gave Father Cavallo a meaningful look. 'We must talk Father. I will call on Sister Celeste to join us.'

Christiano returned. 'I showed him...' His voice trailed away. Mystified, he looked from one side of the abandoned corridor to the other.

The door to the recreation room opened, and Angelica strolled out clutching her sketchpad and his gift to her chest. She nodded and smiled, by way of greeting, but Christiano's face was a mask of stone. He turned to leave.

She reached her hand to his shoulder and gestured as if to ask, *What's the matter?*

He pushed her hand away. 'I'm a priest. What do you think you're doing?'

Her eyes moistened, and her face expressed bewildered betrayal.

He felt a glimmer of regret. 'Tomorrow is my last day at Santa Maria... It's for the best,' he said, and then headed back to the chapel.

That evening, as Angelica lay wide awake in bed, the door to her room creaked open. Sister Celeste tiptoed towards her. The torch in her hand highlighted Angelica's face, forcing her to shield her eyes.

The nun reached her bed and kneeled by her side, gently caressing her cheek. 'Sweet child, it is no longer safe for you here. Abbess Rossini has asked me to come for you. You must follow me to a place of safety, where she is waiting.'

Angelica made a sign as if to ask, *What's happened?*

'I will explain on our journey,' replied Sister Celeste.

Angelica rose out of bed and started to gather some things.

'There's no time for that. We must leave now,' the sister whispered.

As they walked with soft steps through the dusky corridors, Sister Celeste lit the way with her torch.

They reached the preserve kitchen. 'We'll go out this way. It's safer.'

Angelica nodded and followed Sister Celeste through to the shop where the nun unlocked the door to Via Scala. They stepped onto the dimly lit street that flamed their path, like an orange-tinged tunnel encircled by a wall of blackness.

A few feet away, parked on Di Santa Maria Viale, outside the front gates of the convent, Enzo and Ricardo were fast asleep.

The Abbess awoke suddenly, her eyes wide and frantic. Breathing heavily, she clutched at her chest and pushed her covers aside. Moments later, she stood in Angelica's empty quarters and noticed that her sheets were cold to the touch. Deeply distressed, she left the room and entered the bedroom next door, only to discover another deserted chamber. She looked round the lodgings. 'Sister Celeste?' There was no reply.

She made her way to the corridor. 'Sister Celeste! Angelica!' Her voice carried itself down the desolate hallway and melted into oblivion. 'Angelica, where are you? Sister Celeste!' A sudden panic pierced through her body like a scorched blade. Utterly distraught, she ran up and down the passageway. Her cries echoed through the abbey and stirred its inhabitants from their slumbers. Inquisitive nuns appeared at the doors of their dormitories in quick succession.

Sister Carmina approached her. 'What has happened, Abbess Rossini?'

She grabbed her by the shoulders. 'Have you seen Angelica or Sister Celeste?'

Sister Carmina shook her head, wincing from the Abbess's tight grip.

'Has anyone seen them?' the Abbess cried.

The nuns gathered in the hallway where the chatter of anxious voices now dominated the corridors.

'What's going on?' asked Father Cavallo as he came out of his room wearing nothing but shorts and a vest. He scratched his head and yawned.

'Father Cavallo, Angelica and Sister Celeste are missing.'

'Are you certain?'

'Yes of course I am,' she snapped.

'Abbess Rossini!' Sister Immaculata ran towards her. 'The door to Via Scala is open!'

A bolt of fear shuddered through the Abbess's body. She

clutched at her stomach. 'Oh my dear, blessed Lord, what has happened to them?… We must find them! Everyone, move, now!'

Father Cavallo went back to his room to dress, while the rest of the nuns made their way to Via Scala.

The Abbess ran to her office, picked up the phone and dialled a number.

The unexpected ring in the early hours of the morning woke Christiano with a startle. He fumbled for his mobile phone, finally locating it. 'Pronto!'

'Father Christiano!' yelled the Abbess.

He moved the phone away from his ear with a grimace.

'Abbess Rossini, what's the matter?'

'It's Angelica. She's missing!' Her howls were like electric currents speeding through the wires and shocking every cell in his body to full alert.

He bounded out of bed. 'I'll be right there.'

✦ Chapter Eleven ✦

For the height of summer, it was an unusually hazy night with the starlight and moonlight eclipsed behind drifting clouds. While many of the sisters clustered in small, ordered groups outside the front gates of the convent, others paced up and down Via Scala searching in all directions. A few townsfolk in the immediate vicinity appeared at their windows staring curiously at the nuns parading the streets in the early hours of the morning – like women of the night.

The Abbess stood at the centre of Via Scala lost among the tightly woven buildings that defied age. She listened anxiously for sounds beyond the high-pitched whistle of mosquitoes, to hear the faint rabble of voices headed her way.

Meanwhile, Christiano, dressed in grey track bottoms, white t-shirt and trainers, sprinted to the abbey. With his jaw clenched and his intense gaze fixed ahead, he bulldozed through the town. As he reached the piazza, Philippe, who was witness to the commotion outside Santa Maria, felt the wind breeze across his cheek as he ran by.

'Father!' he called, but Christiano continued on, finally arriving at the convent, barely out of breath and his face aglow with perspiration.

Sister Carmina spotted him and eyed him from head to toe. 'Oh Father Abbadelli, I hardly recognised you. Thank the Lord you are here. Angelica is missing and Sister Celeste....'

'Where's the Abbess?'

'She is down by Via Scala—'

'Father!' interrupted Philippe, coming towards him.

Christiano showed little tolerance as he approached. 'I have no time for this, Philippe. Please leave.'

'I want to help. Tell me what is happening.'

Christiano turned away from him, irritated, and scanned his surroundings. A few of the townspeople had appeared at their doors, and some had ventured onto the street to offer their help – but two men stood out from the animated crowd.

Christiano narrowed his eyes in vague familiarity. The men were leaning casually against the bonnet of a silver car, smoking cigarettes, and close enough to witness the events. They offered no assistance; their demeanour was menacing, as if waiting – just smugly waiting.

The very sight of them gave Christiano an uncomfortable feeling of foreboding.

The Abbess appeared from Via Scala and walked quickly towards them. 'A group of teenagers saw them about twenty minutes ago headed for the beach,' she announced in an amplified voice. Then she noticed the men. She slowed to a stop, as did her breath. A feeling of dread snaked its way around her lungs.

'Were they alone?' asked Father Cavallo, who appeared by her side.

She did not reply. Both she and Christiano were preoccupied with the men who were now entering their vehicle.

The engine revved to life, and the car pulled away. The man on the driver's side flashed a malevolent smirk as he tossed his cigarette out of the window, just missing the Abbess.

The car continued on to Via Scala, passing through a gaggle of black habits which rhythmically parted and reunited in an undulation, down the sloping road until the darkness swallowed it whole.

This time Christiano saw the men close-up – the passenger's characteristic scar branded to his memory. 'The man from the corridor?' he asked.

'I'm afraid it is,' said the Abbess, biting a quivering bottom lip, 'and I have just told them where she is.' She held her hand to her mouth and swallowed the lump in her throat.

'Who? Angelica?'

'We must hurry!' she said as she drew a bunch of keys from her pocket and sniffed and wiped away her tears. 'Sister Immaculata, you are to remain here and call the police. Tell them they must get to the beach immediately as Angelica and Sister Celeste are in grave danger. Hurry! Go!'

The nun sprinted to the convent entrance.

'Abbess Rossini…?'

'Please, Father Christiano. There's no time to explain; we must go after them. Go and fetch my car. I will wait for you here.' She handed him the keys.

Christiano reached the little white Fiat and contorted himself to fit his tall, athletic body into the tiny vehicle. He wound down the window, managing to negotiate a little more elbow room. Moments later, he reached Father Cavallo, who squeezed in the back, and the Abbess who entered the front passenger side.

He released the handbrake and looked to the road ahead to find a defiant Philippe blockading their path – his hands splayed across the car's bonnet.

'Philippe! I will not tell you again. Go home.'

'I want to come with you. I am meant to help.'

'Philippe!'

'Father, please!'

Christiano shut his eyes and took a deep breath to calm himself. He opened them with renewed patience and got out of the car. Seeing his cue, Philippe entered the vehicle with the enthusiasm of a schoolboy.

'Thank you, Father. You will see that I can be of great help.'

Christiano said nothing as he sat back in the driver's seat and looked to the Abbess for instruction.

'Follow Via Scala to the beach,' she said.

He slowly manoeuvred round the nuns and a few locals who had offered their assistance – all on a mission to find the two women – and left the last of them behind to continue on foot. The road ahead lay unobstructed by people, just vehicles parked haphazardly along the narrow, sinuous roads of the medieval town.

'Abbess Rossini, tell me what's happening? Why have you called the police? Who are those men?' asked Christiano as he drove.

The awkward silence was relieved by Father Cavallo. 'I would like to know why they are on their way to the beach, instead of safely tucked away in bed at Santa Maria.'

'I thought they had been abducted,' said the Abbess. 'Why are they out on foot, alone?'

After some intense thought, Christiano pulled the letter from his pocket. 'Abbess Rossini, there is something you should know.' He swallowed hard. 'There is a disgruntled nun at the convent. She has been confessing to me. This is a letter from her, left for me outside the confines of confession. As I left my room this evening, I felt compelled to bring it with me.'

He handed it to the Abbess, who now wore an astonished expression. She accepted it, with apprehension and a look so lost it was as if she had no idea what she held in her hands.

'The note in the Bible?' asked Father Cavallo

'Yes.'

The Abbess pulled the envelope open and pored over the letter. A look of increasing incredulity washed over her face with each passing sentence. When she reached the end, her trembling hands flopped to her lap. She stared ahead in dismay, the distressing situation now doubled in complexity and severity. 'And you think Sister Celeste did this?'

He nodded. 'I'm afraid I do. At first, I thought it was Sister Immaculata, but now I see Sister Celeste set it up to look that way. But I had no idea that the victim of her derangement was Angelica.'

'So she means to harm Angelica?'

She continued questioning, partly to herself, as if trying to understand how Sister Celeste's plunge into insanity had gone unnoticed.

'But, why?'

'I am sorry Abbess Rossini, but her confession is protected by the seal of the confessional.'

'May I read the letter?' asked Father Cavallo.

'Yes of course,' she replied, snapping out of her stupor. She handed it to him.

Father Cavallo studied the note with an intense furrow in his brow. 'This is insane. How did she manage to fool us all so well? Abbess Rossini, you must not blame yourself. The woman is clearly irrational, and frankly, cuckoo! At least now we know who's responsible for the newspaper article.'

'What newspaper article?' asked Christiano.

'Father Christiano, how long has this been taking place?' asked the Abbess.

'As far as I know, since before my arrival.'

Sister Celeste and Angelica reached the crumbling stone wall that separated the lengthy road of La Sfilata from the beach – a road that continued straight out of town.

'We'll wait here,' she said.

Angelica shivered with unease as a gentle breeze raised the goosebumps on her skin. With her back to the sister, she surveyed the deserted road and beyond, catching the flicker of red-golden flames on the far distant shore.

Sister Celeste used Angelica's distraction to her advantage and surreptitiously picked up a large rock from the ground. She hid it behind her back.

'Take a seat on the wall. Abbess Rossini will be here shortly.'

Angelica turned to face her, her silhouette lit by the subtle, ambient hue of the streetlights. She gestured with her hands as if asking, *Where is she?*

'She went to find somewhere safe for you to hide. She'll be here at any moment, to take you there herself.'

Perplexed, she sat down on the wall and rubbed her tired eyes.

With a bitter scowl, Sister Celeste raised the rock above her head – about to thrust it down on Angelica's skull – when a speeding car with blinding headlights screeched to a stop just inches from where they stood.

✦ Chapter Twelve ✦

A brilliant white hue saturated the immediate surroundings. Angelica raised her head to see the sister's outline with the rock poised over her. She rubbed her eyes in disbelief as the seriousness of her predicament dawned on her. She sprung up from the wall and staggered back, immersing herself in the light. For what felt like aeons there was no movement, just the chill of dead air crackling like footsteps on a frosted lake.

The headlights switched off and the car doors swung open. The women could see nothing but dancing lights in front of their eyes.

'Angelica!' chanted a mocking voice that raised the hairs on the nape of her neck. Two men left the car and came to a stop by Sister Celeste. Angelica could see two outlines haloed by the light still playing tricks on her, but the familiar, chilling voice had already forewarned her. Both men gradually came into focus. Her wide eyes shot from one to the other.

'It's time to come home,' said Ricardo. He watched her

carefully as she surveyed her surroundings and noticed her linger for a moment longer on the beach, which, in contrast to where they stood, was a nebulous wall of black. 'Don't—'

Before he could finish his sentence, she sprinted into action, hurdled over the wall and vanished into the void.

Ricardo removed a gun from his pocket and pointed it at Sister Celeste. 'Disappear!' he said before the men gave chase.

Sister Celeste strained to see into the denseness. She heard only the muffled sounds of whispers and the stumbles of two men blindly searching. Petrified to the spot, she hardly noticed Christiano screech to a stop behind the silver car.

The Abbess bounded out of the vehicle and marched straight to her, her raging face heavily marked with betrayal. 'Where's Angelica?' she demanded, moving in close to the nun's face.

Sister Celeste recoiled. Her throat contracted so severely no words could flow. She slowly raised her hand and pointed a bony finger towards the beach.

The Abbess gave her a scathing look before she stepped over the wall and came to a stop at the edge of the light, to face the darkness ahead.

'Abbess Rossini, stop!' called Father Cavallo as he reached her side. 'We should wait for the police.'

As the whiff of salty sea air and rotting fish reached Christiano's nostrils, he heaved. Highly agitated, and doing his best not to vomit, he covered his nose as he rushed to join them.

Philippe strolled out of the vehicle and made his way to Sister Celeste. 'Sister,' he greeted, nodding his head.

She observed him uninterestedly for a fleeting moment before returning her attention to the beach.

'Abbess Rossini, what is happening?' asked Christiano as he came to a stop by her side.

'I will turn the car around to flood some light on the beach,' said Father Cavallo. He made his way back to the Abbess's car.

The Abbess grabbed Christiano's arm. 'She's in there all alone. We must help her.' With a distraught look, she fled into the darkness.

'Abbess, wait!' called Christiano in pursuit.

The others stared on eagerly. The sounds of the sea merged with the whispers and blunders.

Moments later, a piercing shot sent a cacophonous ring through the sky.

Sister Celeste, Philippe and Father Cavallo felt a shudder as cold as ice shoot up their spines, followed by a deathly silence where even the ocean waves seemed to still. The silence was shattered by blaring sirens which came to a stop at the wall and the sounds of nuns and townspeople pouring onto the beach.

Enzo and Ricardo raced into the light. Ricardo waved his gun at the terrified onlookers.

'Everyone down,' shouted one of the officers. The police drew their guns and dived behind their vehicles.

Chaos ensued. While some people ducked, others ran around screaming or remained frozen in terror, making it impossible for the police to fire their guns.

Enzo and Ricardo escaped, speeding down La Sfilata and out of town.

Father Cavallo's manoeuvre had unintentionally blocked the road, preventing the police from giving chase. As the car completed its turn, the light panned round to reveal the Abbess lying on the sand, clutching at her stomach. Kneeling by her side was Christiano.

The nuns and townsfolk formed a semi-circle around them. Whimpers of harrowing disbelief haunted the air as Christiano glared down helplessly at the Abbess's bloodstained hands.

She gasped for breath and tried to reach him – desperation on her face.

'Abbess, hold on,' he said. He took hold of her hand. 'The ambulance will be here shortly.'

She gripped his fingers, weakly. Her mouth opened and made sounds as if trying to speak.

He reached in closer.

'Promise me,' she said, squeezing his hand.

'Yes, I promise. Anything for you.'

'Promise… me… you'll get Angelica away from… Santa Maria,' she gasped. 'She needs… you … Please!… Believe… her!'

She fought for her last breath. Her wide, fearful eyes froze over as the sparkle that had once inhabited her body was evicted from its dwellings.

'Abbess Rossini!' Christiano shook her limp body.

Screams and howls reverberated through the night and

the darkness seemed to intensify and hang over them like the angel of death.

Father Cavallo kneeled down by the Abbess, made the sign of the cross, whispered a prayer and gently closed her eyelids.

Farther down the beach, from behind a boulder, Angelica appeared. She walked slowly at first, her steps leaden as the dread rose through her body. She reached the small crowd where Christiano cradled the dead Abbess, dropped to her knees and convulsed with grief.

Sister Celeste shook her head in disbelief. A hoarse whisper escaped her lips, 'What have I done? What have I done?' She stepped back, turned on her heels and fled into the night.

Philippe, who was the only one to notice, chased after her.

The mournful crowd kneeled by the Abbess in wails and whimpers.

Angelica fell by her side and made small kisses on her cheeks. She cradled her face.

There she remained, with muted sorrow.

✦ Chapter Thirteen ✦

Sister Celeste ran desperately along the beach until her knees gave way under her. Though she had distanced herself from the tragedy behind her, she had laboured for every cumbersome step. The sand had swallowed one foot after the other in a relentless battle. To muffle her wailing, she cupped her face with her hands and bent low to press them in the sand. There she remained until a wave lapped at her fingertips and wetted her face. The water's chill quietened her crying. The soothing sounds of the rippling tide acted as a natural sedative, filtering through her body and numbing her senses.

She stared into the darkness at the veiled night spreading infinitely before her. The moon poked its head through the misty sky. No sooner had she registered its light, it was gone; claimed by a drifting cloud. She nodded as if it had spoken to her. Tranced, she stood up, removed her shoes and walked to the water's edge. The lapping foam danced at her feet, enticing her in. The deeper she waded, the higher the level rose, until her garments reached her chest in a wheel of black. Though her body trembled and her teeth chattered, she continued, farther, deeper. The ocean welcomed her in with playful splashes until the sand beneath her feet disappeared and her survival instincts forced her to tread water. Briny tears flowed down her cheeks and reached the end of her chin. They dropped into the ocean to return home in a perpetual flow, as she would.

Beneath her, the ocean depths felt endless. The sea's expanse seemed infinite, its power, terrifying. It had been a long while since she had swum. She remembered being fifteen when her life had turned to hell. Exhausted and breathless, her eyelids leaden and her legs ponderous, she paddled deeper, adding more distance between her and the shore.

The nuns' lamenting sounds were now inaudible; the crowd seemed ant-sized, and the siren lights were a distant blur. She was hypnotised by the infinitesimal flashing lights; her eyelids were closing, closing. Her legs ceased moving. In a moment of pure surrender, the water – like the hand of a mermaid reaching to embrace her – pulled her beneath the sea, where she drifted with the will of the current.

Sister Celeste had managed to evade Philippe, despite his almost immediate pursuit. With all the commotion at the convent, he had left his half-filled bottle of whisky by Neptune's fountain. Nevertheless, the chilling events had sobered even the alcohol running through his veins. He rushed along the beach, panicked and distraught, reliving the moments of his family tragedy – the images of the drowned bodies of his wife and boys were all too strong in his mind. He had been at the graves of his sons when he received the call that a woman had been found floating in the ocean.

He had rushed to the fishing port in time to see the fishermen, who had discovered his wife's corpse, carry her to shore. Her waterlogged face and bulging eyes rendered her unrecognisable. He saw his twins again on slabs at the morgue, their fifteen-year-old corpses battered by the storm's thrashing waves. The visions were a harrowing reminder of his loss.

He forced himself to focus on finding Sister Celeste. The feeling that she had chosen the same fate as his wife, Clarissa, was overwhelming. As he scurried along the beach, he looked up at the cloudy sky and came to a breathless stop. His wife's face appeared in his mind once more. Consumed with despair, he fell to his knees. 'Clarissa!' he cried. 'Why, why did you do it?' He sobbed into his hands. 'I'm sorry! I'm sorry I let you and the boys down. I loved you all so much!' His wailing intensified; his face buried in his hands as he finally allowed himself to feel every ounce of his repressed grief over the deaths of his loved ones.

As he sat in inconsolable mourning, a beam of light filtered through his fingers and caught his eye. He looked up to see a gibbous moon fight its way through the clouds. It beamed a narrow path onto the surface of the ocean – like an arrow guiding his way. His eyes followed the lit path, just in time to see Sister Celeste slip beneath the water, where she remained.

He sprang into action, running into the sea and swimming along the ray of light before diving to its depths. His eyes were of little use as he waved his hands around the murky waters in the hopes of catching a tuft of hair; a feel of her clothing; a glide across her cheek, her arm, a hand; anything. Nothing but liquid slipped through his fingers.

He came up for a quick breath and submerged again. This time he made more pronounced strokes and kicked harder to reach deeper. As he blindly grasped around, something swept the back of his hand. With a swift grabbing motion, he managed to close his fist around what felt like fabric. He gave a strong tug, relieved to feel the weight of the sister behind it. As she drew closer, he wrapped his arms around her and pulled her to shore.

The clouds had cleared, making way for the radiant glory of the stars and the moon, now lending full visibility to the beach. He laid her down on the sand and put his cheek to her mouth. The chill of her blue-tinged lips felt cold against his skin. 'Sister Celeste!' He placed his hands on her shoulders and gave her a shake. There was no response. He proceeded to push down on her chest, maintaining the pressure of several compressions, until her eyes shot open and she coughed and spurted a fountain of water from her mouth.

Relieved, he sat up and tried to normalise his breathing.

The sister was momentarily bewildered. Her eyes searched around and finally fixed their blurry gaze on the man straddled over her. 'You!' she said.

'Are you okay?' he replied.

She grabbed him by the scruff of the neck. 'What did you do?'

'I saved your life.'

She pushed him off her and scrambled to her feet. 'You had no right interfering in something that was none of your business. Stay out of this!'

She dashed for the ocean once more.

He dived at her feet and knocked her to the ground.

'Get off me,' she yelled as she kicked her legs.

He pulled her away from the water's edge and moved his face close to hers. 'Stop this madness!'

Sister Celeste recoiled; her face contorted in disgust. 'It's my right you drunken fool. You wreak of the devil's drink.'

Philippe sat up; his gaze lowered in shame.

'At least I have the courage to put an end to my life,' she said. 'You drown yourself in alcohol every day. A coward's death.'

He looked into her eyes. 'A slow, painful death. The one I deserve.'

'So we both want to die.'

'Not anymore. I have seen the truth.'

'The nonsensical words of a drunkard,' snapped Sister Celeste.

'Then tell me why the sky has been as black as space all night, and the moment your head entered the water, the moon shone its light on your exact spot? I believe God showed me where you were so that I could save you.'

'What for? He's never cared much for me.'

'Because your life is of value.'

She sniggered. 'The moon shone for me too; a message that I should end my life.'

'You saw your own intention, and yours alone.'

'Your interpretation is no more valid than mine.'

'A nun with no faith.'

'Go away before I scream.'

'And bring attention to yourself.' He looked towards the distant crowd. 'I'm sure the police will want to question you.'

She turned to see that an ambulance had arrived at the scene. The police were questioning people. The huddled nuns consoled each other. The familiar ache of guilt swelled in her guts. She wrapped her arms around her legs, and the tears ignited once more.

'We're both drenched,' said Philippe. He felt the coldness of his clothing against his skin. 'We need to get out of these wet clothes and warm our bodies.'

Sister Celeste ignored him. She wiped the silent tears from her eyes and stared out to sea.

Philippe sat next to her, placed his arm around her and pulled her closer. 'We need to keep ourselves warm.'

She turned to him, her face rigid with scorn, but an unexpected feeling of comfort quashed her anger. She melted and made no protest at all. Instead, she found herself snuggling up against him. 'What made you follow me?'

'When I saw you run, I knew your intention.'

'How am I supposed to live with myself knowing I caused the death of the Abbess?'

'You didn't pull the trigger.'

'That makes me no less guilty. I intended to kill a woman, tonight.'

'But you didn't. Perhaps like me, you will one day find a chance to redeem yourself. Or maybe God sent me to save you, to prove to you that he has already forgiven you.'

Sister Celeste burst into tears. 'That I cannot believe.'

'I was led to you, and here you are, alive. Only His will can do this. It's a blessing. If only…' He choked back tears. 'If only I had been there to save my wife and boys.'

'The drownings? That was your family? I remember… I'm sorry.'

Philippe took a deep breath. 'Enough tears. Tonight, my punishment ends. Please, let me help you. Let's go to my house where we can warm up. There are clothes for you there.'

'Go back to your house?'

'Where else will you go? I don't think you're welcome at the convent. At least give them a couple of weeks. You can stay with me.'

'Why would I do that?'

'Do you have anywhere else to go?'

She shook her head. 'I can never go back to the convent. I wouldn't, even if I could. I don't belong there. I never have. I… I have nowhere. No one.'

'Then it's settled. You're coming with me. You'll be perfectly safe if that's what you're worried about. I am a man of honour.'

'And an unpredictable drunk.'

'Then I will make a promise to you. I will not touch a

drop of alcohol while you are staying with me.'

She searched his face for the tiniest hint of a lie but saw a man with wide, sincere eyes. She turned away from him to gaze back at the ocean. The waves lapped just short of her feet, and the tide swept in and out in mesmeric movements. 'I will go with you,' she said. She looked at him. 'What's your name?'

✦ Chapter Fourteen ✦

The wails and whimpers had reduced to woeful sniffles and hushed tears as the business of police and medical procedures took priority. The Abbess lay on a stretcher; her skin cold to the touch. The medic pulled the body bag across her corpse with the indifference of a plank of wood. As the stiff, plastic cover reached her face, calm in repose, Angelica saw the last of the woman she had grown to love and value like a grandmother. She looked on, helplessly, shuddering as the ambulance doors slammed shut. She buried her head in Father Cavallo's shoulder.

Christiano, shocked and pallid, with his clothes drenched in the Abbess's blood, stood next to them using disinfectant wipes to erase the dried red mass caking his hands and arms. No matter how assiduously he wiped, he could not remove the crimson tint which seemed to stick to him like a second skin. A police officer eyed him from head to toe. 'Are you sure you don't need an ambulance? You don't look well. I think you should see a doctor.'

'The medic gave me a thorough check. I'm fine. A little nauseous, that's all.'

'Very well,' he replied. 'I need to ask the three of you some questions. Is the lady able to speak now?'

'You mean Angelica?' said Father Cavallo. 'Oh, she doesn't speak. She's mute. She will write the answers down. May we use your notepad?'

The officer nodded, turned to a clean page and handed his pad to Father Cavallo. 'Do any of you know who these men were?' he asked.

'They work for the Pulsoni family in Tuscany,' replied Father Cavallo. 'Their Boss is Don Primo Pulsoni.'

The police officer motioned to his partner for her notepad. 'Mafioso! How is it this young woman knows them?'

'She, ah… *was* Don Primo's mistress. She was seeking refuge at Santa Maria under the guidance of our dearly departed Abbess.'

Christiano's body stiffened.

'I see,' said the officer. 'Do you know their names?'

Angelica scribbled on the notepad, and Father Cavallo read her words aloud. 'Ricardo Cerri and Enzo Batteli.'

'Do you know which one of them shot Abbess Rossini?'

'I saw only one man carrying a gun,' said Father Cavallo. 'He was the younger of the two. The other man was older and had a scar running down his cheek.' He demonstrated the position of the scar on his own face.

Angelica pointed to Ricardo Cerri's name.

'Just to confirm, you are pointing to Ricardo Cerri's name as being the man with the gun?' asked the officer.

Angelica nodded.

His colleague made a note on her pad.

'And you?' He looked at Christiano. 'You were the one holding her body.'

'Ah, this is Father Abbadelli,' said Father Cavallo. 'He was asleep at home when the Abbess summoned him to help search for Angelica. Hence his civilian clothing.'

'My apologies, Father.'

'No offence taken, officer,' said Christiano. 'I have no idea who the men were. I saw one of them earlier today; the man with the scar, when he strolled into the convent, and then on the streets later on this evening. Here, I only saw their car. They were already on the beach looking for Angelica when I arrived with the Abbess, and it was too dark to see them. I followed the Abbess onto the beach. I think as she scrambled around in the dark, she may have stumbled upon the man with the gun and confronted him. I heard her say, "Leave Angelica alone." I ran towards her voice. Then came the gunshot. I reached her just as she fell against me.'

'Would you say that she shouted at the man?'

'No. Her voice was firm and angry, but only loud enough for those in the immediate vicinity.'

'Is there any other detail you can tell me?'

'No.' He shook his head. 'That's all I remember.'

'Well if you think of anything else, let me know. Unfortunately, with all the chaos we did not get a good enough look at the assailants. It all happened so fast, and what with the street lights so dim. All we saw was the gun, and so we ducked and screamed at others to do the same. They were gone in a flash.'

'Does this mean you won't be able to arrest them?' asked Father Cavallo.

'It will depend on their alibis, which I'm sure will be solid and place them in Tuscany.'

'And no doubt Pulsoni's influence,' muttered Father Cavallo.

The police officer gave him a stony glare. 'Father Cavallo, can you describe the events from your perspective?'

'All I know is that when we arrived the two men were already searching for Angelica on the beach. The Abbess ran in after them and Father Abbadelli after her. I did not hear her speak. A few minutes later we heard a gunshot. I was in the car, turning it around to shed some light on the beach. You had arrived at that point and saw for yourself. The men ran into the light and escaped. He was the only one I saw holding a gun because he passed by the Abbess's car to get into his.'

'Would you be able to recognise him in a police lineup?'

'Positively! But Angelica knows them personally and is certain who they are.'

The officer nodded. 'And how is it that you came to be here?' He directed his question to Angelica.

She scribbled avidly on the notepad. Father Cavallo looked at the words she had written with a sympathetic expression and read them aloud. 'I knew Don Primo's men had found me and I ran away.'

Christiano narrowed his eyes.

'But they still found you,' continued the officer. 'Maybe you were better off staying at the convent and calling the police. Perhaps then, this woman would not be dead.'

Angelica squeezed Father Cavallo's arm and moved in closer to him. 'Officer, she has been through enough as it is.'

The officer maintained a rigid façade. 'My colleague will make a note of your details. In case of further questioning, make yourselves available.' He nodded politely before walking towards the ambulance.

As Father Cavallo gave his details to the policewoman, Angelica turned to Christiano, only to meet with a vacant stare. She looked into his eyes for a shred of acknowledgement but found nothing. Instead, in an undeniable snub, he turned towards the ocean.

Dejected, she made her way to the Abbess's car and got in.

He pretended not to notice and repressed a pang of guilt.

Father Cavallo was now conversing with Sister Carmina. She nodded, gave him a tearful hug, and walked to the huddled group of nuns a few steps away. Then he approached Christiano. 'How are you feeling, my friend?'

'I'll be fine. And you?'

'I have lost a dear friend and colleague. I will grieve her death for a long while, but I must focus on supporting my sisters and ensuring that the day-to-day running of Santa Maria is maintained. It is good that Angelica did not mention Sister Celeste's actions. It is best we keep this in-house. The sisters know to do the same.' He looked around. 'Where is Sister Celeste, anyway?'

'You told them to lie? Don't you think she deserves punishment for what she put Angelica through? Don't you think she should pay for the Abbess's death?'

'My friend, I know you are confused and angry. We are all grieving for a most venerable woman. But this is what she would want. Also, we have an obligation to the Vatican to keep this quiet. It is enough that Sister Celeste made a mockery of us and Santa Maria in that silly excuse of a newspaper.'

'Another matter from which I was excluded. I don't even know what the article was about.'

'Father Christiano, please understand, you were new to the convent, and we did it to protect Angelica.'

'Just a short while ago I was sitting in the car with the Abbess, and now she is gone.'

'The Abbess was fully aware of the dangers of her involvement with Angelica, but she was a woman with the protective instincts of a lioness: a woman of principle. The Lord's intentions can sometimes seem harsh and cruel, but it is our job to have faith. We, as His ambassadors, must be that unshakable faith as an example to others.'

Christiano looked towards the car at Angelica who sat in the back seat. Her head was leaning against the window, and she was wiping tears from her eyes. He lowered his gaze, guiltily.

'Perhaps they will let us leave now. I will ask the officer,' said Father Cavallo.

Christiano watched as Father Cavallo talked easily with the policeman, shook hands with him, and returned.

'Sisters, please gather round,' he said aloud. 'The officer said we can go home. I have arranged for the police to take some of you back to Santa Maria. I know it will be difficult to return. The Abbess's absence will leave a gaping hole at the heart of the convent. We are all very distraught at such a tragic loss, but the Abbess will remain in our hearts and our thoughts for the rest of our lives. In fact, she will insist on it!'

He tried to smile but failed. 'Do any of you feel up to walking back to Santa Maria?' he asked.

A few raised their hands. 'Then those who can, please go now. I can take up to two in the Abbess's car, the police officers have two cars here, they can take six, and I will come back for the rest of you. I will be as fast as I can.'

'I will walk,' said Christiano. 'Another sister can go in my place.'

'Are you sure you're okay? You look sick.'

'I'll be fine. The walk will do me good. I will see you tomorrow.' He left before the old man could protest.

Father Cavallo arrived at Santa Maria. The looming full moon emphasised its eerily gothic exterior as the nuns left the Abbess's car. Father Cavallo instructed Sister Carmina to take Angelica to her room and to stay with her.

'Of course, Father Cavallo.' She took Angelica by the arm.

He nodded with gratitude and made his way back to the beach for the remaining nuns. As he drove, he passed by those who had opted to return on foot. Each tormented face escalated the repressed grief that welled inside him until tears streamed hotly down his face. He slammed his fist on the wheel and gave in to his sorrow – his single opportunity to put his feelings before the Church and his sisters.

Christiano entered the house and stopped with reluctant feet at the door of the kitchen where Marcello and Agostina were anxiously waiting. They had heard him leave the house in the early hours, and later on, the thunder of sirens through the streets. Marcello had called the convent and spoken to Sister Immaculata.

They noticed the splotches of vibrant red on his stark white t-shirt and the unmistakable stains on his hands and arms. Agostina gasped and placed her hand over her mouth.

'What happened, Father? Are you injured?' asked Marcello.

He shook his head and relayed the news with a solemn look on his face, 'The Abbess passed away this evening.'

Agostina burst into tears. She dug her fingers into Marcello's arm. 'How did this happen?' he asked.

'I think it best you speak with Father Cavallo. It's not my place to tell you. I'm sorry.'

'Get some rest, Father. You look as pale as a ghost. Do you need anything?' said Marcello.

Christiano shook his head and made his way down to his room where he removed his soiled clothing, tossed it to the floor and collapsed on his bed. Fatigue weighed through his body. Dull aches throbbed in his arms, his legs, and his back – everywhere. He noticed the photo of Nicolas on the desk opposite. The boy's youthful eyes filled with the expectancy of time, stared back, unaware of what lay ahead for him.

Christiano lay down on the sheets and tried to shut out the night's events. His eyes jittered beneath his eyelids, like ants scurrying from left to right.

Gradually, he melted into a deep sleep, and then the dreams started.

He was back at the beach. The Abbess lay in his arms. As blood seeped from her mouth and the life-force drained from her body, she struggled to utter her last words. Words he had kept to himself. 'Promise... me... you'll get Angelica away from... Santa Maria. She needs... you ... Please!... Believe... her!'

Angelica appeared before him; her gaze lowered to the ground. She looked up. Her grey hood fell to her shoulders as she raised blood-soaked hands from beneath her cloak and held them pleadingly towards him.

Christiano's eyes shot open.

✦ Chapter Fifteen ✦

Steaming walnut-coloured liquid dripped from the spout into an espresso cup eagerly waiting to be filled with the intoxicating brew. Marcello drew the delectable vapour into his nostrils where it circled his head with its invigorating scent. He placed the cup before Agostina who sat at the kitchen table staring into oblivion. He gently massaged her shoulders and planted a kiss on her cheek. 'Are you okay, Gosti?' His caress awoke her from her mesmeric state. She batted her eyelids and patted his hand; an affectionate glint in her eyes that shone with relief. 'When you're around, I'm always okay.'

Christiano appeared at the door impeccably dressed in his priestly garbs. 'I'm off to Santa Maria to see if I can be of assistance to Father Cavallo.'

'Okay, Father. I spoke to him this morning. He knows I intend to stay home with Agostina, today,' said Marcello. 'He has arranged an early evening service. We will be there, of course.'

Christiano nodded. 'I'm sorry that I do not have the

words to help you deal with our loss at this time. I am just as shocked and grief-stricken as you are…'

'We understand, Father. Your words will come,' said Agostina.

He nodded and shut the door behind him. The streets were warming up for another scorching day. It was as if the night's tragic events had never occurred. Christiano walked with pensive steps to the convent. It was the same familiar route he took every day, but today it felt different – empty somehow; devoid of a valuable life, and no one seemed to notice.

He passed through the piazza where a sea of curious eyes was upon him. His feet pounded the pavement harder, faster. His gaze was fixed on the convent. He reached the gates, pressed the buzzer and the gates opened. As he walked through the forecourt, he saw, almost out of his field of vision, the Abbess's orphaned car. The sight of it made him nauseous.

Father Cavallo stood at the entrance. 'It is good to see you, my friend.'

'You too, my friend.'

They shook hands, leaned in and patted each other on the back before they made their way through the corridor.

'How is everyone?' asked Christiano.

'A quiet morning. Most of our sisters are in the chapel.'

'When is the burial service?'

'Due to the circumstances of the death, the police are conducting an autopsy. Maybe in a week. You are staying a while longer, yes?'

'I'm sorry, my friend, I think it best I leave. I will return for the funeral, of course. And I will stay for a couple of days to assist you.'

'I'm disappointed. I hoped the incident would prompt a change of heart.'

They reached the Abbess's office, and Father Cavallo unlocked the door. He held it open for Christiano to enter. 'Let us talk for a moment before we join our sisters in prayer. If it were not for my concern for Angelica, I would be conducting a service.'

'Where is Angelica?'

Father Cavallo took a seat in the Abbess's chair. 'She's in the chapel. I think she is safe at the moment. The shop is locked, and I doubt they will return so soon.'

Christiano flopped down on the chair and rubbed his eyes.

'What's on your mind?' said Father Cavallo.

'The Abbess's dying words.'

'She spoke to you?'

Christiano nodded, about to reply when the phone rang.

'Excuse me,' said Father Cavallo. 'Santa Maria L'adorata... Yes, officer.' He listened intently. 'I implore you to keep searching... Her killers must be brought to justice... Yes, and that's all I ask of you.' He placed the receiver down.

'It's worse than I thought. That was the officer at the scene. Ricardo and Enzo have solid alibis. No gun and no silver car have been found, and there are no silver cars registered to Don Primo, any of his men, their wives, or even their mistresses. With all the chaos nobody managed to get the number plate, including the police.'

'Is Angelica's word not enough?'

'I suspect Don Primo's influence spreads far and wide, which is why it's imperative she leave the convent as soon as possible. No one must know where she is, including the police.'

'And I'm supposed to do that?' said Christiano with a look of disbelief.

'I did not say that, my friend. What is bothering you? What did the Abbess say to you?'

Christiano lowered his gaze.

'Did she tell you something about Angelica?'

'In a way. She asked me to promise her that I would take Angelica away from Santa Maria. She said, "She needs you!" and pleaded for me to believe her. What I am supposed to believe, I have no idea.'

'I see,' said Father Cavallo, his face taking a sombre tone.

'You know something, don't you, about what I'm supposed to believe?'

'You'd better take a look at this.' Father Cavallo opened a drawer at the Abbess's desk, removed the newspaper and handed it to him.

'*Il Cospiratore*. So now I'm to be trusted with this information.'

'It seems she wanted you to know, yes. Take a look at the article towards the bottom of the page.'

Christiano did as instructed. The newspaper headline read: *Mob Boss Mistress Pregnant with the Next Messiah.*

A stunned Christiano looked at Father Cavallo to meet with his sober expression. He continued reading. *The mistress of a mob boss claims to be three months pregnant with the next Messiah. The woman swears she has not been with a man for over a year. The young woman has been in hiding from her mob boss boyfriend for thirteen months at the convent of Santa Maria L'adorata under the care of Abbess Francesca Rossini. She claims the Blessed Virgin Mary herself came to her in a vision and handed her a baby…*

By the time he reached the end, his olive-toned skin was masked in a sickly hue. 'Angelica?'

'It's a lot to take in, I know.'

'I… Ah… Must…' He bounded up from his seat as if it was a mound of burning hot coal, his mutterings barely audible.

'Father Christiano, are you okay?'

The troubled man said nothing. He hastened to the door and made a swift exit.

'Are you coming back?' yelled Father Cavallo.

There was no reply.

The phone rang. A baffled Father Cavallo picked up the receiver. 'Santa Maria L'ador… Monsignor Basso… Yes, of course… He is welcome… So close. We are honoured… Yes, see you in due course.'

His displeased expression revealed the opposite to his words. He grabbed the newspaper from the desk and placed it back in the drawer, tidied up a little and left the office. He made his way to the front gate. Just as he reached the door, the buzzer sounded. A tense Father Cavallo pressed the button and the gates opened. The Monsignor's blue Fiat entered, followed by the Cardinal's limousine.

'Welcome, Monsignor Basso.' He shook the Monsignor's hand. 'And Your Eminence!' He genuflected and kissed the Cardinal's ruby ring. 'Please, please, come in.'

'We're sorry for your loss, Father Cavallo,' said the Monsignor as he entered the hallway.

'Indeed, it is a tragic and senseless loss of a most esteemed woman,' said the Cardinal. 'I met her only once, and her compassionate light was as bright as the stars. We must find solace in the fact that she is by the side of our merciful Lord.'

'Amen,' said the Monsignor. 'Your Eminence, your words are truly heartfelt and wise.'

With his back to the men, Father Cavallo rolled his eyes before making an appropriate reply. He turned to face them. 'Perhaps you would both do me the honour of speaking some of these comforting words to our sisters. They are inconsolable.'

'Of course, let us speak first, and then we shall head to the chapel,' replied the Monsignor.

'Thank you. Your generosity will remain with me for all time.'

They entered the Abbess's office, and each took a seat.

The Monsignor spoke. 'His Eminence has asked me to accompany him as he gathers all the facts regarding this incident. It appears that there are many unanswered questions, and to be honest, all the facts seem to leave us with more questions. Like why the entire convent was on its way to the beach? Who were they after? Who were the men?

Why was the Abbess, and indeed, the convent involved in this incident at all?'

'Monsignor, Your Eminence, I can see that our conduct seems a little incongruous, but I assure you we were merely protecting our own.'

The Cardinal remained silent.

'Who were you protecting?' asked the Monsignor.

The old priest's cheeks glowed.

'Father Cavallo, we have known each other for far too many years. What are you hiding?'

'Monsignor, what can I say…? I'm in a difficult position.'

'I must inform you that His Holiness has requested all the facts regarding this incident. His Eminence has come to oversee the matter personally. He was greatly distressed by what occurred. Is it necessary for us to interview every nun in the convent?'

The Cardinal interrupted, 'Father Cavallo, please be aware that His Holiness has given me the authority to conduct a thorough investigation. We shall leave no stone unturned.'

'And His Holiness will not rule out suspension,' interjected the Monsignor.

Father Cavallo squirmed in his chair.

'I see. Well, it seems I have no choice in the matter.' He paused for a moment before he spoke. 'Just over a year ago, the Abbess's sister brought a young woman to the convent for shelter. She was protecting the poor girl from her local mob boss who had taken an interest in her—'

'Their names?' interrupted the Cardinal.

'The young woman in question is Angelica de Santis, and the mob boss is Don Primo Pulsoni.'

'And the name of the Abbess's sister?' asked the Cardinal.

'Fortuna. I only know her first name,' replied Father Cavallo.

The Cardinal made some notes on a small pad. 'Continue.'

'Angelica was the granddaughter of a dear friend of Fortuna. The old woman had recently passed away. Orphaned as a child, Angelica had no one else. The Abbess did not want to leave her helpless, in the hands of this unsavoury man… So she took her in. Everything was going well until last night when Don Primo's men appeared.'

'If she was so well protected in here, how did this happen?' asked the Monsignor.

'It seems we had a disgruntled nun and—'

'You mean Sister Celeste?' interrupted the Cardinal, fully aware of the answer.

Father Cavallo nodded. 'Yes, she fooled us all. But how did you know?'

'From this,' he said, coldly placing an envelope on the desk. 'This is a letter from Sister Celeste accusing the Abbess of harbouring a prostitute. Obviously this Angelica woman.'

'Well… How would she know to send it to you?' asked Father Cavallo.

'It was sent to the Vatican and passed to me.'

'May I take a look at the note?' asked Father Cavallo.

'No. But I will tell you that it reads like a suicide note.

Has Sister Celeste taken her own life?'

Father Cavallo looked down at his desk. 'That I do not know.'

'So she is not here?'

He shook his head. 'She is not. She disappeared last night, in all the chaos.'

'I see. So we could be waiting for another dead body to appear.'

'Your Eminence, please believe me that I… nobody had any idea…'

'And is it true that Father Abbadelli has feelings for this… prostitute?' continued the Monsignor.

'With respect, Angelica is no prostitute, and Father Christiano is an honest priest who takes his vows of celibacy very seriously. There is nothing even remotely romantic between Angelica and Father Christiano. Of that I am certain.'

'Then why does Sister Celeste say there is?' said the Cardinal.

'She was a disgruntled, disturbed woman who targeted Father Christiano with her insane accusations. Her perspective is hardly that of a well-balanced person.'

'This unbalanced woman may have taken her own life, and nobody saw the signs,' added the Monsignor. 'Now we have a dead Abbess and most likely a dead Sister Celeste, and I hear disturbing news of one of my most promising priests being involved with a prostitute – a woman who should never have been here in the first place and who, I might add, is running from the mob. Does that about cover everything?'

'This is an outrage!' cried the Cardinal. 'This convent has run amok. His Holiness will be very troubled and displeased by this news. This is a PR nightmare—'

'I can assure you this is a very well run convent,' interrupted Father Cavallo. 'The Abbess, God rest her soul, was a unique woman with high moral and ethical standards. She was a deeply religious, compassionate woman, and highly disciplined—'

'Of course,' said the Monsignor, 'perhaps too compassionate.'

'Father Cavallo, is there some vital piece of information that you are withholding?' asked the Cardinal.

'No, I've told you everything.'

'Oh really? So you are not deliberately hiding a newspaper article from us?'

Father Cavallo maintained his composure, despite the knot of dread wringing in his stomach. 'I… It's just the nonsensical words of Sister Celeste. Not worth a mention.'

'Well it's just as well I have my own copy,' replied the Cardinal. 'Did you really think I would not see the article for myself? I make it my business to know everything that affects the Church and His Holiness. You withheld a crucial piece of information from us, which only proves you cannot be trusted.'

'It is a ludicrous, irrelevant piece of information,' protested Father Cavallo.

'Will somebody tell me what we're talking about?' interrupted the Monsignor.

'Father Cavallo, would you like to explain?' said the Cardinal.

He shut his eyes in frustration, opened them seconds later, and began to speak. 'The girl, Angelica, claims to be pregnant with the next Messiah.'

'What? A prostitute? Utterly preposterous and absolute blasphemy!' cried the Monsignor.

'She has committed the ultimate sin against our Lord with such heinous lies. The unborn child is obviously the bastard spawn of this Don Primo?' interjected the Cardinal

'I doubt that very much,' replied Father Cavallo. 'Up until a few days ago he did not know where she was, and Angelica has *never* left the convent since her arrival more than a year ago. She is three months pregnant.'

'What about this Father Abbadelli?' asked the Cardinal.

'No, I placed him here myself less than a month ago,' replied the Monsignor.

'And he left this morning, eager to resume his studies,' Father Cavallo reported.

Their eyes fell on him. A moment of silence spoke a thousand volumes.

He returned an utterly disgusted glare – his face as red as fire. 'With all due respect, I find your accusatory stares an insult, and I will not stand for it.'

'Father Cavallo, you are not being accused of anything. I know you to be a very respectful priest with the highest moral standards,' said the Monsignor.

'Well, she will be leaving soon, anyway. Don Primo will, no doubt, be back to claim his mistress. She is no longer safe here,' said Father Cavallo.

'Maybe I can be of service,' said the Cardinal.

'How so, Your Eminence?'

'Well, she is a Catholic woman, and if she's in danger from this Don Primo, I will arrange for her protection, until the child is born. It will enable us at the Vatican to investigate her claims further.'

'An Immaculate Conception is not the jurisdiction of the Miracles Commission,' said Father Cavallo.

'You mean an *alleged* Immaculate Conception, surely?' said the Monsignor.

The Cardinal nodded. 'Yes, this is true, but I am offering the girl sanctuary, that is all.'

'Something I have just been chastised for doing.'

'Father Cavallo, I suggest you watch your tone. Had the Abbess made the appropriate request I would have helped. You have pointed out that the girl is no longer safe here. I am simply offering you an alternative. She will stay with the Miracles Commission under my supervision until the birth of the child. Then we will help her to find shelter and somewhere safe for them to live.'

Father Cavallo fidgeted uncomfortably in his chair. 'I have seen your scientific experts. Do you intend on running medical experiments on Angelica and the foetus?'

'Of course not, Father Cavallo. We are not the Inquisition,' mocked the Cardinal.

The Monsignor laughed. Father Cavallo did not.

'Where will you take her?' he said.

'She will be hardly safe if I tell you that,' said the Cardinal sardonically.

'I will have to speak with Angelica. It is her choice.'

'Actually, this is my decision. She claims to be carrying the next Messiah. She is now the property of the Catholic Church.'

'How so?'

The Cardinal leaned forward; a glowering look on his face. 'Frankly, I am being courteous, but in truth, you have no say in this matter. Despite her claim, I merely request her presence. She can leave if she is unhappy with the arrangements. I just ask that she is open to what we can offer her.'

'I know for a fact that Angelica will not accept your proposal. She is a headstrong woman.'

'Father, understand that His Holiness is very disturbed by the incident and he is unaware of the full story. One word from me and...' A menacing glare emanated from his pupils. 'I think I have made myself clear?'

'When do you intend to take her?'

'Right away.'

'That will not be possible.'

'Father Cavallo!' protested the Monsignor.

'The Abbess was like a grandmother to Angelica. She is utterly devastated and in no condition to leave today.'

'Where is she now?' asked the Cardinal.

'In the infirmary, sleeping. She was vomiting all night. Sister Carmina, our nurse, says she must not be moved for at least two or three days. She fears for the unborn child's life. Do you wish to speak with the nurse?'

'No, that won't be necessary. I will leave my chauffeur, Johan, here overnight. He will sleep in the car. Make sure

THE PRIEST OF SANTA MARIA

she is ready in the morning.'

'Your Eminence, I must protest,' said Father Cavallo.

The Cardinal raised his hand to hush him. 'She will endure a few hours of discomfort, after which she will have a team of the best medical experts all to herself. Have her ready in the morning.'

There was a knock at the door.

'Enter,' said Father Cavallo.

Sister Immaculata's eyes peered round the door, followed by an 'excuse me'. Her face reddened with embarrassment and she retreated behind the door.

'Ah sister… If you'll excuse me.' Father Cavallo rose from his seat and left the room, to face Sister Immaculata in the corridor alone.

'I'm so sorry for the interruption, Father. I just need to know if His Eminence and the Monsignor are staying for lunch.'

'I want you to listen very carefully, Sister. You are to go and fetch Angelica from the chapel and take her, *personally,* to the infirmary. Tell Sister Carmina she is to stay with her. Tell Angelica to get into bed. Tell Sister Carmina to pull the surgical curtain around her. And,' he said, gripping her arm, 'under no circumstance is she to leave, or so much as move until I inform her that it is safe to do so. Is that clear?'

Sister Immaculata gave him a frightened nod. 'What's happening, Father?'

'I cannot speak of this now. Just make sure you prepare a good meal for the Cardinal. Now go, hurry. In a few moments, they'll be in the chapel.'

'Yes, Father, right away.'

He watched her run down the corridor, making sure she had a good head start before he entered the office.

'I have taken the liberty of letting our dear cook know that you will both be staying for lunch after our little service.'

'We would be honoured,' replied the Cardinal.

✦ Chapter Sixteen ✦

Christiano paced his bedroom like an expectant father; his phone pressed to his ear. An open suitcase lay empty on his bed. The monotonous ring remained unanswered before it finally switched to answerphone. 'Mama, I need to speak with you urgently. Don't bother calling me; I'm on my way home.'

He slipped the phone into his trouser pocket, removed a bundle of clothing from his wardrobe and unceremoniously threw the items into his suitcase. In the bathroom, he swept his toiletries into a bag, showing no care for breakages. The bag was thrown into the suitcase just as haphazardly, and the case slammed shut. As he looked round the room, he noticed the portrait Angelica had sketched for him. He ripped it off the wall and examined it for a moment, staring at the face of a man he no longer knew. He tossed it in the bin, zipped up his luggage and left the room.

At the top of the stairs, an anxious Marcello and Agostina waited for him. 'Father, are you okay?'

'Yes, Agostina. I'm fine. Please stop worrying. You both

knew I was leaving today.'

'Yes, but with all that's happened we thought you would stay, at least until after the funeral,' said Marcello.

'I'm afraid that's not possible. My studies begin tomorrow.'

Agostina and Marcello simultaneously raised their eyebrows.

'Please, just understand that I must leave.'

Marcello walked to Christiano with open arms. 'You may be a priest, but you are like a son to me.' Tears welled in his eyes. He wrapped his arms around Christiano who responded with a heartfelt hug of his own.

'And you are like a father to me.'

Agostina burst into tears and hugged him tightly. 'Father, please say you'll stay in touch.'

'I will,' he replied. He gave her shoulders a firm squeeze. 'Your hospitality made my stay feel just like home.' He kissed her forehead.

'I will get my keys and drop you at the train station,' said Marcello.

'No, you have been more than kind. I will take a taxi.'

'I insist.'

'There is something I must do first. It's best I walk to the taxi office. My luggage is light.'

'Very well, Father.'

Christiano picked up his case and walked to the door. He turned to them for one last time, opened his mouth to speak, but instead, simply nodded and left. He made his way down the alleyway, on to the street, and continued on to Piazza di

Nettuno. As he neared the end of the square, he stopped to take a final glance at the convent. The gates were closed. The innocent exterior concealed the mysteries that lay behind it.

'I've been looking for you, Father.' Philippe walked into his line of sight.

'I must catch a taxi, Philippe. I'm sorry, I have no time.'

'Father, wait!'

Christiano stopped. 'Make it quick, Philippe.'

'Father, can't you tell I'm sober?'

Christiano dropped his suitcase to the floor, and a smile permeated his face. 'Why, yes, you are. What has brought this change?'

'It seems that last night's tragic events had a sobering effect on me… And perhaps the influence of a good woman.'

'Woman! Who is this woman?'

Philippe looked to the ground.

The sudden realisation devoured the smile from Christiano's face. 'Philippe, no.'

'She is a good woman, Father. A woman wronged…'

'She told you her story?'

'All of it, Father. She is truly sorry for what she did. She did not mean for the Abbess to die, and she is truly grateful that God intervened and prevented her from hitting Angelica with that rock.'

Christiano's eyes bulged.

'I have said too much. She did not harm her.'

'It is her actions that resulted in the death of the Abbess, and now Angelica's life is in danger. Angelica did not so much as mention Sister Celeste's conduct to the police, or to us. Philippe, I implore you to run as far away from this woman as possible.'

'Where is your charity, Father?'

Not where this woman is concerned. She needs professional help.'

'No. She needs love, comfort and companionship, and I will give it to her if she will have me. I knew it from the moment I saw her. Sometimes you just know these things.'

Christiano let out a frustrated sigh. 'As you wish, Philippe. I no longer care.' He turned to leave.

'It seems that God did have a plan for me, after all.'

Christiano ignored him and continued walking.

'What about the girl, Father? Angelica. You are in love with her.'

Christiano stopped, made strides back towards him and reached in close to his face. 'I wouldn't go listening to the likes of Sister Celeste. And I would like you to stop such nonsense. I am a priest, and I have a reputation to uphold.'

'She is your destiny, Father.'

'Enough, Philippe!'

'If you leave now, how will your actions be any different from Sister Celeste?'

'Angelica is not my responsibility.'

'Yes, she is, Father. I had a vision last night and…'

Christiano rolled his eyes and turned to leave.

'Father please, you must hear this.' He grabbed his arm. 'She's in danger. Not just from the mafia. There is a man, an influential man who will try to take control of her and the baby. She is not safe.'

'What are you talking about?'

'I saw only a vague vision. He's a man of the cloth. He wears a gold ring with a large ruby. He is a bad man. He means the girl harm. You must protect the baby.'

'Philippe, have you any idea how you sound?'

'What she claims is the truth. She is pregnant with the next Messiah.'

'Everything you are saying you have gleaned from Sister Celeste.'

'I told you I had a vision.'

'Philippe, there is no truth to this.'

'Would you have said the same to the Venerable Mary?'

Ahead of them, the convent gates opened. Christiano watched as the Monsignor's blue Fiat drove onto Di Santa Maria Viale with a man resembling the Cardinal in the front passenger seat.

Philippe followed his gaze. 'He's in there!' he cried. 'The man that means her harm.'

Christiano frowned and then jumped from the vibrational buzz to his thigh. He removed his phone from his pocket. The convent number flashed on the screen. He swiped to answer. 'Father Cavallo?'

'Thank the blessed Lord you answered your phone. I'm in dire need of your help. It's Angelica, she's in danger and not just from Don Primo. The Cardinal has laid claim to her. There is not a hallowed bone in that man's body. Of that, I'm certain.'

Christiano glanced at Philippe who nodded with sageness.

'What kind of claim?'

'He has left his chauffeur here, a tall foreign man who I suspect is Swiss Guard. Angelica is to leave with him in the morning.'

'She can refuse.'

'My friend, something tells me she cannot. Besides, the Cardinal may come back with reinforcements. He has made threats. Please, will you come?'

'Yes, of course.'

'Oh bless you, Father Christiano. Do not come through the forecourt. That's where he's parked.'

'I will come by Via Scala.'

'How long will you be?'

'I'm in the piazza. I'll be there in a moment.'

He hit the end button and dropped his arm limply by his side. His eyes fell on Philippe.

'Best of luck, father. You'll need it.'

Christiano remained frozen, his gaze on Philippe as he vanished round the corner. A group of vocal schoolchildren walked by in twos. They snapped him out of his daze. Their teacher alerted them to avoid tripping over his luggage on the ground. He picked up his case and made his way towards the convent. He skirted by the front gate and walked on to Via Scala where a worried Father Cavallo stood at the shop door.

'Our chauffeur is having a snack in the refectory. He must not see you. I told the Cardinal and the Monsignor you left this morning to resume your studies.'

'Let me see this man,' said Christiano.

They made their way to the corridor, stopped at the corner before the cloister and poked their heads round the wall to see the chauffeur through the glass window. The man sat alone around the large rectangular dining table, munching on some bread and sipping soup.

'He's the same chauffeur from the Cardinal's first visit. I directed him to the hospital when the Cardinal had that episode. You really think he's Swiss Guard?'

'With a name like Johan, I suspect he is, my friend. I have a feeling that if Angelica resists tomorrow, he will force her.'

'Does he have a gun?'

'Possibly, beneath his jacket. I have not been close enough to see.'

Johan finished his dinner, thanked the nun and left the refectory.

They retreated behind the wall as he entered the corridor and made his way back to the forecourt.

'I will make sure he enters his car and stays there. Meet me in the recreation room,' said Father Cavallo.

As Christiano waited for Father Cavallo, his right leg jittered nervously, and a thousand thoughts ran through his mind. He rubbed his tense brow. Minutes later, the Father swept into the room with a carrier bag in his hand. He placed it on the coffee table. 'Right then,' he said as he sat down.

'What exactly are you asking me to do?' said Christiano.

'My friend, I am asking you if you will honour your promise to the dying Abbess.'

'To take Angelica away from Santa Maria?'

'What are you afraid of? I know you have feelings for her.'

'Yes, it seems everyone likes to tell me how *I* feel about Angelica.'

'Are we wrong?'

Christiano's head flopped. 'I don't know. I... feel something for her, something new to me, but I am a priest. I made a vow which I took seriously. How is it that you as a priest who took the same vow can encourage me to break it and toss my career aside as if it were nothing?'

'Because I have never had these feelings. You have, and that means something.'

'Feelings can be controlled. Perhaps I'm just a pawn in everyone's game. Perhaps you wish to rid yourself of the burden.'

'Father Christiano...'

'You know if I do this, my career is over. My family will be scandalised. I have devoted myself to the Church and this... place has turned my life to disarray.'

'The Cardinal means to pass Angelica to his scientists. They will run experiments on her and the unborn baby. Of that I am certain. Once she reaches the Holy See she will become the property of the Church and the Cardinal will do as he pleases. Who will stop him?'

'That's not the purpose of the Miracles Commission. I'm surprised the Cardinal would entertain such nonsense.'

'Unofficially, I believe he is using his status to do as he wishes. I'm not even convinced His Holiness has any idea of his plans. One thing of which I am sure, the Cardinal is not who he seems.'

'What medical experiments could possibly determine that she carries the next Messiah? It's ludicrous.'

'My friend, very few people know what lies in the Vatican vaults. An item with Christ's DNA, who knows!?'

'Let's just call the police.'

'If the police become involved I guarantee you Angelica will be back in Don Primo's hands by the end of the week. In fact, I think the Vatican probably has more influence than the Mafioso. Think carefully my friend, how would you feel if Angelica were back with Don Primo, or being experimented on by the Cardinal's scientists?'

Christiano buried his head in his hands.

'My friend, I implore you.'

'Where will I take her?'

'That's something you must not tell me. You must find somewhere where she will be safe.'

They were interrupted by a knock at the door. 'Enter!' said Father Cavallo.

The door swung open. Angelica stood at the entrance with a small suitcase and the look of a scolded child.

'Angelica, please come in,' said Father Cavallo.

She entered the room and started an intense scribble on her board. She held it up, unashamedly. They both read the message. *I do not want to go with him.*

Christiano cupped his hands over his eyes and made a sigh.

'Christiano will look after you,' said Father Cavallo.

She shook her head.

'It's just until this mess dies down. Maybe a month or

two,' continued Father Cavallo.

'You can't force her to go with me!'

'She's convinced you dislike her. Please tell her it's not true.'

Christiano lowered his head as the guilt rose to his chest and spread like fire to his throat. He rose from his seat and made his way towards her. Her nebulous eyes fixed intensely on his pupils. He felt himself drift through them. 'I'm... sorry, Angelica...'

She turned her attention elsewhere.

He gulped. 'I... was rude last night and days earlier. I didn't mean it.'

'There you go, Angelica,' said Father Cavallo. He rose from his chair and picked up the small bag from the table. 'You could not be in better hands. I'm convinced. Now, Sister Immaculata kindly prepared some sandwiches and pastries for you both.'

She took them, reluctantly, but neither she nor Christiano moved.

'In the name of... Father Christiano, will you do this?'

Christiano made a defeated nod.

'Good, then let's move. I have arranged for Marcello to leave his car outside Via Scala. He says you can have it with his blessing.'

He opened the door to the refectory, and they walked to the opposite side of the corridor where they entered the preserve kitchen, walked straight through to the storeroom and on to the shop.

'Angelica, I would just like a word with Father

Christiano. Would you mind waiting by the door?'

He turned to him. 'My friend, I must be able to trust you. I have to be sure you will not pass Angelica on to the Cardinal at some later date.'

'I need to know something, too.'

'Yes?'

'Do you believe Angelica is pregnant with the next Messiah?'

'My dear friend, pregnant she is, but what I believe is of no significance. I am protecting the girl from harm. Now I ask again, can I trust you?'

They stared into each other's eyes for a few moments.

'You have my word she will be safe.'

Father Cavallo smiled and gripped Christiano's shoulders. 'I thought as much, my friend.'

He went to the door and hugged Angelica. 'Go in peace and know that you are safe and protected.'

She returned his hug and wiped away her tears.

'Good luck, my friend,' said Father Cavallo. They shook hands, firmly. 'It was destiny that brought you to us... Ah, there is Marcello.'

Christiano and Angelica stepped onto Via Scala and made their way to the car.

Marcello stood at the door and waited for Christiano to reach him. 'It is good to see you so soon, but I am sorry to see you go.'

'Thank you for everything, Marcello.' Christiano embraced him.

Father Cavallo placed the luggage in the boot of the car

and helped Angelica into the front passenger seat. He shut the door and wandered over to the driver's side to bid a last farewell to Christiano.

Seconds later, Christiano put the car into first gear and hit the gas.

Angelica turned to the passenger window to shield her tears.

As they drove away, Christiano watched Santa Maria, Father Cavallo and Marcello through the rear-view mirror, grow as distant as a fading memory.

Johan fidgeted uncomfortably in the back of the limousine, his feet crossed as he texted a message on his cell phone. *I will bring her tomorrow.* He hit the send button. He tossed and turned a little until comfortable and shut his eyes.

Moments later, a double *'ping'* alerted him back to his phone. *And what of the cardinal?*

The monsignor took him back to Rome, so I am alone. We are so close, yet…

We can only hope…

Part Two

Pursuit

✦ Chapter Seventeen ✦

A ngelica awoke to a blaze of fiery beams spearing through the waning darkness.

'Beautiful, isn't it?'

She had almost forgotten where she was. She turned to her left to see Christiano focused on the road ahead. His face mirrored the colours of the dawn. She nodded appreciatively and made a quick yawn and a stretch before she removed her sketchpad and pencils from her bag and put graphite to paper.

Christiano's head turned back and forth from the road to her. He marvelled at the skill of her hand. Minutes later, she held a completed sketch that resembled the glory before them. 'A talent I envy,' he said.

She tore it out of her book and gestured it as a gift. 'I can't accept it.' He returned his attention to the road.

Bewildered, Angelica placed the page back in the book and looked to the scenery outside her window. The ocean stretched to infinity. Rows of fishing boats lined the length of the dock, and a skein of seagulls hovered above the sea in a *V* formation.

'There's food in the bag and some water.'

She ignored him.

He had offended her again. He chewed his bottom lip in the fraught silence while he found the courage to tell her the truth. 'I threw the portrait you drew of me in the dustbin,' he blurted sheepishly.

Her head turned to meet the side of his face.

He glanced at her apologetically, before he returned to watching the road. The echoes of sadness in her eyes were imprinted on the road before him. They stared back at him, making him feel guiltier than ever – a guilt too inadequate for words. But he had to try; to say something. 'After everything that happened, I was confused and upset,' he said lamely.

She turned away to face the dawn.

'I'm sorry,' he said. 'I truly am. My actions are unforgivable. I have never treated a work of art, especially of such calibre, with such dishonour. That's why I cannot accept your drawing.'

Angelica shrugged and reached into the carrier bag given to them by Father Cavallo. She pulled out a paper bag filled with an assortment of mini cornetti, took a chocolate one out and bit into it. In two bites it was gone. She returned the rest to the carrier bag and took out a sandwich.

'Also,' continued Christiano, 'that night at the beach, I want to apologise for my actions. I've acted like a man with no heart and a priest without compassion. Please forgive my foolishness on both counts.' He made a side glance towards her. 'I'm truly sorry.'

She nodded with softened eyes and returned to her breakfast. When she had swallowed her last morsel, she scribbled on her board and held it to him. *Where are we going?*

'This is my hometown.'

She scrubbed out the question and wrote, *You don't look well.*

'The sea air turns my stomach a little. I'll be okay when we reach higher ground.'

They drove the rest of the way in silence. Christiano reached the end of a long road and turned left up a hill. Driving sinuously, he passed rows of closed shops and a market square where a few traders were setting up for the day. The car ascended higher with each bend until he took a sharp left and parked opposite a small townhouse of vibrant red stone with a royal blue door.

'We're here. We'll stay at my parents' house for a couple of days until I find somewhere safe for you.' He walked round to the back of the car for the luggage.

Angelica walked to the edge of the road. Her gaze followed the multi-coloured rooftops, shaped like jagged steps down the mountain until they reached the very bottom, where the waves kissed the rocks.

Her sightseeing was interrupted by Christiano clearing his throat as he waited for her at the door. She entered the house and looked around in wonderment. Inside, the rustic interior was a stark white. Dark wooden beams ran the length of the ceiling. To their left was an open door that revealed a long dining table covered with a lacy cream tablecloth, and on the wall behind it, a painting of the Virgin Mary. Her hands were clutched at her heart. Back at the entrance, the narrow passage led to a staircase.

'Who's there?' announced a deep, masculine voice.

'It's me, Papa,' replied Christiano.

The man appeared at the top of the stairs. His frown was replaced with a joyous smile as he bounded down and stopped – somewhat surprised to see a beautiful woman with his son. 'Your mother said you were coming.' He opened his arms and grabbed Christiano in a mammoth embrace; all the while his eyes were on Angelica.

'Papa, this is Angelica. Angelica this is my papa, Emilio.'

'Welcome to our home,' he said, shaking her hand.

She nodded with a smile and then scribbled something on her board. She flashed it at Christiano. *Please, where is the bathroom?*

Emilio's brow creased.

Christiano pointed to a door beneath the stairs.

With Angelica out of sight and earshot, Emilio asked, 'Who is this woman and why does she speak on a board?'

'She is mute, Papa. I'm taking care of her for a short while. Where's Mama?'

Emilio's eyes widened. 'I see. Your mother is in the bathroom upstairs. Are you in trouble, son?'

'No, Papa. She needs my help.'

'Are you involved with this girl?'

'Why do you ask me such questions? I'm a priest!'

'Okay.' He held his hands up in defence. 'It just seems odd…'

'Christiano!' The cry came from upstairs. A woman in

her late forties raced down the steps with an elated smile and outstretched arms. They embraced. 'Are you okay, my son? You sounded so anxious over the phone.'

'I'm fine. Right now I need a little rest. We'll talk later.'

The sound of a toilet flush forced her head towards the staircase. 'Who's here?' The door beneath the stairs opened, and Angelica sauntered into the hallway.

'Mama, this is Angelica,' said Christiano. His gaze met with his mother's frown.

'Angelica, this is my mama, Rosa... Mama, Angelica will be staying with us for a couple of days, if that's okay?'

'Of course,' she replied, beaming a smile at her guest. 'A beautiful name to match a beautiful face.'

Angelica gazed coyly at Rosa as they shook hands.

'Are you both hungry?' As she spoke, her eyes wandered down to Angelica's stomach, who responded by shielding her belly with her hands.

Rosa, open-mouthed with shock, turned to Christiano.

He ignored his mother's expression. 'Angelica can have my old room. I will take Marco's.'

'Okay, son. Show her the way,' said Emilio.

'Then come back downstairs. I will make us some camomilla,' said Rosa.

Angelica gave them both a cordial nod and made her way up the stairs.

Christiano followed behind her. 'I'm tired, Mama. We'll talk after I sleep.'

When they were out of sight, Rosa turned to Emilio with an inquisitive look. 'She is mute!' he said with a shrug.

✦ Chapter Eighteen ✦

The incessant ringing woke Johan. It was 6am. He grimaced with annoyance. The caller ID was that of the cardinal. He sat up like a soldier caught slacking on duty and swiped the display screen. 'Your Eminence.' He tried to disguise the morning croak in his voice. 'I am at the door; about to knock... Yes, Your Eminence, as soon as she's in the car... Yes, Your Eminence, everything was quiet last night... Thank you, Your Eminence. I will, Your Eminence. Goodbye...'

The phone went dead. 'Your Eminence,' he said sarcastically and with a look of disdain. He placed the phone in his pocket, checked his face in the rear-view mirror and used his finger as a toothbrush to scrape the front of his teeth. He slapped his cheeks, rubbed the sleep from his eyes and left the car. As he walked to the convent doors, he tucked in his shirt, put on his jacket and fixed his tie.

He gave the door two hefty knocks and seconds later, noticed the doorbell. He pressed it.

Moments later Father Cavallo came to his call clutching

THE PRIEST OF SANTA MARIA

at his chest and breathing heavily. 'The girl is gone,' he announced. 'The nurse checked in on her in the infirmary about fifteen minutes ago, and she wasn't there. We have searched everywhere, and she is nowhere to be found. Moreover, her personal belongings are missing.'

'But no one came this way last night.'

'No, it appears she escaped through the shop on Via Scala.'

'His Eminence will be furious.'

'I'm sorry, what can I say? It's out of my hands. You may come inside and check for yourself.'

'That won't be necessary.' Johan removed his phone from his pocket and hit the dial button with a scowl. 'Your Eminence.' He gulped. 'The girl ran away last night… from another exit. I'm sorry, Your Eminence… Yes, Your Emi—'

He let out a burdened sigh. 'Please open the gates for me.' He walked to his car.

Father Cavallo shut the door. A satisfied grin dimpled his portly cheeks.

Purple with rage, the Cardinal banged his fists against the perfectly polished wood of his antique desk. 'That meddlesome priest!' He grabbed the pearl handle of his vintage phone and dialled a number, the old-fashioned way.

Father Cavallo was attending to paperwork in the Abbess's office when the phone rang. 'Santa Maria L'ador—'

A rancorous voice fired down the phone, 'Father Cavallo, it has been duly noted that your actions go against the Catholic Church and the sacrosanct orders of His Holiness the Pope. You can expect repercussions. You made a grave mistake making an enemy of me.' He slammed the phone down before Father Cavallo could speak.

Back in his study, the Cardinal stood up and swiped his desk in venomous fury, causing items to spill all over his plush burgundy carpet. He fell into his seat, picked up the pearl handle once again, and this time dialled the Monsignor.

'As I suspected, your friend Father Cavallo is a dishonourable man. When my chauffeur knocked at his door this morning, he was told the girl had run away. I do not believe that she left unassisted, if she has left at all. This Father Cavallo must be made an example of, and I intend to see that he is.'

'My deepest apologies, Your Eminence. You must ensure that he is held accountable for the mess at Santa Maria.'

'My friend, that will be the least of his troubles when I have finished destroying him.'

'Your Eminence, I have been looking further into Sister Celeste's claims about Angelica and Father Abbadelli. It seems he has not enrolled in his studies as Father Cavallo informed us.'

'Do you think he is helping her?'

'From what I know of Father Abbadelli, I would say no, but why would Sister Celeste mention some involvement between them if there was not some shred of truth to it? This harlot may have turned his head.'

'Monsignor Lucca, you have been most helpful. I ask that you make no more enquiries. Leave this to me.'

'As you wish, Your Eminence.'

The Cardinal pressed a red button on the side of his desk. Moments later, two big men entered his office and waited by the door for his acknowledgement. He swivelled his chair round to face them. 'Vito, Sammel. I only needed one of you, but I do so admire your efficiency. Sammel, when Johan arrives send him to see me, will you?'

'Yes, Your Eminence.'

'That'll be all.'

The men nodded and left the room.

The Cardinal swivelled back round to his desk, opened the middle drawer and pulled out a black notebook. He opened it, scanned through his address book and stopped at the letter *K*. He ran his index finger down to the name Kristoff, lifted the phone and dialled the number. It rang for seven rings before it was picked up by an answerphone. 'I have a message from God,' said the Cardinal. He replaced the receiver and moments later, the phone rang. The Cardinal lifted the handle and put it to his ear, without a word.

'What is God's message?' replied a gruff voice.

'Kristoff, my friend, I am glad to find you well.'

'Your Eminence, it is with your prayers and blessings that I remain on this earth.'

'I have some investigative work for you. Are you able to service my needs at this time?'

'Always, for you, Your Eminence.'

The Cardinal flashed a malign smile. 'I would like you to find out everything conceivable about a Don Primo Pulsoni and a Father Christiano Abbadelli...'

✦ Chapter Nineteen ✦

An exhausted Christiano sipped a strong cup of espresso at the dining table of his parent's home. The porcelain clock on the cabinet behind him chimed eleven times. An anguished Rosa sat at the head of the table, to his left. 'Christiano, you look as if you hold the weight of the world on your shoulders.'

He rubbed the sleep from his eyes and took another sip of coffee.

'Son, forgive me for what I am about to ask, but are you responsible for this woman's condition?'

'Nothing gets past you, Mama... No, I'm not responsible. I have been tasked with protecting her, actually.'

'By whom? Is she in danger?'

'Perhaps the less you know, the better.'

She placed her hand over his. 'If you are in trouble I need to know. How can we help you?'

'I will take her to Nonno's mountain cabin. We will leave tomorrow, or maybe tonight.'

'Son, you're scaring me. Who is this woman? Whose

child does she carry?'

Christiano shook his head with a look that showed the full impact of his burden.

'Christiano, please.' Tears formed in her eyes.

'Mama, do you remember what happened to me when I was ten?'

'Why do you bring this up?'

'I want you to tell me the story.'

She remained silent for a moment as she gazed at him inquisitively.

'Please, Mama, I just need to hear it again. Not the bedtime story version for a child. Just tell me what happened.'

'You're the one who knows, son. My information came from you.'

'But I was so young. You remember it like it was yesterday, don't you?'

'How could a mother forget such a thing?'

'So, please Mama. I have good reason to ask.'

'Okay, son. You were at school. It was playtime, and the teacher sent you to take out the trash. It was a punishment because you were disruptive in class.'

'Yes, I remember that.'

'When you reached the bins you saw a beautiful woman who reminded you of the Virgin Mary. She was standing by the bins holding a baby in her arms. She looked troubled and told you her son was in danger. She asked you to look after him and handed him to you. You took him and ran straight out of school. We had no idea where you had gone.' She wiped the corners of her eyes with a tissue.

'You disappeared for three days and nights. I was beside myself with worry. An old hermit saw you walking through the woods with your arms outstretched as if you were holding a precious package – but there was nothing there.'

'That's the point, Mama, there was. I was holding the baby.'

She nodded and started to cry. 'When they brought you back to me, I noticed the mark.' She touched the cruciform mole beneath his left eye.

'I asked you how you got it and what you told me has remained branded to my memory.' She stopped for a moment and looked straight into his eyes. 'You told me that while you were looking down at the baby in your arms, he reached his hand towards your face and touched you beneath your left eye. You said it burned, but it felt like love.'

Christiano grasped his mother's hand. 'As I grew up, I thought this was a sign that I should become a priest, but I think I was being chosen for a greater task. One that I could never have imagined.'

'What task, son? This woman?'

'Angelica claims to have had a vision of the blessed Mary handing her the Christ child. As she held him in her arms, he disappeared into her womb. A month later, she was pregnant.'

'Are you saying what I think you're saying?'

'I don't know, Mama. I feel like a crazy man.'

'Santa Maria.' She made the sign of the cross. 'Did she tell you this?'

'No, I read it in a newspaper article.' He shook his head. 'It's a long story.'

'How do you know it's true?'

'Mama, a lot has happened these past few weeks. The Abbess and Father Cavallo seem certain that no man has been near Angelica for the past year. Also,' he gulped, 'the Abbess is dead.'

'What?'

'I can't go into detail, Mama. Please just trust me.'

Rosa clasped her hands in prayer and closed her eyes. She remained in quiet reflection for a few moments. When she opened them, she said, 'Do not have doubts, Christiano. It is clear you need to protect this woman and her child. Have faith in this knowledge.'

Christiano nodded and gazed down at the table with a burdensome weight tugging at his shoulders.

'Is there more, son? Have you feelings for her?'

Christiano remained silent for a moment. 'I need to see Father Guido.'

Rosa's face turned pale. 'I'm sorry Christiano, but Father Guido died yesterday. I was going to call, but you called me and left me a message that you were coming. I thought it best to wait until you had arrived.'

His face collapsed with grief. 'How did he die?'

'Peacefully in his sleep. He was an old man. Will you be staying for the funeral?'

'I cannot.' He wiped a solitary tear from his eye. 'In fact, I had better stay away altogether. I think it best that I stick with civilian clothing while I'm here.'

'Son, will this trouble affect your career?'

He sighed and nodded.

Rosa gripped his hands. 'Christiano, it's like you said, God has other plans for you.'

'Yes, Mama.'

Rosa noticed Angelica standing in the doorway. 'Welcome. Welcome. Did you have a good sleep?' She rose from her seat and gestured for her guest to sit down. 'Please.' She pulled out the chair opposite Christiano. 'Take a seat.'

Angelica walked gingerly to the chair and sat down, her gaze on Christiano.

A concerned Rosa looked from one to the other. 'You must be hungry. I will get you something.' She made her way to the kitchen, leaving the two of them alone.

Angelica studied Christiano's anguished face and scribbled on her board. *Are you okay?*

'Yes, I'm fine. Tomorrow, or maybe tonight, we'll leave for my Nonno's mountain cabin, about a couple of hours from here. You'll be safe there.'

A look of anxiety crossed her face. She scribbled on her board. *Are you leaving me there, alone?*

'Of course not. I will stay with you until the child is born and until I find somewhere safe for you both to live.'

Angelica's concern was replaced with relief.

Rosa entered the room with a camomile tea and placed it on the table. She returned moments later with *fette biscottate*, apricot jam, and *cornetti*. 'Would you like some fruit? Figs, perhaps?'

Angelica nodded, and Rosa left the room.

'How are you feeling?' asked Christiano.

She smiled by way of reply, took a sip of her tea and

spread the thick apricot jam on her toast. She took a hearty crunch into the crispbread.

He found himself immersed in her every poetic action.

Rosa entered with the figs and set them down on the table, her eyes on her son. She cleared her throat and woke him from his wistfulness. He caught his mother's knowing stare and lowered his gaze.

'I'm planning a late lunch today. Is two-thirty okay?'

'That's fine with me. I have a few errands to run in town.' He got up from his seat. 'Angelica, I will see you later.'

She nodded and carried on munching her food.

'See you later, Mama.' He kissed her on the forehead, made his way to the front door and shut it behind him.

An awkward silence was left in his place.

✦ Chapter Twenty ✦

A pensive Don Primo sat in solitude beneath an alcove in his restaurant. He fiddled with a lighter in the shape of three bullets welded together. He was almost obscured by the cloud of cigarette smoke engulfing him. On the wall behind him was an enlarged monochrome photograph of a young man with a Clark Gable moustache wearing a forties pinstripe suit, trench coat and fedora hat. Standing to knee height was a young boy with Don Primo's characteristic icy stare. They both stood at the entrance of the restaurant – as it looked some fifty years ago with the stone tiling worn to form a colossal stone façade.

From a table opposite, Enzo watched him from beneath lowered eyebrows. Don Primo swiped his fingers through the snow-white hair that stylishly ran to the top of his shoulders, and continued staring down at the table deep in thought. Everyone was wary of his mood. The general atmosphere in the restaurant was cautious, and the usual banter replaced with reticence.

At the bar stood a waiter wiping smudge marks from a

glass. He held it up to the light to ensure its spotlessness. His meticulous ritual was interrupted when the phone rang. 'Aquilon Ristorante,' he announced.

He listened intently. 'One moment, please.' The man glanced towards Don Primo with a worried expression and walked towards him with hesitant steps. He cleared his throat as he reached the table. Don Primo looked up. 'What is it, Fabio?'

'Don Pulsoni, Sir, excuse the interruption, but there's a man on the phone who says he can help you… ah…'

'Spit it out, Fabio!'

'Find Angelica, Sir.'

'What?'

'That was his message, Sir.'

Don Primo held out his hand, and Fabio handed him the phone. He glanced at Enzo as he pressed it to his ear. Enzo stared back through narrowed, curious eyes.

'Who is this?' demanded Don Primo.

On the end of the line, the Cardinal wore a smug smile as he sat at an opulent dining table in a room lined floor to ceiling with polished mahogany and marble. A uniformed servant placed a plate of *trippa alla romana* before him.

'Am I speaking with Mr Pulsoni?'

Don Primo's eyes narrowed. 'This is he. I ask you again to tell me who you are.'

'I am Cardinal Cäsar Beltz, and I have a proposition for you.'

'You said you can help me find Angelica. What would you know about her?'

'Ah, there is a lot I know, Mr Pulsoni.'

Don Primo's jaw tightened. 'If you knew as much as you say, you would know to watch your step.'

'Mr Pulsoni, please, I am not calling you for a confrontation, I assure you. I am offering you my services in exchange for yours, plus an added bonus for you.'

'And your proposition is?' Don Primo was growing impatient.

'If I could direct you to someone who may know where Angelica is…'

'Is she no longer at the convent?'

'They claim she has run away.'

Don Primo's face glowed with newfound possibility. He glanced at Enzo with a glint in his eyes.

'I understand she was your mistress. Is that right?'

'That's none of your business.'

'Please, Mr Pulsoni, do not misunderstand me. I have no interest in your personal affairs. I am willing to offer you five hundred thousand euros for her delivery to me.'

Don Primo was stunned. 'What do you want with her?'

'One million and you ask no questions.'

He raised his brow. 'I'd have to think about that.'

'As I expected.'

'Make it two million, and you *may* have a deal.'

'Come now Mr Pulsoni, let's be reasonable. One and a half is my last offer.'

'You're a Cardinal you say?'

'Yes.'

'Then I'm guessing that your interest in Angelica relates

to a newspaper article and some unlikely miracle. The Virgin Angelica doesn't quite have the same ring. Make it two, and you can call her the Queen of Sheba for all I care.'

'You drive a hard bargain, Mr Pulsoni. Two it is. And it is a bargain considering I have already gathered all the intelligence you will need to find her. Do I have your word you will not ask any questions or back away from our deal?'

'You have my word.'

'Then we are in business.'

'I want all the money upfront.'

'I can have half the amount couriered to you by the end of business day, today. How's that?'

'Understand that I will not pass Angelica on to you until I have *all* the money in my possession. I expect the rest on delivery.'

'I concur.'

'Who is she staying with?'

'There was a young priest at Santa Maria who, as I understand it, was quite fond of her.'

Don Primo's face grew a dark shade of red.

'And she was apparently quite smitten with him.'

Don Primo's hand formed a fist.

'They may have stolen away together in the late hours. Who knows, they may have eloped. The priest is being investigated, but as we cannot find either of them, there is nothing we can do.'

'I see,' said Don Primo, seething. 'And what is this priest's name?'

'Father Christiano Abbadelli. In my humble opinion, a

good place to start is with his hometown. But you'll need to act fast.'

'His parents?'

'Emilio and Rosa Abbadelli. He has a brother, Marco, who is married with two children. So you have a few bargaining chips if need be. I'm certain they'll know how to get in touch with him.'

'Well let's just say it will be in their best interest,' replied Don Primo.

'And if it doesn't pan out you can always trace their steps back to the convent and have a quiet word with a wretched priest named Father Cavallo… when the heat dies down, so to speak.'

'I have no idea what you're talking about.'

The Cardinal smiled wickedly. 'Do you have a pen handy, Mr Pulsoni?'

✦ Chapter Twenty-One ✦

Despite the urge to ram his foot down on the gas pedal, Ricardo drove along the motorway at normal speed under strict instruction to keep his activities within legal limits – as much as possible. The sun's radiating shards targeted his head with the precision of a laser beam. He pulled the visor down, wiped the sweat from his forehead, and fiddled with the air-conditioning controls, further decreasing the ambient temperature.

Enzo looked irritated by his tinkering but said nothing. Instead, he lit a cigarette and turned his attention to the landscapes whizzing by his window.

'You think this priest is the father?' Ricardo asked.

Enzo drew the cigarette smoke deep into his lungs and let out a succession of smoke rings. 'Probably.'

'If she was my woman, I'd tie them up and make them watch each other being tortured.'

Enzo rolled his eyes. 'All you need to know is that right now Don Primo *prefers* him dead. That means only if we get the chance. Don Primo will get him eventually.'

'How can you be so laid back? We have to get him, for Don Primo.'

'Listen to me!' growled Enzo. 'Our priority is to get Angelica. Killing the priest is a bonus. We can get him another time when he lets his guard down, and he thinks he's safe. Whatever the case, he's a walking dead man.'

Ricardo smiled and nodded. 'I like it when they relax and when they think they got away with it and, *BAM*. Oh, the shock on their face when you're holding a gun to their balls.'

Angelica, Rosa and Emilio were finishing their lunch when Christiano returned from his shopping trip. He entered the hallway, wearily dropped his bags to the floor, and followed the remnants of gnocchi and pesto into the dining room. 'Sorry I missed lunch, Mama. I picked up some supplies for the cabin.'

Angelica scribbled on her board and held it up. He read it silently. *I am sorry for your loss.*

'Thank you,' he said.

'Would you like some lunch, son?'

'No thank you, Mama. I had pizza.'

'Ah, from Vittorio's.' She looked at Angelica. 'His favourite pizza place since he was a little boy.'

Angelica smiled.

'I've decided to leave for the cabin tonight. I just need a couple more things in town and a haircut.' He ran his hand through his hair. 'Mama, will you take Angelica shopping and buy her whatever she needs?'

Angelica fidgeted uncomfortably.

'As your pregnancy progresses, you'll need the appropriate clothing,' he added.

She nodded, reluctantly.

'Of course, son. Let me clean up, and we'll go.'

Angelica rose and began to gather dishes from the table.

'No, that's fine. I'll do it. Please go and rest. You look so tired,' said Rosa.

Angelica looked relieved, gave her a hug and left the room.

'She is a sweet young woman,' said Rosa.

'I can tell she has feelings for you, son,' said Emilio.

Christiano collected the plates from the table, ignoring their comments.

The front door opened and they all turned to the dining room entrance. 'Marco!' announced Christiano with a smile.

'Little brother!' Marco grabbed Christiano by the back of the neck and pulled him closer. 'What's this?' he said, noticing his civilian clothing.

'It's called, off-duty.'

'Since when do you ever stop being a priest?'

'Perhaps I'm mellowing.'

'You? Never!'

They laughed.

Marco's smile faded. 'I'm sorry about Father Guido.'

Christiano repressed his grief behind a nod. His expression transformed to delight as Marco's wife and children entered behind him. 'Lina!' He hugged Marco's wife. 'And little Emilio.' He bent down and kissed the toddler in Lina's arms, noticing her little bump. 'You hardly show, when are you due?'

'In four months.'

'And how many more after this one?' he added.

'One of us has to keep the Abbadelli line going,' replied Marco.

As Christiano chuckled, he noticed two eyes peering from behind Lina. 'Lissandra! My how you have grown.' He playfully lifted her up into the air. She hugged him tightly and kissed his cheek. 'She grows prettier by the day.'

'Papa said you'd come with some mysterious woman,' said Marco. 'Where is she?'

'Upstairs.'

Marco nodded and continued to stare at Christiano as if waiting for more information.

Christiano's face was as expressionless as a blank canvas.

Marco's gaze drifted to his parents. 'Mama, Papa, as you know, it's our anniversary, and Lina's parents have gifted us with a weekend break to Venice. It's all last minute. Will you be able to look after the children?'

'Of course,' said Rosa, pleased. 'Are they staying from now?'

'No, I'll bring them later. Is that okay?'

'Yes, of course. I can't wait to have them.'

He turned to Christiano. 'How long are you staying, brother?'

'I'm leaving tonight.'

'That's a pity, I hoped you'd be staying for at least a week, so we can catch up.'

'Another time, Marco. I promise.'

'Are you okay? You look tired and so skinny.' He flicked his arm. 'Where have all those muscles gone? Have you stopped your yoga?'

'I'm fine. I've been too busy to practise.'

Marco raised his brow. 'You really have mellowed. Are you sure you're okay?'

'I'm good.'

Marco nodded, unconvinced. 'Well, look after yourself and make your visit longer next time.'

'I will.'

After they had gone, Christiano turned to his parents. 'I had better go, too... Mama, you look after Angelica.'

'Yes son, I will guard her with my life.'

At a few minutes past four, Ricardo turned into the Abbadelli's road and parked a few metres from the red stone house in a space that offered a clear view of anyone coming or leaving.

Moments later, the men caught sight of Rosa and Angelica leaving by the front door and continuing on foot past rows of townhouses in an assortment of shades.

'Will you look at that?' Ricardo's grin consumed his entire face. 'Lady Luck is on our side. What are the chances?'

Angelica's attention was on Rosa who was busy chatting, both of them oblivious to the danger that lurked just a few paces away.

'Should we grab her now?'

Enzo spotted four men in their twenties leave the house opposite their parked car.

'It's too risky, let them pass. I'll follow on foot. You follow with the car and park close to where they stop. We'll wait for an opportunity.' He left and pursued them round the corner.

Angelica and Rosa reached the shops where the streets buzzed with locals and tourists and entered a store with a pregnancy mannequin in the window modelling a red sundress. Enzo waited opposite while Ricardo found a parking space a few stores down, closer to the town's exit. He locked the car and made his way to Enzo, unaware that Christiano was waiting to have his hair cut in the barber's shop close by.

Half an hour later, the women left the store with bags of clothing and walked arm in arm along the bustling streets. The sweet aroma of freshly baked pastries wafted on the air like a trail of crumbs, leading them all the way to the market square.

Rosa approached a stall lined with olive-filled buckets and began speaking with the middle-aged trader. Angelica stood by her side as she sampled a Sicilian black olive, but soon found herself distracted by a stall selling a colourful array of scarves. She broke away, ventured towards it and picked up a shawl. She felt the texture of the delicate fabric.

'A beautiful shawl for a beautiful woman,' said the trader.

Angelica smiled.

'The scarves are hand-dyed by nuns at a convent in Crete. The vibrant colours will complement your dark looks. Please, try it on.'

Angelica wrapped the shawl around her neck. As she

admired its beauty in the mirror, a blurred figure came to a stop behind her. Her gaze glanced at the spot where the figure stood and the blood drained from her cheeks. She spun round to meet with Enzo's solemn stare. They remained rooted for a few moments, their eyes doing all the talking.

A passing stranger bumped against Angelica, breaking the concentration between them.

Angelica ran.

'Hey, my scarf! Hey!' called the trader.

Angelica continued her desperate escape. As she pushed through the crowd, she collided with an obstacle with such force that the world around her blurred into a fuzzy haze of sounds and images. A vice-like grip clasped around her wrist, and all sounds merged into a cacophonic medley. She tried to move, but the grasp was firm. The coldness of steel poked into her ribs. The reverberations gradually formed crisp, coherent words as the faces before her merged into one. Ricardo's mouth stretched into a malign grin. 'Now, while I'm not allowed to harm you, I will kill that bitch I saw you with. You know I'll do it.' Angelica relaxed. 'That's more like it.'

The trader's cries alerted Rosa to Angelica's absence. She bustled her way to the protesting woman who continued to shout and point at Angelica. 'She stole my scarf! Polizia!'

Ricardo ripped the shawl from Angelica's neck and pulled her away. It danced on the breeze and landed gracefully on the ground.

As Rosa continued steaming through the crowd, a violent

shove from behind sent her hurtling forward. She hit the concrete with a startling thud. A bolt of pain shot through her left wrist. Disoriented, she heard a whisper in her ear, 'Stay down, or you'll be sorry.' She tried to look up but saw only the perpetrator's feet walking in the same direction as Angelica and the man. A group of people surrounded her.

They reached the car and Angelica was bundled into the back seat. Enzo entered from the other side and buckled her in while Ricardo jumped into the driver's side and quickly manoeuvred the car out of the space.

His actions coincided with Christiano leaving the barber's shop and coming to a stop close by the car.

Angelica pounded her fists on the window in a desperate bid to catch his attention.

Momentarily stunned, Christiano lurched forward with the prowess of a panther. He clasped the tips of his fingers on the door handle. His mind, shocked and confused, fought with the unimaginable predicament before him.

The car pulled away and dragged him to the ground. He bounded up, unhindered, and raced after them.

Ricardo speeded up regardless of the hazards on the road. People jumped out of the way, but Christiano's determined sprints were still catching up with them.

The car in front came to an abrupt stop. Ricardo hit the brakes and blasted the horn. He shouted obscenities at the driver who reversed with leisure into a parking space. This gave ample opportunity for Christiano to reach them.

With a mammoth leap, he landed on the boot as if the

soles of his shoes were magnetised.

'What the fuck!' shouted Ricardo. He pulled away with urgency as Christiano clung on.

Angelica and Enzo turned to the back – Angelica, distraught, riveted her eyes on Christiano. His concerned face stared back for a moment before he continued his climb to the roof.

'Determined bastard!' Ricardo increased the pressure on the gas, only to find himself fast approaching an old three-wheeled truck travelling at a snail's pace. 'Let's see how he handles this!' He slammed his foot on the brakes.

The car screeched to a stop, and Christiano's body was flung several feet through the air.

Angelica watched in horror. A rush of deep crimson spread across her face as his body crossed before her eyes as if in slow motion. She wanted to scream. Her mouth contorted. Her body convulsed. Every pulsing vein was about to explode.

'Christiano!' His name thundered from the deepest caverns of her throat like the eruption of a dormant volcano.

He landed a few feet away in the open-back truck.

'Take that!' shouted Ricardo as he hit the steering wheel with his palms.

The distant sound of sirens blared behind them.

Ricardo reached for his gun. 'I'll make sure he's dead.'

Wild with fury, Angelica pulled his head against the headrest and made frenzied scratches to his face. She peeled threads of his flesh.

'Get her off me!'

He turned his gun towards her. Enzo knocked it out of his hand. 'You crazy fuck!' he yelled. He then subdued Angelica and released her grip on Ricardo's face. 'Get us out of here!' he roared.

Ricardo pressed his foot to the pedal and swerved round the truck as he struggled to recover. His face stung, and blood seeped from his wounds. As the car sped away, Angelica stared back for a sign of movement. There was none.

A seething Ricardo dabbed at the painful scratches as he drove. 'You bitch! You're a wild animal. If it weren't for Enzo, you'd be dead!'

'And you would have been next!' shouted Enzo. 'When Don Primo gives an order you damn well follow it. Are we clear?'

His words had a sobering effect on Ricardo who glanced at him in the rear-view mirror. 'It was an instinctive reaction.'

'And one you wouldn't have lived to regret.'

'You won't tell Don Primo, will you?'

'Right now, the police are our problem.' Enzo turned to look at the speeding car fast approaching them. To his relief, the driver of the old truck flagged them down.

✦ Chapter Twenty-Two ✦

It was early evening when Angelica found herself grudgingly back in the town she had fled more than a year previously, hoping never to return. To her, it was a nefarious place that held her darkest secrets; the demons in her life that she wanted to bury forever. As the car reached closer to its destination, her troubled past bubbled in her mind like a pot of raging water.

Minutes later, Ricardo drove into the small, gated, staff-only car park of Don Primo's eatery and parked by rows of bushes that provided excellent seclusion from the restaurant's many clandestine activities. He opened the back door for Angelica who remained seated and motionless, concealing her anguish behind a mask of defiance.

The blood on Ricardo's face was now dry, and in some places, his skin felt numb. In others, it stung like hell. He wrenched her out of the vehicle.

'Take it easy,' said Enzo, who latched onto Angelica's arm. 'You know Ricardo, you look as if a cat pounced on your face and clawed you in a frenzy.' He sniggered as he guided Angelica inside.

Ricardo frowned, painfully, and checked his image in the car's wing mirror. 'That bitch!' He gently pressed his wounds. Scowling bitterly, he stared at them for a moment. 'We'll see who gets the last laugh, old man.' He followed them through the side door of the restaurant.

They entered a long corridor with marble flooring of burnt sienna and polished stone-washed walls. Enzo stopped by a solid steel door to his left. 'There's no point knocking. I didn't see any light from the car park window.'

'He must be downstairs,' said Ricardo. He opened an opaque glass door to his right to see Don Primo making his way up the stairs.

Don Primo stepped into the corridor, his icy stare straight ahead. 'Bring her into my office.'

Angelica was ushered inside and came to a stop by an umber-coloured sofa.

Don Primo stayed outside for a few minutes, talking with his men before he entered and shut the door behind him. Angelica stood up straight and met his narrowed eyes with a deadpan stare. What followed was a short silence that felt decades long.

Don Primo finally spoke, 'So, I heard another miracle happened today.'

Angelica remained silent.

'Am I going to have the pleasure of hearing your voice?'

She remained as still as a stone statue.

'Well, perhaps another time, then. By the way, Ricardo's face is priceless. It seems we've gained some balls at this convent of Santa Maria, or is it this priest? Who, by the way, will soon be dead, if he's not all ready.'

Angelica repressed the tears that wanted to spill like blood from an open wound. She pursed her lips but remained silent.

'So,' he said, 'Angelica's in love with a dead man.'

A surge of rage erupted through her body and vented itself as a thunderous roar. She pounded her fists against his chest.

'There she is!' He grabbed her arms and thrust her backwards. Angelica fell onto the sofa behind her. 'Stand up!' he shouted. He bent down, grabbed her neck and pulled her upwards. 'You dare to hit me! If that bastard priest of yours isn't dead, he'll wish he was.'

He leaned into her face and spoke through gritted teeth, 'I'm going to cut off his balls and feed them to him in front of you.' With a terse look, he let her go. 'Immaculate Conception my culo. You're nothing but a whore!'

With all the juice she could muster, she spat at his face.

He froze, taken by surprise and retaliated with the mighty force of a back-handed slap.

To his utter shock, his hand rebounded; his energy deflected on impact with Angelica's face.

While a rippling pain radiated the length of his arm, Angelica felt that she had been kissed by an angel.

His arm dropped limply to his side, but his expression remained unflinching. All the while a chaotic medley of confusion ricocheted through his mind.

He pulled the steel door open with his good hand. 'You

two get in here! Ricardo, tie her to that sofa. You are to stand outside this door. No one comes in or out without my permission.'

'Yes Boss,' he said as he tied her up.

'Enzo, you go home to my sister, she's been driving me crazy all night complaining that I keep sending you away. Come back tomorrow morning.'

'Boss.'

As Enzo reached the door, Don Primo added, 'You're lucky you two didn't fuck this up. I was losing my patience.'

Ricardo tied the last knot which secured Angelica firmly to the sofa. 'I'll be outside if you need me, Boss.'

The door clunked closed leaving them alone once more.

Don Primo smiled in amusement. 'You'll regret the day you left me.' He moved in close to her face. 'You mean nothing to me, now. You're damaged goods. In fact, you've always been damaged goods.'

He left the room and stopped outside to speak to Ricardo. 'Don't let her out of your sight.'

'Yes, Boss.'

'When the restaurant closes, take her down to the wine cellar and keep her there. You are to stay in the restaurant all night.'

'Yes, Don Primo.'

'I don't want you engaging in conversation with her. Is that clear?'

'Yes, Boss.'

'Don't tell her she's being sold.'

'Yes, Boss.'

'And no retaliation for what she did to your face. Am I clear?'

'Yes, Boss. I would never…'

'Lock the door behind me.' He left by the side entrance that led to the car park.

Don Primo's driver, who was waiting in the white Mercedes, got out of the car and opened the door for him. Don Primo entered.

'Straight home, Boss?'

'Yes, Benito.'

On the drive home, Don Primo sat in silence, his arm as limp as a piece of string. He tried to move his fingers but winced, quietly to himself. He took out his mobile and spoke the word 'Cardinal' into the phone.

'Calling, Cardinal,' replied a robotic male voice.

The phone was answered in three rings.

'Mr Pulsoni,' echoed the Cardinal through the phone.

'I have her,' he said.

'Excellent news! You are a man of your word. I shall send my representative, Sammel, to collect her, with the rest of your money of course.'

'What time will he be here?'

'By about noon tomorrow. Does that work for you?'

'That's perfectly fine. The sooner, the better.'

'Splendid!' said the Cardinal. 'Until tomorrow then.'

✦ Chapter Twenty-Three ✦

Spasms of pain struck like lightning bolts through Christiano's brain, rousing him to consciousness. With each attack, he could see kaleidoscopic veins of light in his mind's eye. His eyes cracked open to a haze of colours and unfocused shapes.

'He's awake,' said a tearful Rosa. 'Christiano!'

'Just give him a moment,' said Emilio.

His vision gradually focused. His mother and father stood over him. Their faces were worn with concern.

'What happened?' he croaked.

'I'm sorry, son,' said Rosa, sobbing.

In an instant, his memory transported him back to the moment he left the barber's shop. 'Angelica!' He swiftly sat up. Every inch of his body screamed in protest.

His father tried to calm him.

Rosa burst into tears. 'I turned away for a moment to sample some olives, and she was gone.'

Christiano noticed the sling around her arm. 'What did they do to you?'

'I'll be fine, son. A man was dragging her away. I was chasing them when I felt a push and the next thing I know I was on the ground. Then I heard a whisper in my ear telling me to stay down or I'd be sorry.'

'Is it broken?'

'No. It's a sprain. The doctor said I'll be fine.'

'Don't blame yourself, Mama. This is my fault. I should never have asked you to watch her. I underestimated the danger.'

'Who were those men?' asked his father.

'They are men from her past. All I know is that they work for a Don Pulsoni in Tuscany.'

'Mafioso?'

'Look, I'm sorry I got you all into this. I must find her.' He pushed the bed sheets aside.

'That's not a good idea, son,' said Emilio. He held his hand out to stop him. 'You've been injured.'

'I feel fine,' said Christiano. He weakly pulled himself to the side of the bed and suddenly wrinkled his nose as a rotting smell drifted to his nostrils.

'You landed in a fishing truck. It saved your life,' said Rosa. She wiped the tears from her eyes.

Emilio embraced his wife and turned to Christiano. 'The police want to question you.'

'Are they here?'

'I managed to persuade them to come back in the morning. The doctor said you need the rest… You were lucky. Is there anything you need?'

'Right now, I need a shower.' He gripped the bed with

both hands and with his arms as weak as two broken branches, heaved himself up.

'Let me help you, son,' said Emilio.

'No, I can do it. Please, just leave me to get ready.'

'The doctor left you some painkillers.' Emilio pointed to the box on the bedside table as he guided his wife out of the room.

Christiano shoved two pills into his mouth and staggered to the bathroom for a shower. He scrubbed vehemently in a camouflage of soap to remove all remnants of rotting fish from his hair and body. All the while his mind was focused on finding and rescuing Angelica.

He entered his room to find his father waiting for him. 'Son, we need to talk.'

Christiano said nothing as he casually walked to his suitcase and removed his clerical suit.

'You're in obvious pain. You need to rest.'

'I have no time for pain,' replied Christiano as he dressed.

'What's so important about this girl?'

Christiano looked at him. 'Mama didn't tell you?'

'Yes, she told me a fairy tale of biblical proportion.'

He continued to dress. 'I made a promise to someone that I would look after her and I failed.'

'So, you call the police. You're a priest, not a secret agent.'

Christiano buttoned his shirt and put on his Roman collar.

'Christiano!' his father snapped. 'These people are dangerous. You need to leave it to the police.'

'No!' he cried.

Emilio was shocked into silence.

An immediate look of regret spread across Christiano's face. 'She's my responsibility. I will find her.'

Emilio let out a burdened sigh. 'Then is there anything I can do to help you, son?'

'Thank you, but no. I don't want you involved. Like you say, these are dangerous people. I'll deal with this my way.' He looked round the room. 'Where's my cell phone?'

'It smashed in the accident.'

'I'll need to use the landline.'

'You can use the one in our bedroom.'

Christiano flopped down on his parent's bed with the decrepit limbs of an old man. He lifted the receiver and dialled a number.

Father Cavallo was attending to paperwork in the Abbess's office. He lifted the phone. 'Santa Maria L'adora…'

'Father Franco. It's me, Christiano.'

'It's not safe for you to call me. Is our friend okay?'

'Father,' he gulped. 'She… I…' The words refused to leave his lips.

'You're scaring me, my friend.'

'Don Primo's men have her.' He bowed his head in shame.

'How did this happen?'

'That I do not know. She was with my mother… It's a long story. The fact is they have her, and I intend to get her back.'

'And how will you do that?'

'You leave that to me. I just need to know where this Don Primo lives.'

Emilio and Rosa stood outside the room with their ears pressed against the door. Their eavesdropping was interrupted by the doorbell.

'The children! I forgot they are staying a few nights,' said Rosa. She made her way down the stairs and opened the front door to see two happy children run inside. Marco saw her tearful face and bandaged arm. 'Are you okay, Mama?'

'No. He's insisting on going after her.'

'I'll go and talk to him. Are you sure you can manage now, what with your arm? It is too much.'

'Your father will help. Don't worry. Go have fun with your wife.'

'Thank you, Mama.' He gave her a hug.

'Now go talk some sense into your brother.'

He nodded and ran up the stairs.

Back in his parent's bedroom, Christiano made notes on paper. 'Do you think there's anyone there who could help me find Don Primo?'

'I don't think so, my friend. Abbess Rossini's sister, Fortuna, was a local baker. She is long gone, though. Her old bakery was on the road that enters the town. It used to be called *Torte e Dolcetti*, but who knows if it still exists.'

Christiano jotted the name down on the piece of paper.

'That's at least something. Thank you. I promise you that

I will get her back. I won't let my guard down again.'

'God be with you, my friend.'

Christiano put the phone down with a deeply pensive look on his face.

He left his parent's room to find Marco in the hallway. 'I heard you had a little accident. Is everything okay?'

'I'm fine.' He limped back to his room.

Marco followed him. 'Do you forget how small this town is? I heard you were thrown from a moving vehicle. What happened? The truth! I want to know about this Angelica?'

'You can stop worrying about your little brother.' Christiano packed his suitcase. 'I can take care of myself.'

'Christiano, please. You've gone from model son to rogue. I've never seen you like this.'

Christiano brushed past him without a word and dropped his luggage in the hallway. He entered the room next door and tossed Angelica's belongings into her suitcase.

Marco silently observed his every move.

Christiano dropped the suitcase in the hallway, picked up his own and carried them downstairs. He placed them beside the stack of supplies purchased earlier that day.

'Mama is worried sick,' continued Marco as he tailed him down the stairs. 'I don't like to see her like this.'

'There's nothing I can do about that.'

He left the house with as many items as he could carry and grimaced from pain as he placed the supplies in the boot. He returned for the remaining luggage.

Marco watched him but offered no assistance.

'Mama, where are the keys to Nonno's cabin?'

She walked to the hall dresser, removed the keys and handed them to him. 'Son…'

Christiano shook his head and continued out of the door. Emilio grabbed his arm and pressed a bundle of cash into his hand. 'Stay safe.'

With his gaze lowered to the ground, Christiano nodded and left.

✦ Chapter Twenty-Four ✦

Christiano reached the hilltop town in the early hours of the morning. He parked on the outskirts of a medieval citadel of monotone stone buildings that stretched up to the crest of a hill. Each structure progressively towered over the next and continued higher and higher as if on a quest to reach the heavens.

He took two painkillers, waited for a few more minutes until seven o'clock and then left his vehicle. He made his way on foot along the tapered winding pathways. The sun's basking rays warmed his shoulders as he walked beneath aged stone archways and continued along a succession of circuitous roads, in what seemed like an infinite spiral. Along the way, he passed a few locals going about their business and tourists who had arrived early for a tour of the old town.

As he walked, the aroma of freshly baked bread wafted to his nostrils. His grumbling stomach reminded him that he had not eaten since yesterday lunchtime. His nose followed the welcoming scent to a young woman inside a bakery stacking hot freshly baked rolls. Above the door, in fanciful lettering, were the words *Torte e Dolcetti*. Unable to believe his luck, he entered the shop and pretended to look around.

The young woman glanced up with a smile that showed a glimmer of intrigue at the bruises on his face. 'May I help you, Father?'

'Yes, two *sfogliatelle* and a double espresso, please?' He eyed a cross with ruby inlays dangling from her neck.

'What flavours would you like?'

'Two almond, please.'

The woman nodded and smiled, placed the pastries into a paper bag, and turned away to make the coffee.

As she prepared the machine, Christiano eased in with his first question. 'Is Fortuna here?'

The woman froze for a moment, and the atmosphere turned palpably tense. She returned to her task of pouring the coffee into a Styrofoam cup and placed a lid over the top. 'Fortuna is no longer here, Father.' She turned to face him and handed him the items.

'Do you know where I might find her? I'm a good friend of her sister. It's important I give her some news.'

'I was unaware that she had a sister. What's her name?'

'Abbess Francesca Rossini.'

'Her sister is a nun?'

'Yes, I am a priest at the convent where her sister was the Abbess. I have come with urgent news of her tragic passing.'

The young woman stood speechless. With her contemplative gaze on Christiano, she nervously chewed on her bottom lip and fiddled with the cross around her neck. 'What happened to your face?' she eventually asked.

'I was in a car accident. It looks worse than it is.'

She nodded as if accepting his story and walked to the shop entrance. She glanced outside before she shut and locked the door. 'Come this way.' She ushered him round the till and into an office.

Christiano entered the cubicle-sized room and leaned against a desk.

'May I ask your name, Father?'

'Of course, I am Father Abbadelli. And you?'

'Maria Falco, Father. May I ask how Fortuna's sister died?'

Christiano looked to the ground and spoke with a tremble in his voice. 'She was killed by one of Don Primo's men.'

The woman scowled at the mention of Don Primo.

Christiano remained silent.

'The truth is I don't know where she is,' she admitted. 'She moved away from here over a year ago. The exact same time as…' She stopped speaking.

'The exact same time Angelica went missing?'

'You know her?'

He nodded. 'I do. She was under the Abbess's care, until…' He lowered his gaze. 'Please tell me what happened.'

'One day everything was normal, and by the next morning, Fortuna and Angelica were gone. She left me a note stating that she'd put the bakery in my name. I was her assistant, you see.'

'What happened when Don Primo's men came looking for her?'

'I was terrified, but I knew nothing. I showed them the note hoping they would believe me. They must have because they left me alone after that.'

'How do you know Angelica?'

'I was at school with her until that awful… thing happened to her. She didn't come back after that. Nobody ever speaks about what happened, before or after the rape. Such a tragedy.'

Christiano's guts somersaulted. An injection of bile hit the back of his throat. 'Well, she has come a long way since then.' He feigned knowledge of the incident.

'How old were you?' He downed his double espresso to remove the taste of sick in his mouth and tossed the cup in the bin.

'I was thirteen. We are the same age.'

Christiano swallowed hard as a feeling of lightness swirled around his head. 'Forgive me. Although I am aware of the incident, I am lacking in certain elements to gain a complete picture. How did she become Don Primo's mistress?'

'Father, you are asking a lot of questions about a subject no one would dare mention in this town. Please do not go making enquiries of this kind around here. Even a priest will find himself in danger.'

'Of course, it's just that the subject came up and Angelica was… *is* under my care at the convent since the Abbess's death.'

'What do you need to know, Father?'

'Please, just tell me everything you know.'

'Fortuna was friends with Angelica's grandmother, Esta. She told me that Don Primo had the rapist killed. Well, that was the little whisper around town. There was no proof. The man wasn't from this town. He was a vagrant passing through, but what he did to her was horrendous.'

Christiano repressed the tears that wanted to spill from his eyes. 'Why did Don Primo have the man killed?'

'He came into his town and committed a serious crime. Don Primo would never put up with that. Fortuna said that Don Primo took responsibility for her after that. Her parents had died two years earlier in a car crash. She had only her grandmother, but she was old and unwell. When Esta died, Angelica was sixteen and a stunner. All I heard was that she became Don Primo's mistress.'

'At sixteen?'

She nodded.

'Okay, why not his wife? Is he married?'

'Yes. He was married long before Angelica, and he has children around my age. She would never have been able to give him that anyway, so it's just as well.'

'What do you mean?'

'About what?'

'Why wouldn't Angelica have been able to give him children?'

'Look, perhaps this is getting a little personal.'

'Please, believe me, I have only her best intentions at heart.'

The woman looked down as if feeling cornered. 'I heard that due to the complications and horrific wounds inflicted on her during her…ordeal that it left her unable to have children. I told you, the man was a savage. What he did…' She shuddered, unable to finish her sentence. She looked up at Christiano. 'From what I heard, I'm surprised she even lived through it. She never spoke again, anyway.'

'Forgive me for pushing this line of enquiry but how are you so certain that she cannot have children?'

'It's a small town, Father. The officer who was in charge of the case is a friend of my papa. The case was going to court, the man had been caught, and so the doctor submitted a report. Then the man mysteriously died. He was found dead in his cell. They said it was a drug overdose but how he came by the drugs…as I said…anyway, it never went to court.'

'What did the report say? Did you see it?'

'No, I was just a teenager. It was a very sad case. All I know is that the doctor made sure he stressed the point about her infertility to ensure the man went away for a long time. Well, anyway, you know the rest. After she became Don Primo's property, she had a guard with her wherever she went. Don Primo's wife knows, but nobody dares mention it. I suppose, what can she do?'

'Do you know where I can find Don Primo?'

She shook her head. 'I have said too much already.'

'Please, I ask just one more thing.'

She made a burdensome sigh. 'He owns a restaurant about half an hour's walk from here. It has a stone front, and it's called *Aquilon Ristorante*. Be careful, Father.'

'Thank you. Please, keep this to yourself.'

'Like I said, these are deep, dark secrets no one ever speaks about round here. I owe Fortuna everything, and I know how much she loved Angelica. But please, you must leave through the back alley. I don't want any trouble.'

She showed him into the kitchen area and through a short passage that led to an alleyway. 'Turn left out of here, walk all the way to the top and turn right. That will lead you back onto the main road. Keep going for about half an hour until you pass beneath two successive arches, follow the road round and take the first right. The restaurant is on that road.'

'Thank you. You've been very helpful.'

Christiano left through the back door, turned left as instructed and found his way back onto the main road. With his appetite quashed, he put the *sfogliatelle* into his rucksack. As he walked, Maria's words haunted his mind. He ducked into an alleyway, collapsed into a squat, and allowed himself to wholly grieve Angelica's tragic story.

The white Mercedes stopped before the electric gates at eight in the morning. Benito pressed the button on a remote control and the gates crept open at the pace of an old Galapagos tortoise. He parked close by the side entrance to the restaurant and opened the door for his Boss. As he left the vehicle, Don Primo's face was like an impenetrable fortress. His right arm was in a sling, and his bandaged hand limply held a greasy paper bag. They entered the building through the side door.

'Wait in my office,' he said.

Benito did as instructed and Don Primo continued

through the opaque door on his right and down the stairs to the restaurant.

Ricardo was awakened by Don Primo's clomping. He quickly tidied himself up, hoping to look as if he'd been awake all night.

'Boss,' he said as he stood up.

'How was it last night?'

Ricardo noticed his arm. 'What happened Boss, are you okay?'

'I asked you a question.'

'She didn't give me any trouble, Boss. She's asleep, I think.'

'Did she speak again?'

'No, Boss, like I said, she was quiet.'

'I'm keeping the restaurant closed today. Call the staff and tell them not to come in. Tell them they'll be paid, just the same.'

'Yes, Don Primo.'

'And make sure all the men come in today. I want them here for when this man arrives at noon.'

'Sure thing, Boss.'

'After you've made all the calls, you can go home and sleep, but be back before noon.'

'Yes Don Primo, thank you…Boss.'

Don Primo made his way behind the bar, walked beneath an alcove and entered an extended room lined with wine racks. Angelica was tied to a sofa in a part of the cellar normally used for staff breaks. Her eyes remained closed. He stared at her for a while. A glimmer of fondness spread across his face. She opened her eyes and his demeanour hardened. He untied her and tossed the paper bag at her. 'Breakfast.'

She opened the bag, removed the pastry inside and bit into it like an animal ravaged by hunger.

Don Primo sat down opposite her. 'If you were hungry you should have asked Ricardo for food.'

She eyed his bandaged arm as she ate.

'So we're still not talking?' He stared at her for a while. 'Just tell me this one thing.'

She looked at him with seeming lack of interest as she chewed.

'Why did you leave?'

She stopped eating and scribbled on a notepad lying on a coffee table nearby. *I was sixteen. You had no right.*

Don Primo maintained his composure and made a slight nod of his head. 'You never complained at the time.' He scratched the top of his nose. 'You gave me the impression you liked me.'

Angelica scribbled avidly.

Don Primo's eyes moved along the sheet, reading the words. *I was young and naïve. You treated me like a princess, but then I grew up. You would never have let me go.*

His face remained blank. 'You're right. Nobody leaves me until I say so.'

Christiano passed beneath the two successive arches and followed the road as instructed by Maria. He stopped just before the right turn, a dead-end road, and noticed the restaurant opposite. The impressive stone façade lent the premises the look of a fancy cave entrance. It took up a substantial amount of space along the closed road, no doubt a pricey piece of real estate for the privacy it afforded.

As Christiano surveyed his surroundings, he saw the familiar frame of Ricardo leave by a side door in the car park and enter a vehicle remarkably like the one he was thrown from only yesterday. As the gates opened, he swiftly backed himself round the corner and hid in an alcove.

He peered out as the car drove by, confirming Ricardo as the driver. As the vehicle disappeared round the curved road, he looked back to the restaurant to see the gates coming to a close.

He made a dash for the narrowing gap and just managed to slip through. He headed straight for the bushes, took a giant leap over a hedge and landed with a soundless thud on the dry mud. His face contorted with pain as the impact and movement took its toll on his bruised body. He grimaced and took slow, deep breaths to stop himself from crying out. He shoved two painkillers into his mouth and leaned against a bush to normalise his breathing.

Now it was time to wait.

✦ Chapter Twenty-Five ✦

As mid-morning smiled on the old Tuscan town, Christiano realised he was starving. He rummaged in his rucksack for one of the *sfogliatella* he had purchased from Maria and bit into the crumbly pastry. His stomach welcomed the influx of food as the bitter-sweet marzipan settled on his tongue. All the while he maintained a vigilant eye on the building opposite.

Enzo had been the first to arrive at around nine. He had parked next to a white Mercedes, which Christiano guessed belonged to Don Primo.

As he satisfied his appetite, a car reached the electric gates and entered the car park. Two stout men in their fifties made their way through the restaurant's side door. Soon after, another car arrived, and for about half an hour the gate sporadically opened and closed, five more cars pulling in and parking. Each time, one or two men left their vehicle completely unaware of Christiano's surveillance.

By now, Christiano's limbs were numb and aching; the hard, lumpy ground pushed against his already bruised flesh.

Despite the welcoming shade of the surrounding trees, he sweated from the rising midday heat. He took a sip of water and wiped his brow.

Twenty minutes before noon, Ricardo drove into the car park.

The Cardinal's limousine made its grand entrance into town. Behind the wheel, Johan was dressed in a grey suit complete with a chauffeur's cap. The privacy screen was up and the intercom off, shielding Sammel in the cab. His wide glinting eyes ogled the wads of cash neatly lined and stacked in an orderly fashion. He shut the briefcase and placed it next to him, on top of a folded copy of *Il Cospiratore.*

It was now a quarter past noon and forty minutes before the last movement. Christiano made a thorough scan of his surroundings before he dashed for the window opposite. He sneaked a peek through the glass, into an office. A man sat on a sofa, reading a newspaper. The door ahead of Christiano opened, and an authoritative figure with milk-white hair and a bandaged arm entered the room. Following behind him, he recognised Enzo and the characteristic scar running from his right eye.

The distant sound of an approaching vehicle carried on the wind. He darted for the bushes, slipped between two hedges and dived to the ground, wincing as he landed on his right arm. He stuffed two painkillers into his mouth as he peered through the foliage at who had arrived.

The Cardinal's familiar black limousine waited patiently

behind the retracting gates. It entered and stopped in a space close by the hedges. Its large presence overshadowed the white Mercedes. He recognised the chauffeur, who stepped out and opened the back door. Christiano was surprised that it was not the Cardinal leaving the car, but a tall man of athletic build with chiselled features and hair gelled into half-inch spikes that resembled peaks of meringue. Cuffed to his wrist was a briefcase.

Angelica's fate dawned on him.

The side door to the building opened and Enzo stepped in front of the entrance.

'You wait here,' said Sammel.

Johan nodded.

Sammel strutted towards Enzo and offered his hand as he reached him. Enzo did not return the gesture but motioned for Sammel to raise his arms. He did as instructed and Enzo proceeded to frisk him. Satisfied, he gestured for him to enter.

As the door shut behind them, Johan relaxed and leaned against the bonnet of the limousine. He removed a packet of cigarettes from his top pocket, pulled one out and lit it, taking slow, savouring puffs.

Christiano searched the ground to find a fallen branch close by. He picked it up and tested its strength and firmness by making a few practised waves through the air and hitting his open palm. Satisfied, he removed his shoes, emerged from the bushes and methodically made his way to the unsuspecting chauffeur.

Johan was checking for messages on his phone when

Christiano reached him. He remained oblivious as Christiano slowly raised the branch above his head.

The sweat on Christiano's face dripped like rain. He steadied his breath. A burst of guilt flashed across his face as he brought the stick down with a heavy hand on Johan's head.

The dazed chauffeur dropped to the ground. His cell phone fell to his side.

Christiano slipped the phone into his pocket, scooped Johan beneath his armpits, and pulled him into the bushes. He released him on the ground and checked for a pulse. The man was still breathing. He made a sigh of relief and searched the chauffeur's pockets to find a packet of cigarettes, mint-flavoured chewing gum, a wallet with a drivers' licence identifying the unconscious man as *Johan Asper,* and two sets of keys, one of which was for the car. He placed the items on the parched earth by Johan's head and proceeded to remove the man's clothing.

Johan's phone vibrated silently in Christiano's trouser pocket. He pulled it out to see the name, *Frya,* and the photo of a naturally tanned and smiling face with deep-set and intelligent eyes.

He ignored the call, placed the phone on the ground, and removed his penknife and wallet from his own pockets. He placed them on the ground by the phone and began to undress. He rolled his clothes into a ball and tucked them beneath the nearest bush. He dressed in Johan's uniform and placed most of the items from the ground into his pockets, slotting Johan's phone into the top cavity of his blazer.

With his penknife open and poised for use, he departed from the bushes and proceeded to slit the tyre of every car in the parking lot, but one.

✦ Chapter Twenty-Six ✦

Sammel Gruner sat on the umber-coloured sofa in Don Primo's office sipping ice-cold water from a glass beaded with condensation. As a seasoned veteran, working as a bodyguard for the rich and famous, he was accustomed to danger and fully trained in combat. However, ten to one did not carry good odds. He was outnumbered and in someone else's territory with only his wits as his weapon. Beneath the cool exterior of his dark suit and shades, he excelled in concealing the knot of dread wringing his guts into a twisted mass.

From behind his desk, Don Primo scrutinised him for any weakness, any sign that he could use to his advantage. He saw none. 'I gather my money's in the case.'

Sammel's legs gripped the briefcase at his feet. 'That is correct.' He spoke in a sharp, accented tone that was a stiff as a corpse, to the point, and replete with efficiency. 'The briefcase contains one million euros, the second instalment of the two million as arranged with His Eminence.'

Don Primo's eyes glinted like diamonds. 'Enzo, get away

from that window and call Ricardo to fetch Angelica.'

'Sure thing, Boss.' He entered the corridor where seven thugs waited silently for orders and made his way down the steps to the basement restaurant. Ricardo sat opposite Angelica maintaining a scowling gaze, to which she looked impervious.

'The Boss wants her upstairs.' He glanced fleetingly at Angelica before heading back to the office.

'It's time,' said Ricardo. He grabbed her arm and yanked her from her seat, a triumphant smirk on his face.

Angelica resisted, dragging her heels as he laboured to pull her through the empty restaurant up every step until they reached the top.

Back in the office, guilt seeped through Don Primo's mind like rot on a fallen apple. 'Where are you taking her?' he said.

'As far as I know, that information is on a need-to-know basis. I am fully aware of your agreement with His Eminence,' replied Sammel.

Don Primo stamped his cigarette into the ashtray and was about to rain thunderbolts on Sammel when the door opened.

Angelica, pushed roughly from behind, stumbled into the office. With her presence now in the room, his guilt intensified. He remained seated, unable to meet her gaze, his anger quashed.

Angelica stared with curious dread at the stranger with the briefcase at his feet.

'Keep her hands tied,' instructed Sammel as he stood up.

'What's going on?' Angelica turned to Don Primo.

Hearing her speak for the first time forced his head up, but now was not the time to acknowledge it. Instead, he turned to Sammel who was walking towards him.

Sammel placed the briefcase on his desk. 'Here is…'

'Not in front of her!' snapped Don Primo.

'As you wish.' He turned to Ricardo. 'Take her to the car and tell my driver I'll be there shortly.'

Don Primo slammed his fist on the desk and stood up. 'Let's get something straight, I give my men orders, not you!'

Sammel's already chiselled features hardened. He clenched his jaw, sucking it all in. 'Of course. My apologies.'

Don Primo nodded at Ricardo, who proceeded to drag Angelica out of the room. She resisted, shouting abuse at Don Primo. *'Bastardo! Bastardo!'* She spat on the ground as she disappeared round the doorway.

'Let's just get this done,' said Don Primo.

Ricardo gripped Angelica's tied hands and pushed her through the side door and into the car park.

She continued to resist, dropping to the ground like a dead weight.

He scooped her up and carried her the rest of the way to the limousine. She kicked and writhed in protest.

With his head lowered, a disguised Christiano waited outside the car. He opened the back passenger door with speedy efficiency and Ricardo dropped her inside, knocking her head on the way in.

As Ricardo bent down to buckle her seatbelt, the height

of his ear danced teasingly across her vision. She bit into it savagely.

He yelped, pushed her head away and stopped to stare at her, his raging eyes plastered with incredulity. He raised his fist for a brutal retaliation, but instead, a smug grin returned to his clawed face. He dropped his fist to his side, leaned in close to her ear and said, 'If I haven't already killed him, I'll give your lover priest your regards as I finish the job... slowly.'

She spat, just missing her mark as he slammed the door with a sneer. 'She's all yours!' he said, heading back to the building.

Christiano swiftly entered the driver's side and locked the doors.

As soon as Ricardo had entered the building and the door was shut behind him, Christiano started the engine, reversed the limousine and rammed through the gates at high speed. He manoeuvred the car along the snaking roads like a Formula One driver.

Everyone in the office scrambled to the window to see what was left of the gnarled and twisted gates crashing to the ground.

'What the hell...' said Sammel. 'Is this some kind of trick?'

Don Primo turned to him in shock, then back to an equally bewildered Ricardo and Enzo. 'Don't just stand there, go after them.'

The men followed them, each man poised for action.

Ricardo reached his car and pulled on the door handle.

'Don't bother,' said Enzo. He pointed to the car's tyres. The rest of the men followed his staunch fingers to see that every tyre in the car park was flat.

Don Primo came out of the building. 'Why isn't anyone moving?'

'The tyres, Boss,' said Ricardo.

Don Primo looked at the cars, noticing that the tyres of his own Mercedes had been slashed.

Sammel reached his side. 'What happened?'

'Your chauffeur took off with her, that's what. As far as I'm concerned that equals delivery. And you'll pay extra for the broken gates and the tyres.'

Sammel's startling six-foot-five frame cast a shadow over Don Primo. 'We'll see what His Eminence has to say about that.'

'I wasn't asking,' said Don Primo unfazed by his size.

Sammel warily turned his head from left to right, realising that Don Primo's thugs had formed a circle around him. He gulped, took a deep breath and suddenly tilted his head with curiosity.

Ahead of him, amidst the bushes, was a white protrusion that seemed odd against the starkness of the dark mud and green foliage. He made his way towards it.

Don Primo followed him, beckoning with a nod of his head for Ricardo and Enzo to follow. They all peered over Sammel's shoulder as he knelt down for a closer look.

With slight trepidation, Sammel reached out and touched the item. As he snapped his hand back, it took milliseconds for his eyes and brain to register. He pushed the bush aside to find a solitary hand lying across the dry mud.

'Is it attached to a body?' asked Ricardo.

Sammel pulled the hedges apart and bustled his way through the bushes to see an unconscious Johan stripped down to his pants. 'It appears so.'

The others entered behind him.

He felt Johan's neck for a pulse. 'And he's alive.'

'Who is he?' asked Don Primo.

'Johan, my chauffeur.'

Four nonplussed men stood staring at Johan's partly clothed and unconscious body.

Enzo was the one to notice the heap of black clothing tucked beneath a hedge. He pulled it out. 'I think we can guess who our fake chauffeur is.' He held the priestly garments in the air.

'That bastardo priest,' said an astonished Don Primo.

'Well he's a resourceful priest,' said Sammel. 'I'll give him that.'

Don Primo's face grew crimson and his body trembled with rage. He looked at Ricardo. 'Didn't you notice the chauffeur was the priest?'

'I didn't look at him, Boss. Plus, I've never seen him close up.'

Don Primo pointed an accusing finger at his men. 'You two were supposed to take care of this.'

Ricardo sent a scathing glare at Enzo.

'Go back to his home town and visit his family. I want answers.'

'Yes Don Primo.' They started to leave. 'And,' he said,

walking towards them – he leaned in, sotto voce – 'I want you to kill the entire family.'

Sammel gently slapped Johan's face. He gradually came to, grimacing from pain, and put his hand to his head. He pulled away blood-stained fingers. 'What happened?' he murmured.

'That's exactly what we want to know,' replied Sammel.

'I was smoking by the car and that's the last thing I remember.'

Don Primo knelt down and picked up a large branch from the floor. 'There's blood on here.' He showed it to Sammel.

'Well Johan, His Eminence is *not* going to be pleased with you. Come on let's get you inside.'

Angelica eyed the dark glass concealing the identity of her knight in shining armour. The limousine had slowed its pace, not that it was any less conspicuous. She lifted her leg and banged her foot against the screen. Seconds later it glided down.

Christiano removed his cap and winked at her through the rear-view mirror.

'You're alive,' she blurted with joyous relief.

Christiano swerved to avoid hitting a parked car. 'You're speaking!?'

A girlish giggle left her lips. 'You made it happen.'

'Me… How?'

'When I saw you flying off Ricardo's car, something just

ripped through me. I discovered it was my voice, screaming your name.'

'That's wonderful. You have the voice of a melodious harp.' He chuckled and shook his head in disbelief. A concerned expression replaced his joy. 'Did they hurt you; lay a finger on you?'

'I'm okay. I can't believe you came for me.'

'Of course. I made a promise.'

'Is that the only reason?'

Their eyes met in the rear-view mirror. Hers searched his for the right answer.

'I'll untie you soon. You're safe now. I won't let them take you again.'

They reached the town's boundary and Christiano parked the lengthy vehicle with little care for its safety. 'We'd better hurry. They'll be close behind.' He entered the back and untied her.

She wrapped her arms around him, unabashedly. 'I thought you were dead.'

His heart fluttered. He felt intoxicated. 'I'm tougher than they realise.' His speech was barely audible.

She gripped him tighter.

With their bodies pressed together, he could not deny the feelings coursing through him. He cupped her face in his hands and they gazed at each other; their foreheads touching; the warmth of their breaths teasing each other's lips. Inching ever closer.

Christiano came to his senses. 'We must leave.' He pulled away.

She nodded, disappointed.

'It wasn't the promise. I came because I care about you.'

She smiled and leaned in close to his face again, wetting his cheeks with her tears. 'Thank you.' Her eyes sparkled with gratitude.

'We really must go,' he whispered, clenching his jaw to stop his lips from meeting hers.

As they moved apart, Angelica caught sight of the newspaper on the seat by her side. She picked it up and briefly scanned the article. Her eyes grew wide with shock.

'It was Sister Celeste's doing,' said Christiano. 'She has caused a lot of trouble. I will answer your questions shortly. But now, we really must go.'

Angelica placed the newspaper beneath her arm. Her face wore a frown as they walked.

Christiano tried to comfort her. 'You know hardly anyone reads those papers. I, myself, only discovered it through Father Cavallo.'

'Then how is it all the wrong people managed to get a copy? The Abbess is dead. You were nearly killed.'

'It will blow over.'

'How? Don Primo will never stop and neither will the Cardinal, it seems.'

Christiano stopped walking and turned to her. He gently gripped her arms. 'I made a promise to keep you safe. We will go somewhere where they will never find us.' He affectionately brushed her cheek. 'Don Primo and the Cardinal did not count on someone like me by your side.'

She smiled. His words filled her with relief and comfort.

'You can fight them all off, can you? Then tell me, what were you going to do if that man had got into the car with me?'

'To be honest, I hadn't thought that far ahead.'

She nodded, amused. 'And what happened to the man whose clothes you're wearing?'

Johan lay on the sofa in Don Primo's office holding an icepack to the wound on the back of his head. Alessandro, the youngest of Don Primo's men, entered the office with some uniforms for waiters and chefs. He handed the pile to Johan.

'Thank you,' he said sheepishly. He proceeded to put on a pair of black trousers and a white shirt – a little self-conscious of the stares as he was dressing.

'What happened, exactly?' asked Sammel.

'It was like I said, I was having a smoke, and the next minute, I awoke to see you kneeling over me.'

'Was anything else taken, apart from your clothing?'

He shook his head.

'Where's your phone?'

'I accidentally left it at home, today.'

'Are you sure? I have never—'

'Your man will live,' interrupted Don Primo. 'What about my money?'

'I'm sorry but no delivery, no money. If security was better around here…'

Don Primo pounced like a one-armed wolf, pinning Sammel to the wall. His men stood behind him, sniggering at the giant held by the neck with just one hand. 'That doesn't work for me,' said Don Primo.

'Perhaps we can come to some arrangement, after all,' said Sammel, struggling to speak with a hand wrapped around his throat.

'The only agreement I will make is one where I'm paid.'

'If I could just call His Eminence. I must follow his orders.'

Don Primo let go of Sammel and walked nonchalantly to his desk. 'Go ahead, call him.'

Sammel rubbed his throat. The redness in his skin slowly retracted as oxygen moved unhindered through his lungs once more. He removed his phone from his pocket and dialled the number as he approached the door to take the call outside.

Two hardened men in their fifties blocked his path. Their arms were as well muscled as their protruding bellies were large.

'Let him pass. He's not going anywhere,' said Don Primo.

Sammel entered the car park and waited for the Cardinal to answer his call.

'I hope you have good news for me.' The Cardinal's voice echoed through the earpiece.

He winced. 'Your Eminence, I am sorry to tell you that the priest has escaped with the girl.'

'Sammel Gruner, are you calling to tell me that you have lost her again?'

'With respect Your Eminence, I had nothing to do with losing her the first time...'

'Enough!'

'Yes, Your Eminence.'

'What happened?'

Sammel recounted the incident to the Cardinal.

'Johan seems to have no wits about him at all. I will deal with him on his return. In the meantime, get a taxi back, or rent a car.'

'Yes, Your Eminence, but we have another problem.'

'And what would that be?'

'Don Primo wants his money. I'm outnumbered here. If he's not paid, I don't think we will return at all.'

'Well, you have only yourselves to blame.'

'May I make a suggestion, Your Eminence?'

'If you must.'

'He has already sent his men after them. May I suggest keeping him involved and perhaps getting him to deliver the girl to Rome? I am better able to take care of him there.'

'Are you suggesting I pay him?'

'Not only are you willing to pay him for the undelivered package but you will give him one million more if he brings her to Rome.'

'Are you out of your mind?'

'Rest assured, he and his men will never leave Rome.'

'And I will be two million worse for it.'

'A small price to pay for the delivery of the girl and the elimination of all witnesses, Your Eminence.'

A rush of dead air met his ear. 'Pass the phone to Mr Pulsoni, will you Sammel.'

'Yes, Your Eminence.' He made a relieved, if not satisfied

grin, as he headed back into the building. 'His Eminence wishes to speak with you.'

Don Primo took the phone and held it against his chest. 'Alessandro, have Enzo and Ricardo left?'

'Yes, Boss. They went to get Ricardo's wife's car.'

He moved the phone to his ear. 'Cardinal.'

The Cardinal maintained an imperious composure. 'Mr Pulsoni, Sammel tells me that you have already dispatched your men to fetch our precious package. Am I correct?'

'You are.'

'Then we are still in business. Are we not?'

'I'm not sure. I may just take my money and keep her.'

'Now, now, Mr Pulsoni, I am a man of my word. You may have the money with my blessing, and there is another one million if you deliver her to Rome.'

There was silence as Don Primo churned it all around in his mind.

The Cardinal continued, 'How wealthy do you want to be Mr Pulsoni? Can you imagine the immense advantage that comes with a direct connection to the Vatican? I can make you a very wealthy man, untouchable by God himself. How would you like to be under the Vatican's blessed employ?'

'What sort of work are we talking about?'

'The sort your unique talents call for, Mr Pulsoni.'

Don Primo scratched his chin. 'Okay, I will deliver her to Rome. And, I accept your offer of employment, but on my terms. If I don't like the job, I don't do it. Is that clear?'

'Crystal, Mr Pulsoni.'

'Then we have a deal.'

✦ Chapter Twenty-seven ✦

The afternoon sun made its last tribute to the day as the car journeyed back to Christiano's hometown. Enzo rubbed his bloodshot eyes while Ricardo concentrated on the road ahead with a vexed look on his face. 'I knew I should have killed the priest, but that bitch went crazy and you stopped me. It would have taken me a few seconds to pump some rounds into the back of that truck.'

'And what about the old man driving? He would have been a witness. Would you have killed him too?'

'Why not?'

'Listen to you.' Enzo's face was contemptuous. 'As far as I'm concerned I made the right call. The police were fast approaching and we would have been caught.'

'I would have shot them too. So Don Primo pulls a few strings. It wouldn't be the first time.'

Enzo rolled his eyes. 'Okay tough guy, next time you do it your way. I made a judgement call, and at the time it was the safest choice.'

'Yeah, these *safe* choices seem to be happening a lot lately.'

'What the fuck is that supposed to mean? Who do you think you are, talking to me like that?'

Ricardo shrugged and maintained his gaze on the road ahead. He did not see or anticipate Enzo's blatant slap across his cheek.

The car veered to the opposite side of the road.

An oncoming vehicle sped towards them. Its horn made a protracted sound as Ricardo gained control of the steering wheel. They missed each other by a hairsbreadth.

Ricardo made an unceremonious stop on the side of the road and pulled his gun out, holding it to Enzo's head. 'You think you're so tough, old man?'

Enzo glared into his eyes. 'Pull the trigger, if you think you're a man.' He pressed his forehead against the barrel. 'Then you'd better run, coz Don Primo and *my* wife, who happens to be *his sister*, will want to know why I'm dead. You won't ever stop running.'

Ricardo visibly gulped, bringing a smile to Enzo's face.

'And, you'd better look down.'

Ricardo felt a dig in his side. His eyes wandered down to see Enzo's gun firmly planted in his rib cage.

Christiano took his eyes off the road for a moment to glimpse Angelica sleeping peacefully by his side. He let out a sigh of relief and turned back to the road. His bruised face was finally relaxed and free from the anxieties that had consumed him over the past twenty-four hours.

Johan's phone buzzed in his pocket. He pulled it out and once again saw the photo of the mysterious Frya displayed on the screen as the phone continued to buzz. Despite his curiosity, he was not about to answer the call. He turned the phone off and placed it in a hollow slot on the dashboard.

Enzo and Ricardo arrived at the Abbadelli's home in the early evening. The street lamp just outside the door shone a wan but fiery illumination upon the red stone house, singling it out among the paler homes beside it. Spats of light fought through the gaps of the rose-pink drapes ornamenting the dining room window, and the sounds of rustling waves drifted like smoke to the top of the mountainside. It was a picturesque scene of idyllic bliss.

'Let's get this done.' Enzo's words sliced through the tranquillity with a sharp knife.

They made their way to the house, and Enzo disguised his intent behind a gentle rap on the door.

Inside, Rosa, Emilio and the children were having dinner.

'I'll go,' said Emilio, rising from his seat. As he opened the door, Ricardo charged with the force of a herd of buffalo, knocking him to the floor. Enzo shut the door behind them, and Ricardo dragged Emilio by the scruff of his clothing through to the dining room. He pointed his gun at Emilio's head.

Rosa screamed as the unimaginable unfolded before her. The children burst into tears and what followed was a chaotic medley of terror-filled cries bouncing off the walls and round the room.

Enzo placed a firm hand over Rosa's mouth, frightening her into a silent sob. Her body visibly trembled. The children seemed to mimic her stifled howls and reduced their cries to a whimper.

He leaned in close to her. 'We just want to know where he is.'

'Who?' said Emilio.

Ricardo stamped on his face.

Rosa made a muffled scream.

Enzo gripped her mouth tighter and pulled her chin to his face.

Terror-stricken eyes stared into his.

'You scream again, he dies. You understand me?'

She nodded, unable to stop her quivering.

'Now, I will ask again. Where's the priest and Angelica?' He let go of her mouth.

She shook her head. 'I don't know.'

'Wrong answer,' said Ricardo, kicking Emilio in the stomach repeatedly.

'Please, stop! He went after Angelica.' Her choked words were filled with desperation and pleading. 'I haven't seen or heard from him since.'

Ricardo left Emilio lying on the ground badly injured and barely conscious. 'Let's try this another way.' He walked to Lissandra and pulled her in close to him. 'Such a cute little girl, what's her name?'

Rosa gulped. 'Please, she's just a child.'

Enzo nudged her head. 'He asked you a question.'

'Lissandra.'

'And your name?' asked Ricardo.

'Rosa.'

'Okay, Rosa, if you want Lissandra to live...' He displayed his gun. 'You'd better tell us where they are.'

The amplified sound of a cocking trigger rang through Rosa's ears. Her sodden face was distraught with tears. 'She's just a baby!'

Ricardo accepted her answer with a contemplative nod and proceeded to shoot Emilio in the leg.

Rosa bounced up in her seat, screaming hysterically. Emilio curled up in silent agony, his mouth swollen shut from Ricardo's kicks.

Enzo gripped her mouth. She gasped for breath, helplessly trying to reach out to the children.

'The next bullet will be for her,' said Enzo pointing at Lissandra. 'Do you hear me?'

She nodded, her eyes wide with understanding.

Satisfied, he removed his hand from her mouth.

'He was going to take her to our mountain cabin,' she blurted.

'Where?' said Enzo, reaching for a pad from his pocket. 'Write it down.' He placed the pad and a pen on the table.

She grasped the pen in her trembling hand.

'It's just as well I damaged the left hand, wasn't it?' said Enzo leaning into her face as she wrote.

She reeled away as she scrawled the information on the now tear-stained paper.

'There, that wasn't so hard was it?' Enzo picked up the pad and wiped away the wetness before he gazed at the instructions. 'Now, is this all true?'

'Yes, I swear to you. It's the exact location.'

Enzo looked at Ricardo. 'Maybe we should take one of the children with us,' he said.

'No! All the information is true. I swear to God, to the Virgin Mary herself.' She made the sign of the cross. 'Please, leave the babies alone.'

'I'm sorry that won't be possible,' said Ricardo pointing his gun at Lissandra's head. He cocked the trigger.

The single gunshot resounded through the room. Ricardo's eyes were wide with madness as drops of blood ran from the single bullet hole in the centre of his forehead. He dropped to his knees and fell against the table. Lissandra screamed.

Rosa's confounded gaze moved to Enzo.

He casually placed his gun in its holster, all the while his eyes resting on hers. He motioned his head towards Lissandra.

Rosa rushed to her side, feeling her face, her head and her body for injury. She sobbed with relief as she hugged her and cupped her angelic face in her hands. 'You watch nonno, okay.' The little girl nodded bravely.

Rosa guided her to Emilio's side and proceeded to remove a tea cloth from the table. 'You tie this here.' She pointed to Emilio's leg, above his wound. 'Just like papa and nonno taught you to tie a rope. You remember?'

Lissandra nodded, competently tying the cloth around her grandfather's leg.

In the meantime, Enzo grasped Ricardo from beneath his

armpits. 'Get out of town for a while. Until this blows over.' He dragged him around Emilio's curled-up body to the front door and dropped him on the floor before returning to the dining room. 'Go somewhere where no one will know you. Understand?'

Rosa nodded with a look that was only too convinced of the ominous inferences in his words.

Satisfied, he opened the front door, dragged Ricardo's body to the car and left without another word.

✦ Chapter Twenty-eight ✦

Marcello's car bumped against every rock and lump of protruding mud on the dirt track leading to the cabin. The towering trees trapped the darkness around them. It was like being inside a sarcophagus.

Christiano reached a row of poplar trees which offered the perfect seclusion and parked.

'Well this is it!' he said, switching the engine off. The eerie sounds of the indigenous night creatures screeched through the silence. The car's headlights illuminated a small cabin in the distance. He cut the lights, enveloping them in blackness.

Angelica's haunted eyes stared into the shadows. 'What is this place?'

'It's not as scary as it looks.' He reached his hand to the back seat and retrieved a large torch. 'I spent many a night here with my grandfather. This is where he gave me the knife I carry. Some of my fondest memories are here.'

'How long ago did he die?'

'Many years ago. I was just fifteen. We kept the cabin as a family getaway.' He switched on the torch and handed it to Angelica. 'I'll get the luggage. Just make your way to the door.'

She shook her head with a look of dread.

'Okay, just stay by my side.' He looked amused.

They stepped out of the car and Christiano walked round to the boot where he collected as many shopping bags and luggage as he could carry.

Angelica noticed a couple of bags left behind and picked them up. She shone the torch on the cabin, illuminating the path as they walked.

'There's no internet access here and no electricity,' said Christiano. 'You live the old-fashioned way.'

'It's just as well it is summer,' she replied.

'Yes, it can get pretty cold up here in the winter. As you'll discover in a few months.'

They climbed a set of stone steps, and Christiano unlocked the front door, pushing it open for Angelica to enter. A stale odour drifted to their nostrils as they entered the cabin. They set the bags down on the limestone floor, and Christiano immediately set about lighting his newly purchased camp lanterns, putting them on their highest setting.

The lamps revealed an open-plan room with a large stone fireplace, a wooden dining table, a three-seater sofa and a small kitchen. There was a closed door to the right.

'This is beautiful,' said Angelica, looking up at a ceiling of wooden beams with a myriad of intricate cobwebs joining one to the other.

'Yes, it was my grandfather's pride and joy. He built it himself with his father.' He looked up at the ceiling. 'It seems we have some uninvited guests.'

'Or, perhaps we're the uninvited guests.' She smiled.

'Indeed.'

'What was his name?'

'My grandfather? Christiano Abbadelli. I was named after him.'

Angelica noticed a range of rifles hanging on the wall. 'Are you a hunter?'

He looked at the guns with an expression that showed he had forgotten they were there. 'Goodness no. They were my grandfather's. He was a collector.'

She clutched at her stomach.

'Are you in pain?'

'No, it's been a while since I last ate.'

'Of course. I knew we would arrive late.' He pulled some food items out of the shopping bags and laid them out on the table for her. 'Please, sit down and eat.'

She took her seat and spread apricot preserve on a *biscottate*. As she crunched on the toast, she watched him remove supplies from the bags and place them on the table.

'We'll put them in their rightful place in the morning,' he said. Her steady gaze was making him feel a little self-conscious.

'Where will I sleep?' she asked.

'You'll take the bedroom through the closed door. I'll take the sofa.'

She frowned. 'It's shorter than you are. Your legs will be

dangling off the end. Let me have the sofa.'

'No, that's out of the question. I'll be fine. I have an inflatable mattress which I will set up tomorrow. My discomfort will only be for tonight, and there's not much of that left.'

'Thank you… I mean for everything you've done.'

He made a modest nod. 'How does it feel to be speaking after so long?'

'It's strange. My throat's a bit sore. I suppose I need to exercise my vocal cords a little more before it feels more natural. Does my voice sound normal?'

'It's a little hoarse and there's a slight drawl, but as I said, beneath is a harmonic chord. It'll take time… Actually, I've been meaning to ask. Why the board? Didn't you learn sign language?'

'I did. The board was for those who couldn't sign. I used to sign with the Abbess…' Her voice trailed off as the grief rose to her throat. Her eyes moistened.

'Come, I'll show you to your room.'

She followed him into a bedroom made entirely of wood-log walls. A simple bed was tucked to one side of the room with a small wardrobe at its side. A black cast-iron stove stood opposite, and towards the corner of the room was an en-suite bathroom, its entire space devoured by a cramped shower cubicle, toilet and sink.

He pulled some blankets from a large bag and placed them on the mattress. 'We'll make the bed properly tomorrow. I'll make this place a home for you…until the baby is born.'

She nodded with a slight smile.

'I'll be right outside if you need anything.' He reached the door.

'Christiano!'

He turned to her.

'Can I call you Christiano?'

'Of course.'

'Do you think you'll ever go back to the Church?'

'Even if I wanted to, I don't think they'd have me.'

'I'm sorry.' Her face was riddled with guilt. 'It's all my fault… You know,' she said, thoughtfully, 'he may be just one crooked Cardinal. Take the Abbess and Father Cavallo, both good people of the Church. And you, of course.'

'I'm beginning to think they're the exception.'

'Perhaps, if we find a way to expose him…'

'If we did that we would just be alerting him to your whereabouts. Besides, the Vatican protects its own. How could we prove anything? He has far too much power and influence. He even got to Don Primo.'

Angelica's eyes sank to the ground. 'Don Primo cares only for money. That's his sole motivation.'

'Don't let this worry you anymore. You're safe now. Get some sleep. Okay?'

She nodded as he left the room and watched him with a sorrowful look as he shut the door behind him.

✦ Chapter Twenty-Nine ✦

Age-old trees of oak, beech and poplar soared high above Enzo's car as he sat with adrenaline-fused eyes, chewing gum and staring into oblivion. A breathtaking sight of a red-orange hue filtered through the branches and the dawn had set the sky on fire, but his only concern was how the hell he was going to get himself out of this one. He was growing too old for a life that left a bad taste in his mouth and an ever-mounting body count. He wanted nothing more than to retire.

The phone rang, waking him from his stupor. The caller ID flashed with Don Primo's name. He took a deep breath, braced himself, and answered the call. 'Boss.'

'What happened at the house? I didn't hear from either of you.'

'We didn't want to wake you. We were driving all night to get to this cabin where the priest's mother told us he would be.'

'You're there now?'

'We just got here.'

'What happened back at the house?'

'The message was delivered and received.'

'Who was there?'

'Just the priest's mother and father.'

'Good. You can go back another time and deliver another message to his brother and his family. Now, how are you approaching the cabin?'

'Ricardo wants to steam in like a bull in a china shop.'

'That's not a good idea. Let me speak to him. I don't want any screw-ups. If it comes from me, he'll listen.'

'Ah... He went for a piss in the forest.'

'Okay, you give him my explicit warning not to fuck this up.'

'Sure thing Boss, as soon as he gets back to the car. And you leave our approach to me. I got this.'

'You'd better because this time I won't be so forgiving.' The line went dead.

Enzo tossed the phone on the passenger seat with a look that was drowning in its own faeces, cupped his face in his hands and rested against the steering wheel. The horn let out a blast. His head snapped up. The silence rippled towards him. He stepped out of the car, went directly to the boot and opened it to see the lifeless body of Ricardo slumped in the back. The small hole in his head stood out like a third eye. 'You crazy son of a bitch.' He slammed it shut.

He locked the car and made his way into the forest on foot, meandering through the landmarks Rosa had mentioned. The fresh air injected life into his blood. He felt light and fuelled with long lost vigour. He wondered what his wife would think of moving to the mountains. He longed for them to be as far away from Don Primo as was physically possible. He reached the cabin and found Christiano's car shielded behind rows of poplar. He hid behind some trees and surveyed the chalet.

Rays of sunlight warmed the log walls of the lone cabin as daylight took its hold on the day.

Enzo watched for a few moments until he was sure there was no sign of movement. He cautiously stepped forward, scrambled for the nearest window, and peered inside. The sofa opposite was piled with unkempt sheets. As he ran his eyes round the rest of the room, he felt cold hard metal press against the side of his head. He gulped, his eyes wide as he raised his hands in the air.

'Take it easy,' he said, slowly turning his head. The rifle met with his forehead. He found himself staring down the barrel at one of Christiano's vibrant blue eyes, glaring back at him like a viper.

'I'm a friend.'

'Friends do not kidnap their friends.'

'I had no choice. I had to go along with it. Ask Angelica. I'm the one who helped her escape with Fortuna.'

Christiano held firm, his gaze unflinching.

'Look, I, ah…saw you…in the car park slashing those tyres and I said nothing. I was trying to find a way to get Angelica out of trouble, and I was praying to God, and there you were… It was like he answered my prayers.'

Angelica strolled out of her bedroom and looked towards the sofa for Christiano. Instead, she saw Enzo through the window; a shotgun pressed to his head. She drew back in shock and ran outside calling, 'No, Christiano. No! He's a friend.'

She reached Christiano's side and placed her hand on his shoulder.

'He can't be trusted,' said Christiano, holding firm.

'Yes, he can. He has to act the part in front of Don Primo.' She gently pushed the barrel away from Enzo's head.

Christiano let the shotgun drop to his side while Angelica proceeded to wrap Enzo in a mammoth embrace.

Enzo returned the hug, lifting her in the air. 'You can talk now, hey. You nearly shocked me to death when you yelled in the car. Where did that come from?' He rubbed her cheek like a loving uncle.

Christiano walked away, glaring at Enzo as he disappeared into the cabin.

'Come inside,' said Angelica, running her arm through his. They entered the cabin, and she gestured for him to sit down while she took the seat next to him. 'Why didn't you warn me that you were coming for me?'

'Don't forget I had no idea where you were. I found a way into the convent to check if it was you, but I was caught.'

Christiano stood at the stove, heating the coffee boiler. 'That's true. Father Cavallo and I caught him.'

'Then at the market. I was hoping you'd get away if I showed myself to you. It was difficult because Ricardo was with me all the time.'

'Where is he now?' asked Angelica.

'Well…ah…' He turned to Christiano. 'Look, my friend, you're not going to like this, but…'

A look of red dread crossed Christiano's face.

'Look,' said Enzo, his guilty eyes on Christiano. 'You have to go somewhere where no one will know where you are. This place was always a risk because it's traceable. Anyway, that's how I found you here.'

'You went to my parents' home, didn't you?' said Christiano in a whisper. His fists gripped at his sides and his jaw was as tight as a clamshell.

Enzo raised his hands in the air, his palms facing Christiano in submission. 'They're okay. It got heavy in there. I needed to act the part to get answers. They wouldn't have believed I was on your side.'

'What did you do?' said Christiano, making a menacing move towards him.

Enzo's solemn face spoke volumes. He stood up as Christiano reached him. 'Look, I was never going to let it go too far.'

He grabbed him by the collar.

'Easy!' said Enzo pulling out his gun.

Angelica shot up from her seat. 'Christiano! Please. Enzo!'

He pushed Enzo to the wall and lifted him up, surprising him with his strength. 'Did you hurt them? The children?'

'No, the children are fine. Rosa is fine. Ricardo roughed up your father a little and shot him in the leg.'

Christiano gripped Enzo by the throat.

'I'm warning you,' he said in a choking voice. He cocked his gun.

'Christiano, please,' said Angelica.

'I shot Ricardo,' said Enzo. 'He was going to kill them all. Even the children. I had to kill him. He was out of control. He's in the boot of my car.'

Christiano's stern expression melted away. He let him go.

Enzo straightened himself up and put his gun away. 'You're one tough priest,' he said, rubbing his neck.

'Where are they now?' asked Christiano.

'I don't know. I told them to get as far away as possible. Don't worry, your father will live. It was just a leg wound.'

'He'd better be okay.'

'Christiano, I'm so sorry,' said Angelica. She placed her hand on his shoulder.

He shrugged it off and moved away from her. His moistened eyes stared at the ground.

'It's not safe for you here,' said Enzo.

'This was supposed to be our hideout.' Christiano punched a mirror hanging on the wall. The glass shattered, sprinkling glass fragments to the floor. He pulled away without as much as a wince though his knuckles were bleeding.

Angelica rushed to his aid. He pulled away and retrieved a towel, which he proceeded to wrap around his hand.

She turned back to Enzo, hiding her hurt. 'What are you going to do? You've risked your life for me.'

Christiano could do little to disguise the look of betrayal on his face.

'I will tell him that when we got to the woods, Christiano was out hunting and caught us and that Ricardo was shot and killed.'

'So not only am I being accused of hunting innocent animals, you're going to tell Don Primo that I killed Ricardo,' said a confounded Christiano.

'Once you two have left, the trail will go cold. He'll never find you.'

Angelica shook her head. 'I don't know, he's very resourceful.'

'I'll keep him off track. I just need help with one thing.'

'What?' asked Christiano.

'I need you to help me bury the body.'

'I may not be a priest anymore, but I still have the same ethics and morals, whether the Church accepts me or not.'

'Hey, I'm on your side. I saved your family. He would have killed them all.'

'So now I owe you?'

'This is not for me. I'm trying to save Angelica and *your* baby.'

Angelica and Christiano looked at each other but said nothing.

'His body needs to be buried somewhere it will never be found. A deep grave. You know these parts better than I do.'

Christiano took a deep breath and rubbed his pulsing temple. 'Okay. I'll do it.'

'Thank you,' said Enzo. 'And after that, you're going to have to knock me out.'

Christiano shot him an, *are you serious* look.

'Sorry, my friend. 'It has to look authentic.'

Enzo shovelled the last mound of mud over Ricardo's grave, patted the surface and smoothed it over. Christiano had chosen a valley strewn with wild flowers and a small stream. He had dug up some overgrown bushes and thickets that had hijacked an entire area and buried the body deep in the soil.

With a look showing he could stand no more of this, Christiano proceeded to arrange the weeds and plants back over the spot, which was now Ricardo's eternal resting place, doing well to conceal its appearance.

'I don't suppose you could say a few words, could you Father? I didn't like him much, but I never thought I'd be forced to kill him.'

Christiano sighed. 'Eternal rest grant unto him, O Lord, and let perpetual light shine upon him. May his soul, through the mercy of God, rest in peace. In nomine Patris et Filii et Spiritus Sancti. Amen.'

Enzo stared at the ground and made the sign of the cross, repeating, 'Amen.' Then he looked up at Christiano. 'Thank you, Father.'

Christiano returned a hardened stare and walked away.

Enzo gazed at the unmarked grave for a few moments longer before heading back, wisely following a few steps behind Christiano.

Inside the cabin, Angelica was closing the last suitcase, having re-bagged the camping equipment and the rest of their items.

Christiano entered looking sombre.

'Thank you for doing this,' she said. 'I know it was hard for you. That it goes against your principles—'

'Think nothing of it,' he interrupted. 'I have made my peace with it.'

Angelica was crestfallen. She felt helpless and guilty.

Enzo entered. 'Right, are you ready to leave?'

'Yes. We just need to get this stuff to the car,' she said, lifting a couple of bags from the floor.

'You rest, we'll do it,' said Christiano, trying to take them out of her hand.

She pulled away, defiantly. 'I'm pregnant, not an invalid.' She stared at him for several seconds, now angry at feeling so indebted to him, and marched past him, towards the car.

Christiano watched her, appearing shocked at her outburst.

'You don't know much about women, do you Father?' Enzo chuckled as he picked up a few bags and followed her to the car.

With the luggage all packed, the three of them stood in suffocating silence in the cabin.

Enzo finally spoke, 'You're going to have to knock me out?'

'Is that really necessary?' said Christiano.

'It must be done. Don Primo will never believe him otherwise,' said Angelica.

'How will we know if you're okay when you come to?' said Christiano. 'What if you need medical attention?'

Enzo snickered. 'Be a man! Come on hit me.' He slapped his own face and punched at his own chest.

Christiano clenched his fists.

'Come on, pretty boy.'

Christiano's fist smashed into Enzo's eye, followed by an

uppercut to the bottom of his chin.

Enzo hit the ground with a thud.

'How's that?' he said to an unconscious Enzo.

He turned to Angelica whose mouth was agape. 'I've made sure he has a good black eye to show for it. Come on, let's go.'

✦ Chapter Thirty ✦

Marcello's car cruised along the country lane with an anguished Christiano at the wheel. Sixteenth-century farmhouses rose in the distance secluded behind stone walls bearing cracks and fissures that mirrored the worn face of time. His glazed eyes were mesmerised only by the road markings rolling by in a precise, hypnotic rhythm. Angelica was sound asleep with her head pressed against the door. Flashing past her window was an intoxicating sea of bountiful vineyards bearing swollen grapes ripe for the picking and budding vines that would one day make a fine bouquet. Christiano peered at her, catching the image of her hair highlighted with a dazzle of orange flecks from the setting sun. He took a deep breath and forced himself to look away. He was angry about what he had been forced to do, yet when he looked at her, all he wanted to do was to save her. He felt himself sinking deeper into the pit of quicksand that had become his life, and he could see no way out that did not involve him abandoning Angelica altogether and fleeing the country.

He prayed, silently to himself. *Father, after all my sinful deeds I can no longer stand before you the man I was. A priest. Your servant. I no longer know who or what I am. I ask for the strength and a message to find my way back to you. Show me if this woman is worthy of carrying the Messiah. Is it true? Could it be true? I find myself without the faith for such miracles, yet we share a vision from the Madonna herself. I am lost. Confused. Unbelieving. Wandering a dark wilderness trying to seek the light. I ask for a message, a sign…*

Tears streaked his face; his throat lumpy and sore. He swallowed, trying to finish his prayer, when Angelica stirred. He quickly dried his face with his hand.

'Where are we going?' she murmured.

'I have no idea. I'm just driving in the hopes that something will find us.'

'Like that?' She pointed to a sign suspended across two stone pillars either side of a driveway, leading to a quaint building in the distance. 'Hotel Tramonto,' she said.

Christiano shrugged. 'Why not!?' He made a sudden swerve and drove through the pillars.

'Will it be expensive, do you think?'

'Don't worry. I have money.'

It was nearing twilight when Enzo stirred. His ringing phone sounded like an earthquake erupting in his eardrum. His jaw ached, and his throbbing eye felt like it was being hit with a hammer. He winced, covered his ears and shut his eyes. He sighed with relief when the ringing stopped, and he managed to raise himself with the aid of the nearest chair. The room spun, and his vision danced before him. He sat down to find his bearings before searching for the bathroom.

'Not bad for a priest,' he said aloud as he stared into the mirror. He washed his face with cold water, his skin sensitive to the touch, and gently dabbed himself dry with the only towel left behind.

He was now as ready as he could be to face Don Primo. He removed his phone from his pocket. There were ten missed calls. He hit the call button feeling a punch to his stomach with every ring.

'Enzo, where the fuck have you been? I've been calling you and Ricardo. What the hell is going on with you both?'

Enzo gulped. 'Boss, its Ricardo… He's dead. He's lying here dead.'

'Wait, just slow down. What happened?'

'We… ah… I'm in pain Boss. My head… He knocked me out. He surprised us.'

'Enzo you're not making any fucking sense. Just sit down somewhere, relax and start from the beginning.'

Enzo sat down, playing his role like a star and ensuring that his stress-releasing breaths were loud enough for Don Primo to hear. 'When we got to the cabin, it was early morning, just after we spoke. We approached the nearest window, to take a look inside, and the next minute we heard the sound of a shotgun being broken and loaded. We turned and saw the priest pointing the rifle straight at us. He must have been out hunting. Ricardo went for his gun and before he could reach it, the priest fired off two shots to his chest. He went flying back and landed on the ground. I knew he was dead. I went crazy. That's when I made my attack. I knew he needed to reload and I wanted to kill that son of a bitch with my bare hands. But as I reached him, he hit me in the face with the butt of the rifle. That's the last thing I remember. I just woke up. They're gone. It's just me and Ricardo's dead body.'

'Enzo, listen to me. I don't want you coming back here with a dead man. I need you to bury the body.'

'What will we tell his wife?'

'She knows the job. I'll compensate her.'

'I'm sorry Don Primo. We screwed up again. This priest... He's a clever bastard like he's always a step ahead. Like God is helping him.'

'No. We're the ones with the Cardinal's blessing, therefore, God's blessing. Get it done and come home.'

The receiver went dead, and Enzo breathed a sigh of relief.

On the other end of the phone, Don Primo sat in his restaurant enveloped in a fog of smoke. About twenty cigarette butts lay discarded in the ashtray. With a deeply pensive look on his face, he brushed some fallen ash from the tablecloth. He narrowed his eyes, reached for his phone and selected a number.

The phone was answered in two rings. 'Paolo, it's been a while. I have a job for you.'

✦ Chapter Thirty-One ✦

Two gaping holes on fire blazed from the devilish eyes of the beast pinning Christiano to the ground. It flashed its serrated teeth as it inched closer. The smell of rotting flesh repelled his nostrils as a dense, sebaceous liquid dripped from the beast's mouth and slid across Christiano's cheek. He gawped in terror as it sprouted two more heads with extended necks. Each head turned to the other menacingly before it returned its demonic gaze on him and zigzagged its way to his face. A furnace of fire exhaled from each mouth.

Christiano's eyes shot open. He whipped his head round the dim hotel room, his breathing laboured and his body dripping with sweat. From the sofa where he lay, he could see Angelica sound asleep on the bed, her chest rising and falling in rhythmic beauty. He exhaled with relief and flopped his head back on the pillow. But he was still restless, and his mouth tasted like sawdust. He rose and made his way to the fridge, removed a bottle of water and took a big, long gulp as he pushed the curtain aside to take a look outside.

The darkness twinkled, and the bright half-moon shone like daylight on the distant mountains. He let the curtain drop and noticed Johan's phone on the dressing table. He picked it up, took his seat on the sofa and turned it on.

A short, succinct text message appeared. *Type 'Frya'.* He narrowed his eyes and swiped the slide-to-unlock feature on the phone. The keyboard flashed up. He typed in *Frya*, exactly as it was written and found himself with complete access to the phone. The text icon indicated another message. He tapped it and sat up in his chair, his eyes wide. *We are on your side. Johan's work for the Cardinal has been a cover to help us find you. We've been waiting for you both. Please come to Rome where we can help you to understand what is happening. We will get you to safety. Trust no one at the Vatican. Return a text or call when you see this message. Frya Attar, a trustworthy friend and ally.*

He rubbed his perplexed brow as his confused mind attempted to assimilate the information. He opened a nearby drawer in search of writing paper and proceeded to jot down some notes before leaving both the phone and the paper on the table. He then used the hotel phone and dialled a number by memory. A distant ring echoed through the receiver.

'Pronto,' replied a meek, tired voice.

'Mama, 'Are you okay? Is Papa okay?'

'Oh Christiano, thank God you're alive. They forced their way into our home. The one with the crazy eyes held a gun to Lissandra's head. I've never been so scared in my life. What have you got yourself mixed up in?'

By now, tears welled in Christiano's eyes, and he felt as if a lump of coal was lodged in his throat. 'Is she all right?'

'You know Lissandra, she's a courageous little one with a heart of pure love.'

Tears dripped from his chin to his lap. 'And what about Papa?' Christiano's voice was hoarse.

'He was beaten up pretty badly and shot in the thigh, but the worst is over. It will be a slow recovery, though.'

Christiano shut his eyes and held back the tears and sounds that could expose his anguish.

'Thank God we can trust our doctor to leave the police out of this,' continued Rosa. 'That crazy man would have killed us all if that other one didn't shoot him. I was scared he was lying to me and meant to harm you both. I was beside myself, but I had to get them out of there.'

'You did the right thing, Mama. He was a friend. He found us and warned us to leave.'

'So you're not at the cabin anymore?' she asked.

'No, but it's best you don't know where we are.'

'Is Angelica okay?'

'She is well. Another strong one.'

'Give her my love, son.'

'I will, Mama, and you give Papa my best. I'm sorry I can't visit him. Kiss the children for me. Tell Lissandra I am proud that she is such a brave girl, and tell Marco I'm truly sorry.'

'Son, before you go let me have your number in case I need to contact you. Please, I just need to know that you are only a phone call away.'

Christiano thought for a moment. 'I have a temporary mobile, but only get in touch in an emergency, and stick to text messaging. When we hang up, I'll text you, so you have the number.'

'Thank you, son. Please, look after yourself and that child. It's clear something of great importance is happening here. I am proud that God chose you.'

When he ended the call he did as he had promised, sending her a message that read, *Do not worry about me, Mama, Cx.*

Then he lay back on the sofa, his eyes wide with anguish.

Enzo arrived at the restaurant headquarters in the early hours of the morning. Normally he would have gone straight home, but Don Primo wanted to see him. He dreaded what lay ahead as he drove over the mangled gate and parked by Don Primo's Mercedes.

He entered the building and proceeded down the steep steps, reaching the restaurant, dense with smoke, to see Don Primo and a few of his cronies at a round table. They were in the middle of a poker game; drinking liquor and munching on nuts and pastries.

'Hey, room for one more?' He maintained a steady tone.

'For my brother-in-law, of course,' said Don Primo. 'Alessandro, shift over, make room for Enzo.'

Enzo walked cautiously to take the seat that had been made available to him. Don Primo put his arm around him and pulled him closer. 'Are you okay? That's quite a shiner. That priest doesn't act much like a priest – murder, knocking people out, getting women pregnant.'

Enzo lowered a guilty gaze. 'Yeah, he's something else.'

'You want a drink? Francesco, bring another glass for Enzo.'

The waiter came over with a single glass on a silver tray. He placed it by Enzo, and Don Primo proceeded to pour him a whisky, while Vincenzo dealt a card to each man.

'Bella came to me complaining of how much she has missed you. She made your favourite pastries and left them here for when you get back. Vincenzo, pass the cannoli. She wants me to stop sending you out on jobs. That wife of yours, ah! What my sister wants, she gets.'

Vincenzo passed the plate to Don Primo, who placed it by Enzo.

'You know, Boss. I miss Bella too, and it's been a long few days.'

'I know, I know. Take the week off. Rest, recuperate, do something nice with my sister. Just have one drink with us before you go.'

Enzo nodded and picked up the glass.

'So tell us, what was it like when you killed that bastard priest's family?'

Enzo braced himself and knocked back the whisky in one gulp.

'Fun as always.' He chuckled, picked up a cannoli and took a big, satisfying bite. As he chewed and swallowed, a strange feeling came over him. He grabbed at his neck, labouring to clear his throat as an intense feeling of nausea rose from his belly.

His pleading eyes fell on Don Primo who returned an arctic cold stare; his face was like the moon shrouded behind a cloud. 'I know the priest's parents are still alive.' His voice was a galaxy away.

Enzo's spine arched and his body convulsed. He gasped for breath and clutched at his throat as foam bubbled from his mouth.

'And I have had a sneaky feeling you helped Angelica run away.'

Enzo's excruciating struggle reached its finality; his pained expression trapped on his face as his lifeless body froze in the chair.

Don Primo rose from his seat with a sour, twisted look. 'Benito.' He motioned with his head as he spoke.

Benito stood up, removed the car keys from his jacket pocket and proceeded to follow Don Primo out of the building.

'What do you want us to do with him, Boss?' asked Vincenzo.

Don Primo stopped in his tracks, but he did not look round. 'Feed him to the pigs,' he said, continuing to the exit.

Part Three

Epiphany

✦ Chapter Thirty-Two ✦

Angelica awoke from a nightmare. Her chest heaved, and her usual olive-toned glow was more like porcelain. In her dream, Enzo had come to her, foam seeping from his mouth. He gasped for air as he told her not to worry, that he regretted nothing and he had made his peace with God. Tears rolled down her cheeks as she tried to gather herself and make sense of the dream. She picked up the hotel phone unsure of what to do. Then she saw Christiano lying sound asleep on the sofa. An immediate sense of peace washed over her. She replaced the receiver and decided to shrug it off as a bad dream. Instead, she rose from the bed and made her way to the window.

Scatters of light streamed in through the curtain gaps. She lifted the drapes and looked outside. It was a bright, crisp morning and for a second she imagined she was on holiday. She noticed the mobile phone on the dressing table, picked up the sheet of paper beneath it, and examined it.

Johan – Cardinal's chauffeur undercover (but for who?) Who is Frya? Who does she work for? Why is she interested in

us? Trust no one at the Vatican? Should we trust her? Rome?
Don Primo – Cardinal connection?

With a bemused look, she placed the sheet back on the desk.

Deep in thought, Don Primo sat in the back seat of his Mercedes as the car cruised its way to the restaurant. His phone rang. 'Pronto!... Paolo, what do you have for me?'

A guttural voice sounded through the phone. 'One call and a text message were made to the priest's mother's cell phone. The call came from a Hotel Tramonto, and the text from a cell phone owned by a Johan Asper.'

Don Primo arched his eyebrows. 'Is that so?' He made a warped smile. 'Can you access the text message?... If you can, yes. And text me the information on this hotel... Good work, Paolo. Excellent. You'll get a bonus for this.'

He ended the call and retrieved another number from his cell phone. A double beep signalled the arrival of a text message – Paulo's text with the hotel address. He smiled, but ignored it and tapped his finger against the Cardinal's name. He put the phone to his ear.

'Your Eminence,' he mocked.

Miles away in Rome, the Cardinal sat in a plush chair at his desk. 'Mr Pulsoni, what a pleasant surprise.' He picked up a pen and started a doodle on a blank notepad. 'Do you have news for me?'

'I can deliver Angelica to you, but I want two million more.'

'Now, now, Mr Pulsoni, Sammel already left you one

million as a gesture of my goodwill. The deal was another million when you bring her to me. Now you're asking for two? I thought we had a deal.'

'Your Eminence, do you trust the people in your employ?'

'Implicitly. Why?'

'Someone is not who he claims to be. How much would a name be worth to you?'

The Cardinal narrowed his eyes. 'How did you come to possess this information?'

'I have my sources.'

'I think another million is a big ask, but I do value my privacy.'

'Well I'm a reasonable man, how about I give you his name and one day you do me a favour?'

'What kind of favour?' replied the Cardinal.

'I have no idea, but I'll think of something.'

The Cardinal stopped doodling. He gripped the pen with rigid fingers and made the mark of a large X on the sheet. He stamped the centre of the letter – his hand trembling with rage. 'You have a deal Mr Pulsoni.' He smiled as he spoke, to disguise his animosity.

Don Primo smirked. 'Your chauffeur, Johan Asper, is not who he seems.'

He dropped the pen and sat up in his seat. 'Johan! That's ludicrous. The man came to me with the highest recommendation, and he has been in my employ for three years. How did you come to this conclusion? Who is your source and what did he tell you?'

'The priest has his cell phone.'

'Well, as I understand it, that insolent man stole his clothing. It must have been in his pocket. Really Mr Pulsoni, is this all you have?'

'Just ask your man Sammel what the chauffeur told him when he asked him if the priest had stolen his phone.'

The Cardinal pressed an intercom button at his desk. 'Sammel, come to my study.'

'Yes, Your Eminence.' The tinny voice sounded through the speaker.

Moments later, Sammel entered the study and shut the door behind him.

'Sammel, did you ask Johan if the priest had stolen his phone?'

'I did, Your Eminence.'

'Why did you ask him that particular question?'

'I thought that if he had there might be a way to trace it and find the woman and the priest.'

'I see.' The Cardinal nodded. 'And what was his reply.'

'He told me that he had left it at home that day.'

Don Primo heard his reply down the phone. A satisfied grin dimpled his cheeks.

'And you are certain he was not mistaken?'

'His own words were, "No, I accidentally left it at home." But, Your Eminence, I was sure I saw him with it that very morning. Then, just yesterday, he informed me of a change of telephone number, claiming he had found a better tariff.'

The Cardinal's eyes formed slits. 'And you do not think this is a coincidence?'

'It's possible Your Eminence, but all too convenient. I believe he is lying.'

'And did you intend to inform me of your suspicions?'

'To be honest, Your Eminence, your questioning has confirmed my doubts.'

The Cardinal returned to the phone. 'Mr Pulsoni, you may be correct after all. If so, you shall have your favour.'

'Oh, I am correct, *Your Eminence.*' He stressed the last two words, smiled and ended the call.

The Cardinal turned to Sammel. 'As soon as we have that bitch in our possession, I want you to kill Pulsoni and his men. Is that clear?'

Sammel nodded. 'Crystal, Your Eminence.'

The Mercedes pulled into the car park, and Don Primo entered the restaurant to be greeted at the door by Vincenzo and Alessandro. 'Did you get rid of the body?'

'Yes Boss,' said Vincenzo.

'I told my sister that he and Ricardo never came home last night. She thinks I've sent out a search party.'

'The pigs had a feast, Boss,' said Alessandro with a snicker.

Don Primo shot him an icy stare.

Alessandro gulped.

'You two are going on a little trip with Benito and me,' said Don Primo. He looked at the text message sent by Paolo. As expected, the address of Hotel Tramonto was on his phone. 'Make sure you're armed. This time I want the priest dead and Angelica in my possession.'

✦ Chapter Thirty-Three ✦

It was now mid-morning, and Christiano opened his eyes to shards of morning light spearing the dark hotel room as if desperate to burst through the drawn curtains. He swallowed the stale parchedness in his mouth. Every inch of his body throbbed in pain. His cushioned landing may have saved his life, but diving behind bushes and all-night driving and sleeping on sofas were not aiding in his recovery. Besides, it had been a while since he had practised any yoga. He raised himself from the sofa like a decrepit old man to find the bed ahead of him empty.

'Angelica?' He looked round the room. Fear set in as a hollow silence lapped at his ears. He repeated her name but received no reply. A sudden bolt of adrenaline rushed through his veins. He bounded off the sofa just as the bathroom door opened.

A concerned Angelica, wet and wrapped in a towel, looked towards him questioningly.

He flopped back in his seat, and his short-lived relief was replaced with scorching cheeks as he averted his eyes to the ground.

Angelica shielded her modesty behind the door.

'I'm sorry. I didn't see you when I awoke,' said Christiano. 'I was half asleep and jumped to conclusions.'

'It's okay,' she said, quickly shutting the door.

Christiano huffed, perplexedly rubbing his forehead with rigid fingers. He rose from the sofa and drew the curtains back. The sun devoured the wan light, revealing a messy room, which he proceeded to tidy.

Several minutes later, the bathroom door opened and a dressed Angelica entered the room – her raven tresses glistening wet and tied in an unkempt bun, and her skin and eyes glowing with renewed vibrancy.

She looked round the tidy room.

Christiano grew self-conscious. 'A habit I can't seem to break. Tidying up…that is.' His cheeks glowed.

'Most women would find it endearing.'

He smiled faintly. 'Look, I'm sorry about what just happened…'

'It's fine. We're in a unique situation. There's likely to be some awkward moments.'

His face relaxed.

'Perhaps next time I will leave a note,' she said.

'It's not my intention to make you feel like a prisoner.'

'I understand. I'm not so reckless that I would leave the room without letting you know where I'm going.'

'It's probably best we stick together at all times,' he replied.

'Of course. You're right… Look, I want you to know how grateful I am for how much you've given up for me.

That you rescued me. To be honest, I'm surprised Maria was so forthcoming.'

'It was probably my clerical suit,' he said, making light of the situation. 'It seems to have an effect on people. I have been forced to hear confession in the strangest places.'

She smiled with interest. 'And what was your most awkward location?'

'It would have to be the old gentleman in the men's room.'

She chuckled. 'And what did Maria confess?'

Christiano's expression betrayed him.

Her smile faded. 'You know, don't you?'

'I do. I'm sorry. I didn't mean to invade your privacy.'

'Do you know everything?'

He nodded.

'Yet you still have doubts.'

'She told me you can't have children, yet you're pregnant.'

'Would more proof really make a difference?'

He continued to stare without offering a reply.

'Right, well if you must know…' Angelica fixed an intense gaze on him '…I became pregnant…'

She continued speaking impassively. 'Don Primo arranged a secret abortion for me. I caught an infection, which led to scarring and the result was two severely blocked tubes. The doctor informed me that I was infertile. Not even IVF would work. Anyway, what did that mean to a thirteen-year-old with no mother and father? Nothing!'

'I'm sorry you endured such a horrendous ordeal… I can't imagine… But maybe this doctor was wrong about your infertility. After all…' He pointed to her belly.

'Right, well, you're a man of the bible. I'm sure a studious priest such as yourself will be familiar with Luke 1:34 to 37.'

His eyes remained on her for a moment before he made a reluctant reply. 'I am.'

'And I bet you can quote it right off the top of your head.'

'I can.'

'Bearing in mind that I did not leave the convent since my arrival more than a year ago, humour me, please.'

He swallowed the dryness in his mouth. 'Then Mary said to the angel, "How can this be, since I do not know a man?"'

Angelica nodded. 'Please continue.'

'And the angel answered and said to her, "The Holy Spirit will come upon you, and the power of the Highest will overshadow you; therefore, also, that Holy One who is to be born will be called the Son of God. Now indeed, Elizabeth your relative has also conceived a son in her old age; and this is now the sixth month for her who was called barren."' He stopped again.

'Please finish, Christiano.'

'"For with God, nothing will be impossible."' These last words were a mumble. He lowered his head in shame.

'You're a priest who does not believe in miracles.'

He raised his head to meet her eyes once more. He gulped, and his face wore the look of a scolded child.

Her sense of betrayal showed on her face as she stared at him unforgivingly. Then she said, 'As I have to report my every move to you, I'm going to get some food.'

The white Mercedes cruised along the motorway with Vincenzo in the front passenger seat next to Benito, and

Alessandro and Don Primo in the back. The air was as cool as the atmosphere. A pensive Don Primo stared hypnotically at the splurge of images shooting past his window. His ringing phone brought him back to full alertness. 'Pronto!'

'Mr Pulsoni, thank you for that little bit of intel,' said the Cardinal, getting straight to the point. 'My men are dealing with the situation and Johan will soon find himself in a disagreeable predicament. Have you made any progress?'

'The matter is in hand. Do you have my money?'

'I have a filled suitcase here waiting for you. I will instruct Sammel to text you my address for the delivery of our precious package.'

Angelica munched on the remnants of her pasta, washing it down with a glass of orange juice.

Christiano watched her as he bit into his last triangle of pizza.

The entire meal had been eaten in silence and Christiano was feeling guilty. 'Could we just start again? I'm sorry I offended you. I have no excuse other than feeling overwhelmed. You're a very brave woman and I have the utmost respect for you. I mean that.'

'Despite what you know of me and the fact that you don't believe me?'

'Because of what I know of you and despite what my head tells me.'

She made a faint smile that relaxed her frowning features. 'If I'm honest, I'm glad you're here. The thought of facing this alone...' She shook her head. 'I know it sounds far-fetched, and only a rare person of extraordinary character would stick with me through all this.'

He nodded, modestly, and his attention moved to the copy of *Il Cospiratore* folded on the table. 'Why did you bring that with you?'

'I came across an interesting article at the cabin, but with all the commotion I forgot to mention it.' She unfolded the paper and pointed to the circled article close to the one about her. 'It states that over the past few years women have been disappearing from all over the world, and the one thing they have in common is that they all claim to have an Immaculate Conception.'

Christiano took the paper. A look of growing concern washed over his face as he read. 'You think the Cardinal is behind this?'

'My gut feeling is that he is. My situation is not so different from these women and he came after me.'

'But what are his reasons? Surely, he doesn't believe...' His voice trailed off.

'Well clearly he does, otherwise, why is he after me?'

'You're right. I'm sorry. But, if you're the one carrying the next Messiah, then these women were hoaxers.'

'Yes, but, don't you see? He wasn't about to take any chances. I believe he's responsible for these disappearances and if it wasn't for Father Cavallo and yourself, I would be another one of his victims.'

'Okay, let's say you're right. What do you think he does with them?'

'Who knows? Maybe he has his scientists run tests on the

mothers, or he waits for the babies to be born.'

'What tests could possibly confirm that any of the babies were the next Messiah?' said an exasperated Christiano.

Angelica shrugged. 'For all we know he has the women killed.'

'Killed?'

'The man is clearly a sociopath,' she replied. 'If there's a reason for his madness he must be privy to some information and he is trying to gain control of the next Messiah or stop him from being born altogether.'

'We've been waiting for the second coming for over two thousand years. It's not something the Church considers a threat.'

She raised her eyebrows. 'Are you so sure about that? Men like the Cardinal are sitting on a throne. As far as the faithful are concerned, they are the incarnation of God in the flesh. Whatever they say is God's word. God's wishes to the masses who must obey and follow for fear of His wrath. What if they don't want to relinquish their throne to the true Messiah? They stand to lose all their wealth, power, influence – everything.'

'Not necessarily; the Messiah would more likely spread his word with the influence they already carry. What better way than to use the Church for this good?'

'When my child arrives – the child of God – there will be a clean slate. A new dawning. None of the old models will fit the new world. The Messiah needs no one to spread his word. Those seeking the truth will be drawn to him.'

'Angelica…!'

She remained firm. 'I know it. It's part of me like a fact. I can't explain it. I think you're struggling with this because if you dare to believe me, then everything you have ever stood for will be a lie and you don't want to face it.'

'I have devoted my entire life to the Church, to becoming a priest, and you come along and tell me that for all these years I have been wrong.'

'When the Messiah first came to earth in human form, was he a Catholic?'

'And Jesus said to Peter, the first Pope, "I say to you that you are Peter, and upon this rock I will build my Church, and the gates of hell will not overcome it. And to you I will give the keys of the kingdom of heaven,"' he quoted.

'Throughout history, the Church has attracted men of questionable character. If hell was not supposed to overcome it, why is it men like the Cardinal are able to abuse their power?'

'You go too far,' said Christiano.

'I know that deep down in your heart you believe me, but your ego won't let you accept it.'

He leaned back in his chair, frustrated.

'Christiano, you have to face this. Sooner or later you will have to submit to belief or leave. You say the Church has been waiting for the new Messiah, yet you don't believe me.'

He looked down.

'Soon, it won't be enough for you to just be here. I have the Messiah growing inside me. Your belief is all that should keep you here. Anything else, whatever your reasons, will not be enough. Maybe your role was to get me to safety and that's all. Maybe we'll soon part ways.'

He looked at her, his eyes not wanting to hear any more.

'Time will tell.' She motioned to stand, but he grabbed her hand, holding it gently down on the table. 'Please, don't!' he muttered. His eyes pleaded.

She sat back down, softening. 'I was raised a devout Catholic too, but something inside me is changing. It's like these lies are dispersing clouds and the truth is no longer obscured. I see these men for who they truly are. They are not men of God. I'm sorry Christiano. They are self-serving men who have succeeded in controlling the masses for hundreds of years, and they have committed heinous atrocities. Do you deny this?'

'What do you want me to say?'

'You can't deny that much of the Vatican's vast wealth was built with Mussolini's bribe money. Yet we all choose to ignore these facts and continue to believe in the Church.'

Christiano frowned. 'These heretical words will not sit well with God.'

'And now *you*'re putting words in God's mouth.'

Christiano leaned back shaking his head.

'The Cardinal is a dangerous man. He is full of narcissism and he lusts for nothing but wealth and power. He is after me to kill me or imprison me. You have seen this for yourself.'

Christiano sighed and made a subtle nod in agreement.

'*Il Cospiratore* headquarters is in Rome. Maybe we should go and speak to this journalist.'

'That would be a bad idea,' replied Christiano. 'I have

been tasked to watch over you. We need to find a safe place to hide. It's not our fight. My instincts are to get you and the baby to safety. We are not detectives. This is not about exposing the Cardinal, or the Vatican, however deep this conspiracy runs. Let's keep this simple, okay.'

'I saw that piece of paper with all those questions. Why does it mention Rome followed by a question mark?'

Christiano took Johan's phone from his pocket and placed it on the table. Then he fished out the piece of paper and unfolded it. 'Out of curiosity, I turned the chauffeur's phone on today, as you slept, and there was a message for us by a woman named Frya. She claims that the chauffeur's work for the Cardinal is just a cover to find us, and she wants to help.'

'Now complete strangers want to help us and you're still struggling to believe.'

He rolled his eyes and turned the phone on. 'There's a new message. *Please trust us. We are your friends. Return the call so that we can talk.*'

He showed Angelica the message.

'Do you think it's a trick?' she asked.

'I don't know. The Cardinal could be behind this, but I have to admit, I'm curious. We have to move on anyway and we can always leave the phone here.'

'Okay, let's call from our room,' said Angelica.

They made their way to their hotel room in silence, the anticipation creating an almost palpable atmosphere. Christiano placed the phone on the desk, hit the dial button and switched to loudspeaker. The phone was answered in one ring.

'I'm so glad you called,' said an elated voice.

'Are you Frya?' asked Christiano.

'Yes, and I'm here to help you both to safety.'

They glanced at each other with raised brows.

'What makes you think we need your help?'

'Please believe us, Christiano. Our family has been preparing for this task for over two thousand years.'

'Firstly, how do you know my name? And secondly, for what task has your family been preparing?'

'Johan told us your names. As for our task, we are here to help the Messiah.'

Christiano looked up to meet with Angelica's astonished expression.

'You bear a mark beneath your left eye. Am I correct?' continued Frya.

'And what would that mark be?' asked Christiano.

'An equilateral cross in the form of a mole.'

He narrowed his eyes.

'Is our angel there? The one carrying the Messiah.'

'This is a bad idea,' said Christiano, about to end the call.

'No. Please, Christiano. Give us a chance. I know it's a lot to take in, but we are genuine.'

'Call us back.' He ended the call.

'Can you believe this?' he said to Angelica, just as the phone rang. He took a deep breath and answered the call.

'We can come and get you from wherever you are,' said Frya keenly.

'For all we know, you're working for the Cardinal,' said Christiano. 'How else would you know all this stuff?'

'The Cardinal is an unholy man, but if it wasn't for him, we would never have found you.'

'And how did you know he would lead you to us?'

'It is written. We would love to tell you more, but we must show you.'

'How many of you are there?' asked Angelica.

'There are three of us. Johan, who is nursing a bruised head, my father and me. It is wonderful to hear your voice, Angelica. Are you aware that you bear an identical mark to Christiano?'

Angelica sat up in her chair.

'If I describe it and you find it, will you believe us?'

'Where is it?' replied Christiano.

'You must part Angelica's hair in dead centre. Two inches up from the back of her neck is the same mark that you have beneath your left eye.'

He raised his brow, took the phone off loudspeaker and blocked the receiver. 'Do you know about this?'

She shook her head.

He unblocked the mouthpiece. 'We will take a look and call you back.' He ended the call.

'How would they know such a thing?' asked Angelica.

'I doubt it's true.'

'The perpetual doubter. Why would they take such a risk?'

'Well, let's have a look, shall we.'

Angelica turned her back to Christiano and bowed her head.

He delicately parted her hair and searched for a mark in

the proximity described. As the wisps of hair parted, beneath the strands, he saw a black cruciform mole, closely resembling his. His mouth dropped open.

✦ Chapter Thirty-Four ✦

The white Mercedes reached the gates of Hotel Tramonto and made its way steadily along a narrow lane skirted by vast, pristine lawns where golfers teed off in the distance. Inside the car, the men's faces wore severe expressions like armour. As the hotel drew nearer, its impressive gothic façade of sun-yellow stone formed a castle with turrets of beige brick and terracotta-coloured rooftops. A large staircase with stone balustrades led the visitor to the hotel entrance.

Benito parked across two spaces as if marking his territory.

'Vincenzo, Alessandro, you come with me. Benito, keep the motor running.'

Benito nodded. 'Boss.'

The men strutted to the hotel with Don Primo in the lead and entered the reception area carrying with them a palpable air of foreboding.

A cold shudder coursed through the receptionist's body and her hairs pricked up like the quills of a porcupine. She straightened her posture, visibly gulping as they approached.

'Yes sirs, how can I help you?' Her voice quivered.

'We're visiting some friends of ours who are staying here,' said Don Primo.

'Do you know their room number?' she asked.

'No.' He removed a wad of cash from his wallet and placed it on the desk. 'How about we give you their names and you tell us where they are?'

She looked at the money, then back at Don Primo, feigning a smile that tried to conceal the fear in her eyes. 'What are their names, Sir?'

'Christiano Abbadelli and Angelica de Santis.'

She typed the names on the keyboard. 'Ah, I have a Mister and Mrs Abbadelli, here.'

'Is that so?' he replied. 'And what room are *Mr and Mrs Abbadelli* staying in?'

'I'm sorry, but they checked out. You missed them by a couple of hours.'

'Do you have the number plate of their car?' he asked.

'Ah, let me look.' She glanced at the monitor. 'Oh, yes, I was on duty yesterday when they arrived. I asked them for their number plate, but the man, ah, Mister Abbadelli, said they were tired and he would get it for me later… But then they left.'

'Did you hear them mention where they were going?' he asked.

She shook her head, gulping as she stared into his steely eyes. 'I'm sorry, Sir. They mentioned nothing.'

Don Primo grabbed the money from the desk. 'If you know what's good for you, you won't have lied to me today.'

She shook her head. 'No Sir, I wouldn't lie. I don't know

anything. But…you could check with the waiters in the restaurant.'

As she finished speaking, Don Primo's phone rang. He checked the caller ID to see Paolo's name flash on the screen. Before answering, he gestured with his chin towards the restaurant, indicating for his men to enter.

They dutifully left.

'Paolo, you have news for me?'

As Paolo spoke, Don Primo watched his men interacting with one of the waiters.

'From Johan's phone?' he asked… 'You managed to access the messages?' His eyebrows arched. 'And what did these messages say?' He listened intently to the answers. A look of surprise sprang to his face. 'And where did these messages and calls come from?… Rome! I see. And from whose phone?… Frya Attar,' he repeated. 'Well done Paolo! Can't you trace their whereabouts?… Keep monitoring. He may switch it back on. In the meantime, text me this Frya woman's address, will you?'

As he ended the call, his men re-entered the reception area.

Vincenzo shook his head.

'That's okay,' said Don Primo. 'It looks like they're doing our job for us. I suspect they are on their way to Rome.' Just as he finished speaking, his phone pinged.

He smiled. 'And we have an address, where at the very least, we will get some answers.'

Angelica placed the last delectable morsel of pastry into her mouth, enjoying the sweet hint of orange zinging its way to each taste bud and leaving her mouth as fragrant as an orange grove. She rummaged in her bag, pulled out a book and started reading.

Christiano concentrated on the road ahead, twisting his head as if trying to release the tension in his neck.

'How long until we get there?' she asked.

'It should be another two hours or so.'

'I've heard about this place,' she said.

'And what do you know of it, tell me?'

'That it's filled with the most exceptional artwork. That there's a huge dome of mosaics filled with biblical illustrations dedicated to the Madonna.'

'And did you know that the mosaics date from the thirteenth century and are the work of Pietro Cavallini?'

She shook her head. 'I can't wait to see it. What else can you tell me?'

'Well, according to legend, at the moment of Christ's birth a well of oil sprang from the ground where the church now stands, and it flowed to the Tiber all day.'

'Is that really true?' she asked with an unconvinced expression.

'Asks the woman who's carrying the next Messiah!'

She giggled. 'Point taken. The story certainly makes the church something of an enigma.'

'And it keeps the tourists coming,' he replied.

They both glanced at each other and chuckled.

Christiano breathed deeply, catching Angelica's gaze from the corner of his eye. A hesitant silence desperate with yearning settled in the air.

'I thought you'd left that book back at the convent,' he said.

'I would never part with this book. I was lavished with so many expensive gifts by Don Primo and I left them all behind when I ran away. You gifted me with the greatest treasure of all, apart from this ring my parents gave me before they died.' She wiggled her little finger where the heart-shaped gold ring took permanent residence.

'You flatter me.' He glanced at her again, a coy smile leaving his lips and a light glint in his eyes. 'It seems we have both encountered some big changes.'

'My life at the convent was good,' she said, 'but the first day I saw you, something changed.'

'What do you mean? Changed how?'

'I'm not exactly sure. I walked into the refectory with that large bowl of soup and…'

'You noticed me that day?'

'Yes, of course. Why?'

'I didn't think you could see anything beneath that oversized hood. That's all I saw, along with your delicate hands peering out from long sleeves, and that ring.'

'Oh, I saw you,' she replied.

He chuckled. 'It's a beautiful ring, by the way.'

'Thank you. I was twelve when I received it and over time it has grown too small. Now it fits on my little finger. I will never remove it.'

'Well, your fingers may swell with your pregnancy, but I promise to find a safe place for it until you're ready to wear it again.'

She peered at him through smiling eyes. 'That's sweet, thank you.'

'It's me who should be thanking you. I think you may have saved me from a life I was not destined to live.'

'Well, that's a change of tone. Where's this coming from?'

'I don't know.' He shook his head. 'The duplicate moles... everything that's happened!'

'Well, all I know is...' She hesitated.

'What?'

Her eyes moistened. 'Nothing.'

Christiano pulled the car to the side of the road and cut the engine. He turned to her.

She avoided his gaze.

'You know, only weeks ago, I was fresh out of the seminary having taken my priestly vows. And now I have this task and these feelings...'

'Feelings?' She turned to him.

'Yes, feelings... It was all I could do to stop myself from kissing you in the Cardinal's car.'

'I longed for that kiss.' She chewed her bottom lip and eyed his cherry red lips. 'What I wanted to say, before... It's as if everything is erased. Now I can't imagine a moment when you were ever absent from my life.' She placed her hand over his.

'I wish it were that simple.' He pulled his hand away as if it weighed a ton.

'If not dangerous,' she replied.

'It's not the danger. I don't want to take advantage of

you. If you are indeed pregnant with the Messiah, how am I worthy to touch you, to be with you?'

'You are the only man who has ever been worthy.'

A look of deep veneration shone from his pupils. 'And you're the only woman I've ever wanted to be with... But whatever this is, it is beyond delicate for the both of us. We must be sure. We must tread carefully. This is not to be rushed.'

'I understand. I know what I want, but I understand.'

'For now, let's get you to Rome, okay.'

She nodded and feigned a smile, her eyes tearful.

Christiano switched the engine on. 'I think it's for the best,' he said as he continued to drive.

Subtle tears glided down her cheeks. 'Yes,' she whispered, facing the window.

✦ Chapter Thirty-Five ✦

Rome greeted them with the gentle smile of the afternoon sun. Christiano parked the car, and they walked along a street alive with the sounds of life, in the antiquated city which never seems to tire. Cars hooted, mopeds rumbled by, and people laughed and called out – natives and tourists alike, each day wandering through a metropolis of ancient structures ingeniously built to withstand the millennia.

Christiano took hold of Angelica's hand and they entered Piazza Santa Maria in Trastevere. The crowded piazza was brimming with people dining alfresco round the surrounding restaurants, and tourists sitting on the stone steps of Rome's oldest fountain, nibbling on snacks, taking photos and basking in the sunshine.

They stopped and looked round the piazza with a combination of intrigue, fear and anticipation.

Angelica looked at Christiano, whose eyes were narrowed and scrutinising. 'You seem as nervous as I am.'

'It could still be a trap. Just because they knew of your

mole, it doesn't mean they're on our side.' He continued to survey the area. 'Maybe this is a bad idea. We should have found a hotel first. I should have come alone.'

'We're in this together, remember. Do not exclude me from something that God himself has involved me in.'

He sighed. 'You're right. I'm treating you like a child. Just don't let go of my hand, no matter what.'

Angelica smiled. 'You mean like a child should not let go of her father's hand?'

He rubbed his eye and chuckled. 'And I'm doing it again.'

'Yes, you are. But I will hold your hand because I want to.'

'Well, that's good enough for me,' he replied.

They continued past the fountain and stopped outside the twelfth-century Romanesque church.

'This church,' said Christiano, 'as it stands today, replaced a basilica from as early as possibly the third century. It's one of the oldest churches and one of the first dedicated to the Madonna. Also, you'll be interested to know that in one of the chapels is a very rare seventh-century painting on wood of the Virgin. *The Madonna di Clemenza*. If we get the chance to see it, you'll love it.'

'I wish I had the time to do some sketching.'

'Maybe some other time,' said Christiano. 'Are you ready to go in? We're half an hour late. Frya and her father may have left.'

She nodded. 'As ready as I'll ever be.'

Inside the church, their eyes fell upon a sea of people

covering every corner and crevice of the basilica. A coach load of tourists gathered beneath the centre of the semi-dome staring in wonderment at the mosaics featuring the Madonna and Christ and listening with intrigue to their guide's tales. Other visitors were looking skywards, captivated by the gilded wooden ceiling, whilst others pointed at the varying widths of the twenty-two granite columns lining the nave.

Angelica's eyes were wide with excitement.

'I have visited here before,' said Christiano, staring at the sights before him. 'It is beyond sensational.' He shook his head in veneration and turned to Angelica.

His mouth dropped open.

'What?' she asked with concern.

Christiano's stomach rose to his throat, his eyes fixed on the golden hue haloing Angelica's face. He resisted the deepest urge to collapse to his knees and kiss the feet of the woman before him. His eyes filled with tears as he swallowed the lump lodged in his throat. *'You are Her.'* His voice was a choked whisper.

Angelica began to notice people staring and pointing towards her. 'What's going on?' she said, finding her focus drawn to two people in the distance close to the apse. Before she could point them out, she found herself being dragged outside.

As soon as Angelica passed the doors, the halo blended into the afternoon sun.

'What's the matter with you?' She stared at Christiano with an irritated expression. 'I think I saw them…'

'You don't understand.' He noticed that some people had followed them to the door and were looking their way. 'You were…glowing.'

'Glowing? What do you mean I was glowing?'

A female voice sounded to their side. 'I'm sorry. We didn't realise that was going to happen.'

They turned to see the familiar image of Frya from Johan's phone, and an older man with the distinguished looks of Omar Sharif, whom they had also seen in photos on the phone.

'You saw it all the way from the apse?' said Christiano.

Frya nodded reverently and slowly walked towards Angelica. 'Yes I did, and it was the most breathtaking sight I have ever seen.' She held out her hand towards Angelica who raised hers in return. Frya kissed it as soft tears spilled from her eyes.

'This is my father, Kurush,' she said.

Kurush walked forward with his hand outstretched, taking hold of Angelica's and kissing it. 'Forgive me for not greeting you with the respect you deserve.'

Angelica's cheeks were crimson.

'I have been waiting for this moment since before I knew what I was waiting for, but we mustn't attract any more attention.'

'Why did you choose this place?' asked Christiano.

'Believe us, our suggestion was not as random as you think, and what we witnessed only serves to deepen our belief. We will explain more when we are alone,' replied Frya. 'Will you come with us?'

Christiano and Angelica looked at each other with the questioning expressions of: *Should we trust them?*

Frya noticed and said, 'Please, there's nothing we want more than to make this all clear to you, but not here. It's best we show you.'

Christiano clenched his jaw and gripped tighter onto Angelica's hand.

She looked up at him for his thoughts. His deep blue eyes were dark with foreboding. 'Yes, we will come with you,' she said.

'Angelica, wait,' said Christiano. 'Excuse us for a moment.' He pulled her aside.

'I and many others just witnessed a miracle. Now it's even more imperative that I keep you safe. I'm not sure about them, okay.'

'I know in my heart they are here to help us. I feel it… You ask me to trust you. Can't you trust me?'

'Okay,' he replied unwillingly. 'But any sign of trouble and we're leaving.'

'I promise I will listen to you.'

They turned back to them.

'We will come with you,' she said.

✦ Chapter Thirty-Six ✦

Don Primo and his men reached the Cardinal's residence in the twilight hours. The Mercedes stopped at a set of opulent, wrought-iron gates, supported by two stone pillars topped with snarling gargoyles whose ruby eyes sparkled red like the devil. Their bat-like wings were outstretched as if poised to pounce on unwanted visitors. The words *Dei Verbum* were sprawled across the gates in a large, medieval font of gold lettering.

Each one of Don Primo's men peered through the windscreen, mouths agape at the palatial home protected by high walls and security cameras.

'We should have asked for more money, Boss,' said Vincenzo.

'There's always time for renegotiation, Vincenzo. Especially when you have the upper hand,' replied Don Primo.

'What's that mean, Boss?' asked Alessandro, pointing to the words on the gate.

'What's going on here? You think he's better than us? When you go through those gates, you are to act like you live this life every day. Got it?'

'Yes, Boss,' they said in unison.

Dei separated from *Verbum* as the gates sailed open. The car entered the stately grounds and drove along a gravelled lane, round a Botticelli water feature, and parked close to the front of the palace.

Sammel stood at the door, scrutinising their every movement with the utmost distrust. 'Gentlemen,' he said as they walked towards him. 'We meet again. No Angelica?'

'Don't concern yourself with that, Sammel,' said Don Primo. 'She will be here soon enough.'

Sammel looked unconvinced as he moved aside to allow them entry.

Don Primo matched his stare with a scowl as he entered a vast, moon-shaped hallway lined floor to ceiling with white marble flooring veined with glistening copper threads. At the centre of the floor was a large crest – a design of a shield emblazoned with a medieval gold cross and the now familiar words *Dei Verbum* written in calligraphy, running along its horizontal and vertical aspect. Ahead of them was a corridor with seemingly no end.

Another of the Cardinal's men, Cedric, a short stout man, stood firm as a wall at the entrance to the corridor. 'Gentlemen. Follow me,' he said.

Don Primo took the lead and sauntered with a commanding air behind Cedric who stopped at a set of mahogany double doors and rapped lightly on the polished wood.

'Enter,' replied the Cardinal.

'Gentlemen,' said Cedric, opening the door.

Don Primo breezed in and came to a stop on a plush burgundy rug in the study.

'Ah, Mr Pulsoni.' The Cardinal was seated at an antique desk with intricate auriferous carvings. He stood up and made his way to Don Primo.

'Your Eminence,' replied Don Primo. His eyes reflected walls that shone like gold bars. He subtly eyed his surroundings to see a library beyond the desk which occupied all the wall space, leaving just enough room for two rectangular windows. An imposing spherical fireplace stood in the centre of the room crowded by luxurious sofas and armchairs – a place where one could sit with a book for a relaxing read.

'It is good to finally meet you in person,' said the Cardinal reaching him and offering his hand.

Don Primo shook it, much to the annoyance of the Cardinal.

'No Angelica? I was led to believe she would be with you.'

'Your Eminence, do not mistake her absence for a problem. I know where she is.'

'Then why do you not have her?'

'My payment includes you not having to concern yourself with the minor details. I ask that Your Eminence trusts me that I will have her soon.'

'I see,' said the Cardinal. 'Please, do sit.' He gestured towards a sofa.

Don Primo took a seat and crossed his legs.

The Cardinal sat opposite him and momentarily removed his cap to reveal white, lustrous hair with a distinctive streak of silver running through the centre. He scratched his head and replaced his cap. 'Is there anything I can do to assist you?' he asked.

'That won't be necessary. However, I would like to know your plans for Johan. Is he here?'

'He has been off work due to his head injury, but I have ordered him to come at six this evening to drive me to an unexpected dinner engagement. He will not leave this place. His actions have been too suspicious.'

Don Primo nodded, returning a smug smile. 'Do you concede to my men interrogating him?'

'Of course, do with him as you wish. My only interest is his motive for working for me under false pretences all these years.'

Don Primo nodded. 'Oh, you will know everything, Your Eminence. I assure you.'

✦ Chapter Thirty-Seven ✦

Angelica and Christiano sat in a country-style kitchen watching Frya prepare a camomile tea. Three brick arches, each with an alfresco depicting fields of lavender, separated the kitchen from the lounge.

Frya turned to them with the cup in her hand and placed it down by Angelica. 'So you have been running since that night at the convent?'

'We have,' said Angelica. 'I think poor Christiano has been the worse for it. He was thrown from a moving vehicle. He waited for hours to rescue me from Don Primo's restaurant, hiding behind some bushes in the unbearable heat. He has done all the driving and spent the little sleep he has managed on sofas half his height.'

'It's a pity we didn't manage to get a message to you earlier,' replied Johan, entering the kitchen.

Christiano stood up, noticing the bandage on his head. 'My sincere apologies,' he said.

Johan smiled, and they shook hands. 'It's not as bad as it looks. Anyway, my doctor here,' he said pointing at Frya, 'informs me that it's coming off today.'

'Are you a real doctor?' asked Angelica.

'Yes. Although Johan makes it sound like I've been playing nurse.'

'Nevertheless, if I had been aware of your intentions…' continued Christiano.

'I understand. You were protecting Angelica and the Messiah. I would have done the same… Had you not intervened though, I would have explained who I was and brought her straight here.'

'What about the man with you at Don Primo's restaurant?' asked Christiano.

'Admittedly, the first time at the convent would have been far easier, but I had a plan for Sammel.'

'Oh, ah, here's your phone,' said Christiano handing Johan his cell phone.

Johan took it, touched his head and made a mocking wince.

Christiano smiled. 'Just the same, where Angelica goes, I go.' His expression grew serious, and he eyed them intensely.

'Of course, Christiano,' said Kurush, strolling into the room. 'We would have contacted you to meet us. I know that you are just as imperative to this mission.'

'What makes you so sure about all the information you have? How did you know about the moles on our bodies?' asked Christiano.

'Do you remember the first time Johan drove Cardinal Cäsar Beltz to Santa Maria?'

'Yes, the day the Cardinal had that strange attack. Come

to think of it, it was the moment Angelica passed through the cloister.'

'Is that what happened?' said Kurush, raising his eyebrow. 'Well, Johan here noticed the Cardinal reading a conspiracy theory newspaper on the drive to Santa Maria. On his arrival at the convent, he locked it in his briefcase, which was a strange thing to do with a sensationalist newspaper. He was clearly hiding something. Johan's suspicions were heightened when you helped the Cardinal to his car, and he saw the cruciform mole beneath your left eye. That very day, he purchased a copy of the newspaper, read the article and told us the news.'

'But how did you know of the mark in the first place?' asked Christiano.

'And, that this particular Cardinal would lead you to us?' followed Angelica.

'It is written,' replied Kurush. 'The Cardinal was easier to locate than we thought. We were guided to Rome, to the Vatican in particular. This left us with the choice of the Pope, the Cardinals and anyone else who worked at the Vatican. We knew to look for an emperor who had strayed. Among other characteristics mentioned, Cäsar Beltz fit the description by name alone. He was our man.'

Angelica and Christiano returned a quizzical look.

Kurush chuckled. 'Please, follow me to my study where it will all become clear.' He led them up a short staircase and stopped outside a closed door. He removed a key from his pocket and unlocked the door. Before entering, he turned to face them. 'What I am about to show you may seem like something out of a storybook, but please indulge me while I recount the events of my life.'

The room they entered was large and rectangular in shape, reminiscent of an old, stuffy library. Beams of light from a patio door highlighted the dust particles in the air. The doors led to a terraced roof garden, where a table and sun chairs occupied the space.

To the right, Kurush approached a tidy desk. An antiquated wooden box stood out from the other items. The tanned wood was light in colour, and the main body was covered with meticulous hand carvings of a starry night. He motioned for the others to come closer.

Angelica and Christiano sat down on two chairs facing Kurush.

'From the age of fifteen, I was given a special task by my mother to look after this ancient wooden box,' he said, taking a seat. 'This has been passed down to each generation of our family for over two thousand years.'

He pulled open the lid and slid the wooden panel inside to reveal a long strip of fabric. 'This,' he said, holding it up and eyeing it with admiration, 'is a swaddling band given to my ancestor, Jannara, by the Madonna herself, when he visited Jesus.'

Christiano straightened his back and leaned forward. 'Are you saying that your ancestor was one of the wise men from the bible accounts?'

'Indeed I am.'

'That's not possible,' said Christiano, leaning back in his seat and shaking his head.

'And it came to pass, when the Lord Jesus was born at Bethlehem of Judea, in the time of King Herod, behold, magi came from the east to Jerusalem, as Zeraduscht had predicted; and there were with them gifts of gold, and frankincense, and myrrh. And they adored Him, and presented to Him their gifts. Then the Lady Mary took one of the swaddling bands, and, on account of the smallness of her means, gave it to them; and they received it from her with the greatest marks of honour,' quoted Kurush.

'Where is this text from?' asked Christiano.

'From the non-canonical Arabic Gospel of the Infancy of the Saviour,' replied Kurush.

'The Gospel of Matthew 2: 1-12 does not mention this,' announced Christiano.

'Yes, we are aware of this but please indulge us for a little longer, will you.'

'May I hold it?' asked Angelica.

Christiano glanced at her with incredulity in his eyes.

'Of course,' said Kurush handing it to her.

Angelica held the fabric close to her face, staring at it with an almost reminiscent expression.

'Did you have it authenticated?' asked Christiano.

'I did not. The cloth itself would indicate this time period, but even if it was authenticated, that in itself would not prove that it was the swaddling of baby Jesus. Also, please understand that I did not want to draw attention to it. It's a family heirloom, and I was explicitly told it stays in the family.'

'You bring us all the way to Rome for a box and a strip

of fabric?' said Christiano.

Angelica put the swaddling band to her nose and breathed in the smell.

Kurush smiled, exposing a glint of self-assuredness in his eyes. 'Please allow me to show you something profound.' He held out his hand. 'Please.'

Angelica handed the cloth back to him.

He rummaged through the middle drawer of his desk, and his hand emerged with a box of matches. He removed a match and struck it.

They stared at him curiously as he proceeded to put the flame to a section of the cloth.

Angelica gasped.

The flames engulfed the fabric and burned fiercely for a couple of minutes without spreading, before gradually dying out. To their amazement, the area was completely unharmed, untouched, and free of any scorch marks.

Angelica drew in her breath.

'A flame retardant fabric, perhaps?' said Christiano.

Kurush chuckled. 'You are quite the sceptic.' He then proceeded to place the fabric in its proper compartment in the box and closed the lid. He lit another match and held it to the wood. They watched as the flames did nothing. Not even a scorch mark appeared.

'This box was meant to reach me in this time. It has withstood house fires and was even retrieved unharmed from the bottom of a river, once, but it has always remained intact and its contents secure. It was my destiny that the message inside reaches me.'

'What message?' asked Christiano.

Kurush opened another compartment in the lid of the box to reveal clockwork circuitry.

'An astrolabe?' asked Christiano.

'Similar, but not quite,' replied Kurush. 'It is some kind of advanced locking mechanism set to open in the future.'

'And it did not burn, rust or malfunction, and the wood did not rot when it fell in this river you mentioned?' asked Christiano.

'It did not. It's like something otherworldly,' replied Kurush.

'Where's the message?' asked Angelica.

'Right here,' said Kurush, swivelling his chair and picking up a frame from a chest behind him.

Encased in a double-sided glass frame was a piece of parchment paper with writing on the front and reverse. He placed it on the table.

'Ancient Greek,' said Christiano.

'Yes.' Kurush nodded.

'You had it translated?'

'I translated it myself. I'm a Professor of Babylonian Studies, and I'm also fluent in Ancient Greek and Latin. It was a message for me by Jannara.'

'Why you?' asked Christiano.

'Each generation did their duty of looking after the box. It was pure instinct. There was never any doubt about keeping it safe. The box conjured in each of us the same instinct we would have for protecting our child. Perhaps because of the swaddling cloth that once covered the baby

Jesus. We had no choice. My mother first showed me the box when I was five years old. She told me I went into a trance and muttered the words, "I am Jannara". She was shocked. Every generation kept a note of their experiences, which was passed down with the box, and nothing like this had ever been noted. She knew this meant something. She waited until I was a teenager, about fifteen, and handed it to me again. The same thing happened. And this time she was able to record it and play it back to me. From that moment my career path was decided and I set about learning to translate the inscription on the inside top of the middle compartment.'

'No one had done that before?'

'Yes, but I wanted to be able to read it myself. To be sure. Plus, I didn't want to be influenced by the generations before me.'

He opened the box and showed them the inscription carved in cuneiform writing.

Christiano ran his hands along the surface, feeling the dents and carvings of the symbols.

'What does it say?' asked Angelica.

'It says, *I am Jannara. On the fiftieth year of my second and final incarnation, follow the status of each Royal through the sign of stauros, to the unknown, where what I have concealed can be retrieved by my hand only, at the hour that seals the night.*'

'The sign of *stauros*?' said Christiano. 'You mean the Greek word for cross?'

'Yes, that's right. However, originally, the stauros meant

upright stake. It did not resemble the cross we know today. Over the millennia it came to be the symbol we know of as the cross on which Christ was crucified.'

'So how did you deduce that it was meant in its modern context?' asked Christiano.

'It was quite clear, not least because the positioning of each star formed the shape of a cross. And specifically, the Greek cross. Thus the use of the word stauros. In Greek Orthodox religion when they make the sign of the cross, they move their hand from right to left.' He demonstrated on himself.

'As opposed to the Catholic church where we cross left to right,' said Christiano.

'That's right. So the use of the word stauros made a clear distinction as to the sequence for opening the secret compartment,' replied Kurush.

'And you're the reincarnation of this Jannara?' asked Angelica.

'I believe so.'

'Tell me more about the message,' said Christiano.

'Of course. You see the spiral design?' He pointed to the lid of the box.

Christiano and Angelica moved forward for a closer look.

'My fiftieth birthday, at midnight, was the time chosen for me to open the box. The clockwork circuitry inside' – he pointed to it – 'was an ingenious, timed, locking mechanism that would only open on the designated night by pressing a pin into each of these minute pin holes. The Prophet Zarathustra, the founder of the Zoroastrian faith – the faith of the Magi – spoke of four Royal Stars. Each pinhole represents one and forms the stauros – hence the sequence by which I was to push a pin into each hole.'

'But there are five stars,' said Angelica.

'Yes, this one, in the centre, is what Jannara refers to as the unknown. It materialised in the sky for the first time that night, five years ago, and disappeared the moment I plunged the pin into the central hole. It was all over the papers the next day. I have a copy here if…'

'Yes, I remember reading about it in the paper,' interrupted Christiano. 'It appeared just beneath the Pole Star and flickered for about five minutes before disappearing. And it has never been seen since. It was named *The God Star.*'

'That's correct. That was our star. Now to the translation on the parchment. It is long, and I have transcribed it into a notebook for you to read yourselves. You will need to keep an open mind.'

He pulled on the middle drawer and removed a small black notebook, opened it to the relevant page and placed it on the table before them.

'Will you read it aloud please, Christiano?' requested Angelica.

'I will, but first, I read Ancient Greek too. I would like to study the parchment for myself if that's okay?'

'Of course, Christiano. I would expect nothing less,' replied Kurush.

Satisfied, Christiano picked up the book, cleared his throat and read aloud, *'I am Jannara, son of Damasius, of the faith of Zarathushtra, a Magi born in Babylon at the time of King Herod and the coming of the new age. My brethren, Caspar, Balthasar, Melchior and I were the chosen ones to follow the Star that would lead us to the new Messiah, the King of the Jews, as the wise ones predicted before us and the signs in the heavens confirmed.*

'*We followed the star to the east, and during our journey were called upon by King Herod to reveal the child's whereabouts. We found him in Jerusalem at the home of a relative and requested his audience. His father granted our wishes and my own eyes fell upon the heavenly creature, the Saviour predicted to summon the new age and save the Jews from their persecutors.*

'*When I looked upon the Saviour's face, my life was changed, implicitly. His mother, Mary, allowed me to hold him in my arms, and his fingers touched my face, and my heart ripped open. I wept like never before, as I have wept many times since. I believe his essence lives in my body and now guides my life through its motions. I still feel the lightness with which he has left my mind and body.*

'*We gave him our gifts, and before our parting, Mother Mary gave me one of His swaddling bands as a gift. I thanked her reverently. Her angelic presence was filled with such humility and peace.*

'*As we journeyed home that same Star that had guided us to the Messiah, guided us safely back to our homeland, avoiding the route of Herod's kingdom.*

'*Once home, we shared our experiences with our tribe and elders, showing them the swaddling gift from the angelic Mary.*

'The elders bid us celebrate this honour with a feast and a great fire, whereupon we made our prayers upon the swaddling and I was called upon to toss it into the flames.

'I watched as the fire claimed the swaddling for its own, and I celebrated with my brethren until dawn. Upon waking I was witness to a miracle, discovering the swaddling was still whole and untouched, and as sacred as the moment it was gifted to me by His mother. I held it, and kissed it and laid it upon my eyes, calling upon my elders to bear witness to the miracle that was. And we knew without doubt that it was the truth. And my elders gave it to me, the treasurer of our tribe, for safe-keeping.

'That same night a vision was bestowed upon me, whereupon I saw His mother, Mary, and Joseph standing before me. A circle of light crowned Mary's head, and she welcomed me with the same reverent smile. She opened her mouth to speak, but the voice was not her own. It did portend of the future demise of the Messiah.

'The voice then commanded me to fetch the swaddling with which the Lady Mary had gifted me. I retrieved it from my home and presented it to Her, upon which She continued, "Listen carefully to my words Jannara, as the Messiah himself chose you for this task. You must construct a box from the wood of the Cypress. In it, you will place the swaddling for safekeeping. In the lid of the box, you must construct a secret compartment into which you are to place a piece of parchment that recounts this vision in full detail. This compartment must remain sealed and can only be opened upon your second incarnation and by your hand only."'

Christiano stopped reading and glanced at the others.

'Please, Christiano. Carry on,' said Angelica, poised at the edge of her seat.

He returned to the notebook and continued. 'At which point she waved her hand to the skies and there appeared a spiral of light with five stars, each one more luminous than the other. The central star, the one I did not recognise, was the brightest of them all. The others I knew as Zarasta's Royal stars, Aldebaran, Antares, Fomalhaut and Regulus.

'A light appeared running from Aldebaran to Antares and from Fomalhaut to Regulus and ended on the central, unknown star, which shone brighter. Then once more, each star dazzled one by one in the order of Aldebaran, Antares, Fomalhaut, Regulus, and then the unknown star.

'The voice spoke once more, "Jannara as I speak, so my words and the vision drawn upon the heavens are imprinted in your Soul for eternity. The secret compartment will remain locked until the fiftieth year of your second and final incarnation, and must only be unlocked by following the exact sequence of the Royals, as shown on the heavens. You are to scribe the following riddle on the underside of the main compartment. 'I am Jannara. On the fiftieth year of my second and final incarnation, follow the status of each Royal through the sign of stauros, to the unknown, where what I have concealed can be retrieved by my hand only, at the hour that seals the night.'

"As you construct the box, the means and knowledge to build the timing device will guide your hand."

'As the voice continued to speak, Mary's angelic vision metamorphosed, as did that of Joseph, to two people in clothing not of my time. On the tips of my toes, I was dragged and lifted *into the air, to face the man who was tall. He pointed beneath his left eye where I saw a cross etched into his skin.'*

Christiano paused and made a visible gulp as the implausible took a hold of his senses and sunk its teeth in. He looked round at the others to see Kurush looking at him with a confident smile and a told-you-so glint in his eyes. Christiano dragged his gaze away and back to the book, clearing his throat before proceeding.

'I was pulled to the left, lined face to face with the woman, whose hair fell from her head, leaving it naked. She turned around and ran her fingers from the centre of her earlobes to the centre of her head. Where her fingertips met there appeared the very same mark. I was thrust back to my place. She faced me now, her hair fully grown. I watched in fright as her abdomen swelled and a baby sprung forth.

'As she held the child in her arms, the voice spoke once more. "Jannara, Mary and Joseph will be reincarnated once more in the time of your second incarnation…" Christiano nearly stumbled over the inconceivable words *"…when the Messiah will be reborn for one last time. The child must be born at a place that will find you on the desert land of Moses' great mountain. You are to ensure the safe passage for the mother and the unborn child."*

'She waved her hand through the air and immediately I was transported to a foreign place where Romans walked the earth. I saw a man on an inverted cross being crucified. His screams curdled the blood running through my veins. Then his body transformed into an obelisk that stood tall and firm. A man appeared dressed in long black robes, with a red sash and a ring

of gold with a large amethyst stone. His hair was a lustrous white, with a streak of silver running through its centre. The man's hands were thick with blood, and it dripped on to the obelisk, which caught fire and devoured him.

'*The voice spoke for the last time. "Follow the road to Rome, to an enclave by the Tiber. There you will find the Emperor who has strayed. He will lead you to the Messiah."*

'*So I say to you, Jannara that was, go forth and ensure you meet the wishes of Mother Mary. You will know what to do, instinctively, as you are Jannara and your Soul is imprinted with the Messiah's instructions.*'

Christiano looked up from the little black notebook through a new set of eyes – like a newborn seeing for the very first time. He found no words nor questions to catch Kurush off-guard and expose him as a charlatan. He was speechless, frightened and fascinated all at the same time – his world upside down, yet, for the very first time, it all made sense.

✦ Chapter Thirty-Eight ✦

Christiano lay on a kingsize bed gazing contemplatively at the concave ceiling above him. The walls surrounding him were papered with trees abundant with robins and butterflies perched on lush, verdant leaves. The black notebook and the framed parchment were by his side.

Angelica breezed out of the en-suite bathroom, changed, refreshed and ready for a little rest before dinner. 'Are you okay?'

With his thoughts disrupted, he turned to face her. 'Do you believe that premonition? That we are the reincarnation of Mary and Joseph?'

'Have you translated the parchment already?'

'I was going to take a look after dinner, but to be honest, I do not see Kurush as an incompetent man. And to fabricate all this would be an orchestration of inconceivable proportion. If he is lying why let me see the parchment at all?' He rose to a sitting position and rubbed his frowning brow.

Angelica kneeled on the floor and gazed sympathetically into his eyes. 'Well, I'm pregnant with the Messiah. It stands to reason I would or could be the incarnation of Mary. And who would I want by my side but my Joseph?'

The tension left his face and his lips spread into a modest smile. He returned a mesmerised stare. 'You are beautiful.'

'As are you.' She allowed her lips to drift closer to his, and their mouths touched, sending a scorching heat through their bodies – their passionate kiss fevered by lifetimes apart.

When their lips parted, he leaned his forehead against hers, finally relenting to the impassioned feelings pulsing through his veins.

'Let me show you something.' She stood up.

'Angelica...'

'Shush.' She spoke gently as she guided his head to her belly.

As his face rested on her abdomen, a feeling of peace wafted through him like a drifting cloud on a sunny day. It reached his heart, shattering all its defences, and in an instant, every doubt in his mind was obliterated. He gasped, unable to breathe as his being was drenched in love so pure that it was unbearable. He buried his forehead against her bump, never wanting to lose the presence of Truth that filled every gaping hole he had ever felt. There he remained, sobbing into her belly.

Part Four

Nemesis

✦ Chapter Thirty-Nine ✦

Johan's face bore a light smile as he arrived at the Cardinal's residence. After all these years of chauffeuring the Cardinal around and putting up with his menial and perverse fancies, he had finally completed his task of locating the Messiah and could now concentrate his efforts on ensuring that Jannara's instructions were followed to the very letter. He looked forward to holding the Messiah in his arms and welcoming him into the world. He walked through the service entrance to a frugally furnished servant's lounge consisting of a four-seater sofa, a television set, and a small kitchen area.

Sammel and Cedric sat at a table, playing poker – smoking and flicking ash into an overflowing ashtray.

The stale, smoky odour nested in Johan's throat and nostrils.

'Ah, Johan, come join us for a game,' said Cedric.

'I would, but I'm here to take His Eminence to a dinner engagement.'

'Oh that's been cancelled,' said Sammel.

'Cancelled? Since when?'

Cedric stood up and walked behind him to the door.

Johan turned to watch him, a sudden gnawing of panic in his stomach. 'What's going on?'

'Nothing,' said Sammel, noticing a white envelope protruding from Johan's pocket. 'What's this?' He grabbed it.

'Hey, that's for His Eminence.'

'Ah, let me guess. It's a letter of resignation,' said Sammel.

'That's none of your business.'

'Everything that goes on in this place is my business.'

Johan gulped and all the moisture drained from his mouth.

'I will pass it on to His Eminence for you.'

'I can do that myself.'

'Okay, I'll come with you,' said Sammel, walking towards him.

Johan backed off and bumped into Cedric who shoved him forward.

'We know you've been deceiving us,' said Sammel.

Before he could make another move, Johan felt a sharp pain explode in his skull. He dropped to the floor unconscious.

Angelica and christiano entered the dining room just as Frya was placing a dish on the table.

'That smells delicious,' said Angelica.

'You must be so hungry. Please sit. Just a few more items.'

'Let me help you,' said Angelica.

Frya placed a hand on her shoulder. 'Just for tonight, let us serve you.'

Angelica nodded and sat down, while Christiano took the seat opposite her.

Alone in the room, their toes rubbed together beneath the table, and they eyed each other like love-struck teenagers.

The front door opened and clunked closed. Kurush sauntered into the dining room. 'I hope you like red wine, Christiano.' He placed the bottle on the table and proceeded to open it.

'I do,' he replied.

'Angelica, I assume you're not drinking. What would be your choice of beverage?' asked Kurush.

'Just water. Thank you.'

He nodded as he poured glasses of red for Christiano, himself and Frya. 'I'll get you that water,' he said.

Frya entered with two more dishes and placed them on the table.

'Johan isn't joining us?' asked Christiano.

'No. Unfortunately, he was called to drive the Cardinal to an unexpected dinner party.'

Kurush returned with a jug of water and poured a glass for Angelica.

'Kurush, how long was it before you fully understood the cuneiform message inscribed into the wood of the box?' asked Angelica.

'A few months. As soon as I realised my destiny, my studies began, and I did not rest until I understood the message completely.'

'It's been a long wait,' said Christiano.

'Indeed it has!' replied Kurush with a raised brow.

'The prophecy states that the Messiah is to be born in the same desert as Moses' mountain. Obviously the Sinai desert,' said Christiano.

'That's correct,' replied Kurush.

'So, how do you plan to arrange safe passage for us to Egypt without Don Primo or the Cardinal's knowledge?'

'Do I detect a sudden *lack* of resistance, my friend?'

Christiano smiled. 'A little, perhaps.'

'Did you translate the parchment?'

'Not as yet, but let's just say there have been far too many persuasive occurrences to deny this truth any longer.'

'That's excellent news,' he said, affectionately slapping Christiano's shoulder. 'After a toast, I will tell you of my plans.' Kurush held up his glass.

The others rose from their chairs, and four glinting glasses were lifted to the light.

'To the birth of the Messiah and the dawning of a new age that will save humanity once and for all,' toasted Kurush.

Their glasses clinked together.

'It's a pity Johan is not with us. His part was instrumental to us finding you both. I honour his efforts,' said Kurush, holding his glass up once more.

They followed his lead.

'To Johan,' said Frya, 'the love of my life. A true soldier and warrior of God.'

'To Johan,' repeated the others.

'Will he be leaving the Cardinal's employ soon?' asked

Christiano as they took their seats.

'Yes,' said Frya, serving salad onto her plate. 'I told him not to go back. That I would give him a doctor's note for one month's leave and by then, we would have disappeared, but he insisted on personally handing in his notice. He wants to be cautious to avoid suspicion.'

'My daughter has been cursed with two stubborn men in her life,' said Kurush with a wide grin.

Frya was not amused. 'Papa, the mission was to find Angelica, and this has been accomplished. He should not have gone back to that place. Am I the only one who recognises how dangerous these people are?'

Johan awoke with a pounding headache. His breathing was hot and heavy. He cracked his eyes open to find his head shrouded in darkness. He tried to move, but his hands and legs were bound securely to his seat. 'Sammel! Cedric! Are you there?'

He heard the patter of footfalls headed his way and a reply by way of an agonising punch to his face. His head flew back, sending a shooting pain through his neck and spine. He nearly blacked out again.

'What's your interest in Angelica?' said an unfamiliar voice.

'Please, I don't know what you're talking about.'

'Tell him what he needs to know, Johan, and no harm will come to you.'

'Sammel. Please. You know me. How could you...?'

Another punch to his face interrupted his pleading.

'Just tell us what we need to know,' said the voice.

'Please, I don't know anything.'

No sooner had he finished his sentence, he felt one of his hands being untied and laid flat on a cold, hard surface.

'What are you…?'

His fingers were aggressively spread apart and held down.

'Please!'

A shrilling scream resounded from his lips as a sharp blade penetrated his skin, cutting into it like a piece of steak and slicing through his bone as if it was made of butter.

He gasped for breath and drool dripped from his mouth as he heard the crunch of his own bone and felt his finger being severed from his body.

The digit was shoved beneath his nose.

The smell of his own blood curdled his stomach. He wanted to keel over from the nausea rising to his throat. *'Pl…ea…se….'* he barely managed.

What followed was a succession of punches to his right cheek.

He vomited into the bag over his head; his breathing laboured; his entire body trembling with shock. The space that his finger once occupied was throbbing with unbearable pain. He felt his mind retreat to a faraway place that grew darker and darker, and smaller and smaller, until there was nothing but darkness.

✦ Chapter Forty ✦

The white Mercedes crawled along the cobbled road before parking in front of the sun-brick Renaissance apartment block where Frya and her father lived. At three in the morning, the streets slumbered as soundly as the local residents.

Alessandro and Vincenzo stepped out of the car with Don Primo, while Benito remained in the driver's seat. 'I want this to go smoothly,' said Don Primo pulling on his jacket sleeves. 'Just Angelica. Kill the rest, but do it quietly. Let's move.'

They reached a set of glass double doors, and Don Primo rapped firmly on the window.

The concierge looked up from his book to see two fingers flashing the peace sign in his direction. Recognising his cue, he nervously stood up and opened the door, standing back to let the men inside.

'You have what I asked for?' said Don Primo.

'Yes, Sir,' he replied as he reached a quivering hand into his pocket and removed a key. He handed it to Don Primo, who slapped a large handful of bills into his palm.

'Thank you, Sir,' said the concierge, pushing the money into his pocket. 'Take the lift to the top floor. There's only one apartment per floor.'

'Make yourself scarce for at least an hour,' said Don Primo.

'Yes, Sir.'

Don Primo moved in close to his face. 'You breathe a word of this, and you will never breathe again. You understand?'

The concierge reeled back and took a nervous gulp as his face turned a pallid shade of death. 'Yes… Sir.'

'Now go,' said Don Primo.

The man hastened into the shadows to be swallowed by the darkness. The guilt of what he was now a party to gnawed at his intestines as he walked. It rose to his head, and the world took a disorienting spin as his chest laboriously heaved to catch a breath. He managed to reach the end of the road where he dropped to the ground – his heart thumping and his face hot with fear. He had known the Attars for four years since their arrival from Switzerland, and they had always treated him with the generosity and respect he had never known from the other tenants. To them, he was a man, not a menial servant. Don Primo's threats had been persuasive. An offer he could not refuse. He rubbed the sweat from his forehead and noticed the blood money protruding from his pocket. In a disgusted rage, he tossed it to the ground and stood up with his fists clenched.

The abrupt ring from his bedside table startled Kurush from his dreams. He scrambled for the phone as he rubbed the sleep from his eyes.

A muffled voice saturated with dread heeded its warning down the phone. 'Get out of the flat, *now*. Avoid the lift.'

'Alberto is that you?'

The phone went dead.

Kurush remained in his bed, the receiver still in his hand and the hypnotic dead tone dulling his senses.

Frya entered his room. 'Was that Johan? He hasn't come home yet, and I'm—'

'We must get out of here, *now*,' interrupted Kurush, scrambling out of bed.

'Papa?'

Kurush reached her side and pushed her into the hallway.

'Papa!' protested Frya.

Christiano came out of his room. 'What's the matter?'

'I will explain later. Wake Angelica. We're leaving.'

Angelica appeared behind Christiano, wrapped in her robe.

'Let's move!' said Kurush ushering them to his study. 'We'll take the roof.'

As he finished speaking, the sound of a key being inserted into the lock downstairs sent a petrifying chill through each of them.

Kurush placed his finger over his mouth to hush them and motioned for the women to enter the study.

The next sound was the front door opening, followed by faint noises and a short gap until it closed.

'Maybe it's Joh—'

Kurush placed his hand over Frya's mouth, his eyes wide with warning.

Whispers and footfalls echoed from the corridor downstairs.

Kurush grabbed a baseball bat from behind the door of his study. Christiano latched onto it. A short grapple ensued before Kurush conceded. He made a ratifying nod and let go. Christiano gently pushed him into the room. Kurush's eyes never left Christiano's as he shut the door, locking him out.

Angelica, who had been the first to enter, realised that he was nowhere to be seen. 'Christiano.' She pushed past Frya to reach the door.

Kurush placed his hands on her cheeks and spoke in a whisper. 'This is what he wanted, Angelica. Please. You and the baby come first.'

'Angelica you must think of the child,' said Frya.

Tears spilled down her cheeks as she allowed herself to be dragged onto a large roof garden bordered with blooming flowers and furnished with lounge chairs, a garden table and a small greenhouse.

Kurush drew the curtains before shutting the patio door and locking it behind them. 'We must hurry. This is not the only entrance to the garden. We're going to make our way to the building next door. Do you think you can climb onto the roof?'

Angelica looked at the rooftop and shook her head.

'The apartment building next door belongs to friends of

ours,' whispered Frya. 'You can't tell from this vantage point, but the buildings practically connect from this roof. There is a gap of about two feet between our roof and the roof garden of their apartment, on the other side. We cross over all the time. Just not in the pitch dark.'

'If you can do it, I can do it,' replied Angelica.

'Good, just follow Frya's lead,' said Kurush.

Frya climbed onto the stone balustrade and hauled herself onto the rooftop. There, she sat down, easing her way horizontally until she was mid-way across the roof before making a controlled slide down the sloping tiles to reach the two-foot gap. Lifting herself into a standing position, she leapt across, landing with the elegance of a ballerina onto the roof garden next door.

The cold stone wall between Angelica's thighs sent shivers through her body. She stared down at the fathomless drop to her left.

'Don't look down,' said Kurush, gently gripping her waist. 'It'll be okay. I'm here for you.' He pulled her up from her waist, moving his hands to the tops of her thighs, and hoisting her up.

Angelica took some of the weight, propelling herself up and onto the roof. She remained captivated by the starry sky, which seemed to close in on her, spinning in a whirlpool as it dived towards her. Her body went limp and her foot slipped on the sloping tiles.

Kurush caught her and eased her down.

'Are you okay?'

'We shouldn't have left Christiano behind.' Angelica

glanced over her shoulder and peered at him through the tear-stained corners of her eyes. 'We have come such a long way. Been through so much.'

'What he has been through to get you here is the exact reason why you and the baby must make it through this. All you need to do is shuffle along to the centre of the roof and then slide down. I will hold you, and Frya will help you to the garden. Okay?'

Angelica took a deep breath and began shifting her buttocks along the tiles until she was halfway across the roof. She waited for Kurush to reach her.

'We're at the last hurdle.' He sat behind her and gripped her waist.

With a deep breath, Angelica slid down the tiles, guided by Kurush, who slipped down with her, maintaining a firm grasp of her waist, his legs supporting her on each side.

When she reached the edge, Kurush took her hands and she slowly rose to her feet.

Frya had placed a large, cushioned bench where Angelica's feet would land, significantly decreasing the steepness of the jump. She stood on the seat and held out her hand.

Angelica reached out and clasped hold of it.

'Take your time,' said Kurush.

'I promise, you'll be fine,' said Frya.

Angelica took a deep breath and hopped onto the cushioned surface.

Seconds later, Kurush leapt down by their side. He hugged them both. 'Well done. Now, let's get inside.'

He retrieved a key from behind a plant pot and unlocked the patio door.

'They're not home?' said Angelica.

'Our friends spend eighty per cent of their time away on business. I watch the place for them. We'll be safe here.'

'And what about Christiano? We should call the police.'

Kurush pulled on the patio door, and they entered a dark room with the stale odour of closed doors and summer heat. He shut it behind him and locked it.

'We've always said no police. If Don Primo has found you, and I don't know how, then the police are always a risk,' said Kurush.

'How are you so sure?' replied Angelica.

'Did you go to the police when you were hiding from him at the convent?'

Angelica sighed. 'No. In our home town, every officer was in his pocket.'

'Exactly. The best plan is to wait until we think it's safe to go back home. Then we will deal with what we find,' said Kurush.

'Even if it's Christiano's dead body?' replied Angelica.

Hidden inside the doorway of the guest bedroom, Christiano stood poised with the bat raised above his head. Droplets of sweat formed beads of liquid glass on his face. His chest was visibly heaving; his expression was strained with tension.

Faint footfalls grew louder on the stairs.

He peered round the doorway to see Alessandro reach the

top of the stairs and walk directly opposite, to the study door. He reached for the handle and gave the unrelenting door a tug.

With his hands firmly grasped around the bat, Christiano crept out of his room.

Oblivious, Alessandro drew back from the study door and positioned his shoulder as a battering ram.

The unexpected whack across the side of his face sent him hurtling against the study door. He landed on the floor with a thud.

Vincenzo bounded up the stairs to see Alessandro's body unconscious and slumped on the beige carpet. Don Primo made his way up behind him and located the light switch. A warm, orange-tinged hue flooded the upstairs hallway.

Christiano was back in his hiding place, straining to keep his laboured breathing silent. He wiped the sweat from his brow and leaned against the wall, trying to normalise his breath.

Don Primo's brusque voice sounded through the hallway. 'Hey, priest. I recognise your handiwork. He'd better not be dead.'

Christiano closed his eyes, making a soundless thump of his head against the wall.

'Angelica, why don't you make this easy and give yourself up. I promise you, I will spare your friends.'

'There's no one here but me,' said Christiano, entering the hallway with his hands raised.

'Will you look at that,' said Don Primo. 'So you're the famous priest.'

'That would be me.'

Don Primo eyed him from head to toe.

Christiano's gaze fixed on his steely eyes.

'Where are they?' he said.

Christiano said nothing, maintaining a defiant glare.

'Get down on your knees.'

He remained standing.

'I said, get down!' Don Primo charged at Christiano, who casually stepped aside and landed his fist squarely on the charging man's right temple. Don Primo staggered, fell to his knees and clutched at his temples.

'Bastardo,' shouted Vincenzo, sprinting towards him. Christiano dropped to the floor and lifted his leg to catch Vincenzo's chest. Using the momentum of Vincenzo's movement, he sent him hurtling through the air. He slammed on the floor behind him. Christiano then jumped to his feet and pounced on the dazed thug and held him down as he continued a succession of punches to his face.

A sharp pain to his skull put an end to his fearless battle and shunted him into unconsciousness. He keeled over Vincenzo, who pushed him off. His body rolled over to face upwards.

Don Primo placed his gun back in his pocket, all the while staring down at Christiano's motionless body. 'He's a tough bastard, for a priest.' He kicked Christiano's leg. 'I don't think they're here. They would have come to his aid.'

Vincenzo wiped the blood from his nose. 'Do you think the concierge told them, Boss?'

'If he did, he's a dead man. Let's give the place a once

over. Get that room open. We'll leave Angelica a note.'

'What about the Cardinal?'

Don Primo grabbed him by the scruff of the neck. 'When I give you an order you do it. You let me handle the Cardinal.'

Kurush was the first to enter the study. He scanned his ransacked office to find the wooden box tossed to the floor. He picked it up and examined it for damage. Seeing none, he placed it back on his desk where he noticed a hand-written message scrawled across a pad. He turned the writing to face him.

Frya came in through the patio doors; an anxious look on her face.

'I told you to wait next door.' He turned to her with a burdened expression.

'They're gone by now, Papa'

'They have Christiano.'

Frya was silent for a moment. 'At least he's alive.'

'For now.' He glanced behind her.

Frya turned to see Angelica standing at the door, frozen and distraught. 'Angelica—'

Before she could finish, Kurush interrupted her. 'They have Johan too.'

She turned to him with a look that was already aware. Her eyes moistened. 'I told him not to go back to that place.' Tears spilled down her cheeks.

He walked towards her and placed his hand on her shoulder. 'I know you did. They're going to call us at 9am. It's not safe here. Let's gather some things and go next door.'

✦ Chapter Forty-One ✦

A dreamy image, vivid with colour, Angelica's chest rose and fell in perfect synchronicity. Christiano found it comforting to watch. He moved across and planted his lips on hers. She smiled and opened her sleepy eyes to look up at him. Suddenly, her smile faded, and her eyes screamed in terror as the distance between them grew rapidly. Christiano was adrift, like an unbound air balloon floating into the night sky.

He watched helplessly, his arms reaching out as Angelica made frantic grasps for his hands. His tormented gaze remained fixed on her shrinking form until she was no more.

Christiano gasped for breath. He opened his eyes just a crack to a disorientation of blurred images, each one superimposed over the other. A sharp pounding in his head was an unwelcome reminder of what had happened. Clanging noises reverberated around him as if he was in the deepest depths of a dungeon, and a metallic smell, putrid with death, clung to the air. He tried to raise his collapsed neck; every movement was excruciating. A round table to his right gradually came into focus. A line of peculiar objects he could not identify lined the stained plastic sheet at the far end of the table.

He squeezed his eyes shut, blinking several times in an attempt to adjust. A row of finger stumps – at least five and a thumb – formed a clear and undisputable image. His head jerked back in shock. He winced from the sharp pain running down his spine, and his eyes now focused on the image behind them.

A barely recognisable Johan, his face caked in dry blood and a mass of swelling and bruising hung his head limply to one side. His eyes were slits; his breathing almost undetectable.

'Johan… Can you hear me? Johan.'

Johan could only move his eyes. Blood and saliva seeped from his mouth. He spoke without moving his lips. A hoarse whisper. 'Christiano.'

In a clinically modern kitchen, Angelica and Frya sat on stools that defied gravity, at a white plastic table supported by a solid leg the width of the table at one end, and an inverted leg built into the wall at the other – like a collapsed Z. Their faces were worn and puffy from hours of crying.

Kurush wore a forlorn expression as he placed a cup of camomile tea on the table for Angelica and a strong espresso each for himself and Frya. He opened his mouth to speak, but thought better of it and propped himself on a stool instead.

'Maybe we should have called the police,' said Frya,

playing with the handle of the cup.

'No, Kurush was right,' said Angelica. 'If we did we would never see them again.'

Kurush downed his espresso and cupped his head in his hands. 'I know you are both suffering, and I wish there were something I could do, but all we can do is wait.'

'Do you think he'll kill them?' asked Frya.

Angelica looked across at her with a knowing glint that caused Frya to collapse her head on the table. Her body convulsed from her uncontrollable tears.

Angelica wiped hers away and tried to maintain her composure. She looked up at the clock on the kitchen wall. A minimalist design: just a faceless iron disk with two hands and no numbers. The hand was seconds away from the hour.

Frya's cell phone rang. They watched it ringing at the centre of the table as if it was something alien.

Kurush reached over and picked it up, looking at the flashing screen. 'It's Johan's phone.'

Frya collapsed in tears again.

He took a deep breath, swiped the answer key, and hit the loudspeaker button. 'Pronto.' He placed the phone at the centre of the table.

'Give me Angelica.'

Kurush looked across at her.

'Don Primo,' she replied.

'So now I get to hear your voice.'

'Why are you doing this, selling me to that madman? Do you know he intends to kill me?'

'So how does an infertile woman become pregnant? It

really must be a miracle. Maybe because you fucked a priest and God blessed you. Or, just maybe you really are carrying the *Messiah*. Either way, it's just about the money.'

She shut her eyes and opened them to dripping tears. 'Don Primo, please. If I ever meant anything to you…'

A mocking laugh assaulted their ears. 'We're long past that now. I don't care what happens to you or your bastard. You're not my responsibility, but you are my meal ticket. I will kill them both if you don't surrender yourself to me within the hour. Is that clear, *my angel?*'

'That's out of the question.'

'Ah, Kurush. The magi.'

Their heads straightened.

'Yes, I know all about the prophecy and your ancestor Jannara. Little Johan had to part with many fingers before he told me that fairy tale.'

Frya yelped as panic choked the breath from her lungs.

'And just to show you how serious I am…'

'No!' resounded down the phone, followed by a gunshot.

The line went dead.

Shock gripped each of them.

Frya fell from her chair. Her body hit the ground where she remained trembling and howling with terror.

Kurush rushed to her side, lay down beside her and cradled her in his arms. 'We don't know that anyone was killed. Frya. Please.' He kissed her head and whispered comforting words into her ear.

Angelica remained stunned and motionless. She looked down at the hysterical Frya, stood up, left the room, and entered the study. She collapsed onto a sofa in the corner of the room and allowed the tears to flow. 'How could you bring us together and then take him away from me?' she said aloud. As she continued her inconsolable tears, she noticed a telephone on the desk opposite.

Sammel and Cedric untied Johan's lifeless body and laid him down on a large sheet of black plastic covering the ground.

Christiano watched them through swollen eyes. He was exhausted and weak. He muttered a prayer for Johan, his mouth dripping with blood.

'Do you think she loves you enough to give herself up?' asked Don Primo, sitting on a chair just inches away from him.

'I hope not,' he muttered through motionless lips.

'You know I had to take Alessandro to the hospital and leave him, like some nameless hobo. If he dies…well, you're going to die whatever happens.' He took a puff on his cigarette, drew in the smoke until there was not a scrap of air left in his lungs, and blew it out in Christiano's face.

Christiano coughed up more blood, much to Don Primo's amusement.

The phone rang.

Don Primo looked at the caller ID. 'A blocked number. Maybe she does love you, after all.' He answered the call with a commanding air. 'Angelica. What a pleasant surprise… Yes, I can be there… Okay, it's a deal. What time?… I trust you're not stupid enough to involve the police… Aren't you going to ask me who's dead?'

He hit the end button with a smile. 'Well if she's coming to save you, she must be madly in love with you. She would never have come for me.'

He scowled at Christiano as he took a tuft of his hair in one hand, straightened his head, and punched his face – once, twice, three times.

Christiano's head flopped to one side, his nose crushed against his face. He gasped for breath through his barely open mouth.

One more punch to his temple and darkness consumed him.

Angelica replaced the receiver. Tears drizzled down her cheeks. A warmth emanated from her womb, filling her with love. She made a faint smile and clutched at her belly. 'Thank you,' she said aloud. She wiped away the tears. 'We'd better go.'

She looked round the stark room with its unadorned walls and its aloof furniture. Nothing there belonged to her. Her entire life lay in her womb, and she may have just heard the murder of the man she loved.

She left the room and trod quietly over the black marble floor, passing by the kitchen with a vigilant eye. The door was wide open, and the sound of Frya's distraught hysterics was sure to drown out any noise she would make. Kurush was still by her side, consoling her.

Angelica glided by like a ghost and left the apartment in a silent whisper, her presence a mere echo clinging to the safety of the surrounding walls.

Outside, the unrelenting sun beat down its scorching heat. The Roman streets were as rich in hue as they were in vigour and life. Another typical day racing by without a conscious breath. She walked with haste as if Satan's bloodhounds were snapping at her heels and the burden of the world's fate was on her shoulders. Whatever choice she made she stood to lose something – if she had not already.

She flagged down a taxi and requested the driver take her to the Colosseum. The journey was tense. Angelica's hands clutched around her bump in a reassuring embrace.

The driver, a short, wispy man, made constant glances at her through the rear-view mirror.

She ignored him by turning her attention to the historical sights on the way.

'Sei una bella donna,' he said. *'Molto bella.'*

She forced a smile. *'Grazie.'* Then she turned back to the window.

Twenty minutes later, the taxi arrived at the Colosseum.

Angelica thanked the driver and paid him.

He left her standing by the entrance, looking lost amongst the hordes of tourists eager to see the most famous landmark in Rome.

A tap on her shoulder forced her to spin round.

Don Primo's steely, narrowed eyes sent a momentary shudder through her. He greeted her with a mocking grin.

She looked into his eyes coldly. 'You will never find peace in this. You'll have nothing but regret and guilt that will taste like bile on your tongue, and all that money is as cursed as Judas's thirty pieces of silver. Do you understand this, Don Primo?'

His smirk faded, and an unmissable glint of fear flashed past his eyes, but it was gone in an instant. Gone and forgotten. He took her arm. 'Your lover boy is waiting for you. You won't cause a scene if you want him to live.'

Angelica released the tension in her arm, making it easier for Don Primo to drag her along. They looked like a father and daughter casually walking the streets of Rome. When they reached the car, Benito opened the door for them and they entered.

As the car cruised the streets, a loaded silence choked the air until Angelica spoke, 'You said Christiano is waiting for me. Did you kill Johan or just shoot in the air?'

'The priest is alive, but not for long. As for Johan, I did him a favour. My men were – how should I put it? Overzealous in their questioning.'

'He was a good man. He has a fiancé whose life has just been shattered. He did nothing to you. You told me you would free them both if I turned myself in.'

He looked at her with twisted features of hatred and leaned into her face until his nose was barely an inch from hers. 'Killing for me is about as burdensome as brushing the dust from my shoe. Do you understand me? That includes you, that priest and his bastard child.'

'Don Primo, I am four months pregnant. I have known Christiano for no more than two months. You know I'm infertile. The child I carry in my womb is the next Messiah. You are about to commit an indelible sin from which there is no return.'

'What is this bullshit? I've had enough of this! You're no

Virgin Mary. You're a whore with delusions of grandeur. Whether he's the father or not, he dies because you love him and I know you fucked him.'

Angelica found herself slapping his face as if her hand was fuelled by its own mind.

His cheek turned crimson with immediate effect, joined by the rest of his face. 'You're dead,' he screamed, 'but first, you're going to feel that bastard child dying inside you.'

His hand formed a fist and he thrust it forward with all his venom, aiming directly at her stomach.

✦ Chapter Forty-Two ✦

'So are we just going to leave them there?' protested Frya. 'No police? Nothing? As if Johan never existed?'

Kurush rubbed his furrowed brow. 'If we involve the police, Angelica confirmed they will die, for sure. And the Cardinal will have Angelica. The mission comes first. You know this. Johan knows this.'

'Papa, they have the man I love. The man I'm going to marry. After all his help. After everything. He's like a son to you.'

'Do you think I take this lightly?'

'I know they're at the Cardinal's house and I think we should confront him.'

'You, yourself, announced how dangerous he is only last night at dinner. And why would the Cardinal be so stupid as to take them to his home?'

'Because he's above the law. Because that is where Johan went. He told us of the basement rooms and the incinerator. Of the man who was taken down there never to be seen again.'

'We don't know if the man was killed. Johan's shift was over, and...' he trailed off, hearing his own vacant justification.

'Papa, I'm going to the house. Are you coming with me or not?'

'And what do you intend to do when you get there?'

'I'm going to take a look around. Knock on the door if necessary. If I suspect anything, I *will* call the police. It's a risk I'm willing to take.'

'I will go,' said Kurush. 'Alone. I'll speak with Angelica. You two would be safer staying here. If I'm forced to involve the police, I want you to flee with Angelica. You know the arrangements.'

'Papa—!'

Before she could finish her protest, Kurush was in the hallway knocking on Angelica's door. He waited for permission to enter but heard nothing. 'Angelica?' The door creaked open beneath his hand. He peered inside to find an abandoned room. 'Angelica?' Back in the hallway, he knocked on the bathroom door. There was no reply. He tested the handle, pushing the door open. The room was vacant. 'Angelica!'

Frya joined him in the hallway. Her eyes searched his. 'Papa?'

The realisation hit them both with the force of a freight train.

'Surely she didn't,' said Frya.

'I think she did,' replied Kurush. 'What kind of mother would risk the life of her child, let alone the unborn Messiah?'

'She is saving Johan and the man she loves.'

'She is sealing the fate of the world. We'd better get to the Cardinal's before it's too late.'

Sammel greeted Don Primo with a wide grin as Angelica stepped out of the car. 'I thought you'd never deliver.'

Don Primo's icy glower sent a clear warning signal to Sammel, who gulped and moved aside to let them in.

Don Primo shoved Angelica forward. 'Get in the house.' He turned to Benito who walked behind him. 'Wait in the car.'

Benito nodded.

Angelica stared directly at Sammel with eyes of raging fire as she entered the orbed hallway. She stopped to gawp at the palatial surroundings. The air whistled past her ears in an eerie silence that caused her hair to stand on end. The entrance was devoid of furnishings, and the sun streamed shards of golden light on the marble floor that created the illusion of a pool of copper while simultaneously veiling the adjoining corridor in darkness.

'Keep moving,' said Don Primo, pushing her into the void.

By the time they reached the top of the seemingly unending corridor her eyes had adjusted. She stood before a dull wooden door which swung open beneath Don Primo's force. She moved through to a sizable, unoccupied kitchen, stopped and turned to him. 'Did I tell you to stop? Through the door opposite.' He nudged her forward to yet another closed door and pushed it open to reveal a steep flight of steps and a drifting odour suffused with death.

Her eagerness to see Christiano was replaced by a gripping fear.

'Move,' he said.

She ventured forward under a wan light, down spiralling stone stairs. With each step, the combined stench of faeces, urine and blood grew stronger. It sucked through her nostrils with her every breath. She stumbled, her head spinning with nausea. Don Primo gripped her arm and led her the rest of the way down until they reached a large cellar that narrowed down to a small corridor. The potent smell increased still further – more metallic now and combined with rotting wood.

Angelica gripped her stomach as she heaved. Lining the corridor were at least six rooms with sealed doors.

Don Primo pulled her to the first one and knocked three times on the rough timbered surface.

A fumbling sound from the other side pulled the hefty door open and a foul, foetid smell charged at her nostrils. Unable to hold back any longer, she stooped and heaved and coughed as bile spilled from her mouth to the floor. She slowly raised her head to see speckles of red leading to a pair of blood-splattered shoes. She followed the line of the trousers all the way to a beefy face, unmistakably Vincenzo's.

A shove behind her pushed her into the room. That's when she saw him, strapped to a chair, his face a mass of blood layering his skin like a mud mask. She reeled back in shock at the unrecognisable features, so swollen that his eyes had been swallowed by his own swelling flesh. 'Christiano!' She rushed forward.

Vincenzo obstructed her path. She turned to Don Primo with a look of pleading. He nodded, and Vincenzo moved aside. She rushed to him, but her moistened eyes obscured her vision.

'You should not have come.' His words were barely audible.

She whimpered, her hands unable to find a space unoccupied by blood and severe bruising.

'Sit down,' said Don Primo.

Vincenzo pulled her away and threw her on the nearest chair.

Sammel entered the room. 'His Eminence is pleased and is coming down to see the catch for himself.'

The distant patter of footfalls turned their attention to the door. Seconds later, the Cardinal entered with Cedric close behind him. A triumphant smirk lit up his portly cheeks. He searched the room with greedy eyes. As his gaze fell on Angelica's scathing glare, his sneer faded. His heart jumped violently in his chest and a crippling intoxication seeped through his veins. Each limb grew heavy with fatigue. He tried to step back, but his feet were cemented to the ground. With all the energy he could muster, he raised an accusing finger at Angelica. 'You…wick…ed, wick…ed wo…man.' He collapsed to his knees. Cedric kneeled by his side, while Sammel rushed to his aid. They laid him comfortably on the ground as he clutched at his chest. His face turned a plum shade as he gasped for breath.

He gripped Sammel's arm. 'K…k…kill the w…witch,' he said.

Sammel stood up, pulled out his gun and pointed it at Angelica.

A bolt of adrenalin rocked through Christiano, recharging the cells of his body. He writhed and fidgeted in an attempt to loosen his ties.

Sammel's face formed a scornful smirk. He cocked his gun.

Angelica squeezed her eyes shut and shielded herself with raised arms.

A cacophonous sound exploded through the room.

Sammel dropped to his knees, a frozen picture of shock on his face. With his perplexed gaze on Don Primo, he turned his gun on him and fired as he hit the ground.

The bullet dropped Don Primo on his back, his gun still in his hand. Deep crimson stained his hands as he clutched at the hole in his stomach.

Christiano's lashings intensified. He stood up, still tied to the chair, and smashed his back against the wall.

Cedric who was still kneeling by the Cardinal, stood up, his gun in his hand, his eyes meeting Vincenzo's.

They froze for a moment.

Vincenzo reached for his gun.

Cedric fired.

The bullet hit Vincenzo between the eyes. His bulky mass sent a seismic shock through the ground as he crashed to the floor – wide-eyed and dead.

Christiano continued smashing the chair against the wall until it lay on the ground in a mound of splinters. He loosened his ropes and lunged forward, grabbing hold of Angelica.

Cedric obstructed the doorway, his gun trained on them.

From the ground, a quivering Cardinal pushed himself up, gripping onto Cedric's trouser leg, and then his arms as he raised himself to standing. 'I'll be damned…' he struggled for breath '…if I would let a whore bewitch me!' He hissed through gritted teeth, his skin as plump and purple as an aubergine. 'Kill . . . . . .her!' He squeezed Cedric's arm.

Cedric cocked the trigger and with his eyes focused on Angelica, he fired the shot.

Time seemed to slow for Christiano, who threw his body around Angelica and fell on top of her.

The slug hit the wall and wedged itself in the plaster.

Another shot fired.

They peered out from beneath Christiano's arms to see Cedric's face smash against the concrete floor.

The gun fell from Don Primo's hand with a metallic clang.

Angelica rushed to him, kneeled by his side and gently gripped his hand. 'Thank you. You saved me. True to your word.'

He smiled at her and gave her hand a weak squeeze. 'It was the least I could do. May God forgive me for the man I was.' With his last word, came his final breath.

She placed her hands over his eyelids and shut them.

A bewildered Christiano stood over her.

She looked up at him. 'He had a change of heart.' She stood up and sobbed into his chest. 'Thank God you're alive.'

Christiano gripped her tightly before he noticed the

Cardinal obstructing the doorway, his face quivering with rage.

Angelica turned, joining Christiano to face him.

A large, ornate, gold crucifix encrusted with emeralds and rubies hung from the Cardinal's neck. He tugged at the bottom end and pulled out a long sharp blade. Its light reflected in their eyes as he moved with seething determination, one incompetent foot after another as he made his way towards them. His voice trembled as he spoke, 'I am a man of God… And I t…tell you in God's own words that only the b…east can be born of a whore. You carry the anti-Christ in your diseased womb and you must…die.' He lunged forward with the knife to meet Christiano's firm clasp around his wrist.

Christiano forced the blade from his grip and slapped him across the face with the back of his hand. 'You're no man of God. Your heart and Soul belong to hell.' He pulled him from the back of his neck towards the table. 'How many women have you killed? And Johan! Who else? Who else, so that you can keep your position? You can't even see how lost you are!'

Christiano forced the Cardinal's hand on the table and faced his palm down. Holding the Cardinal's own knife above his head, he plunged it down impaling the man's hand on the table.

The Cardinal wailed in agony.

Christiano pulled the blade up and hammered it back down once more, lodging the knife and the Cardinal's hand to the table.

The man's shrieks ricocheted round the room. He dropped to his knees, his hand still wedged to the table. Tears streamed down his plump face.

Christiano released his grip. 'Let that be a constant reminder to you.'

He took hold of Angelica's hand, and they left the cellar where they made their way to the kitchen and through to the hallway. At the front door, he pushed the buzzer that opened the front gate and they entered the courtyard.

'Isn't that one of Don Primo's men?' He pointed to Benito seated in the Mercedes.

Benito stepped out of the car. 'He's dead, isn't he?'

'He was very brave,' replied Angelica. 'He saved my life, twice. You know what he wanted you to do.'

He nodded. 'Is his body in the basement?'

'His and Vincenzo's,' replied Angelica.

He stared at the house for a moment before taking a deep inhalation, followed by a burdensome sigh. 'The best of luck to you, Angelica.' He nodded respectfully and made his way to the house.

The exhausted couple continued on foot towards the palace gates.

'We should call the police,' said Angelica.

'We'll make an anonymous call once we're out of here.'

As they passed through the wrought iron gates, Christiano noticed the words *Dei Verbum* embossed on the gates. 'Word of God,' he mumbled.

'What?' said Angelica.

'Nothing.'

Frya and Kurush, who were parked opposite the estate, rushed out of their vehicle. Frya looked eagerly behind them for Johan. She grabbed Angelica's shoulders and shook her. 'Where's Johan?'

Kurush pulled her away and clung to her tightly, all the while his gaze on Christiano, who shook his head gravely.

Frya collapsed in her father's arms, howling Johan's name.

Her father picked up her limp body and carried her to the car.

Christiano opened the passenger door, and Kurush sat her down. He grabbed a bottle of water from the floor, drenched his handkerchief and dabbed her forehead as she continued wailing.

Don Primo's white Mercedes passed through the gates and stopped. Benito called for Angelica. 'You'd better leave before someone calls the police.'

'We're leaving in a second,' she replied. 'Benito, you look after your wife and child, okay?'

He took her hand and kissed it. 'You be careful and if you need anything, call me.'

'I will.' She stared at him for a moment. 'You won't go back to your old ways, will you?'

'I don't know what has happened to me, but I'm not that man anymore. It's as if the veil of lies has been lifted from my eyes and I now know who I truly am.'

'Where will you go?'

'After I've helped Don Primo's wife, I'll take my family and leave the country. I don't know, maybe a Greek island for a while. Can we come with you and help the Messiah?'

'If our paths cross again, we'll see, but for now, go to your family.'

'Can I ah…feel the baby one last time?'

She nodded and placed his hand on her belly.

He breathed in as a rush of peace coursed through his body. He leaned in and kissed her bump. 'Thank you,' he said. 'You saved my life.'

'Benito, one last question. I tried calling Enzo. Is he…'

Benito dropped his head. 'Don Primo realised he was helping you. I'm sorry.'

Tears streaked her cheeks as she watched the Mercedes pull away.

Christiano came to her side. 'Are you okay?'

'It's Enzo. Don Primo killed him.' She burst into tears.

'I'm sorry.' He hugged her tightly against his chest until her tears reduced to a whimper. She looked up at him through sorrowful eyes.

He gently wiped her tears. 'You want to tell me what happened with Don Primo? Why the change? How?'

'We had an argument, and I was so angry I slapped him. He told me he was going to kill the baby and made a fist to punch my belly. As his hand came towards me, it was as if it hit a force field that rebounded towards him. He flew back, hit the door and was momentarily stunned. Then he burst into tears and begged my forgiveness.'

'And Benito?'

'During the process, Don Primo grabbed his arm and he felt it, too. These two hardened men crying like babies.'

'We should leave,' called out Kurush.

As they drove away, the plush house disappeared down the unsuspecting street as if the horrors within it were a work of fiction. They were completely exhausted, and Frya's sobs lay heavy on their hearts.

Angelica placed her hand on her shoulder.

'Did you see him?' asked Frya, turning to Christiano.

'I did. I'm sorry. He was in a bad way. There was nothing I could do.'

She let out a whimper as fresh tears spilled down her cheeks. 'Did he speak to you?'

'We were alone for a short while, and he had lost…' he struggled to speak '…a lot of blood. He didn't think he was going to make it. He said, "Tell Frya I love her and not to worry because the Messiah came to me and told me my work was done. That death does not exist, and the feeling is like passing through a dark doorway and being greeted by the sun." An hour later, he was dead. Although Don Primo fired the gun, it wasn't what killed him. He died from his wounds.'

✦ Chapter Forty-Three ✦

A solitary police car stood out like a blemish on the plush, pebbled driveway of the Cardinal's palatial home. Botticelli's modest woman watched through lofty eyes as water flowed from the shell in which she stood, leaving not a spot of her mildewed skin dry.

A uniformed officer left the premises and entered the driver's side of the car, while a plainclothes detective stood at the door.

The androgynous woman, her short, coal-coloured hair slicked back with handfuls of gel, spoke in a husky voice. 'Thank you for your co-operation, Hans.' Fresh mint masked the stale odour of cigarettes lingering on her breath as she spoke. 'However, I will need the Cardinal to confirm that he has been away since yesterday morning?'

'I will inform His Eminence, but he won't be back until this evening. He is currently in meetings with His Holiness. I cannot interrupt him.'

The detective opened her notebook and scrutinised her own rushed scribbles through large orbicular eyes. 'So just you and your wife were here all day and night. Gertrude, is her name?'

'Yes. She is the house cook. She's shopping at present.'

'I will need her to visit me at the station to confirm your story.'

'Of course. She will do her moral duty,' replied Hans.

'Also, have His Eminence call me at this number.' She handed him a card. 'I will pay him another visit at his convenience, of course. I just need him to reiterate your story so that I may close this absurd inquiry.'

The butler nodded and took the card. 'Is it okay if my wife makes a statement when you visit His Eminence? To save her a trip to the station?'

'That'll be fine,' she said with a nod.

Hans shut the door and walked across the hallway, through the lengthy corridor, and into the Cardinal's study where he approached a bookcase towards the back of the room. He balanced on the tips of his toes as he reached up to the top shelf and pulled the first book downwards. He repeated the process with the last book from the bottom shelf. The bookcase swung open, and a hand wrapped in a white bandage grasped the doorway followed by the body to which it belonged.

'Did they look convinced?'

'Yes, Your Eminence, but the detective insisted you call her to arrange another day when she may call upon you. She would like you to confirm the story so that she can close the inquiry. She called it an *absurd* inquiry, Your Eminence.'

The Cardinal's mouth curved like a sickle. 'Well, I am a

man of God, after all.'

'Indeed you are, Your Eminence.' He walked to the Cardinal's desk and placed the detective's card on the table. 'At your convenience, Your Eminence.'

'Is it time for my brandy?' He winced as he stretched his bandaged hand.

Hans looked at his watch. 'It is, Your Eminence. I will fetch it now.'

'Make it a double, today.'

'As you wish, Your Eminence.' Hans bowed his head and left the room.

The Cardinal returned to the secret chamber and made his way across the irregular stone floor to the centre of the room, where he took a seat by a desk almost identical to the one in his study. The surrounding walls were formed from coarse stone, and hanging on one side was a portrait of the man himself sitting in the Pope's throne. His smile was unable to disguise the nefarious pucker in his lips and the greed in his eyes. A four-poster bed with a wine-coloured quilt embroidered with gold thread was to the left of the portrait. He pulled open the central drawer of the desk, retrieved a cell phone and hit the speed-dial button. There were seven rings followed by a monotone beep. 'I have a message from God,' he said before ending the call.

Moments later, the cell phone's rings echoed through the room. The Cardinal answered, saying nothing.

'What is God's message?' said a gruff voice.

'Kristoff. I am glad you are well. There is always slight trepidation when I call on your services.'

'Your Eminence, it is with your prayers and blessings that I remain in this world. I am sure of it. How may I be of service?'

'I need you to locate some people who, well, let's just say they need to be eliminated from the entire planet. I made the grave mistake of enlisting the services of another. But he was not of your calibre. I know you will not fail me.'

'Your Eminence, as always, you can rely on me. Tell me more about these people.'

'They are all sinners against God, but one, in particular, is like the other harlots you disposed of. However, she has proved to be the most resourceful and dangerous. Do not let your guard down.'

'Dangerous how, Your Eminence?'

'She has bewitching powers that I have experienced first-hand and never seen the likes of before. And she has followers who would risk their lives for her. I have no doubt that she has fornicated with the devil himself and her life must be ended before the beast comes to full term.'

'Your Eminence, please offer your prayers for my protection against this beast, and bless this killing as an offer to our almighty creator.'

'That I will, Kristoff. That I will. Her followers will be easier to locate, and where you find them, you will find her. The details I have are for a Frya and Kurush Attar…'

✦ Chapter Forty-Four ✦

S unlight streamed through partly open blinds. But its penetrating warmth proved futile against the cold barren room where Angelica and Christiano lay in each other's arms. Christiano's wide, tortured eyes drilled through the clinically white ceiling. His battered face had marginally improved, and his head and nose were bandaged. Angelica lay asleep, neatly tucked into his side. A vision of Johan with his missing fingers flashed across his mind's eye. He shuddered, waking Angelica.

She balanced herself on one elbow and gazed at him, attentively. 'I thought if I slept next to you the baby would comfort you,' she said.

'I can't stop myself picturing Johan's last hours. All that suffering. For us.'

'No, Christiano. For the Messiah.'

'Why did you come? Why did you risk your life and the baby's?'

'This again? I have told you, already.'

'It was a serious risk and it could have ended with both

your deaths. Don't do that again Angelica. You and the baby come first. Do you understand?'

'I couldn't let you die…'

'If Don Primo hadn't had that enlightened moment we would all be dead.'

'Well, it's clear God had other plans.'

'That doesn't mean we take crazy chances.'

A light rap at the door ended their heated discussion.

Christiano rose from the bed and opened the door. Kurush stood there.

'I'm about to finalise some plans for our trip,' he said.

'Is Frya okay?' asked Christiano.

Kurush shook his head. 'She's in a lot of pain. The problem is that my own sorrow prevents me from being the rock she needs right now. Johan was like a son to me. We were his only family, and I let him down. The blame for his death lies with me.'

'You mustn't think that way Kurush. Believe me, Johan did not leave this world blaming anyone. He spoke only for his love for you both.'

He nodded, wiping the tears from his eyes. 'When I'm back we'll discuss the arrangements over dinner.'

'Okay, my friend. Be careful.'

Kurush nodded and walked away with his head still bowed in sorrow.

Christiano watched him, helpless to offer any more comforting words.

Angelica nuzzled herself against his back and wrapped her arms around his waist.

He turned to her. 'You're still frowning.' He kissed her lips.

'I feel so guilty that I'm glad you weren't the one killed. I don't know how to be with this feel—' She stopped, noticing Frya peering round the door. Her arms dropped from around Christiano's waist and she stepped away from him.

'Frya, can I get you anything?' Her cheeks burned.

'Where's my father?'

'He went to finalise the plans for our trip to Egypt. Is everything okay?' asked Christiano.

She looked from one to the other and walked away.

Roasted garlic and rosemary sailed through the apartment adding a much-needed homeliness to the dispassionate ambience of their temporary hideout. Kurush, Angelica and Christiano dished segments of garlic bread and portions of pasta and salad onto their plates.

'Do you think Frya will join us?' asked Angelica.

'I doubt it,' replied Kurush. 'She has lost her appetite, and she clearly wants to be alone.'

'I'll take this to her,' said Angelica, leaving the room with a plate of food. She knocked apprehensively on Frya's door.

There was no reply.

'Frya!'

Only the sounds from the salle à manger echoed through the corridor.

'I have a plate of food for you. We're having dinner if you care to join us.'

On the other side of the door, Frya sat in a chair staring out of a large oval window designed like a fish-eye lens. A distorted Rome curved towards her as if enveloping her in its concrete armour. A memory filtered through to her mind. In that very same room, on a visit to their friends' for dinner, they looked out for the first time through the oval window. Johan made faces between a gap in the pane of glass. She heard the echo of her giggle and saw him grab her in his arms and kiss her. The passion of their love ran through her body, giving her butterflies.

'I've never met anyone like you,' said Johan.

'And you never will,' she replied with a cheeky grin.

Their stares lingered as they exchanged numerous expressions. Each and every thought and trepidation flashed across their faces.

'Doctor Frya Attar, your love is as vital as the blood that flows through my veins and the air I breathe.'

'Wow! That's pretty special.'

'I know you're not one for public displays of affection, but we're alone here. You can let your guard down. Give him the night off.'

'Have you forgotten we're guests here? They'll be wondering where we've got to.'

'Frya, I want to spend the rest of my life with you.'

'Is that a marriage proposal in front of this crazy view of Rome?'

He knelt down on one knee and looked up at her. 'Yes.' He gulped in a moment of insecurity.

She caught the momentary flicker in his pupils and

dismissed it immediately. 'Well, Doctor Frya Attar-Asper certainly has an interesting ring to it.'

'I've never been so serious.'

Her face betrayed a glint of vulnerability. She dropped to her knees where her loving gaze met his. 'Johan Asper, I will marry you.'

'You will!?' His mouth burst into a beaming smile. He kissed her hard on the lips.

She placed her arms around his neck. 'I know I can be emotionally detached. I don't know how you put up with me. But if I allowed my heart to rule over my head, I would never have survived as a doctor.'

He gently rubbed his nose against hers. 'I wouldn't have you any other way.'

They kissed before the oval window as the concaving buildings wrapped around them like creeping ivy, imprisoning them inside, and crudely snatching the image from her mind.

The tears rolled down her cheeks. The finger bearing her engagement ring jerked upwards involuntarily.

Angelica let out a sigh and walked away. 'Maybe she's asleep,' she said as she entered the dining room. She placed Frya's plate on the table and covered it with a napkin.

'She'll come around, eventually. Hopefully, our trip to Egypt and our mission will help to alleviate some of the grief, if not distract her from it. It will give her a much-needed reason to carry on with her life. After all, she is to deliver the Messiah,' said Kurush.

'I am so relieved it will be Frya and not some stranger,' said Angelica.

'Nevertheless, you must be nervous,' replied Kurush.

Christiano placed his hand over hers. 'I will not leave your side. I promise.'

She squeezed his hand. 'Are you sure Frya still wants to be involved? This mission has led to the death of her fiancé and...'

'I raised the question with her last night. She has no doubt,' said Kurush. 'She would not dishonour Johan's memory by abandoning everything he worked for and all he endured for the past three years, and especially his last hours.'

'His sacrifice will not be forgotten,' said Christiano.

Kurush stared through the table. 'I'll never forget the day he walked into my classroom. He was a student of mine, you know. Within a month he became my assistant. Such a keen, astute young man with a natural, deep perception of my teachings. When he and Frya met, it was like old lovers coming together.' He looked down to hide his moistened eyes. 'That reminds me. If you'll excuse me for a moment.' He rose from his seat and left the room.

Christiano squeezed Angelica's hand. 'A penny for your thoughts.'

'I don't know. I want to understand that everything happens for a reason, but...'

'Moosh-am!' Kurush's voice sounded from the corridor.

They turned to see Frya standing at the door.

Kurush appeared behind her holding Jannara's box. He

placed his arm around her. 'Please sit down and eat with us.'

'Okay, Papa.' She patted his hand.

With a look of relief, he led her to a seat. 'You'll need your strength for this journey of ours.' He reached for her plate and placed it before her.

Frya's gaze drifted to the family heirloom. 'What are you doing with Jannara's box?'

'I was about to give it to Angelica as a gift.'

'I can't accept it,' interrupted Angelica. Her guilty eyes fell on Frya. 'It should be passed to Frya. It has been in your family for two millennia…'

'No,' said Kurush. 'It ends with me. It should be returned to the Messiah.'

Angelica's questioning eyes remained on Frya.

'He's right. It belongs to the Messiah. Please accept it.'

'Thank you,' she said, brushing the etched spiral design on the lid. 'It's beautiful. To think it was handcrafted so long ago, and to reach us here at this moment in time.'

Kurush nodded. 'I have felt the same for as long—'

'What happened to Johan's body?' interrupted Frya.

The room fell silent.

Christiano lowered his head before looking her in the face. 'All I saw was them taking his body away. I don't know what happened to him.'

'The furnace,' said Frya. 'Johan told me the Cardinal has a furnace in the basement. Didn't you hear the sounds?'

'I heard many sounds. I was disoriented and…'

'Frya, you can see what Christiano has been through,' interrupted Kurush.

'I'm sorry. I'm not blaming you. I told him not to go back to that place, but he didn't listen. They cremated him, and I have nothing. No ashes, no way of giving him a proper burial.'

'I said a prayer for him,' said Christiano. It was just after he gave me the message to pass on to you. Then, I prayed again when they took his body away.'

'Thank you, Christiano. I'm glad he was not alone. Will you say something now?' she asked.

'Of course. It would be my honour.'

They all stood up and bowed their heads.

'This is a prayer from the Book of Wisdom,' he said. He cleared his throat. '*The souls of the virtuous are in the hands of God, no torment shall ever touch them. In the eyes of the unwise, they did appear to die, their going looked like a disaster, their leaving us, like annihilation; but they are in peace. If they experienced punishment as men see it, their hope was rich with immortality; slight was their affliction, great will their blessings be. God has put them to the test and proved them worthy to be with him; he has tested them like gold in a furnace and accepted them as a holocaust. When the time comes for His visitation, they will shine out; as sparks run through the stubble, so will they. They shall judge nations, rule over peoples, and the Lord will be their king forever. They who trust in him will understand the truth, those who are faithful will live with him in love; for grace and mercy await those he has chosen.*'

He made the sign of the cross and continued, 'Brother Johan, go in peace to the Lord and know that you are loved and honoured for your service to Him. May your Spirit live in eternal bliss, and your light shine upon Frya so that she may sense your presence and so that it may be of comfort to her. You are missed, you are loved, and you are cherished by all in this room. Rest in peace, my brother. Rest in peace… Amen.'

'Amen,' resounded through the room.

Tears rolled down Frya's cheeks. 'Thank you, Christiano. That was beautiful.'

He nodded as he rubbed the corners of his moistened eyes.

'Yes. Thank you,' repeated Kurush.

They took their seats and for a few moments soaked in the peaceful ambience evoked by the prayer. Frya's food remained untouched, but her face had grown a healthier shade. Kurush comfortingly rubbed the top of her shoulder. She smiled at him.

'Christiano, your prayer has had a healing effect on us all, I think. You must have been a great priest,' said Kurush.

Christiano smiled, and Angelica caught a glimpse of sorrow in his pupils. 'Are you both religious?' he asked, changing the subject.

'Our ancestors in Jannara's time were of the Zoroastrian faith. Today, there are probably about two hundred thousand Zoroastrians in the entire world. Frya and I prefer to remain detached from any religion, but we are not without God.'

'Yes, it seems quite the opposite, in fact,' said Christiano.

'Even as a child, I saw religion and God as polar opposites. I found religion too rigid and easily misinterpreted and manipulated by egocentric minds. One's connection to God is an intimate affair.'

'I completely agree,' replied Christiano. 'My faith remains, but my perspective has changed. Even though I have not been officially laicised, I could no longer remain in the priesthood.'

Angelica's head shot up.

'Yet look at what God himself has chosen for you,' said Kurush. 'Something more profound and worthy than you could imagine.'

'Yes. At first, it felt like a punishment. Now I see that I have been truly honoured.'

'As have we all. Too many of us misinterpret our disillusionment and lack of fulfilment as having not gathered enough wealth, or love, or the career we wanted. We search and strive for more and more, feeling ever less fulfilled. What we fail to realise is that all our longing, grief and yearning is for our return to the source – to God. But it's like running around searching for a limb that's already attached to our body. Our connection was never lost. Our problem is that we are too fearful to feel – perhaps from lifetimes of feeling forsaken by God – to delve deep and take even just a few seconds to feel His presence within us. It's a great shame that our fear and disconnection only perpetuates the selfish, destructive and superficial world in which we live.'

'I am in total agreement,' replied Christiano. 'At the seminary, I was taught that I was the vessel by which a parishioner could connect with God. That only the chosen are holy in God's eyes. That the word of God flows through our sacred lips. Our hierarchal system puts men like the Cardinal in positions that only help to keep the masses at a distance from God and under the control of the so-called *chosen ones*. The contradictions never end. Yet, on the other hand, a vessel – and not necessarily a priest – is maybe what some people need. I do feel that a healthy mind is better able to differentiate between the true and the false voice of God. Otherwise, you have those with sociopathic tendencies claiming that God has told them to commit murder.'

'Yes, but as with the Cardinal, the message will be as corrupted as the vessel from which it comes,' interjected Angelica. 'The point is that any human vessel is open to corruption and misinterpretation.'

'It's a complicated matter,' said Kurush. 'People claim that the truth is subjective, but not God's truth. God's truth is the ultimate truth and is not easily interpreted by human minds ruled by the ego.'

'Exactly,' said Angelica. 'It's our egos that get in the way. It's the ego that misinterprets; that's prone to madness and disillusionment. I think a healthy mind is one that is aware of its ego and learns to observe it, hear it, and ignore its neurotic patterns. Then the voice of truth can enter.'

'Yet it's the ego that runs the world,' replied Christiano. 'You only have to look at politics and religion to see the chaos and destruction inflicted upon the planet and its inhabitants.'

'People controlled by the false self and thinking they are living authentically. All the decisions made, not just on a small scale but decisions that affect us all,' replied Kurush.

'You only need to look at the state of the world to see the danger of the ego interpreting the Holy Scriptures of *all* the religions,' said Christiano.

'It's the definition of madness,' said Angelica.

'And perhaps a subject on which the Messiah will be able to shed some light for us soon,' said Kurush. 'Which takes us to the next phase of our mission. I have finalised the plans for our trip. We travel by cargo ship, tomorrow.'

'So soon?' said Christiano.

'I assumed you were ready to leave straight away.'

'Yes, of course. It's fine. I'm still getting used to the idea. I don't travel well on the ocean.'

'Ah, yes, your travel sickness. Perhaps, some motion sickness pills will help. The ship will take us to Greece where I have arranged fake passports for us, and from there we will take a normal passenger ferry to Cyprus, and from there on to Egypt.'

'And you are sure this cargo ship is secure?' asked Angelica.

'Yes, the captain is a close friend of mine. His cook, a Greek man, has a cousin who works for port customs in Greece. The cook has arranged for us to enter the country unseen. He has also arranged the fake passports. We need to take photos this evening so that I can hand them to him on board the ship.'

'What time are we leaving?' asked Christiano.

'The taxi is picking us up at dawn. I will pop out this evening and get your pills.'

Christiano nodded, appreciatively.

The Cardinal sat on an oversized sofa in his study, sipping brandy and reading from an antiquated book. A phone rang and buzzed in his vicinity. He reached into his pocket, withdrew his cell phone and accepted the call, and then placed it on the coffee table by his side.

'Your Eminence,' came the gruff voice.

'Kristoff, as always, a speedy return call. What do you have for me?'

'There has been no activity from their cell phones or their landline. In fact, there's no one at home. They're in hiding. The only lead is from phone records which point to a shipping company and suggests they are leaving the country.'

'I suppose that doesn't surprise me. Do you have anything more concrete?'

'The latest call was received from a pay phone earlier today. By then I had bugged the shipping company's phone and managed to catch the details. There is a cargo ship leaving for Greece tomorrow. They'll all be on it.'

'Greece, you say. Whatever for?' Perplexed, he rubbed his head and gazed into oblivion.

'Your Eminence, I suggest that the best way for their elimination is on this ship.'

'And how will you secure a position on this vessel?'

'Your Eminence, it is already done.'

'Well done, Kristoff.' He smirked. 'I won't ask how you managed it.'

'It is best you remain blissfully unaware, Your Eminence.'

'You understand that it's imperative their feet never land

on Greek soil, don't you? I cannot stress this enough, Kristoff.'

'Your Eminence, their bodies will make a hearty feast for our ocean inhabitants. You have my word.'

✦ Chapter Forty-Five ✦

O n the drive to the port, the air was stifled by a mishmash of feelings from grief, to fear and anxiety. All four of them ruminated with closed eyes or stared into oblivion.

Christiano's arm was wrapped around Angelica. The flashing scenery outside his window mimicked the speed at which his life seemed to be moving lately. She nestled into his chest like a purring kitten and shut her eyes. He kissed her forehead, and she smiled, her lids remaining shut.

'Ah, Christiano. I have your motion sickness pills,' said Kurush delving into his travel case. 'I forgot to give them to you at the apartment.'

Christiano took the box and examined the instructions.

'It's probably best you take one when we arrive at the port,' advised Frya, 'so that by the time we travel it will take effect. It's one tablet every six hours. And not more than three in twenty-four hours.'

'You have my gratitude,' said Christiano, placing the pills into his pocket.

Three hours later, the taxi pulled into the port. The sun's rays bedazzled the ocean, and the crisp, fresh air carried a strong hint of fish on the wind.

The nervous passengers alighted their vehicle, stopping for a moment to breathe in the captivating scenery. Christiano had already grown pale, with his nose buried in his sleeve. Angelica, who felt a little queasy, planted her hand into his pocket and removed the tablets. She handed him a pill.

'How long before these take effect?' he asked Frya, swallowing the pilule.

'About half an hour. I didn't realise you became sea sick *before* travelling.'

The taxi driver pulled away, leaving them and their luggage stranded amidst the bustling chaos of moving containers the size of buses, the droning of ships' horns and the cawing of seagulls. Behind them, mustard-coloured buildings with terracotta rooftops were heaped one upon the other in a seemingly haphazard fashion, as if one tremor would send them falling like a stack of dominoes.

'That's our ship, I think,' said Kurush pointing in the direction of a gargantuan vessel with the name *Colossus* scrawled along its side.

'An apt name,' said Christiano breaking into a sweat.

Kurush checked his watch. 'We'd better go and find Costantino. His office is in the building over there.' He pointed at a large, stone edifice, bountiful with rectangular windows lining each façade like a row of columns.

The four of them crossed the road and entered the

building, unaware that they were being watched through binoculars from the deck of the *Colossus*.

The watcher, a man of short stature with broad shoulders and legs like stumps of wood, dropped his hands to his sides to reveal extraordinarily large and nebulous pupils that left little room for the whites of his eyes. A zigzagging scar ran from his ear, across his right cheek and to his nose.

Minutes later, Christiano and his companions left the building with one more added to their number, Captain Costantino. They piled their luggage onto the back of a buggy parked close by and hopped on. With Captain Costantino in the driver's seat, they made their way towards the *Colossus*.

The moment Christiano clambered aboard the vessel, his head plummeted into his stomach, and the world around him swayed in sync with the billowing sea.

'Are you okay?' asked the Captain, grabbing hold of his arm.

'Just a little seasick,' he replied, gripping onto the railings either side of him. His tremulous legs buckled as if supported by liquefying bones.

'We have motion sickness pills on board if you need them.'

'I've just taken one. It will take effect soon. I hope.'

The Captain nodded and continued, 'I will give you all a tour of the ship once we're cruising smoothly to our destination. But first, I will show you to your cabins.'

He opened a cream bulkhead door, and a rush of hot air infused with diesel torpedoed towards them.

Christiano gagged, gripping the side of the door.

'Do you need help?' asked Angelica.

'I'll be fine.'

'You don't look…'

'Please. I hate fuss.'

'Sometimes, it's okay to ask for help, Christiano.' She sighed. 'If you need me just ask.'

As they reached the bottom of the stairs, the wanly lit corridor narrowed to a claustrophobic degree.

'You have two cabins. Close to the stairs and exit. I thought that would suit you better. You can sort the sleeping arrangements amongst yourselves.'

'Thank you, my friend,' said Kurush, slapping the Captain's shoulder in appreciation.

'Why don't you drop your bags and I'll introduce you to the Greek. You can stay for refreshments whilst I make my last checks before we set sail.'

'I think I had better stay here until the tablet takes effect,' said Christiano.

'I'll stay with you,' said Angelica.

'No. Please. You go. You should have a snack and a drink.'

Angelica nodded, and the three of them followed the Captain along a putrid green floor, towards the mess hall.

Herculean in stature and with skin as bronzed as a statue, the Greek was a hazel-eyed man with wild, dark blonde hair that continued to his face to form a beard. 'Captain!' he called out with a voice as deep as a horn.

'Achilleus,' said the captain, 'these are the guests we

spoke of. My dearest friend Kurush, his lovely daughter Frya, and their friend Angelica.'

'Welcome,' he said, holding out his arms in a grand gesture. 'I thought there were four of you?'

'There is, but our friend doesn't sail well. He is resting,' said Kurush.

'Do you have something for me?'

'Ah, yes,' replied Kurush, dipping into his pocket and retrieving a white envelope. 'The photos are in here.'

Achilleus took the envelope.

'I gather you have already received our, ah, gratitude,' said Kurush.

'Yes, thank you. I was very grateful.' He winked and smiled at Kurush. 'Please, there are refreshments on the table over there. My hospitality is the Greek way. Everything in excess.'

'I thought that was the Italian way,' said the Captain.

'No, you got it from us!'

They both chuckled. 'You can see what it's like around here,' said the Captain. 'The Greek and Italian war! I only let him get away with it because he's an excellent chef.'

'Of course. I'm Greek!'

They laughed.

'I must leave you if we are to set sail on time,' said the Captain. He nodded and made his departure.

As the ship progressed on its journey to Greece, Angelica and Christiano shared a single bunk in their Spartan cabin. Angelica awoke to see a contemplative Christiano staring at the gold, amethyst ring around his finger. A minute, ornate gold cross was embedded in the centre of the amethyst stone. He turned and twisted the ring as if it might reveal a secret. 'Does that ring have a story?' she asked.

'This ring was given to me by my mentor, Father Guido, when I was ordained. It means as much to me as my grandfather's knife.'

'It's beautiful. Is he the priest who died recently?'

'Yes. Back in my home town. He was a special man.'

'I have never seen a ring with a gold cross fixed into the stone like that. He must have had it made especially for you.'

'He did,' said Christiano removing the ring and turning it over. 'You can see the inscription. "For Christiano, the follower of Christ."'

Angelica narrowed her eyes and looked closely at the words. 'He loved you dearly.'

'The feeling was mutual.' He placed the ring back on his finger.

'And how are you feeling? You seem much better,' said Angelica.

'I should be concerned about you. I feel embarrassed about this sickness. It stems from a rebellion against my father. I am sure.'

'He wanted you to be a fisherman.'

'He did, and I knew from the first moment of consciousness that I did not. But yes, I'm feeling surprisingly well.'

'Good.' She kissed his lips.

'And how are you feeling about this journey to a foreign land to have your baby?'

'I was concerned about having the baby in the desert, but if Frya will be there, and you, and it's God's wish, then I'm sure it'll be fine.'

'I will hold your hand throughout. There is no need for you to fear anything when I'm with you. You know that, right?'

'That's exactly how you make me feel – safe and secure.' She kissed him again. 'But…'

'What?'

'It's just that there was a moment last night when Kurush said that you would have made a great priest.'

'And?'

'I saw a glint of regret in your eyes. I don't want to take you away from something you love.'

'Yes, but did you hear what I said after? That with everything that's happened, I could no longer remain in the priesthood.'

'I did, but I just wanted to make sure. That's all.'

Christiano placed his hands on her belly. 'You, the Messiah and me. In a million years, I could never have imagined this gift I have been given.'

A look of relief washed over her face. 'I feel the same.'

A clanging knock on metal sounded through the door, followed by a tinny voice. 'We're going to lunch. Are you coming?' asked Kurush.

They looked at each other.

'Actually, I'm starving,' said Angelica.

'We're coming,' called out Christiano.

The mess hall was a hullabaloo of boisterous crewmen, most of whom were familiar with each other.

The four of them dined with the Captain from pressed wooden trays on bolted-down Formica tables, oblivious of the man who sat quietly among the crew, studying their every movement.

'There's certainly more colour to your cheeks, Christiano,' said the Captain.

'Yes. It seems I have found my feet.'

'Well, if you're able to eat you're doing very well... How about I give you all a tour of the bridge after lunch. I have a bit of time?'

'Actually, I'm going back to the cabin,' said Frya.

'What about you three?'

Kurush looked at Christiano and Angelica for confirmation. 'Sounds good,' he replied.

They finished their lunch with small talk and laughter and later entered the funnelled corridor to embark on their tour of the ship.

'Are you sure you won't join us, Moosh-am?'

'I'm not a baby anymore, Papa.' She headed back to her cabin without another word.

'Maybe I should go with her,' said Angelica.

'No. Clearly, she wants to be alone. She is much better since Christiano's prayer, but one little thing may trigger a memory, and she plummets again.'

'Time is the friend of grief,' said Christiano. 'It also selects the sweetest memories.'

The oval bridge with its cockpit-style window faced a transparent sky and a halcyon sea that shimmered like a galaxy of stars. The interior lacked the outdoor splendour – the floor painted with the same putrid green that appeared throughout the ship. Two crewmen stood to attention when the Captain entered.

'As you were,' he said.

The first mate sat back down in his chair facing the navigational instruments and out to sea. Bleeping sonar devices and screens displaying automatic radar plotting, tracking aids and electronic chart displays all added to the layman's confusion.

Angelica looked at the screens and out to sea. 'Is it okay if I go out on deck? I've never sailed before, and it looks beautiful.'

'Of course,' replied the Captain, 'but please stay close to the bridge.'

'I'll join you in a moment,' said Christiano.

Their hands parted with reluctance, and Angelica made her way onto deck where she found a secluded spot away from the prying eyes of the bridge.

She took in the sights around her with the splendour of a child's eye, made a deep inhalation and leaned against the railings with closed eyes. The blustery wind welcomed her like a lover's embrace.

'Hello.' The gruff voice came from behind her.

She turned to the sound and was immediately taken aback by large, nebulous eyes and a zigzagging scar running across the man's cheek. 'H…ell…o.'

'Beautiful, isn't it?'

'Yes, it is,' she responded politely and turned back to the scenery.

Kristoff made a quick scan of the empty deck and narrowed the gap between them.

Sensing his closeness, she turned to face him, swallowing the lump in her throat.

The man smiled and dug his hand into his pocket.

She gulped, feeling a crippling numbness swarm her body.

'Would you like some gum?' he said, pulling out a packet of spearmint gum.

She relaxed and smiled. 'Yes, thank you.' She took a stick.

'Can you see over there?' He pointed. 'That's the direction of Greece.'

She followed the line of his pointed finger out to sea and was temporarily distracted as he surreptitiously removed a small dagger from his inside pocket. Keeping it hidden beneath his gilet, he drew closer still. The blade caught the flash of the sun.

Angelica continued to face the ocean. 'How long have you been sailing?'

Kristoff could not reply, his face was a mass of contorted confusion. He looked down at his trembling hand, trying with all his strength to plunge the dagger into her flesh and end her life.

'Crewman!' called the Captain.

Kristoff shoved the knife back into his pocket and turned to the voice.

'Don't you have work to do?'

The man nodded with a defiant glint in his black eyes and sauntered off without a word.

The Captain's gaze followed him with suspicion. 'Are you okay?' he asked Angelica.

'Yes, he just offered me gum and showed me the way to Greece.'

'I think he was a little taken with our Angelica,' said Kurush.

'If he approaches you again tell him to leave you alone. I like to know my crew, but he was sprung upon me only last night, recommended by one of my longstanding crewmen who had a bad accident doing some DIY work at home. The man sounded half dead. Apparently, he may lose a limb… Anyway, I must be off. It seems I have some unexpected arrangements to make.' He winked at Christiano as he left.

'I'll go and check on Frya,' said Kurush, leaving.

Angelica noticed Christiano's guilty face. 'What's going on?'

'Oh, nothing. I just asked the Captain to marry us tonight, that's all.'

'What?'

He cupped her face in his hands and kissed her tenderly. 'I want to make this real. I cannot spend another moment without you as my wife. Will you do me the honour of spending the rest of your life with me?'

She stared into his questioning eyes as tears welled in hers. 'I never thought I would hear those words from anyone's lips.'

'Why not?'

'Because of the life I've led.'

'Why would you think such a thing? Until you came along, I had never felt anything for any woman.'

'Everything seems to have changed overnight. It's…wonderful. I have a family.'

'Then your answer is *yes*?'

She nodded eagerly, too choked to speak, and buried her head in his chest. 'Wait!' She looked up at him. 'Does the Captain have the proper licence to marry us? I don't want to discover years down the line that we are not legally wed.'

Christiano laughed. 'You think of everything, don't you? It just so happens he used to captain cruise ships where he performed marriage ceremonies all the time.'

'Then yes, yes, yes!' she announced, swooping her lips towards his for a lingering kiss.

Kristoff watched them from a distance. He knew little of the people he had been sent to eliminate, and for the first time in his life, an ominous feeling smouldered in the pit of his belly. The Cardinal was right. Something was different, and it made him uneasy.

✦ Chapter Forty-Six ✦

'I don't want you to go to any trouble.'

'It's no trouble at all,' replied Frya, unsettling the contents of her suitcase. 'Ah. Here it is.' She pulled out a creamy coloured tea-length dress and held it up for Angelica to see. 'This is perfect.'

'It's exquisite,' said Angelica closely examining the lace fabric. She held it against her body. 'Where's it from?'

'Johan bought it for me from a fifties vintage fair.' Her voice choked back tears. 'Although I'll have little use for it in the desert, I couldn't leave it behind. And now look. Who would have guessed we would need it?'

'I can't wear it.' Angelica placed it on the bed.

'Why not?'

'It's too precious. What if it was ruined? I would never forgive myself.'

'I can hear Johan's voice in my head right now, saying, "It would be an honour for Angelica to wear it." Please honour his memory by wearing this dress.'

Angelica's eyes filled with tears. 'If you're sure and

completely okay with this then it would be a privilege to wear it.'

They embraced like sisters.

'I want to thank you for everything you've done. Everything you've sacrificed for the baby and me,' said Angelica.

'Well, if it wasn't for the prophecy,' Frya joked, tearfully.

'I'm glad that destiny brought us together.'

'It's an honour beyond imagining.' Frya wiped the tears from her eyes.

'Despite what it has cost you? I'm not sure I could be as forgiving.'

'This is in my blood, but it was not in Johan's. When we finally trusted him enough to tell him of the prophecy, he begged my father to let him join us. It took two months before my father agreed. He said to him, "Johan, you must be willing to die for this. Otherwise, it is not for you. Take a week to think about it and make sure your answer is an unequivocal *yes* before you commit." He didn't hesitate.'

'If it were not for all his work, you may never have found me.'

'His help was exactly what we needed. He was guided to us, and it was clear it was his destiny, too. I will never forget him.' She wiped away her last tear and smiled. 'Now, let's get you ready.'

Before an alpenglow blaze, Captain Costantino, Kurush and Christiano waited on the top deck for Angelica's arrival.

'It would be impossible to capture a more perfect *mise en*

scène,' said Kurush, admiring the scenery.

Christiano, dressed in black trousers and a white shirt, smiled faintly as he fiddled with his tie. A light perspiration had formed on his forehead and his dilated pupils exhaled a palpable tension. Every few seconds his gaze turned to Kurush, who chuckled and eyed him like a proud father.

The bulkhead door swung open and the first mate stepped out, stopped and waited.

Frya was the first to exit. She walked to Christiano, kissed him on the cheek and stood to his left, nodding to the crewman.

The man peered back inside.

Seconds later, Angelica glided through the door as if on a cloud. Her silky black locks were tied up and away from her face. Frya had matched her hair and make-up to her fifties dress, finishing off with a touch of pearly pink lip gloss.

Christiano stood frozen, wearing the gaze of a man who could not believe his luck.

'Your beauty rivals the likes of Sophia Loren and Claudia Cardinale,' said Kurush as he reached her side. He kissed her cheeks.

'You flatter me.' She laced her arm through his. Together they walked the makeshift aisle towards an anxious Christiano who received her with a nervous tremble.

Captain Costantino cleared his throat. 'Before you are both joined together in marriage, it is my duty to remind you of the solemn and binding vows you are about to make. Marriage is for life, a union of two people to the exclusion of all others. Angelica, please repeat after me. *I do solemnly declare.*'

'*I do solemnly declare...*' She continued to repeat his words, '*...that I know not of any lawful impediment why I, Angelica De Santis, may not be joined in marriage to Christiano Umberto Abbadelli.*'

Christiano repeated the words. '*I do solemnly declare that I know not of any lawful impediment why I, Christiano Umberto Abbadelli, may not be joined in marriage to Angelica De Santis.*'

'I ask you now, Christiano Umberto Abbadelli, do you take Angelica De Santis to be your lawful wedded wife, to be loving, faithful and loyal to her for the rest of your lives together?'

'I do.' His voice was soft and his mesmerised expression mirrored in her pupils.

The question was repeated to Angelica. She stared at him with love-struck eyes as she affirmed, 'I do.'

'Now we move on to the formal vows of marriage... Christiano, you know the vows, would you like to say them?'

Christiano faced Angelica, savouring the moment like a fine wine. '*I call upon these persons here present to witness that I, Christiano Umberto Abbadelli, do take you, Angelica De Santis, to be my lawful wedded wife, to love, and to honour, and to cherish from this day forward.*'

She stared at him for a moment before repeating the vow. '*I call upon these persons here present to witness that I, Angelica De Santis, do take you, Christiano Umberto Abbadelli, to be my lawful wedded husband, to love, and to honour, and to cherish from this day forward.'*

'Now we seal the contract that you have just made by the exchanging of rings. The ring symbolises an unending and everlasting love between you both and a sign of the lifelong commitment and promise that you have made to each other.'

Kurush came forward with the rings.

Christiano's ecclesiastical ring rested in Kurush's palm, its shank circled with a mound of tape to decrease its size. He took it between quavering fingers and turned to face his bride. 'Angelica De Santis, I give you this ring as a symbol of my love for you.' He nervously slipped it onto her finger where it was a perfect fit. He sighed with relief.

She chuckled, feeling the tape with her thumb, her eyes moist with joy.

'I give you all that I am. And all that I have I willingly share with you. I promise to love you eternally and to be faithful and loyal to you through the difficult times and the best of times. May this ring be a constant reminder, a symbol of my words and the vow I have made to you today. Your arrival in my life has led me to my true destiny, and I will spend the rest of my life by your side, honouring you, loving you and taking care of you.'

Angelica took the heart-shaped ring, gifted to her by her parents, between her fingers. Its golden hue reflected the ebbing shimmer of sunlight. 'Christiano Umberto Abbadelli, I give you this ring as a symbol of my love for you.' She slipped it onto his finger, managing to get it midway across his fingernail. As the skin puffed around it, the image was greeted with laughter by all present.

She continued her vows with a smile in her voice. 'I give you all that I am. And all that I have I willingly share with you. I promise to love, cherish and honour you for the rest of my life. I promise to be faithful and loyal to you no matter what obstacles come our way. I give you this ring, a cherished memento from my parents, and I share this love with you as a token and a reminder of the vows I have made to you today. You have cast a ray of light and hope in my world, and I will cherish your love and your company for the rest of my life.'

'Today is the beginning of the rest of your lives together,' said Captain Costantino. 'May you have many happy and cherished years together. And in all those years may all your hopes, aspirations and dreams come to fruition. It is my honour to tell you both that you are now legally husband and wife. Congratulations!'

As the last echo of sunlight was swallowed by the darkness, Angelica reached her lips to Christiano's and the bond of marriage was sealed with a kiss.

The mess hall had been transformed into a room fit for a wedding. Ribbons and balloons hung from the walls and ceilings, and clean white tablecloths lined with red ribbon adorned the Formica tables. A hand-painted sign with the words *Just Married* was attached to the head table, and a three-tiered cake with creamy white frosting took centre stage.

The couple were greeted with a standing ovation by jovial

seamen who had not expected a wedding reception on a regular working sea voyage.

Christiano walked Angelica to their table. Her face was a priceless picture of surprise.

She hugged Captain Costantino and Achilleus. 'Words cannot express our gratitude.'

'Yes. Thank you. It is beyond our expectations,' said Christiano, vigorously shaking each man's hand.

For a few hours, the four of them forgot their troubles, their grief, their anxieties and their mission, as they tucked into their meals, sipped cheap champagne, and enjoyed hearty words and laughter with their new friends.

Angelica relished each moment. A mixture of disbelief and elation rushed through her veins as she looked round the room.

Her eyes were forced to stop on the man from the deck whose intense stare unnerved her.

'Mrs Abbadelli,' said Christiano with a look of utmost pride.

She turned to him smiling. 'Yes, my husband?'

He laughed and kissed her lips. 'This has to be the most surreal sight I have ever seen.'

'I was thinking just that.' She looked back at the man to see him chatting to another crewman.

'Is everything okay?'

She turned back to him. 'Better than I could have ever imagined.'

Their lips met again.

'You two save that for later,' said Kurush.

They chuckled.

'I'm sorry, it seems my father has had a little too much to drink,' said Frya, looking a little annoyed.

'A toast!' said Kurush rising from his seat and clinking the side of his glass.

The room fell silent.

'I have known Angelica and Christiano for a fraction of time, yet they are as intrinsically a part of my life as my own daughter. I am honoured to know them and to call them family. I am glad they found each other, and I am blessed to be a witness to their union. I am sure you will all agree what a handsome couple they make. Please join me in a toast to Angelica and Christiano.' He raised his glass. 'May they live an eternity in love.'

The room was filled with an unmelodious medley of cheers and the ringing and clanging of glasses and cups.

As the evening progressed, an inebriated Kurush made his rounds to every crew member in the room as if on a mission to share his exuberant laughter and nonsensical conversation. When he reached Kristoff, he slapped his shoulder and moved his face close to his. It was as if their alcohol-infused breaths formed a cloud. 'That is a bad scar you have, my friend. What happened?'

'I was attacked on my way home from work one evening, many years ago.'

'Did they catch the man who did it?'

'There were three of them, and they no longer breathe,' he replied with a wry smile.

Kurush stared at him for a moment. 'Ah!' He waved a

crooked finger at him. 'You're a funny man.'

Kristoff responded with laughter.

Kurush felt a tap on his shoulder and turned to see another drunk smiling crewman.

Kristoff surveyed his surroundings ensuring that each person was preoccupied with some activity or other, or too drunk to pay attention, and surreptitiously poured a clear liquid into the champagne glass in Kurush's hand.

The syrupy solution dispersed and blended with the fizz rising to the top of the glass.

'Drink up, my friend,' he said slapping him on the back.

Kurush chortled and downed the bubbly in one.

'You like your drink, ah?'

Kurush nodded, feeling light-headed. He wandered off and dropped to the nearest chair.

Kristoff's mouth formed a sardonic smile as he turned his attention to the object of his intention.

Christiano took the motion sickness pills from his pocket, removed one from the packet and placed the box on the table.

'You haven't had any alcohol have you?' asked Angelica.

'No, I thought it best not to mix the two.' He picked up his glass of water, about to take the pill when Frya's and Angelica's frowns caught his attention.

Kurush had risen from his seat, his face a sinister shade of red. He stumbled between men so intoxicated they could barely stand, his body stooped over as he clutched his stomach. He dropped to the floor.

The three of them rushed to his aid, the Captain following closely behind.

Frya felt her father's pulse. 'We'd better get him out of here.'

Christiano lifted Kurush like a weightless sack and propped him beneath his armpit. The captain took the slack on the other side, and together they carried him to his cabin and laid him on the bunker.

'These are not the symptoms of over-drinking. Something's wrong,' said Frya, as she crouched beside him.

'Could it be food poisoning?' asked Angelica.

'Food poisoning?' repeated the alarmed Captain.

'It can't be,' said Frya, shining a pocket light into her father's pupils, 'we all ate the same food.'

Kurush vomited, soiling her in the process.

Christiano gagged and dashed out of the room.

Angelica found him in the corridor; a light sweat on his forehead. 'I can't find my pills,' he said, frantically searching his pockets.

'You put the packet on the table, remember?'

'I'll go back and get them.'

'No. You had better go and lie down. I'll go.'

The mess hall was still a party, too many merry men making too much noise. What was at first a wonderful surprise had suddenly turned into a rowdy affair.

Kristoff saw Angelica enter the room and walk to the head table.

He downed his whisky while his hungry gaze followed her every movement.

Two drunk and blithesome crewmen unintentionally strolled into his line of sight.

He rose from his seat and bulldozed them aside, making his way towards her. 'Have you lost something?' His hot breath steamed the side of her face, and the waft of whisky unsettled her stomach.

She turned to find him inches from her. His nebulous eyes protruded like a dead fish.

'No, it's fine.' She visibly gulped, averted her eyes from his and headed straight for the door. She rushed back to her quarters, stealing glances behind her before stopping at Frya's door. The smell of vomit breezed towards her as she entered the cabin. 'Is there anything I can do?'

Kurush was markedly better, lying peacefully in bed, but his body was weak and wet with perspiration.

'I've given him an antiemetic,' said Frya. 'We'll see how he is through the night and in the morning.'

'Well, if you need anything, let me know. It seems that Christiano has lost his motion sickness pills. Will the antiemetic work for him?'

'It does help to relieve nausea, but it does little to prevent motion sickness. I'm sorry, I have nothing else.'

'Not to worry, we have a couple of packets on board,' said the Captain. 'I'll fetch them for you.' He left the room, leaving the two women alone.

'Are you okay?' asked Frya. 'You look terrified.'

'It's nothing. I'm sure.' She pressed her hand against her chest. 'I'm just concerned that both Kurush and Christiano are unwell, and there's this…'

'What?'

'This strange man paying me a lot of attention.'

'You're a beautiful woman. He probably likes you that's all.'

'Perhaps. It's just that everywhere I turn he seems to be there. Do you think the Cardinal could have found us?'

'I don't think so. We covered our tracks well.'

'So you think I'm just being paranoid?'

'After what we've all been through, I wouldn't rule it out, but even on a large ship you will see the same people in the communal areas.'

'You're right. I'm reading too much into this.'

'Well, there's nothing anyone can do tonight. When the Captain returns, you should mention it to him. At the very least, he will warn him off in the morning. In the meantime, let's keep our cabins locked.'

'Yes, I'll do that. Look, thanks again, for everything. The dress was beautiful. I will give it to you in the morning.'

'You wore it well,' replied Frya. 'You look stunning, and the ceremony was magical.'

They gave each other a hug and Angelica made her way next door to find that the smell in her cabin did not fare better.

Christiano's head was buried in the porthole.

'Is that helping?'

He turned to her, his face pallid and his eyes drooping and moist.

'You've been sick, haven't you?'

'In the sink. I cleaned it up as best I could. Do you have the pills?'

'I couldn't find them, but Captain Costantino is bringing you the ones they stock on board. Come, lie down here.'

By the time she helped him to the bunker, there was a knock at the door.

'Who's there?'

'Pietro, the first mate. The Captain sends his apologies, but he had to tend to a dispute between two crewmen.'

She opened the door, cautiously.

'The Captain sends his apologies, but it appears that our supply of motion sickness pills are missing.' The words squeezed through the tight gap in the door. 'He doesn't understand how when he filled the order himself. He promises to look into the matter in the morning. It's all madness and mayhem tonight. It's not usual that we have a wedding on board.' He smiled.

'Okay. Thank you, anyway.' She returned a polite smile and shut the door.

Christiano's bloodshot eyes tried to focus on her. 'There isn't any, is there?'

'No. It seems they have mysteriously vanished.'

'What are the chances?' His speech was now slurring.

'Exactly.' She pulled on the cabin door ensuring it was securely locked before removing her dress and carefully laying it out on the top bunk. She slipped on a long t-shirt and slid in next to Christiano.

'Let's try to get some sleep, okay.' She lay his head on her belly and gently stroked his hair. 'Hopefully, things will be better in the morning.'

He smiled, faintly, and weakly lifted his left hand in the

air and tried to remove Angelica's ring from his finger.

'Why are you taking it off?' she asked.

'I don't want to lose it. Please, help…'

Angelica gave the ring a few tugs before it finally relented. She slipped it back onto her little finger. 'Do you want your ring back?'

'No,' he murmured. 'Not until I buy you one in Greece… We had a good night, didn't we?' He smiled frailly, his eyes misty and unfocused.

'We did, but it's best you try and sleep,' she whispered gently.

'A great wedding,' he repeated as he drifted to sleep, making further mutterings about a bad wedding night.

✦ Chapter Forty-Seven ✦

In the pulsing heat of the engine room, the crewman's terror-filled eyes stared down in disbelief at the dagger protruding from his chest. Kristoff waited patiently for him to die. Examining his last moments through his caliginous eyes; watching the motions of his dying body with the eager curiosity of a savant. No one ever died in peace. He could write a book on the subject and draw from his extensive knowledge and experience as a professional assassin. It was his art. He had disposed of many, killing indiscriminately, savouring the high it gave him. He was like the Highlander after decapitating an immortal and gaining all his power. The intimacy of the blade far outweighed the gun's impersonal distance. He craved the feel of the person's flesh; the ice-cold prickle of the skin. He could be but an inch from his victim's eyes; a witness to his own reflection as the bringer of death – the Grim Reaper himself. The ecstasy he felt as the blade savagely ripped through the epidermis was his carnal pleasure.

Tears trickled down the man's cheeks. His agonised face

screamed soundlessly the pain he could not express.

Kristoff placed his ear close to the fading man's mouth. He lived for the last breath. It came as expected, a hiss, similar to the sound made when he would step on a snail shell as a child. He was fascinated by the hissing sound as the hermetically sealed home released all its air and sealed the fate of the snail.

The dead man's frozen eyes pictured the horror of his death.

Kristoff withdrew the knife, wiped the serrated blade on the man's shirt and checked the mirrored surface for remnants of blood. The face of a demon reflected back at him.

It was the early hours of the morning and most of the crew who were not on night shift were fast asleep in the comfort of their cabins. Most of them would be too drunk to respond to the shrill of an alarm. This poor soul was one of the lucky ones as far as Kristoff was concerned. The rest would die most likely in pain from the explosion – screaming in agony as they lost a limb or burned alive. Others would drown. Whichever way you looked at it, only he would get away. He would make sure of that.

He proceeded to plant the bomb to blast in thirty minutes' time and, as a precaution, set an emergency remote detonator on his cell phone. He left the deceased body and the monotonous drone of the engine room muffled behind the locked door and bounded up the clanging metal carcass of the ship's bowels, where another crew member, carrying two cups, stood waiting for him to pass.

'Are you taking Torin some coffee?' asked Kristoff.

'Yes, we're both on duty.'

'He wondered where you'd got to.'

The unsuspecting man continued past Kristoff who plunged the knife into his back, penetrating his heart with the precision of a surgeon. His back arched in a violent spasm. He hurtled forward, his body hitting every step and landing at the bottom in a twisted, bone-shattered mass.

Crimson-coloured coffee crawled across the floor, but there was no time for his usual ritual. He removed the dagger, wiped it clean and dragged the body into the engine room, leaving rusty track marks in his wake. He locked the door and checked the vicinity before heading up the stairs to resume his plans.

His next stop – the bridge.

Captain Costantino awoke with a start. There was something bothering him on this trip – a foreboding feeling in the pit of his stomach. For days before the voyage, he had recurring nightmares of a raging fire on his ship, and each dream became more vivid. Now he was seeing the dead, mutilated bodies of his crewmen strewn around the vessel. Arms separated from legs, entrails lining the corridors and pieces of bloodied flesh papering the walls.

He stood by the sink, splashed cold water on his face and stared into the mirror as he wiped his skin dry. The icy dread in his eyes perturbed him. He dressed and made his way to the bridge for a cup of coffee and a chat with his second mate.

The ship's creaks and rumbles sounded like a hungry old whale with arthritic joints. The lights above him flickered, transforming the corridor into a dark, dank cavern. There was fear in the air. It smelled metallic. He reached the metal door and noticed that it was slightly ajar.

He slid it open and a set of black pupils looked up at him through murderous eyes. A bloody blade in hand and standing legs straddled over the second mate whose neck was slit open spurting sanguine liquid like fountain water.

The second mate turned his glassy eyes on Costantino and reached out his hand in pleading. His last desperate gaze suspended on his Captain.

The reality of Costantino's nightmarish dreams spread across his face like the plague. With his eyes fixed on Kristoff, he stole a sideways glance to his left where the general alarm activation switch felt a million miles away. Its blood red hue demanded his attention.

Kristoff followed his trail and smiled with devilish glee. He tossed his serrated blade from hand to hand and bit his bottom lip. 'Let's see if you can reach that switch before I gut you like a fish.'

✦ Chapter Forty-Eight ✦

The ear-splitting shrill of seven short blasts could have woken the dead. Christiano and Angelica shot upwards and turned to each other with a quizzical look that seemed to suspend in time.

The long alarm followed. Its screech left a high-pitched ringing in their ears. Christiano scrambled for the life jackets in a nearby cupboard and rushed to place one on Angelica and then on himself.

'What do you think is going on?'

'I don't know, but we'd better follow protocol.' He finished clipping his jacket and made his way to the porthole to take a look outside. The ocean was as calm as a mirror. He turned his head from left to right. 'I can't see anything wro—'

A sudden blast ripped through the ship, knocking them both off their feet. Sounds of tearing metal and gushing water followed as if the ship was being torn in two.

Christiano crawled across the floor to Angelica, pulled her up and held her close to his chest. 'Whatever happens, stay close to me.'

As they reached the cabin door, Angelica looked up at him with cold dread in her eyes.

He cupped her face. 'Do you trust me?'

She nodded, tears streaming her cheeks.

'I won't let anything happen to you.' He kissed her lips before pulling his sleeve over his hand and grasping the searing metal handle.

The door buckled from the other side causing two large concaves. It relented like a joint being ripped from its socket. Hot, dense smoke, heavy with toxic fumes, hurled towards them in a rapid wind motion that enveloped them in a cloak of smog.

'Cover your mouth,' shouted Christiano above the cacophonous clanging of alarms and the blood-curdling screams of crewmen being devoured by the advancing flames.

A coughing sound at the doorway revealed Frya struggling with her unconscious father, who she was dragging as best she could along the sweltering linoleum floor. 'I need to get him off the ground.'

Christiano pulled him over his shoulder. 'Get to top deck and stay close together. Walk in front of me.'

The agonising screams chased around them like taunting spectres. The women caught sight of a human torch scurrying to the end of the blazing corridor. His flesh melted like plastic off his face, leaving bulging eyes burdened with the torment of hell.

They screamed as he dropped to the floor, his agonised cries silenced by the flames cremating his body.

The bulkhead door at the top of the stairs flew open. The Chief Officer yelled, 'Abandon ship! Get to the lifeboats.'

The women scrambled up the clanging metal steps, their legs leaden with fear. Angelica gripped the bannister to hasten her ascent. Her palm sizzled on the scorching metal. She screeched, shaking it vigorously and held it out to see a deep red mark running from her hand to her elbow.

'Keep moving,' yelled Christiano.

She shook it off and continued to clamber up steps that felt steeper and more cumbersome by the second. When they finally reached the top, an explosion of mass proportion sent a crippling tremor through the vessel. Seismic vibrations rumbled through their bodies as the ship wavered from side to side, enough to send them bouncing against the railings behind them.

Frya grabbed the handle and pushed on the bulkhead door. Its weight felt like a ton of scorched metal. 'It's stuck,' she yelled.

Angelica pushed the door with all her strength. It relented but an inch. 'There's something on the other side.'

Behind them, the fire crawled towards them as if its conscious purpose was to seek out and devour the living. Sounds of whipping, crackling and buckling grew ever closer as did the rise in humidity and the diminishing oxygen.

'We don't have much time left,' yelled Frya.

Christiano stepped forward and gave the door a kick. The obstacle on the other side moved slightly before bouncing back. He followed with a succession of hard kicks – giving little chance for the object to rebound onto the door

– until there finally appeared a gap large enough for the women to pass.

Angelica was the first to slip through, tripping over the hindrance at the doorway. She looked across to see the Chief Officer's corpse – his left eye a black, empty hole, his right wide and vacant. She squealed, kicking back with her legs.

Frya followed behind her and caught sight of the dead body.

'This is the work of the Cardinal,' yelled Angelica. 'How did he find us?'

Frya helped her to her feet. 'I don't know, but right now, we need to move that body out of the way before my father and your husband burn or suffocate to death.'

'Hurry up out there!' Christiano's tinny voice echoed desperately through the door.

Angelica placed her arms beneath the dead man's shoulders, and Frya took hold of his legs. Together they pulled his body to one side.

Christiano pushed the door open and with Kurush still slumped over his shoulders, he stepped onto the deck. He welcomed the influx of oxygen, albeit smoky, which filtered its way to his lungs and relieved him from the slow suffocation of the corridor.

Fire raged from the cargo holders. Miniature explosions detonated from all directions. The sky, ablaze with light, could have been mistaken for the burning furnace of hell.

'We need to get to the lifeboat,' yelled Christiano, and no sooner had he finished speaking than another blast erupted from one the cargo holders. A large fragment of metal torpedoed through the air. The three of them stood spellbound as it glided towards them.

The ship dipped to one side, and they tumbled to the ground. The sharp-edged missile missed their heads by a micro-second, wedging itself in the decking where it remained a blazing torch. Kurush slipped through Christiano's grip like melted butter, and his body slid towards the mouth of a hungry ocean. Christiano's hands grasped at empty air as Kurush's descent continued.

He stretched his torso across the deck and propelled himself in the same direction. As his body slid down the sloping deck, he stretched his arm as far as he could and just managed to grasp one of Kurush's fingers. With his other hand, he clasped his wrist and began to haul him up. Frya and Angelica knelt by his feet and clamped their arms over his legs until Kurush was back in the safety of Christiano's grip.

'I have him. He's fine. Now, get to the lifeboat. I'm right behind you.'

The women reached the bright orange vessel.

'Are you all okay?' The weary voice of Achilleus approached them from another angle. His right foot dragged behind his left; his maimed and bloody arm across his chest. 'You need to twist the handle and pull the door towards you.'

Angelica did as instructed.

As Frya helped Achilleus inside, Angelica lingered outside for Christiano who showed little patience. 'Angelica, please get inside.' He placed Kurush on his feet at the foot of the boat. 'I'm right behi…' His words trailed off. His eyes widened and his dilated pupils glazed over.

'Christiano?'

His gaze wandered down to Angelica's questioning face. She stared into his unfocused eyes – his contorted face a frown of disbelief as the blood visibly drained from his skin.

Kurush fell away from his arms and tumbled into the vessel.

'Christiano!' Angelica groped his shoulders. 'What's the matter? Christiano!' She shook him as his mouth opened but no words found their way to his tongue. He grabbed at his left shoulder as he dropped to his knees.

'Christiano!'

Behind him, Kristoff wore a mordant smirk. He pulled the knife from Christiano's back and kicked him aside, making an easy path within reach of Angelica.

Christiano writhed on the floor, his spine twisted and his hand attempting to reach the spot – as if it might alleviate the pain. 'Get…on the…boat.' The words strained through his throat. Angelica tried to rush to him, but Kristoff stood in her path.

He brandished his blade at her before proceeding to pull out a larger knife with a lethal serrated edge. With a blade in each hand, he flashed pearly white teeth that reflected the orange flicker of flames. 'Before I separate your head from your body, you *will* renounce your bond with Satan?'

'My bond is with the Almighty.'

He bent his head to one side and gazed at her as if she were a different species. 'There's something about you.

You're not like the others.'

'So you're the one who killed all those women and their unborn babies.'

'And you will be the most interesting kill of them all. Move away from the door, or everyone on that boat dies.'

She followed the tracks of his feet as he stepped backwards.

'Keep coming,' he said, beckoning her with his blades.

They stopped a few feet away from the lifeboat.

'You're not even going to fight me? I was told Satan had endowed you with the powers to protect his child.'

'One day you'll answer to God for all that you've done.'

Kristoff's eyes widened; his black dilated pupils covered their entire sockets. He raised the knives in the air. The reflection of the flames set the blades on fire. They flickered in his eyeballs. 'This kill is sanctioned *by* God. You carry an abomination, and you must die.'

Angelica maintained her composure, her fearless gaze focused on eyes that looked like empty sockets, ablaze. She looked across at his hands futilely quivering with determined force, yet Kristoff's arms remained suspended in the air.

He stared at them as if they were alien, trying to move them with all the strength he could muster. He turned his dumbfounded gaze on Angelica. 'What are you?' he managed to say before he found himself taking off through the air.

Firmly attached to his hip was Christiano, ramming him with all the might of a bull. They landed several feet away on the sloping ground and wrestled in a tangled embrace as they tumbled down the deck.

'Christiano!' cried Angelica, watching helplessly as her husband vanished into a forest of shadows and flames.

Frya rushed to her side. 'I saw what happened. Angelica, I'm—'

'He's gone,' she mumbled, immobilised and numb.

'I know.' She placed her hand on Angelica's shoulder, her face worn with grief. 'We need to get to the boat,' she whispered gently.

'It wasn't meant to be like this.'

'I know. Please Angelica, the baby. We don't have time.'

Achilleus appeared behind them and grasped hold of Angelica's arm. 'We must go now!'

Together with Frya, they pulled a stunned Angelica to the lifeboat.

Achilleus threw her into her seat and positioned himself next to her, buckling her in with his one useful hand. 'This is not a fairground ride. It's going to get rocky.'

Frya locked the door and made her way to the helm.

The next explosion tore the ship in two. The screeching metal carcass careened to an extreme angle sending cargo containers the size of coaches spilling into the sea.

Frya frantically pumped the release lever, and the lifeboat slid off its davits. It nosedived into the water like a playful whale, submerging into the sea and causing crashing ripples around them before it sprung to the surface. It danced on the stormy waves as Frya steered the boat like a native seaman, taking them a safe distance from the swirling vacuum.

Only the four of them had made it to safety.

A tortured Angelica rose from her seat and pushed her way past Achilleus. She pulled the door open, slumped on the floor and looked towards the sinking mass before her.

The ship's mast, now a flaming beacon, was the last evidence of the ship's existence – the rest of its body submerged beneath the ocean.

'Christiano,' she whimpered, unable to steer her gaze away from the hypnotic flames.

The Italian flag, a fluttering blaze, sank towards the devouring ocean, offering its last heroic wave before fizzling out.

Nothing but a hole as black as space was left in its place.

✦ Chapter Forty-Nine ✦

Hans drew the curtains open, and shafts of powdered light illuminated the Cardinal seated at his desk across the room. His bandaged hand gripped a newspaper. 'That will be all, Hans.'

'Your Eminence,' he said, bowing his head and leaving the room.

The Cardinal's virulent eyes stared at the headline. *Italian Cargo Ship Sinks in the Mediterranean Sea.*

The article went on to describe that the Greek coastguard found only one survivor on the lifeboat, the ship's cook, who was currently in hospital with a broken and severely gashed arm in need of several stitches, and a minor leg injury.

The Cardinal called Kristoff's cell phone and left the usual cryptic message. As he waited for the equally cryptic return call, there was a knock at the door.

Hans entered the room. 'Your Eminence, your physician is here.'

'Let him in, will you.' He placed the cell phone in his desk drawer.

The doctor, a distinguished gentleman of wizened years, entered the room clutching his black case. 'Your Eminence, how are you feeling?'

'Ah, Doctor Conti, my hand feels imprisoned inside this wretched bandage, not to mention the unbearable stabbing pain. Please tell me you are removing it today and supplying me with more potent relief.'

'You're in luck, Your Eminence. It is coming off today, and I'll be prescribing high-strength painkillers to be used at your discretion. Only if you feel pain.'

'Your blessings will be thousandfold.'

'Received with gratitude,' replied Doctor Conti as he proceeded to unravel the gauze from the Cardinal's hand.

'Do you think there'll be much scarring?'

'They were deep lacerations, Your Eminence. Most likely there will be some scarring, yes.'

Doctor Conti lifted the last segment of fabric, and they looked eagerly down at the Cardinal's hand.

'Will you look at that?' said Doctor Conti. 'It's as if the very hand of God came down and made his mark upon you.'

The Cardinal gazed down at the perfect markings of a Greek cross in the centre of his right hand. He was not amused.

✦ Epilogue ✦

Four-and-a-half Years Later: Bedouin Camp,
Sinai Desert, Egypt

The sun's unrelenting rays beat down upon a sea of barren desert stretching for miles in all directions. Its blazing heat reflected a haziness that blinded the eye. A solitary tamarisk stood defiant. Firm. Erect. Shooting up from the arid sand. Its branches and leaves spread out to form a vast tent-like structure. A golden eagle lay on the shadowed surface. Its body rigid. Dead.

Aker, a lanky, hazel-brown-eyed boy with bronzed skin, kicked a homemade football put together from paper, plastic bags and a rope. Ten or more children chased behind him unable to catch him. He kicked the ball. It rolled beneath the tamarisk and bounced off the eagle's taut lifeless body. He approached the bird, picked it up and held it out for the others to see.

The crowding children parted like the Red Sea to make way for a little girl. She was small in proportion to the others and much younger at four years old. She looked up at Aker with her deep malachite eyes. 'Let me see. Let me see.' She bounded up and down on the spot.

Aker lowered his hands to her eye level. 'It's dead. There's nothing we can do. By the looks of its wound, it was catapulted with a rock.'

The child smiled humbly and pressed her ear to its body. She closed her eyes for a moment and then opened them and announced, 'He wants to live.' She kissed his feathered torso.

The creature opened his eyes in a daze and found himself staring into the face of the little girl. She smiled at him in adoration.

The children gasped as they crowded round with baited breaths.

'Aker, open your hands,' she said.

Aker did as instructed. The bird fidgeted, lifted its wings and hopped to a standing position in his palms. He pecked his head towards the little girl and brushed her cheek with his beak.

'You're welcome,' she said. 'Go fly and be free. Nothing will ever hurt you again.'

The children gasped in awe as the eagle took flight and soared through the sky until it reached the size of a black dot and disappeared from their sight.

'Salvatrice, how did you do that?' asked Aker. 'It was dead!'

She grinned and said, 'Magic', before running away, her hands suspended above her head to feel the touch of the air.

The others followed behind her shouting playfully and chasing the ball.

They reached a private enclosure bustling with men, women and children going about their daily chores. In the moderately sized camp was an adobe structure which formed a T-shape – what looked like the main building. Smaller huts were sporadically spread around the encampment.

In one corner, a few children dipped and swam in a crystalline rectangular pool, welcoming the icy-cold water on their scorched bodies. The surface glistened like diamonds enticing flies to their deaths.

A queue of people snaked its way to a building where a native nurse stood in the doorway and questioned the next person in line. She was busy making notes on a clipboard. A father held his child who lay unconscious in his arms.

Frya came to the door with a pregnant woman, saw her out and welcomed in the new patient.

Salvatrice ran towards them and touched each person in line as she scurried past until she reached the man with the child in the front of the queue. She skimmed the girl's head with her fingertips. The unconscious child opened her eyes.

Salvatrice stopped at the entrance, wearing a beaming smile. 'Is there a baby in there?' She touched the woman's stomach.

The woman gasped and clutched at her bump. 'I felt a kick.'

Frya smiled with knowing. 'Your mother has been looking for you. It's story time with nonno.'

'Okay,' said Salvatrice who swivelled round and ran to her mother. Seconds later, she reached a woman busy hanging washing on a clothesline nearby.

'Salvatrice, where have you been and why are you following those older children?'

'I don't follow them, they follow me.'

Angelica stifled a chuckle. 'Of course. Nonno is waiting for you inside.'

Salvatrice casually hummed as she strolled through the door.

Angelica finished hanging the clothing and stopped for a moment, her eyes locked inside her mind. A sorrowful tear escaped each eye, rolled down to her chin and cascaded to the ground. She picked up her basket, headed indoors and walked past Kurush and Salvatrice who were sitting cross-legged on the floor.

Kurush looked her way.

Angelica avoided eye contact, pulled aside a curtain and entered another room. The Spartan bedroom consisted of two military-style beds and a hand-made wooden wardrobe. Angelica slumped down on one of the cots. The sun filtered through a hole partly covered with a beige makeshift curtain.

She raised her hand and stared through moistened eyes at Christiano's ecclesiastical ring. A fresh piece of tape had been recently applied to keep it in place.

'Angelica, are you all right?' said Kurush from behind the partition.

'I'm fine.'

'Angelica, please. I know what today is.'

She buried her head in her hands and made quiet whimpering sounds.

'Please let me come inside.'

She closed her eyes and sighed. 'Okay.'

Kurush entered the room, sat down next to her and placed his hand on her shoulder. 'I'm sorry. Is there anything I can do?'

'Instead of celebrating my wedding anniversary, I'm grieving the death of the only man I ever loved.'

Salvatrice entered the room and stood in front of them. 'Are you okay, Angelica?'

'You must call me Mama around here, Salvatrice.'

The girl smiled. 'How can I call you Mama when you're *my* child?'

Angelica's face softened as she looked at the paradox before her.

'You know it's just for safety, Salvatrice. No one must know who we are,' said Kurush.

'But we are safe here. My Father has protected this place. He speaks to me every night in dreams and visions. He told me about today. He told me you'd be sad and he gave me a message for you.'

Angelica's eyes froze on Salvatrice. 'Mm...message?' The words could barely leave her lips. 'About Christiano?' Her face lit up but then dimmed in sudden fear.

'Why are you afraid?'

'I'm not. It's... Just...' She shut her eyes and opened them again to see the wise four-year-old still giving her a quizzical look. 'Must you always look through me?'

Salvatrice remained silent.

'Salvatrice!' She immediately regretted her tone, flopped her head into her lap and burst into tears. After a couple of heartbeats, she looked up. 'I'm sorry I yelled. It's a difficult time. You know the sacrifice Christiano made to get us here. You know how much he loved you.'

The young girl smiled. 'Yes, and you will be happy with my news.'

'Salvatrice, the message, please,' interjected Kurush.

'My Father told me that Christiano's heart is *still* filled with love for you and for me.'

'*Still?*' Angelica gulped and stood up. 'Salvatrice what do you mean, *still?* The words rasped through her throat.

'My Father told me that Christiano is fast asleep.'

'Asleep?' questioned Angelica.

'Salvatrice, do you mean a coma? Ah... Like Snow White?' asked Kurush.

'Yes.' She nodded enthusiastically. 'He hurt his head badly and fell asleep like Snow White.'

Angelica's surroundings seemed to all but once move in on her. She gasped for breath and clawed at her chest, trying to catch it. Kurush bounded up from the bed as she collapsed to the ground. He caught her in his arms and set her down on the floor. In her mind's eye, she could see Christiano, his eyes closed; his expression still and reposed like the face of a corpse in an open casket. Her hand reached out as if caressing his cheek. 'Christiano,' she muttered.

Four-and-a-Half Years Earlier

The two men rolled like tumbleweeds down the sloping deck, speeding through fire and knocking against sharp, unidentifiable obstacles – both maintaining their grips like two vices. Their descent to the ocean depths was shielded by a large cargo container loosely hinged in mid-air. It creaked beneath their weight as if this one more pressure was just too much to bear, and at any moment it would plunge into the sea and take them with it.

Both men were indifferent to the danger. With Kristoff pinned to the ground, Christiano had the advantage; his hands clamped around his neck in an indomitable grip.

The assassin's hands were cemented to Christiano's wrists, pushing against him with all his strength. The sweat on their bodies sizzled. The heat from the scorching fire was hazardously close. The groaning cargo container continued to hinge up and down like a seesaw. Each movement threatened them with imminent death.

Sweat dripped from Christiano's forehead into one of Kristoff's eyes. It stung, forcing it to shut. The assassin's face strained purple as he wrestled to catch a breath, but Christiano's wide eyes were red with fury, his tremulous hands seeking their own vengeance.

Kristoff's battle was coming to an end – his lungs, devoid of air were on the verge of exploding. His hands made a desperate crawl to Christiano's face and futilely pulled on his skin, but the life force that resided inside him was abandoning his body with the indifference of a drifting cloud. His eyes glazed over. His grip barely a touch.

The deck rumbled, and another explosion ripped through the ship. A loud creaking noise from above sent a large piece of rigging crashing down on the cargo container.

The ship careered to the right, and Christiano's grip was lost.

Kristoff gasped for breath as a large influx of smoky air was sucked into his lungs.

The container gave way and squealed all the way down to the sea.

Both men instinctively grabbed hold of the large pole that had dropped down. They stared at each other as they clung for their lives.

'You nearly had me.' Kristoff coughed up his words. 'You would have been the first.'

'And the last,' replied Christiano.

Kristoff sniggered. 'You will find that I am like a cat with nine lives. God has blessed this mission and keeps me safe to fulfil his deeds.'

'God plays no role in your depravity. You follow a madman with his own agenda. You believe the lies he spins because you think it will save you, but it won't.'

Kristoff's eyes pierced Christiano like daggers. 'When I find your whore wife, I'll hack off her head and send it to the Cardinal in a box made of gold.'

'Over my dead body.' Christiano's face glowered like the raging fire around him.

'As you wish,' said Kristoff releasing one of his hands from the pole. He proceeded to punch at Christiano's knuckles and dig his nails into his flesh. He released one of his legs and began kicking at his ribs.

Christiano lost his grip and slid sideways towards the ocean. He tightened his legs round the pole.

Not a man to give up, Kristoff skimmed along the pole

and began a flurry of kicks to Christiano's head.

His skin split like a zipper, exposing part of his skull and oozing with blood. He fought to stay alert, bearing the pain through gritted teeth. His thighs clenched tighter round the pole.

A hair-raising screech sounded from above, and a large metal chain descended upon them – landing square on the pole. It bent like a piece of elastic and broke off from its base before it made its slippery slide towards the sea with Christiano and Kristoff clinging on. As they made their ungraceful plunge down the deck, Christiano eyed a bright red rope in his line of sight. He grabbed it and released his legs from the pole.

Kristoff followed his lead but missed the rope. He managed to catch hold of Christiano's foot. The pole continued on to sea, and their lives now depended on the rope's stability. Woozy and heavy with fatigue, and with Kristoff's hefty mass, Christiano could barely hold on. The rope slackened and in one sudden movement jerked downwards, taking them with it.

Christiano maintained his hold, with Kristoff's hands clamped firmly around his trainer, like a lost soul trying to prevent his plummet to hell. The assassin looked up at him in venomous desperation as the trainer, unable to hold his weight, began to slip off Christiano's foot.

His face flashed with panic. He made a swift grab at Christiano's calf and clung on with taut, desperate hands as the trainer came off and made its final run down the deck.

With Kristoff's nails digging into Christiano's skin, the

blood combined with the sweat left a slippery surface. Kristoff's nails clawed their way down his leg and glided off his sock. He glared in cold terror as gravity, playing its role as the grim reaper, dragged him into the darkness. His nails scraped all the way down the deck, and his mouth emitted a monotone screech that grew ever distant until it was no more.

Christiano let out a heavy sigh when all sight and sound of him was gone. Barely able to hold on by his fingertips, his sweaty hands were also losing their grip. At that moment, he relented to death and muttered a prayer. 'Most sacred heart of Jesus, I accept from your hands whatever kind of death it may please you to send me this night...'

The rope came loose, and Christiano's fate was moments away. His surroundings were an unintelligible blur as he made his speedy descent down to the sea. His voice grew louder. '...with all its pains, penalties and sorrows; in reparation for all of my sins, for the souls in Purgatory, for all those who have died tonight and for your greater glory.'

The ship made a sudden dive to the right. He shut his eyes and shouted, 'Amen', ready for the morbid outcome, but his body landed against a cushioned surface. His eyes formed slits surrounded by a blur of orange. He forced them wider to see a bright orange valise to his left.

He let out a cry of relief and shook his head in disbelief as tears streamed from the corners of his eyes. With his waning strength, he lifted his hand to the Velcro flap and made a few hapless attempts to pull it, before his hand, limp with fatigue, flopped to his side.

He felt himself drifting, the pain in his head like a chisel to his brain as his surroundings grew as dark as a cavern. Angelica appeared in his mind's eye. She smiled lovingly and blew him a kiss. 'Come find me.' Her voice blasted like a horn and shocked his eyes open. With renewed vigour, he raised his hand to the flap and gave it a hard tug.

The ship made a sudden dive. He grasped his hands around the lifeboat valise as the vessel, and what was left on it, began sinking into the sea. As the valise hit the water, it emitted sounds of puffing and hissing as the lifeboat wrestled to meet its challenge of inflating to a full-size raft.

Christiano gripped on tightly and thrust himself inside as its plastic orange skin enveloped him. A roof sprung over his head and ensconced him in the raft. With the persistent throbbing in his head and his vision obscured by the blood streaming from his head, he fought to remain conscious as he felt in his pocket for his grandfather's knife. He located the painter line that secured the raft to the ship, and cut it before he flopped down where he lay and tucked his body into a foetal position. With his arms wrapped around his shivering, cold torso, he relented to the fog eating through his mind.

Another explosion lit up the sky, and the ship took its farewell dive. The inflatable raft twisted and fought against the current as the water sucked it down to its sinister depths before setting it free.

It sprung to the surface in jovial buoyancy as if making a victory dance.

The sea claimed the last of the ship's mast and the fire

fizzled out. A sheet of darkness was left in its wake.

The life raft floated on the now calm waters, and Christiano's world faded to black.

THE END

GET FOUR OF ANGELICA'S EXCLUSIVE SKETCHES, PLUS ONE OF MY SHORT STORIES

Building a relationship with my readers is very important to me. I occasionally send newsletters with details on new releases, special offers and other news relating to my novels.

If you would like to join my mailing list, you can get the four sketches and my short story by signing up at https://www.subscribepage.com/thepriestofsantamaria

ENJOY THE BOOK? YOU CAN MAKE A BIG DIFFERENCE

Reviews are the most powerful way for me to gain attention for my books. As much as I wish, I don't have the financial resources of a big-time publisher. I can't take out full-page ads in newspapers and magazines, nor can I place posters in the perfect locations to catch a potential reader's attention.

But what does help me immensely is when a reader leaves an honest review. This is by far the best way to gain the attention of other readers and has more power than any advert!

So if you enjoyed the book, I would be very grateful if you could spend just five minutes to leave a review on the book's online selling page (you can make it as long or short as you like).

Thank you very much.

ABOUT THE AUTHOR

Alexandra Kleanthous is the debut author of *The Priest of Santa Maria.* She is currently working on the second book in the series. You can find her online at https://alexandrakleanthous.com/. You can connect with her on Facebook at https://www.facebook.com/priestofsantamaria/ and if you feel to, you can send her an email at alex@alexandrakleanthous.com.

Printed in Great Britain
by Amazon